The

Daughters

of

Foxcote Manor

ALSO BY EVE CHASE

The Wildling Sisters

Black Rabbit Hall

The
Daughters
of
Foxcote Manor

✳

PUTNAM
— EST. 1838 —

G. P. PUTNAM'S SONS
Publishers Since 1838
An imprint of Penguin Random House LLC
penguinrandomhouse.com

Library of Congress Cataloging-in-Publication Data

Names: Chase, Eve, author.
Title: The daughters of Foxcote Manor / Eve Chase.
Description: New York: G. P. Putnam's Sons, 2020. |
Identifiers: LCCN 2020013903 | ISBN 9780525542384 (hardcover) |
ISBN 9780525542407 (ebook)
Subjects: GSAFD: Suspense fiction
Classification: LCC PR6103.H45 D38 2020 | DDC 823/.92—dc23
LC record available at https://lccn.loc.gov/2020013903

Printed in the United States of America
1   3   5   7   9   10   8   6   4   2

BOOK DESIGN BY KATY RIEGEL

For my family

What is the meaning of life? That was all—a simple question; one that tended to close in on one with years. The great revelation had never come. The great revelation perhaps never did come. Instead, there were little daily miracles, illuminations, matches struck unexpectedly in the dark; here was one.

—VIRGINIA WOOLF, **To the Lighthouse**

The

Daughters

of

Foxcote Manor

Body Found
in Woods

A body was discovered yesterday in the wooded grounds of a house in the Forest of Dean. The death is being treated as suspicious. Shocked locals told the *Enquirer* that the property, Foxcote Manor, is owned by the Harrington family, who moved in earlier this month after a fire at their London home. A resident from the nearest village, Hawkswell, who wishes to remain anonymous, said, "We're all just praying it was a terrible accident. This sort of thing shouldn't happen in a quiet place like this. Or to a family like the Harringtons."

1

——— ✻ ———

Rita, Forest of Dean, 4 August 1971

The forest looks like it'll eat them alive, thinks Rita. The light's gone a weird green and branches are thrashing against the car's windows. She tightens her grip on the steering wheel. The lane narrows further. Wondering if she's missed the turning to the house or if it's around the next corner, she takes a bend too fast, then slams her foot on the brake.

Rita sucks in her breath, her eyes widening behind the Morris Minor's insect-spattered windscreen. She's not sure what she was expecting. Something smarter. More Harrington. Not *this*.

Behind a tall, rusting gate, Foxcote Manor erupts from the undergrowth, as if a geological heave has lifted it from the woodland floor. The mullioned windows on the old house, a wrecked beauty, blink drunkenly in the stippled evening sunlight. Colossal trees overhang a sweep of red-tiled roof that sags in the middle, like a snapped spine, so the chimneys tilt at odd angles. Ivy suckers up the timber-and-brick gabled façade, dense, bristling, alive with dozens of tiny darting birds, a billowing veil of bees. It's as far from the Harringtons' elegant London townhouse as Rita could possibly imagine.

For a moment no one in the car speaks. Unseen, in the trees, a woodpecker drums its territorial tattoo. Sweat trickles down the back of Rita's left knee. Only now does she register her hands are shaking.

Although she's done her best to disguise it from Jeannie and the children, she's been panicky ever since they turned onto the forest road, almost five hours after leaving London. It's not just the worry she'll kill her precious passengers. Every so often her vision has actually shuddered, disoriented by all the soaring trees, the lack of sky, and the knowledge of quite how hard a tree trunk is when hit at fifty miles an hour. Now they've survived the journey, she covers her mouth with her hand. Everything's still going too fast. How on earth has she ended up *here*? A forest. Of all places. She hates forests.

It was meant to be a London nannying job.

Fourteen months ago, Rita had never been to London. But she'd dreamed of it longingly, the Rita she might be there, far away from Torquay, everything that had happened. And the metropolitan family—just like the Darlings in *Peter Pan*—who'd embrace her as their own. They'd live in a tall warm house that didn't have a coin-gobbling electricity meter, like Nan's bungalow did. She'd get a bedroom of her own, with a desk and a shelf, perhaps a view of the churning, thrilling city. And the mother she worked for would be . . . well, perfect. Someone delicate and kind and soft. Cultured. With tiny earlobes and fluttery birdlike hands. Like her own mother, whom Rita hazily remembered. Everything she'd lost in the accident. And that a bit of her kept searching for.

On the morning of the interview, she'd gazed up at the Primrose Hill house's sugar-white stucco and cascading wisteria, and immediately known this was it. Her new home. Her new family. She could feel a tingling sensation, like the first fizz of pins and needles, as she'd knocked on the smart front door, her heart scudding beneath her best blouse that didn't look best in London. Now it's her second-best blouse, packed in the boot along with any other clothes—practical, plain, rarely long enough in the arm or leg—she could salvage after the fire that tore through that London house last weekend. Even after the long cycle at the launderette, her clothes still whiff of smoke.

Rita glances across at Jeannie in the passenger seat. Wearing a new haul from Harrods, she is defiantly dressed for London, clutching a black patent leather handbag as if for dear life. She looks fragile, upset. Her recent weight loss is painfully obvious in that cream crepe skirt, tightly belted, another hole in, a powder-blue cashmere twinset, and a white silk scarf, wound like a bandage around her stemlike neck. And she's wearing those sunglasses again, the tortoiseshell ones, with lenses big as Hartley's jam-jar lids, she always puts on after a night of crying.

Jeannie hadn't wanted to leave Claridge's. (Rita neither: she'd never stayed anywhere she hadn't had to make her own bed before. The maid wouldn't even let her help with the tricky mattress corners.) Jeannie certainly hadn't wanted to come here: "Monstrous place. Walter's way of isolating me," she'd whispered last night, out of the children's earshot. Peering up at Foxcote Manor now, Rita can't help but wonder if Jeannie was right.

When she'd started the job, everything was different. She remembers Jeannie reading her reference out loud on the day of the interview, her slowly spreading smile, her hands stroking the sun of her heavily pregnant belly. "'Loyal, kind, and adored by my four children. Brilliant with the baby. Not so good on laundry or cooking. Very nervous driver. Would hire again in a heartbeat.'"

Walter hadn't been particularly interested. A reserved man with a carefully curated mustache, sinewy in a slim-cut brown suit, he'd been friendly but businesslike. After briskly shaking her hand, he excused himself, blew some kisses in the direction of the kids, and rushed out to work, trailing the faint soapy scent of shaving foam. Back then, Walter was happy to leave all of the domestic decisions to his wife. He ran the Harrington Glass headquarters in Mayfair, not the family house. And he seemed perfectly nice. If there had been warning signs, Rita didn't spot them.

She'd never wanted a job so much. Carefully lowering herself to the sofa, she'd laced her hands together tightly, so they couldn't fidget, and crossed her untidy legs at the ankle, tucking them in, as Nan had instructed ("It'll make you look smaller, love. More feminine"). She tried very hard not to smile too much, to appear a serious professional, older than her twenty years. Worthy of such a plum post.

Jeannie had called the then-five-year-old Teddy into the drawing room. "He's delicious," she said. And he was. Rita had to fight the urge to ruffle his curls. Then-twelve-year-old Hera appeared, less obviously delicious and, as if to compensate for this, offering a slice of cake—Jeannie called it *pâtisserie*—on a bone-china plate with a minuscule silver fork. As Hera shyly explained how to pronounce her posh name—"*Here*-rah"—Rita took the plate. It tipped and the cake, in horrifying slow motion, slid off and landed in the deep-pile carpet next to the potted aspidistra. Hera giggled. Rita caught her eye, then disastrously giggled too, and tried to disguise it as a coughing fit. Obviously she'd blown it spectacularly and would be sent packing back to Nan's bungalow, cloying small-town life—and her own ugly secret. But that giggle, Jeannie told her afterward, had won her the job. She wanted the baby to have a fun young nanny, not some cross old boot.

But the baby never heard Rita's giggle. Or anyone else's. She's a tiny ghost doll, stiff, white, frozen in time, a presence constantly felt but never, God forbid, mentioned. And Rita . . . well, what is *she* now? Not just the fun young nanny. And she's got more than what they'll eat for tea weighing on her mind.

Even the trees seem to peer down at her accusingly, shaking their leafy heads. "Our little arrangement," Walter calls it. When he suggested it two days ago, Rita didn't want any part. She felt such disquiet about his motives. "You want to *think* about it?" He'd snorted. "This is a job, not a dessert menu, Rita." The choice was stark: agree or leave ("immediately, without a reference"), and he'd hire someone more compliant.

"I have to remain in London, what with the business, so you must make notes on my wife's state of mind." Walter smoothed his rapidly retreating hair. "Keep me informed of her moods. Appetite. Quality of mothering. I'll expect your absolute discretion, of course. My wife mustn't find out."

Rita's mind had raced. First, if she left, where would she go? How would she live? Nan had died a few months earlier—not a bad case of indigestion, after all—and the council had reclaimed her bungalow. She had been determined to give Nan a proper send-off and a gravestone. The cost had wiped out her savings.

And she couldn't bear the thought of walking away from Jeannie, Hera, and Teddy when they needed her most. It'd be like giving up on them. Or saying, "I can't help you anymore," even though she's sure she *can*—she knows about grief, the way it scars you, not on the skin but on the soft suede of the soul inside. (And how it is to grow up different, like Hera, the one who doesn't fit.) So yes, surely better she "report" on Jeannie this summer, fudging whenever necessary, than some strict new hire, she reasoned. Even this morning it felt like the right decision. But now that they're here, enclosed by these somber, looming trees, in a spot so remote it feels like they're the last survivors on the planet, she's no longer sure. Her mouth is dry and metallic. It tastes of betrayal.

"Rita?" Jeannie touches her lightly on the arm, interrupting her spiraling thoughts. Jeannie's voice is thick with the morning's medication, the reason Rita is driving. ("Funny, I see halos," Jeannie observed over Claridge's flawless poached eggs at breakfast.) "Are you ready?"

"Oh, yes! Sorry." Rita's cheeks blaze. Her conscience lies too close to the surface.

"Well, let's get this bloody awful thing over with, shall we?" Jeannie whispers grimly. Rita nods and grapples with the gearshift. Forcing a smile for the children, Jeannie says in a loud, bright voice, "Well, hello, Foxcote! This *is* exciting. Come on, Big Rita. Drive in."

2

Sylvie, Kensal Town, London, Now

I heave the last cardboard box from the house to the car, hands on the bulging base so bits of me don't fall out into the street and cause a scene. I glance back at the house, my eyes stinging. Is this it? My family home, like the marriage I've stuck with for so long, finally excavated of me?

My married life has been bookended by moving boxes. Arrivals and exits. Whoops and sobs. When we first moved in, nineteen years ago, I was five months pregnant, a busy makeup artist with a carry-on case always packed, ready to easyJet off for a shoot abroad at short notice. I didn't own a salad spinner. I'd never changed a nappy. My engagement ring—antique gold, pea-green emerald— had belonged to Steve's great-aunt and made me smile every time I looked at it. The wedding would happen after I'd lost the baby weight (not all of it). I'd wear an ivory lace vintage dress and T-bar shoes, just the right side of Courtney Love. We'd dance to Pulp's "Common People." We'd be married forever.

I couldn't have imagined this street changing either.

Cheap for Zone 2, it was home to a kebab shop, a resident loon, who shouted abuse at lampposts, and a thriving drug den. The front doors were painted a council rust red. Now those doors are mostly sludgy shades of charcoal gray. The kebab shop is a much-Instagrammed florist, selling dragon-red dahlias. There are five Sophies living on the street. Probably fifty juicers. If we had to buy our house now, we wouldn't be able to afford it. We? That mental slip again. Keeps happening.

I say, "Good-bye," under my breath. I've been moving boxes out of the house into my tiny apartment for the last month, tentatively, while Steve's at work. Now it's done, I feel elated. But my heart aches. I can't shut it as easily as the front door. So many memories remain in that house, stored like sunlight in a jar: Annie's ascending height marks penciled on the bathroom wall; the baby-pink rose we planted to mark the grave of Lettuce, Annie's rabbit; folders of tear sheets, editorial magazine work I did when starting out, well over twenty years ago, happy to be cool rather than properly paid. I've no storage space now. No garden, either. And way too many bills to settle on my own.

A *trial separation,* Steve still calls it. He didn't believe me when I first told him six weeks ago. We were eating prawn linguine in silence. I'd been away that week, working on a countrywear catalog shoot in the Highlands, involving lots of corduroy, shivering models, and driving rain. Steve had forgotten the bin day—crime A—so we'd be stuck with the recycling for another two weeks, and the bin was stuffed full already. But really it was about something else—other layers of rubbish built up in our marriage (crimes B-Z).

I watched Steve decapitate a prawn with his fingers, humming under his breath. His face—the angular dark brows, the childhood

BMX scar on his chin—was so familiar it was as if I couldn't see him. "What have I done now?" he said, not looking up at me.

I put down my fork. The words just tumbled out. "Steve, I can't do this . . . us . . . anymore." A moment passed. Steve blinked rapidly. He waited for me to apologize or blame my hormones. The music shuffled on to Lou Reed's "Perfect Day." Normally we'd quip about the irony. We didn't. It felt like nothing would be funny again.

"But I love you," Steve stuttered, floored. And at that moment—8:11 P.M., 19 June—I knew he meant it, he really did, but also that he couldn't imagine life without me, which is not quite the same. Then I thought about our eighteen-year-old daughter, Annie, out in Camden celebrating finishing her last A-level exam, sweetly oblivious, and I burst into tears. What was I *doing*?

Love. Stability. An unbroken home. The moment Annie slid into the world, unfathomably precious, I'd promised her all of this. I didn't mourn my lost freedoms, even though my career soon shrank like cashmere in a hot wash. I could no longer travel or work late into the night. I was exhausted. Even my feet were fat. But there was no getting around it, I was also deeply, shockingly happy, maybe for the first time in my life. My magnetic north had flipped. So yes, I'd get motherhood right. That was all that mattered. I'd give Annie absolutely everything I had.

To this end, I've done my very best to forget about Lisa from HR—early thirties, balayage blonde, spilled her Negroni on my best Isabel Marant dress at Steve's office Christmas party—and, I'm 55 percent sure, the woman he plays doubles with at the tennis club—and other encounters I've sensed but not been able to prove these last few years.

If you learn as a kid how to bury painful things—for me, everything that happened in a forest long ago, the sort of questions that'll stop my mother dead in her tracks, with a coronary grimace—you get pretty bloody good at blocking things out. And keeping secrets. Only secrets don't go away completely, it turns out. Like moths in a wardrobe, they nibble away, hidden, before you notice the hole.

As Annie's schooldays drew to a close earlier this summer, I felt an internal shift, one I hadn't expected. Like a gear change on my bike, a strange freewheeling feeling, then a clunking into place. A little voice in my head started to whisper: You're forty-six years old. If you don't leave now, *when*? What sort of example are you setting for Annie anyway? She'd want you to be happy.

Annie didn't quite see it like that. "So you've been living a lie all this time? *Pretending?*" she stuttered when I broke the news, desperately trying to make our separation sound like a Gwyneth-style conscious uncoupling (admittedly, a stretch). I couldn't bear to tell her about Steve's affair, since that's an adult mess, and my own humiliating business, a symptom of our breakup as much as its cause. Also, despite everything, he's always been a brilliant father. So I said, "We're united in our love for you, Annie. That's the most important thing." Which is true. But when I tried to hug her, she pushed me away.

"Why didn't you warn me? You know what, Mum? It's been like this all my life, you going *la, la, la,* everything's great, just don't ask too many questions."

I flinched, sensing I'd tapped into something else, more subcutaneous, a vein of resentment that went beyond Steve's and my split.

"And it's *bullshit*."

The next day Annie decamped to my mother's cottage in Devon for the summer, where Granny's sympathetic shoulder was waiting. "Right now she's lying on the sofa, eating a tub of my homemade caramel ice cream, watching reruns of *Girls*," my mother reported back reassuringly on the phone later that evening. "Of course she doesn't hate you! No, stop it, Sylvie. You're a wonderful mother. But it's a bit of a shock. She feels duped. She needs time to digest it. We all do," she added, which I took as a small dig.

I hadn't warned Mum, either. We both share difficult news on a need-to-know basis. Like mother, like daughter.

"Let her have a carefree summer by the sea. I'll take good care of her, don't you worry. But who'll look after you?"

I laughed and said I was quite able to look after myself. Yes, really. But after many years of wifedom, I needed to find out who I was.

"Who *you* are?" she said quietly, after a beat or two of fully loaded silence, then swiftly changed the subject.

Annie quickly sorted herself out with a waitressing job and a boyfriend. On the phone she'll often claim, not wholly convincingly, the signal's dodgy and promise to phone back later, then doesn't. If I ask about the new boyfriend—"Dotty about him," Mum says—Annie immediately shuts down the conversation, as if I've lost the right to her confidence. Can I meet him? Silence. When will she come back to London and see my new apartment? "Soon," she says, often with a muffled giggle, as if the boyfriend is there in the background, nuzzling her neck. "Gotta go. Love you. Yeah, miss you too, Mum."

At least she's having fun, I reason as I park the car on my new street that's not nearly as nice as my old one and grab the cardboard box out of the boot. I can hear the building's summer pulse already.

Out of its open windows, the competing sounds of cooped-up children, hip-hop, radio commentary—*"Goal!"*—and the opera singer on the second floor, throat open, practicing her scales. A group of hooded teenage boys watch me idly, leaning back against a graffiti-spattered wall, smoking weed. I smile brightly at them, refusing to be intimidated, and climb determinedly up four flights of stairs, the last bit of my married life weighty in my arms.

The block is what estate agents call "industrial cool," a mix of council and private with concrete communal walkways and balconies overlooking the Grand Union Canal. Slightly edgy. My apartment—with two small bedrooms, the nicest one ready for Annie, yet to be used—is owned by an understanding old friend, Val, and usually rented as an Airbnb. It's an immaculate vision of pink gallery-picture walls, whitewashed Scandi floorboards, Berber rugs, and enormous, hard-to-kill waxy-leafed houseplants. More important, it's only a couple of tube stops from the old house, so Annie can move between Steve and me easily, as she pleases. Or not.

I drop the box to the floor and wish there was someone I could shout to "Put the kettle on!"

Silence chases me around, like a cat. I flick on the radio and open the balcony's glass doors, arms outstretched, head thrown back, pretending I'm in an old French movie. The city rumbles in, smelling of canal, diesel, and beer-soaked late-July heat. I lift my face to the sunshine and smile. I can do this.

Even after I've lived here a month, the view from the balcony is a novelty, as though big gray London's cleaved open its hidden green heart and let me in. The color of matcha tea, it's an urban highway for dragonflies, butterflies, and birds. Other interesting wildlife: a thirtysomething, who likes hats, plays guitar, and sings—weirdly unselfconscious, not in tune—on his canal-boat deck in the evenings. A resident heron. Displaced from my old home, I've felt a funny kinship with that tatty urban heron—awkward yet stoic, no spring chicken—and can't help but see it as a symbol of my strange new freedom. No sign of it yet this morning.

I rest my arms on the balustrade, my dark curls starting to frizz, and my mind restlessly twitches forward, like the hand of a clock, to work, the earliest acceptable time to drink a glass of wine, then Annie. Images bloom in my mind. Mum yomping across a beach, toddler Annie on her shoulders; Annie curled up on the sofa, like a silky mammal, in a nest of cushions with a hoard of electronic devices; her freckles, persimmon stars, impossible for a makeup artist's brush to replicate. I miss those freckles. I miss her. And I can still recall, as if it happened hours ago, the precise sensation of running my fingertip over her first tooth, hidden under the sore scarlet gum, intent on surfacing.

Out of the corner of my eye, the heron, my freedom bird, swoops down and turns into a statue on the bank. I smile at it. My mobile rings. Not recognizing the number, suspecting spam, I flick it to voice mail. It rings again. "Hello . . . Sorry? . . . Yes, Sylvie. Sylvie Broom . . . What?" My breath catches. The heron's huge wings hinge open and it holds them there, still, open, frozen at the first intention of flight. Time slows. The words "an accident" snag the baked London afternoon. And with a clap of feathers and air, my heron's gone.

3

Rita

A pheasant bolts up from the overgrown verge, making Rita start. She waits for it to scrabble safely into the forest, then shunts the car through Foxcote Manor's gates. A metallic scraping sound makes her wince. She hopes Jeannie didn't hear it. She needs this first day to go smoothly, without any bad omens.

"The car says ouch," announces Teddy from the back seat. He's lying across it, his head on the pillow of his big sister's lap, one bare foot pressed against a window, undone dungarees strap swinging. He has been dozing for most of the journey while Hera's sat in a state of brittle vigilance, her cheeks squirrel-stuffed with Black Jacks. "But don't worry. You scraped it on the other side this time, Big Rita. So it matches," he adds sweetly.

Rita turns to Jeannie. "I'm *so* sorry." And even sorrier about agreeing to take secret notes for Walter. Only she can't say this.

Jeannie shrugs and smiles, the first real smile all day, as if she rather likes the idea of a new scratch on her husband's car. Rita doesn't understand the Harringtons' marriage. Every time she thinks she does, something overturns it. Like the knife.

Two days after the fire, Jeannie confided that she'd hidden the dead baby's things from Walter—who had banned "any reminders"—under her bed and feared she'd never see them again. Rita immediately offered to retrieve them. She knew firsthand that memories had to be protected, like rare jewels: the enormity of tiny things.

Crawling on her elbows in the fine ash under the Harringtons' marital bed, snagging her cowlick, Rita eventually found the flesh-pink velveteen shoe bag, stuffed like a belly, with a cot blanket, frilled bootees, and a silver Tiffany's rattle that the baby never got to shake. But as she was trying to exit, almost stuck—always harder to get out of tricky situations than into them, she'd noted—she spotted a small kitchen knife tucked into the mattress wire, just below the pillow, as if awaiting Jeannie's hand to dangle over the bed to grab it. Still spooks her. Rita doesn't know what to think. Does Jeannie feel threatened by her husband? Has he ever hurt her? Walter would say his wife is paranoid, the knife another worrying sign of her tragically churned mind, the illness that's shamed the family. But Walter would say that.

After all, it was Walter and his doctor who had sent Jeannie to The Lawns a month after the baby died. Rita, dispatched to collect her eight long weeks later, will never forget it, the country-house façade, the dead-eyed women drifting around the gardens in long white nighties. She'd got talking to a sweet old lady, rocking a pillow in her arms. She said she'd been there for fifty-three years and hadn't had a visitor for forty. Rita had had no idea such places existed. And she vowed to make sure Jeannie never went back.

"Here. We. Are." Rita turns off the engine. The hush is thick and soft, like her ears need to pop.

Looking around, she notices a small brown car, violently pocked with rust, parked under a slump of honeysuckle. It's not the only thing in a state of disrepair. Foxcote's struggle with the forest was clearly lost some time ago. Fat tree roots have punched clean through the garden wall in many places, leaving nettles to swagger through the cavities and thorny brambles to reach across the drive, as if intent on crawling inside the house. The whole place has gone to seed. Rita hopes the energy of the children will lift it.

"Whoo!" yells Teddy, throwing open the car door and launching himself toward Foxcote's timber porch. Air rushes in, smelling sharp and chlorophyll green and oddly familiar to Rita, something long forgotten. It makes the fine hairs on her arms bristle statically, as if rubbed against a balloon.

"What are we actually *doing* here?" Hera hurls the question, like a rock, from the back seat.

The mood takes a perpendicular dive. At first Rita says nothing, careful not to step on Jeannie's toes. She watches, tensing, as Jeannie pushes her sunglasses into her dark wavy hair and eyes her thirteen-year-old daughter in the rearview mirror, with a look of wary tenderness.

Hera glares back with unblinking eyes of such a pale Arctic blue you can see right to their backs—Walter's eyes. Her fringe falls jaggedly over her forehead. Last week she used the blunt kitchen scissors to give herself a haircut that made her mother actually scream.

When Jeannie still says nothing, Rita twists in her seat. "We're escaping the grimy city for the summer," she says cheerily, even though she loves London in August, its fractious energy and greasy hot dog heat. "While the house is being done up."

Jeannie shoots her a small grateful smile.

"But you've always hated Foxcote Manor, Mother," Hera points out. Teddy, literal and trusting, doesn't really understand what's going on. Hera understands far too much and won't stop prodding at her parents' version of events. She didn't miss her parents arguing in the hotel foyer earlier: Walter holding Jeannie by the arms, as if to impart some sense to her; Jeannie snapping her head away, refusing to look at him. Something about Hera's expression today makes Rita think of a simmering pan of milk about to boil over.

"Not at all," Jeannie lies softly.

Rita bites the inside of her cheek and feels awkward. She knows Jeannie had no choice but to come here. Not if she wanted the children to stay in her care. She'd felt a punch of shock when Jeannie confided she has no access to the family's money, either, only housekeeping, that a privileged married woman has less freedom than her nanny.

"But—" begins Hera, enjoying having her mother's full attention for once.

"That's enough," Jeannie interrupts. "Not today, okay, darling? And stop gorging on sweets. You'll ruin your tea."

Hera slams the car door. Rita watches her stomp toward the house on her mottled plump legs. If Jeannie has halved in size since the baby died, Hera has doubled. Rita finds sweets wrappers everywhere—in Hera's pockets, under her pillow. Last month, she was caught stealing from her school's tuck-shop, twice.

Something was damaged in Hera the night the baby was lost. Rita has tried to get her to talk about it many times. But Hera closes up like a clam. All Rita knows is that the events of the last year are somehow externalized in Hera, the turmoil a shadow in her pale eyes. And it's her job to contain Hera's flare-ups and shelter her and Teddy from the worst of their parents' humdinger rows, which shake the house to its foundations. (Rita often feels about as useful as an umbrella in a force-nine gale.)

"Bodes well," says Jeannie.

"Don't worry. She'll come round." For some reason, Rita's got faith in Hera. The febrile girl touches her heart. "I'll grab some luggage and settle her in." She unfolds her long legs from the cramp of the driver's seat and strides around to the boot, knowing it's not luggage she's after.

As the lid lifts with a satisfying clunk, Rita exhales a breath she didn't know she was holding.

"So has your precious cargo survived?" Jeannie calls from inside the car.

"Yes!" Rita calls back, grinning. Her natural optimism returns. "Alive and well."

"I told you it'd be fine wedged between the suitcases, Rita."

A glass conservatory shrunk to finger-doll size, Rita's terrarium is the only possession she cares about. The only thing she owns that has no practical purpose. On the night of the fire, after tugging Jeannie and the children down the smoky stairs in the dark, she'd tried to return for it, but the blazing heat beat her back. She rescued it the day she went to get the baby's things. It was like reuniting with an old friend, a dear silent companion. Housing the most perfect mossy rock and, among other plants, a maidenhair fern she's named Ethel and another she's grown from a tiny black spore (Dot), the terrarium is the one constant between her unlikely nanny's life and Life Before.

Since she was little—though always the biggest in the class, least likely to be chosen as an angel for the nativity play or, later, asked to a dance—her dead father's botanical plant case has been on her windowsill. She gazes into it as other young women might into a mirror. If she squints through the half-moon of her lashes, she can retreat inside its glass and crouch down in all the landscapes she's ever created: the beach made from a handful of sand; a baby bonsai, its trunk like a twisted gray school sock; the prairie of dandelions rescued from a paving crack; all her old selves at different ages, different sizes, traveling the world in her mind, containing it, controlling it with her fingers. Keeping the scary big one out.

Resisting the urge to carry the terrarium safely inside the house first, she extracts the children's suitcases and walks around to the front of the car, the weedy gravel crunching beneath her feet. She stoops down to Jeannie, who has not moved. "Shall I grab your bag too?"

"No, no. I'll manage. You go in, Rita. I need a moment." She unclasps her handbag and rummages inside for a cigarette.

Rita hesitates, fearing Jeannie might jump behind the wheel and drive back to Claridge's, or even to the house that ignited on the anniversary of the baby's birth. A fact no one mentions. The firemen blamed the antique palm-tree lamp in the drawing room for starting the blaze. But Rita's not so sure.

The moment tautens, like a thread.

"Fear not. I'm only having a ciggy, Rita," Jeannie says wryly.

Rita colors and smiles, reassured. But as she walks toward the house, she hears the gassy whoosh of the lighter and the muttered words: "Although I'd much rather burn this bloody place down."

4

Hera, 4 August 1971

When I peered out of my bedroom window that morning, a year ago last week, the London sky was blue and still, and it felt like the whole city was holding its breath, waiting for our baby's first cry to peal across the rooftops. She wasn't meant to come for another two weeks. I'd circled her due date in my flip-top calendar with a red felt-tip heart. But neighbors had already started dropping off Pyrex dishes loaded with toad-in-the-hole and coronation chicken. Mother, who'd started to walk like a cowboy, had also had "little twinges": the words made me think of garden birds on the wing.

After lunch I helped her lay old towels on her bed, then newspapers on the floor, and we giggled about the nonsense poetry they stamped on our fingers. I tried not to think about what the newspapers were there to soak up and concentrated instead on what it would be like to hold my new little sister. (I'd done a deal with God to secure a sister, an ally, the best friend I'd never had, but I'd forgotten to make Him promise she'd stick around.) She'd be raw-looking, like an oversucked thumb, and would grow up to be a slightly plainer version of me. I imagined cradling her in my lap and people saying, so my mother could hear, "Oh, you're such a good big sister, Hera. She's lucky to have you," and me shrugging modestly, as if I'd not been practicing, using the neighbor's cat, for weeks.

But then the twinges flew away. It felt like a party had been canceled at the last minute. We waited around. Aunt Edie arrived, creating a sizzle, as she always does. Aunt Edie has declared herself too clever for marriage and wears a white shirt and navy slacks and works on a newsmagazine that sends her abroad to dangerous places, armed with a pen. She's been shot at twice. She has love affairs with war photographers. She finds kids' stuff boring. Whenever she came with us to feed ducks in Regent's Park, she'd stifle coffee-stinky yawns and check her man's watch. I loved her just for this.

"Don't let us keep you from the front line, Edie," Mother would mutter, a bit vinegary, making me wonder if she found feeding ducks boring too, but wasn't allowed to say so. Mother was much fonder of Aunt Edie when she wasn't actually there. She became a useful reference point in arguments with my father, waving like the vibrant flag of an exciting new country. Women like her were the future, my mother would declare, beating the cake mix harder and harder, so that shreds of it flew into the air and landed in unexpected places, like my father's raised eyebrow. Edie was living the sort of life Mother would have if she hadn't got married so young—at nineteen—and had me (six months after the wedding). It always made me feel bad when she said that. Like I'd come along and stopped her being her, dragging her back into a time before television.

Anyway, that Tuesday our life still resembled one of my mother's *House & Garden* magazines. The napkins were fan-folded on the dining-room table, which was polished like a mirror. I was plump then, not fat. Mother was still completely sane. She wore an apple-print dress that rocked over her bump as she moved, like it was enjoying itself. Aunt Edie had popped over and brought some things for the baby, a silver rattle and a yellow blanket, soft as butter. When my mother wasn't looking, she nibbled off the price label with her teeth. It was obvious from my aunt's expression she'd mistimed her visit—she'd thought she was safely two weeks from the birth. And now she was stuck. Like us. Like the baby.

Soon Mother was orbiting the drawing room, her hand on her lower back, blowing out in puffs, like a boiling kettle, then straightening with a short, breathless laugh, herself again. Teddy didn't like it. Aunt Edie didn't like it. She said, "Christ, Jeannie, do you want an ambulance?"

Mother bellowed back, "No, I want to be a man!"

It wasn't just Mother's words that had roughened: she'd started to look different by then, sort of ugly. Her face was flushed and swollen. Even her feet had gone pulpy: I could press my finger into them and lose my nail. When she paced in front of the sunlit window in her apple dress, her tummy was no longer high or round but slumped, as if whatever was inside was too heavy to be held there much longer. The thought of something so big leaving her body, through the same tiny secret slit as the one between my own legs, worried me. I couldn't work out the mechanics of it. But I took comfort in knowing it'd been done before.

Daddy came home early from work, tugging off his tie. He

brought Mother a glass of water, which she shooed away, like he'd done something wrong. After that, leaving Aunt Edie and my mother alone, he sat on the metal steps that spiral down to the patio. He lit cigarette after cigarette and frowned, as if the baby's arrival needed serious mental preparation. He'd been doing this a lot as my mother's belly had got bigger.

At one point the phone rang in the hall. Mother and Aunt Edie exchanged funny looks as Daddy scrambled up to answer it and hissed something to the caller before clapping the receiver back on its cradle. After that, he stood there glaring at the phone, the cigarette burning down to an ash wand in his fingers, then falling onto the floor. When Mother asked who it was, he didn't answer. Aunt Edie was pretending to read *House & Garden*. So it was me who let in the midwife.

Mother started to grab on to the sofa with her fists, as if trying to stop it galloping across the room. Her curls clung to her forehead, oily and dark. "Time for you to go to bed," she managed through a gritted smile. She hugged me. She smelled different. "You'll have a new sibling by the morning." Then she sucked in air loudly, adding, "Stay upstairs with Big Rita, okay, darling?" I couldn't get away fast enough.

On the top floor, Big Rita emerged from Teddy's bedroom with her huge smile, like the seaside was inside her. Her skirt was still soaked from Teddy's bath and she had a white caterpillar of bath foam caught in her hair. She hadn't been with us long then—a few weeks, her nickname already stuck—and every time I saw her, it still felt like a nice surprise. I'd expected to dislike her, as I had all the other mother's helps and nannies who'd been brought in after the death of Nanny Burt two years ago. (Sharp left-handed smack and a frown like the fork print in her pastry pie lids: I never liked Nanny Burt, either.) But I liked Big Rita. She asked me questions. She filled a room. Her hands were as big as Daddy's. But she never used them to slap. And if Teddy woke in the night, scared of the shadows under the bed, I'd hear her say, "The safest place in the entire world is exactly where you are, Teddy." Like bad things happened outside houses like ours. Never inside them.

Also, Big Rita isn't pretty, not obviously. It probably shouldn't matter. But it does. I've spent my whole life with people staring at my mother's face, then glancing at me, observing I didn't get her looks. Pretty people wait for you to notice them, rather than noticing you. I could tell straightaway that Big Rita was a noticer. She has wide eyes, the color of a wet beach. I loved the ordinariness of her name too: it made me think of ice-cream parlors and chips in a newspaper cone, stuff I'm not allowed. ("Best not, until you lose the puppy fat, darling," says Mother, who never stops watching her figure. Or mine.) I wanted *her* name instead of my own. I hate having to repeat my name—"Hero?"—and spell it. Also, Hera is the Greek goddess of marriage, which isn't even funny. Mostly, though, I just liked Big Rita for liking me. When Daddy jokingly said I was an acquired taste, like a Brussels sprout, she whispered behind her hand, "My favorite vegetable." I'm not sure anyone has said anything nicer to me than that. Unlike other nannies, she'd take us into the city, to museums and galleries, or mudlarking along the Thames, where we'd pocket tiny grubby treasures, our feet squelching, the metallic smell of the river on our cold pink finger-tips. Until you washed the finds over the sink, you never knew quite what would be revealed.

That night was the same. We were both so excited. I couldn't sleep. I asked her to tell me the story of her glass plant case again. Sitting on the edge of my bed, she explained in a low, soft voice how terrariums were once called Wardian cases, and designed so that people could grow plants in the polluted London air or transport them on long journeys overseas, and how it had changed botany forever, and the contents of Kew Gardens, and then, when my eyelids grew heavy, my head filled with ferns, she stopped talk-ing and tugged the sheet over my body. It was too warm for a blanket.

I woke in the stuffy dark to bloodcurdling screams coming from the floor below. Mother was dying. I clamped my pillow over my head. I wanted whatever would happen to happen so that she wouldn't be in pain anymore. Big Rita came in to check on me. There would be a beautiful baby in the basket tomorrow, she said. But when she pushed the hair off my face, I felt a tremble in her fingers.

An hour later, I opened my window and knelt with my chin on the cool sill, my eyes on the rooftops, the pink sun rising. I was there when the ambulance pulled up outside the house, where the milk truck usually stops with a cheery chink, and when the midwife ran down the steps, the big lantern light above the door spotlighting the bundle in her arms.

The shock of what I saw emptied my brain, then my stomach.

And it hasn't come back. I keep trying and trying, but I just can't remember: whatever I saw is scratched out, like a face from a photograph. Daddy says this is for the best. I must forget everything I might have seen that night and remember I've always had a ridiculously vivid imagination. And never ever mention it again.

5

Sylvie

"Would it help to talk about what happened?" I ask gently, edging closer to Annie on the big white sofa. I've still got a niggling hunch she's not told me everything about Mum's accident, that something's building inside.

Annie shakes her head and chews on a rope of her long red hair, mashing it flat as a ribbon. I loop my arm around her shoulders. Under her sweat top, she feels young and frightened and shuddery. I notice that she's gripping her phone and hope the new boyfriend has called to offer some moral support. Maybe he can reach her.

A boat chugs past on the canal. Even this sounds different from normal. The world has shifted. Darkened. The rippling shadows on the wall look like people falling.

"Granny's in the very best place she could be now, Annie." A brilliant specialist unit in London—the local unit she needed was full. *Thank God,* I think, for the umpteenth time, clinging to every scrap of good news. "I'm going back in an hour. Come with?"

Annie nods and tries to smile. But her face is stiff with shock. Her eyes are wet green glass. She's been crying on and off since it happened three days ago. We both have. But we're crying for different people: Annie for Gran-Gran, as she used to call her; me for Mum, not just the woman I call most days to chat to about nothing much or squabble with, but the unspoken thing that exists in the space between us, deep and rippling like a sea, so gigantic and elemental and complicated I can't put it into words.

"Or I can drive you to Dad's, if you'd rather be there," I bluster on guiltily, clumsily trying to normalize the fact that Annie's now got two homes, two bedrooms, all that to deal with too. I don't want her to go anywhere. She's been staying in this apartment for the last couple of nights, and it's been such a comfort to have her close again. In the early hours, I've sat on the edge of her bed and watched her sleep, like Mum used to watch me. Or my big sister Caroline did, swinging down from the upper bunk bed, her caramel-colored hair dangling, hissing, "Sylv, you awake?" until I was.

Caroline will be here in four days. But America feels even farther away this morning, and I'm terrified Mum will have taken a turn for the worse by the time my sister flies in from Missouri.

"Can I get you something to eat? A nice biscuit?" I think how Mum always says *a nice biscuit* when just *a biscuit* would do, and grief thunders through me again. I have to remind myself she's in a coma. Her heart still beats. She's not brain dead.

So where is she? I imagine her pinioned inside her own skull, incredulous and frustrated, demanding to be let out. *This isn't my time!* She has a calendar full of busyness. Decades of life still waiting. Stuff to do.

"No thanks," I hear Annie say, through the white noise in my head. "I can't face food. I feel kind of sick." She buries her face in my neck, like she used to as a little girl, her cheeks sticky with tears, eyelashes butterfly fluttering against my skin.

I hold her tight. My eyes slowly close. I haven't slept for more than a couple of hours at a time since it happened, endlessly jolting awake, slippery with sweat, my heart scrabbling in my chest.

The accident keeps flashing in staccato bursts. I can picture it all: the spray of blood up the cliff wall; the ocean boiling under the churn of the helicopter's propeller as Mum was lifted from the rocky ledge; Annie running along the cliff path, frantically trying to catch a signal to call me.

Then there are the photographs on Annie's phone. Taken a moment apart, the split second that separates a casual cliff stroll from catastrophe. One shows my mother smiling for the camera in her green North Face anorak; the next, just sea and sky, my mother extracted in an instant, like someone sucked out of an airplane window.

"Granny's going to be all right, isn't she, Mum?" Annie mumbles from under my unwashed curls.

"She . . ." I hesitate. Mum told white lies too. She sugarcoated the darkest of truths for me and Caroline. Rubbed the edges off them in the hope that they wouldn't hurt so much. I can't help myself. I do the same. "Granny will be just fine, hon."

※ ※ ※

After Annie's left for Steve's—*home,* as she calls it, inevitably: it'll always be the family house—I stand beside Mum's hospital bed, adjusting to her not being at all fine. When a doctor gently suggests that, given the uncertainty, I may want to get her affairs in order, I try not to scream like someone who's googled "head injury" and "coma" late at night and scared themselves witless. Also, Mum's affairs? It'd be easier to hack into the Kremlin, frankly. "Okay," I say, trying to hold it together, like Mum would.

When he's gone, I hold her warm, slack hand—the hand that once patted plasters onto my scuffed knee, that still writes random one-line postcards sent from home: "Glorious weather! You should see the lupins"—and my tears fall and bloom on the white hospital sheet. I can't help but feel she's secretly conscious, saying, "Buttercup, hang in there." And I mumble it back to her, "And you, Mum," only my voice goes raspy, all the things I can't say, haven't said, sticking in my throat.

Lying flat, her swirl of bandages like a turban, she looks younger. This cheers me because I know she'd *love* that, even if she'd pretend not to. ("Better old than dead!" she likes to say, then slaps on the retinol cream every night.) Her shaken brain might be bleeding, the left side of her face swollen, but her bone structure stands out, revealing the face that was scouted by a modeling agent decades ago. Who she was before Caroline and I came along and she and Dad left London for the rural good life—chickens and beaches and Argyle cardigans—and she basically turned into Linda McCartney. I smile, thinking how she's never quite lost her fashiony tics. Like muscle memory. I'll see it in the way she'll swing on a coat, with a small flourish, or lift her chin for a family snap. She's always had a model's protean ability to inhabit different versions of herself. Overwriting. Shape-shifting.

I touch her cheek with the back of my hand. Papery and dry. In need of rose face oil, massaged in under my warm palms. Or some moisture-boosting hyaluronic acid, finger-patted into her pores. If I had my makeup kit with me, I'd get to work and dust her cheekbones with blush too, salve her chapped lips and varnish her bare toenails, all the little things we do to keep life's darkness at bay. That's what I do. What I've always done. Toss handfuls of glitter into the deepest, dirtiest shadows.

As I sit watching her for almost an hour, something new and unsettling begins to dawn. Mum's not indomitable. I'm childishly staggered by this. She may die. She may not come back as herself, memory intact. So what will be lost exactly? She's the keeper of all our family secrets. What if there were things she still wanted to tell me? Questions she was waiting for me to ask? But I can't ask them now. Maybe I'll never get the chance. The truth about what really happened in a remote forest in the fading sun-bleached summer days of 1971 has been brutally, unexpectedly yanked out of reach.

6

Rita

S hocking business, isn't it?" the woman whispers, lurching into
the aureole of personal space that normally separates strangers.
Foxcote's front door bangs shut behind Rita, with a suck of air, sealing the dimly lit entrance hall like the heavy lid of a wooden box.
"Just terrible," the woman continues heatedly, as if Rita had an-
swered.

Rita's unsure if she's referring to the loss of the baby or the other
thing—the much more salacious gossip about Jeannie. She smiles
politely, well practiced in the art of giving nothing away, and rests
the children's suitcases on the floor with a thunk. Registering the
hissing sump of a log fire on the far wall, she feels something in her
chest tighten. This dilapidated old house would go up like a bonfire.

"The poor Harringtons. One thing after another, eh?" The
woman shakes her head. Her hair doesn't move. It's stiff and streaky
brown and gray, like a barn owl's wing. "What a hoo-ha."

A dull banging from the floor above snaps Rita's attention back
to the children. Teddy? Yes, Teddy. She can hear him giggling.
Sound travels differently here, not bouncing off the walls, like it

did in London, but seeping into the wood, like a spill of warm oil. Another muffled bump. A shower of plaster. Rita's big eyes roll upward.

The ceiling's low—she could touch it with her fingertips—and the flaky plaster is crisscrossed with thick black beams, the sort you get in farmhouses, creating the dusty nooks and crannies so beloved of crawling insects and, most likely, mice. She can only imagine the daddy longlegs count in such a place. The walls are wood-paneled and studded with oil paintings—landscapes, dogs— and dusty bunches of dried flowers. At least nothing looks too precious. A woodwormed console. A rustic settle bench. A disintegrating upholstered chair. All listing slightly on the bare floorboards, as if on the deck of a ship. She has a sensation of tipping too, as if she's on the verge of falling into something. But she's not sure this has much to do with the floor.

"Mrs. Grieves." The woman's handshake is strong, her palm rough against Rita's young skin. "But you can call me Marge." She lifts her lantern jaw, revealing a raised mole inhabited by one prominent wiry black hair. Rita tries hard not to look at it. "Housekeeper." Marge smiles. Her teeth are grayish and oblong, chipped and irregularly sized, and make Rita think of Stonehenge. "Live out. Hawkswell born and bred."

Housekeeper. Could make life difficult. She'll need to get on with Marge. "I'm the nanny—"

"Big Rita, yes, I know," Marge interrupts. She sweeps a sharp, beady gaze over Rita's length. "Well, I can see why that nickname stuck."

Rita struggles to maintain her smile. ("Six blimmin' foot at thirteen!" Nan's friends used to marvel, making her stoop and shrink, so embarrassed she couldn't breathe.) She takes in Marge's muscular forearms; the broken capillaries on her cheeks; the stout, shapeless figure. Late forties? Rita can't tell. Everyone over thirty looks ancient.

"Soft on the kids. Devoted as a Great Dane. Snapped the wing mirror off the car. Throws reds in a white wash." Marge licks her lips. "Mr. Harrington told me all about you," she adds, with a note of unmistakable rivalry.

Rita wishes Walter had thought to warn her too. Divide and conquer. She can imagine him thinking that. (Also, she hasn't buggered up the white wash for months.)

"I can turn my hand to anything, Rita. You'll find I'm extremely flexible," Marge says, in a manner that suggests the contrary. "I can get here in no time, any hour of the day." She nods toward the door. "That's my trusty motor out front."

Rita recalls the rusting heap of metal under the honeysuckle.

"Faster than it looks, actually," Marge says with a sharp sniff. "I've worked these country houses for years. Ever since my husband died. Drowned in the Severn. Tsk." She clicks her tongue, as if remembering his stupidity. "The tidal surge."

"Gosh, I'm so sorry." Rita looks at her feet, then steals a sidelong glance up the stairs. What *is* Teddy doing?

"I manage just fine on my own." Marge speaks with grim pride, as if she's pummeled her life into shape against the odds.

Rita warms to Marge a bit more then. They share the common ground of independence, at least. In London there was camaraderie among the domestics, most of them unmarried, dispensable, burrowed into the attic bedrooms or with roommates in cramped flats. The live-outs would emerge early in the morning, worker bees, swarming from grimy districts into London's wealthy streets and mansions to look after other people's children—feed them, delouse them, iodine the gashes on their knees. They'd keep the houses unmarked by their charges, and then, as night fell, they'd scramble onto buses or sink back underground, returning to their lodgings, leaving no trace, as if they were never there at all.

"Not that the work's a piece of cake."

"Of course not," Rita rushes to agree.

"Houses don't do well not lived in round here. Turn into a right shambles, they do. The forest reclaims them. Damp. Mildew. Mice. Wood beetle. No point keeping the place if you don't use it."

Rita nods. She struggles to understand how anyone could have a whole house they didn't use, let alone care about. What she'd give just to have a tiny flat of her own.

"If it weren't for me, there'd be dog roses growing through the rafters."

Rita laughs, rather liking this idea. But another loud thump from upstairs—more showering plaster—sobers her again. She needs to Teddy-proof. Check there are no low windows open. No heavy furniture leaning perilously against uneven walls. If there's an accident waiting to happen, Teddy will find it. "I'd better check on the children," she says, picking up the suitcases again. "Sounds like Teddy's making himself a bit too much at home."

"This isn't an easy place to live." With no warning, Marge grabs the sleeve of Rita's blouse. Her nostrils flare. She releases the sleeve, sizing Rita up. "Know the forest, do you?"

Rita shakes her head. Her heart starts to beat faster. If you lose both your parents on a lonely forest road and you're plucked from the smoking wreckage, a half-dead thing, you have nightmares about trees. But she refuses self-pity. She was six. And the memory of the car crash is, mercifully, a blank.

"Didn't think so. A Devon girl, Mr. Harrington said."

"That's me." Sky and ocean. Just thinking about it makes her long to look out of a window and see a paintbrush streak of horizon, the gray-green smudge where water meets cloud. She remembers sea salt, its fine crystal crust on her lips, and her mouth waters.

"You'll need to keep your wits about you here, then. Adders. Death cap mushrooms. Ticks. As for branches in a high wind? By the time you've heard the creak, it's too late. Old mines open up under your feet. Oh, yes, there's a pile of felled tree trunks near the garden gate. If Teddy climbs on that, the whole lot will come tumbling. Roll him out like puff pastry."

"Well, it's good to be warned," she manages, trying to seem undaunted. This place sounds like a nanny's nightmare. Through the window, the green mass sways queasily.

"Poachers. Dangerous lot. But the foresters shouldn't give you any bother, if you leave their sheep alone. Ancient grazing rights." She stops. Something fires in her eyes. "Oh. I beg your pardon. I should warn you about Fingers Jonson."

"Fingers?" She's beginning to wonder if the woman is slightly unhinged, or if the fuggy heat and woodsmoke in the room are distorting her own judgment. Also, she really needs the toilet. It was a long drive.

"Loner. Tall. Albino. Wanders the woods. Our Green Man."

Rita pictures the mythic man of folklore, a face formed of twisted sticks and leaves, acorns for eyes. Horrible. A large moth batters against the window.

"Oddballs are drawn here. Always running from something. Fugitives. Druggies. Price we pay for living in the last bit of wild in England."

Rita's hands instinctively fist. She'd lay down her life for Hera and Teddy. "The children will be safe with me, Marge."

"You do seem very sure of yourself for such a young woman, I must say." Marge sniffs, irritated by this. "I suppose at your size, you're more than a match for any man."

Feeling the familiar tightness in her chest, hearing the whispery chant of old school playground insults—"Rita Rex," "Rita Heifer," "Mr. Rita Murphy"—she decides she'll have to make a break for it.

"And it'll shred those shoes of yours." Marge nods down at Rita's feet as she places one brown Clarks sandal on the stairs. She hates her feet. More than this, she hates people looking at them.

There's a rush of fresh air and yellowy-green light. Rita turns to see Jeannie in the doorway.

"I was wondering if you could be a darl—" Jeannie stops. Her face falls. "Marge," she says, quickly rearranging it.

"Mrs. Harrington." Marge smooths down her overall in rapid, jerky movements.

"I wasn't expecting you to be here today," Jeannie says.

"Your husband asked me to help bed you in," Marge says, managing to sound both obsequious and superior.

At the mention of Walter, Rita colors. The damning words "our little arrangement" start fluttering in her head again, trapped there, like the moth at the window.

"*Bed* me in, Marge?" Jeannie recovers a smile—she's well practiced at maintaining a gracious front, and then, Rita suspects, going upstairs to scream into a pillow. "Goodness. I'm thirty-three, not ninety."

Marge ignores this and her eyes dart to Jeannie's ring finger, as if to check the wedding band's still there.

With an unpleasant bump, Rita's mind lands back on the sleety evening in December when she'd pressed her own engagement ring into the hands of a bewildered tramp on Waterloo Bridge, then carried on walking, tears rolling down her face. Earlier, she'd called Fred to confess. She can still hear the tremble in his voice: *You betrayed me, Rita.* And the line—and the future she'd thought was waiting back home—gone dead, cutting her adrift.

"I've given the house a good airing," Marge continues. "The fire will help get rid of the damp, Mrs. Harrington."

"You can call me Jeannie now."

"Do I have to?" Marge says after a beat, in a voice that could pickle onions.

Last year, returning from The Lawns, Jeannie also insisted that Rita call her by "my name, not my husband's." It felt strange at first, but she has gotten used to it. She's gotten used to many things she'd once thought extraordinary.

"As you wish, Marge." Jeannie walks across the room—her patent leather heels clopping—and turns to the large silvered mirror above the console. She balks at her reflection, as if she were expecting someone different.

Marge hovers. "You'll be happy here, Mrs. Harrington. I'll make sure of it," she says firmly, as though happiness were something that could be conjured with a bit of elbow grease, like shine on a parquet floor.

"Thank you." Jeannie's smile falters. A silence spreads.

"And the children will have tree sap running in their veins before you know it," adds Marge. "The forest will knock the city out of them, don't you worry."

Jeannie's eyes widen. Rita stares at the floor, hit by a sudden nervous urge to giggle.

"Well, I'll start on dinner," continues Marge, undefeated. "How does a bit of lamb sound? Spuds?"

"Don't trouble yourself. A simple nursery supper will be fine. Rita can rustle something up."

"But Mr. Harrington instructed that *I* cook you supper." Marge shoots an offended look in Rita's direction.

"Well, I instruct you not to. You've worked very hard to get the house ready. Go home and put your feet up."

Marge stands stubbornly in the entrance hall, as if held there by a deep taproot. "You look so tired, Mrs. Harrington. Thin as a rake. If you're here to convalesce, you must have a good square meal."

"*Convalesce?*" Jeannie manages a small laugh and lifts her hair from her neck, airing it. "Dear me."

"Well, I'll let you get on," says Marge, sounding unrepentant, turning to the front door.

Rita follows Marge's smudged reflection moving across the mottled sky of the mirror. As soon as she's gone, Jeannie says, "My god, she's not changed a bit. Damn it, she's clearly been enrolled as one of Walter's spies."

A rush of shame and guilt hisses through Rita, like hot water in a pipe. *Our little arrangement.* Somewhere in the house a cuckoo clock squawks, a shrill mechanical mimicry of the real birds outside.

Jeannie sits on the bottom step of the stairs. She rests her face in her hands and peers up at Rita through her long curled lashes. "We need to talk, don't we?"

Her stomach flips. Jeannie *knows*. She gestures upstairs. "The children . . ."

"Oh, they'll survive." Jeannie pats the stair. "Sit next to me."

Rita lands heavily, simultaneously horrified and relieved at being exposed. All that's left is to confess first. "I'm so sorry, Jeannie."

"Sorry? What on earth are you talking about?" Jeannie looks at her, bemused. "Gosh, you really are a funny old thing, Rita. I wanted to say *thank you*. For coming with us. Really, from the bottom of my heart."

Robbed of her confession, she doesn't know what to say.

A lozenge of toffee-brown sunlight penetrates the dappled, dirty window, revealing a cyclone of dust motes, rotating in the middle of the hall.

"I won't lie to you, Rita, you're in for the most boring summer of your life."

She can feel heat crawling up her neck like a rash.

Jeannie studies her with a puzzled expression that softens into one of sympathy. "Fred's no longer on the scene, is he? Your butcher chap. I suppose you don't need to travel back home to see him at least."

"No," she stutters, floored that Jeannie even remembers Fred's name. She's always assumed she ceased to exist for the Harringtons outside her job. Maybe she does. Toward the end of her engagement—although she'd had no idea it was the end, not until that phone call—Fred used to say she'd got so suckered into the Harringtons' London life she'd not got one of her own; she'd attached herself to the family like a limpet to the side of the *Titanic*. For some reason it felt too exposing to reveal the deeper reasons she stayed, so she chattered about the salary she was saving, much better than anything she could earn back home, the little house they'd buy one day. She knew he'd never understand the way being in a family, even as staff, bolted down something loose and rattling inside. Nannying wasn't just a job. It felt necessary on a level she didn't really understand. When she wasn't working, she felt lost, unrooted. Fred was a good man—and half an inch taller. But there were lots of things she couldn't tell him.

"You're unlikely to find new romance here," continues Jeannie, with a sigh. "I warn you now."

This suits Rita just fine. After what happened with Fred, she's sworn off men for good.

A sharp rapping sound. They both turn. And there's Marge standing in a doorway, clutching a jailer's bouquet of keys in one hand and, in the other, held high, laces dangling, a pair of large scuffed leather boots. "I just swiped these from the woodshed, Rita. Belong to our woodsman and carpenter, Robbie. He won't miss them. As I said, you'll need a good pair of shoes. Look about the right size, eh?"

Men's boots. Embarrassing.

"Well, I'll leave you in peace then." This seems unlikely. Marge doesn't move. The battered leather boots crouch beside her, like dogs awaiting instruction.

"Is there something else, Marge?" Jeannie says tightly.

"I don't know if it's my place to say this . . ."

Then *don't* say it, Rita silently pleads, remembering how Mrs. Pickering from number 35 had begun with "You can always have another, Jeannie," in the same way. Jeannie's hands start writhing in her lap. They always betray her.

Marge licks her front teeth. "I heard about your baby, Mrs. Harrington," she says, the words hurrying out, as if prepared in advance. "I'm so sorry for your loss."

The silence stretches. Rita remembers the morning after the baby was born: the stew of newspapers she cleared up from the master-bedroom floor, soggy with blood; the forgotten heap of stained towels on the window seat; the ferric blast in the air. The empty cradle.

Marge starts to shuffle back into the corridor.

"Wait," says Jeannie suddenly.

Marge stands to attention. Rita braces.

"Thank you." Jeannie's hands are still on her lap. Her diamond ring glitters in the earthy brown light. "For acknowledging my baby existed. Not many people do."

Marge's relief is almost palpable. "Oh, I forgot. One last thing."

That's it. She's never going to leave, Rita thinks.

"A man phoned earlier this afternoon. Before you arrived. Asking to speak to you."

Jeannie straightens instantly, like a thirsty plant, watered. "Not Walter?"

"Most definitely not." Marge's eyes narrow. She watches Jeannie more carefully. "Called three times. But he wouldn't give a name."

Oh, no. Something in Rita flattens. Not *him*. Not here.

"How odd," says Jeannie weakly. The air in the room thins. A moment passes.

"You have a lovely evening, then." Marge retreats, her bunch of keys clinking.

Jeannie covers her mouth with her hand. Rita sits very still, not daring to say anything, listening to Jeannie's breath quickening, all that damage and desire threading between delicate diamond-weighted fingers.

7

Hera

Don Armstrong used to be Daddy's best friend. They were at Eton together, and in the old school photo that Daddy smashed against the wall at Easter, they're grinning at each other rather than at the camera, like they're in on a joke. Years later, Don took Daddy to the party where he met my mother. The legend goes that outside the party, her stiletto heel snapped off in the pavement grating. Don gave her a piggyback ride to the taxi. Daddy sat in the cab and escorted her safely home to her room in Kensington. "A team effort," Mother used to say.

In my parents' wedding album they're there again, arms thrown over each other's shoulders. Don, best man, looks pretty much the same as now—tanned, broad-faced, all his features fighting to be top dog, dirty-blond hair. Daddy used to joke—in the days when he made jokes, and Don's love life was an amusing topic of conversation, rather than a seeping open wound—that Don had kept his hair because he hadn't gotten "bogged down" with a family or done a proper day's work in his life. Don inherited a fortune of stocks and shares, Daddy a doddery old glass company and an unprofitable quartz mine in Africa. Don got adventures. Daddy got meetings and cone furnaces and striking workers to worry about.

Don would go traveling a lot. Mother would gaze out of the window and say things like "Walter, when did we last see Don? I hope he's not in a fix somewhere," and her voice would always sound a bit too high.

After a while—days or weeks, we never knew—Don would pitch up on the doorstep again, crumpled from a flight, eyes blue beads in the tan of his face, the pockets of his sun-faded khaki jacket stuffed with stories and presents for me and Teddy: a tiger's tooth; a gold Indian bangle; a wooden mask with slits for eyes that laughed in my nightmares.

At dinner he'd do astonishing things like helping Mother in the kitchen, something my father would never ever do in a zillion years. "Budge up and let me baste the potatoes, Jeannie," he'd say, making a huge mess, all the dripping flying everywhere, potatoes skidding across the counter, while my mother leaned back against the refrigerator, laughing, not at all bothered by the oil slick gleaming on the kitchen floor, as she normally would be.

Afterward, the conversation would no longer be about what the Pickerings had done to their front garden ("To pull up those old roses!") or whether the Smith-Burnets had bought a holiday house in France. We'd be transported.

Don would sit in Daddy's chair. No one else was ever offered it: the leather was molded to my father's shape, like a saddle. Don would lean back, the ice crackling in his whiskey glass, and as he talked about his travels, it felt like the globe in the drawing room started to spin on its axis. Marrakesh. Paris. Bombay. Hunting game in Kenya was his favorite thing. He relived it as he talked: the eardrum-crack and shoulder-punch of the gun; the thrill of a huge beast falling. "The closer you are to death, the more alive you feel," he'd say.

Occasionally my father would mutter something about the heat of his glass furnaces or the depth of the Namibian quartz mine he'd inherited from a favorite uncle, which he calls "my most expensive, difficult child" and refuses to sell. But neither could beat the mineral gamy smell of lion's blood and Teddy would shush him. And Mother would still be leaning toward Don, elbows on her knees, chin in one hand, all the places she hadn't been and things she hadn't done stamped like postmarks in the furrow between her eyebrows. (Daddy never took her traveling with him. She had to stay at home with us. "Hold the fort," he'd say.) After Don had left, she'd get a funny distance in her eyes, not dissimilar to the look she had in the car journey down to Foxcote yesterday. She thinks I can't see behind those big dark sunglasses, but I can. I can see through everything.

Don never stayed long. And he didn't stay long *that* weekend, either. Just one night in the guest room, while Daddy was abroad on business: he'd been away for over a month. I caught Mother leaving the guest room the following morning, her face glowing, her hair all messed up, mascara on her cheekbones, like she'd been unpicked and sewn back together overnight. And it was about three months before she announced she was pregnant and the baby's due date.

Before then, once a month, it felt like it was raining inside the house. Mother would go to bed with an aspirin and a hot-water bottle. There would be small spatters of blood in the lavatory bowl, and I'd know that the baby she and Daddy kept trying to have—the one who was meant to be close in age to Teddy but kept getting further away—hadn't worked again. And I'd pray it would work. But not like this.

I don't know what made me do the math. Pore over my biology book. I guess I just knew. And I'm pretty sure Daddy did too. When I think about it now, and I still think about it a lot, the thoughts hopping and biting like fleas, everything bad that has happened to us is Don's fault. And he's gotten away with all of it.

8

Sylvie

My days develop a frenetic rhythm. Trying to keep the gnawing dread at bay, I bounce from moment to moment in a blur
of busyness. Between hospital visits—and calling Mum's phone to
listen to her voice mail over and over—I become obsessed with
turning Val's perfect pink apartment into a home. I want Annie to
hang out here, not just to stay out of a sense of duty.

When Caroline arrives from America, I need her to approve of
the place too, rather than assume it's a reflection of her mad little
sister's metropolitan midlife crisis. I throw old Welsh blankets over
the pristine white sofa and cook Mum's recipes from my childhood:
red velvet cake, mushroom quiche with soggy pastry, and a briny
fish pie.

The world of work feels like it exists on a different plane. One on
which I can no longer function. So I bat off all new commitments,
including a five-day catalog shoot in Greece, reasoning that just because I'm self-employed, it doesn't mean I can't have compassionate
leave. As my agent, Pippa, waspishly points out, I can, I just don't

get paid. "Take as long as you need," she says—then, more steely, "but not too long." We both know it's a risk dropping off the radar when so many other makeup artists—younger, hungrier, with churning Insta feeds and instructive YouTube videos—are competing for work. I don't tell Pippa my hand is not steady enough to do a cat's-eye flick right now, that I barely sleep, and every time someone asks, "How are you?" I have no idea what to say.

There's no language for this strange, shifting place I'm inhabiting, unable to grieve, yet reeling from loss, the days raw with every chatty phone call I don't make, emails I don't send, the Christmas plans Mum and I always start discussing, madly, in August. I arrive at the date in the diary when we were going to see a new exhibition at the V&A. And I imagine the afternoon happening, in a parallel what-if universe, us walking past the Greek statues, Mum saying, like she always does, "I could live in here."

As I'm surviving on coffee and adrenaline, the weight drops off. (Satisfying, even in a crisis.) My heart feels like it's running 10Ks in my chest. In the mirror, I observe a violent twitch in my left eyelid. We think other people don't notice them, like so many things, but they do. And yet. The man in the black canal boat, the one who plays guitar and wears a battered fedora, giving him a sexy, rakish air, has started smiling at me whenever I walk past on the towpath, furrow-faced after a hospital visit. Or I'll be on the balcony, ruminating, heron-watching, and catch him peering up at me. He might be a nut or in need of glasses, but his smile always looks like a question. Once I smiled back.

Steve phones. "You're not all right, are you?" Passive-aggressive. Annie must have said something. "You sound manic, Sylvie. It's bonkers you being at Val's flat at a time like this. Come home, babe. Let me look after you."

The offer is so tempting—in a cowardly, "screw it, I'm done" sort of way—that I have to sit down.

I could slot back into my marriage, my house, our joint account, like a spoon in the cutlery drawer, *and* end Annie's resentful shuttle between bedrooms. But something in me resists. I think of Annie's words: *So you've been living a lie all this time?* How I've plugged painful, awkward bits of my life for so long. So I grip on, like a woman dangling from a window ledge by her fingertips.

"You've always been your own worst enemy, you know that?" Steve says, hanging up, reminding me why I left.

Caroline saves me, blowing across the Atlantic, emerging from customs in a fluttering marquee of lime-green linen, sweating and grinning, like a bomber pilot who's survived another rough tour. (My sister hates flying and becomes religious when airborne.) We hug and I inhale the comfort of her American house with its stoop and comfy snugs, her big, riotous, loving family and three slobbering dogs—as well as the thousands of miles she's traveled, all the months we've been apart.

Caroline's married to a haulage company director, Spike, the loveliest man, built like a grain store. They have five children under nineteen, including Alf, a seven-year-old with Asperger's, who very much needs Caroline around. (We Skype a lot.) We are as different as sisters could be. She's big, blond, steady, and solid, like a Labrador. I've always been the scrawny dark one, nervy, light on my feet, like a witch's cat. Oh, yes, and Caroline has managed to stay happily married, like our parents.

"Still dressed for a funeral I see, sis." She grins. Me wearing black is one of our jokes. She holds me by the shoulders. "And traitorously skinny! I've put on six pounds since Mum fell, mainlining cookies, and you've shrunk a dress size. How is this even possible? Are you just eating steaks and foraged berries or something fashion crazy? Is your breath gonna smell like a caveman's?"

I laugh. The relief of her is physical and enormous.

"Or . . ."—she narrows her eyes—"you're not, are you?"

"Not what?"

"Having animal nonmarital sex?"

"Oh, my god, *no*! Caro, I am so far from having sex that I may as well join an order." For some stupid reason, I think of the man in the fedora on the boat.

She lifts an eyebrow. "Why are you going red, then?"

"Hot flush."

"You know I don't believe that! You still look thirty. It's incredibly annoying."

"Yeah, yeah." But I can feel my grin stretching wide. How confusing it is to feel so ridiculously happy to see someone when the reunion is occurring for the very worst of reasons.

We're soon chatting at a hundred miles an hour until the gap between us closes and her transatlantic accent slips into British and it's as if we saw each other yesterday. Then we're kids again. I'm lying in the lower bunk bed, reaching up to touch her fingers dangling down from above. We're walking back from school along the overgrown Devon lanes, bulging school satchels digging into our shoulders, grabbing wild flowers—oxeye daisies, Queen Anne's lace—from the bank to give Mum at teatime. Mum's turning from the sink, wiping sudsy hands on her A-line denim skirt. It all rushes at me, sucking away my breath, nipping back time, like a belt.

"What's the matter?" she asks, shooting me a sideways look. "Have I got too fat to wear green or something? Do I look like a hedge?"

"No. You look gorgeous." I lift her bag into the car's boot. A carry-on. Not staying long, then, I think, a bubble of sadness in my chest. "I've missed you, that's all."

She slips an arm around my shoulders. "Same."

❈ ❈ ❈

The sight of our magnificent mother lying sessile on her hospital bed, suspended in the fathomless murk of a coma, her bodily functions outsourced, makes Caroline burst into tears.

I did warn her. But nothing really prepares you. I take her hand in mine. Her palm is hot and damp. She hates hospitals. They're up there with flying on her anything-to-avoid list. She had so much surgery as a kid it's not surprising. "I can't believe this. I thought she was invincible. She's never ill! She never even gets colds. Oh, Sylvie, I feel so bloody guilty for living so far away."

"If you'd lived next door, it wouldn't have stopped it." I hand her a tissue. "Caro, there's a chance if . . . *when* she wakes . . ." I stall. The subject has its own weft, too many layers. "Her memory might be affected. You should know that."

I watch this information percolate through my sister's features.

Like me, she'd never have imagined that so much family history might vanish with Mum, like a Polaroid image left in stark sunlight, fading to a skeleton-gray silhouette, then gone.

A moment passes. She links her little finger in mine and shakes it. I smile at her, relieved. Growing up, we used to do this all the time. It was our secret way of saying, *We're sisters, that's all that matters; we won't talk about the past, where the monsters live.* "I just want her better," she says.

"Me too."

We stare at Mum quietly for a while. The machines beep and buzz. "You know there's a small chance she can hear us?"

"Oh, wow. Really?" Caroline leans closer to the bed. "I've got your wedding photo here, Mum." She digs into her handbag and pulls out a small framed photo of our parents outside Hackney register office. (Beaming at each other, eyes shining, they look like they can't believe their luck.) She places it on the table to remind the nursing staff that Mum's an individual, a woman with a story, not just a gray-haired patient in a backless gown, daft enough to fall off a cliff. "There. Stunning."

The curtains rattle back. Kerry. My favorite nurse on account of her nonmedical professional snort of a laugh, which reminds me of Mum's. I make the introduction, then pull out the newspaper article about the rescue I've kept for Caroline and show it to them both.

"Ooh. Not every day I get to change the IV on a celebrity," Kerry says.

"I wish you could see this, Mum." Caroline shakes out the newspaper. "You've only gone viral."

Mum's accident had coincided with charged public debate about funding for coast guard emergency services. Since the first instinct of most onlookers was to take photographs—what clickbait she made, lying so perilously, enthrallingly, close to the abyss!—the story found its way into social media, the local Devon papers, then spilled, in a surreal way, into the mainstream press.

"Not far off a Kardashian," I say.

We wait for Mum to smile or say, "The Whatishians?" feigning ignorance to amuse us. But she doesn't. Mother. Her sense of fun. Her secrets. Silenced.

❊ ❊ ❊

"Aren't you two a bit old for a sleepover?" Four days later, Annie emerges from her bedroom, wearing the pajamas I bought her in Paris and a guarded look of daughterly dismay. I suddenly remember crawling into Caroline's sofa bed in the early hours, unable to bear the idea of her flying back to America. We'd been up half the night, talking about Mum's prognosis, Steve's affair, Caroline's acne rosacea, and Annie's conditional offer to read math at Cambridge, which we agreed was insanely exciting, and proof that one day she'd run the world. We sobbed and laughed. We drank way too much. The incriminating wineglasses are still on the coffee table, along with empty Doritos bags, a violent sight at eight A.M.

"Your mother's led me astray, Annie. She always does. And now it feels like a coyote's died in my mouth. Come on, we'll budge up." Caroline pats the side of the bed. Her accent is more American this morning, as if part of her is already over the Atlantic, back with Spike and the kids. Although I know she's desperately torn about leaving Mum, I can sense how much she longs to be with her own family again. I almost forgive her for leaving.

Annie flops down on the bed, picks up the remote, and flicks on the telly. The news starts to roll. Our eyes glide sleepily to the screen. The weather: warm and cloudy.

"There's something I haven't told either of you," Annie blurts. The temperature in the room instantly drops. "It was my fault. Granny fell because of me."

"What?" Wine throbs behind my eyes.

"Annie, don't be daft," says Caroline, with a small laugh.

"You don't understand. If I hadn't tried to take a photo . . ." Annie begins. Her voice breaks.

"Oh, sweetheart, you think that makes it *your* fault?" I say. "The cliff edge crumbled and she slipped. It's bad luck. Hideously bad luck."

"Selfies are even more dangerous! People are always falling off cliffs while taking selfies. They step back and then . . . Argh!" Caroline stops abruptly, seeing the horrified expression on Annie's face, me shaking my head. "Sorry. God. Sorry. There I go again. Me and my big mouth."

"See what I've had to put up with all these years?" I joke, trying to change the mood.

Annie almost smiles.

Caroline wiggles up on the pillow. "Come on, tell us all about your new chap then, Annie."

Annie's expression darkens. She shakes her head.

Caroline glances at me. A question zips like a current between us.

A new sort of anxiety starts to marble inside me. I've been focused so much on Mum this past week, I barely know anything about Ed. No, not Ed. Elliot. "Right," I say, my voice coming out too high, fake cheery. "Pancakes? Those big fat Nigella ones with leaky blueberries. What do you think?"

"Tired of pancakes, tired of life." Caroline nods.

"I feel a bit sick. Can't face anything." Annie twists out of the bed and plants a foot on the rug.

"Wait." Caroline flings open her arms. "Before I skedaddle. Last group hug. To stop the 747 falling from the sky. You know I'm totally neurotic."

Annie stays: Caroline's the teen whisperer. We both fold into her arms and we stay like that awhile, buttressed against the outside world. It's the first time I've been properly still—or held—since Mum fell. Something in me loosens. Tears start rolling down my cheeks.

"Now, ladies," Caroline says, switching to her firm mom-of-five voice, "before we get too maudlin about things, I think we need to remind ourselves that our patient's tough as old boots, right?"

I nod and rub away my tears, igniting hungover sparks on my inner lids, the shape of a skeletal tree, a red vein forest. Suddenly Mum feels closer. She never gives up. Neither shall I.

"Annie?" Caroline asks.

"Right," says Annie weakly.

"There." Caroline hugs her close again, kissing the top of her head. "That's more like it, Annie. Don't blame yourself. And never forget this is Granny Rita we're talking about, okay?" Caroline shoots me a glance. Understanding flows between us, a secret sisterly transmission, and when she speaks again, her voice is soft, barely audible, like a private thought exhaled. "I reckon our Rita's survived much worse."

9

Rita

A darkling mood is spreading through Foxcote, tender as a bruise. As each hour is squawked in by the cuckoo clock on the landing, Jeannie seems to drift further away. Four days they've been at the house now, and no signs of improvement.

Rita may be what Nan would call "born cheerful," but she still feels the contagion of Jeannie's sadness, the sag of energy under Foxcote's eaves. Even the forest seems to mirror it, the air cloying, still and warm, boiling with insects. Above the trees the clouds hang low, white, and heavy, like damp laundry on a line.

Rita really hadn't expected another "episode" to strike so soon. Or for Jeannie's decline to be so steep-sided, like one of those old mine openings in the woods, their mouths gummy with moss, hidden under leaves. And now her loyalties are torn. Quite how dishonest is it right to be? She has promised to inform Walter—that's the arrangement, and as Jeannie's husband, he'd argue he has a right to know. She's not so sure. "Don't mention anything to Walter, will you?" Jeannie mumbled yesterday morning, and the cup of tea Rita was holding had jerked in her hand and sloshed on her wrist.

The possibility Walter might use information—*her* information—against Jeannie makes Rita want to slide out of her own skin in shame. What if Walter and those terrifying private doctors of his decided this new slump in Jeannie's spirits warranted a return to The Lawns?

Last night she lay awake, tossing and turning, wondering what to do, thoughts scuttling like the mice under the rotten floorboards. She woke up none the wiser.

Brevity seems the only answer. "Friday. J still has migraine. Lost appetite," Rita writes, sitting at the desk in her stuffy bedroom, the top of her thighs grazing the rough underside. Chewing the pen, she gazes at her terrarium—the ferns love the ravishing low light—then back at the pad. No, even this small amount of detail is damning—Walter will spot the signs, stupid—so she scrubs it all out, slaps the notebook shut, and shoves it into the desk drawer. She hates that notebook. And she dreads Walter phoning again.

He called a couple of days after they had arrived, sounding rattled—Jeannie, Rita had said, was out having a stroll—and told her the Namibian mine had collapsed during a busy shift. It was a god-awful disaster. He needed to go out there immediately and wouldn't be able to visit at the weekend, as he'd hoped. Rita tried to imagine the suffering taking place at that moment, those poor people buried alive. She thought about the children who'd lose parents, how their lives would be unrecognizable from what they'd been seconds earlier. It put the problems at Foxcote into perspective. And yet she still couldn't help but be enormously relieved Walter was going abroad. She assured him everything was fine at Foxcote. Jeannie was perfectly cheerful. No need to worry.

Her first lie. It had slipped out surprisingly easily. Even though her fingers left sweaty prints on the black Bakelite phone. But he would ring again: a man like Walter will always find a way to check up on his wife even from the other side of the world. And she'll have to tell another.

She also needs to hide Jeannie's state of mind from Marge, who Jeannie is convinced is in Walter's camp.

Keeping Marge away is difficult. The more vigorously Rita politely refuses the housekeeper's offers of help, the more determined she is to give it. She arrives without warning for spurious reasons, her rusting car coughing up the drive, trailing a boar's tail of exhaust. Rather than knock, she lets herself in using her own keys, then stomps around, obstinate, unstoppable, flapping dusters, slopping mops, and snapping out sheets, armed with gristly sausages, homemade pork pies studded with globs of yellow fat, and enamel pitchers of creamy milk—"to build Mrs. Harrington up again"—and questions, endless questions. "Did you get a good look at the baby, Rita? Was there a funeral?" Rita explained the baby was taken away in an ambulance. No, she didn't see her. No funeral: Jeannie was too sick, not coping, and Walter thought it better if they all pretended nothing had happened. Marge listened avidly, hugging a bottle of Ajax to her bosom. "All that maternal love." She sighed, as if deriving a small shiver of pleasure from the drama. "Nowhere for it to go."

Rita wishes it would find its way to Teddy and Hera.

But Jeannie doesn't leave her bed, a four-poster with the age-pocked texture of the stocks in Hawkswell, the nearest village, and a swag of cobweb hanging off its upper rail. She doesn't even gaze out the bedroom window, through the thick ivy, at the twitching, summery woods. The light hurts her eyes, Jeannie says. Rita leaves the windows ajar, but the dark red curtains stay closed, inflating in the breeze, like lungs.

The trigger was the news of the phone calls. Rita's sure of it. The migraine struck on their first night shortly after Marge appeared with those embarrassingly big boots and told them about the man who'd called three times. Who else would it be but Don?

As long as she's worked for the Harringtons, Don Armstrong has been around. First, it seemed, just as an old family friend, an irreverent raconteur, who arrived at the house with charm and boom. But then Don started to look at her in a way that made her feel odd and uncomfortable. And she'd dream of him, waking in a twist of sheets, slick with sweat and self-loathing. She began to notice he'd call during the week, when the kids were at school and Walter at the office, asking to speak to Jeannie. Phone cradled against her ear, Jeannie would talk to him in a hushed voice, with an intimate cadence, stroking her pregnant belly in small circles.

After the baby died and Jeannie was "no longer herself," as Walter put it, everything changed: no one came round at all. In the grocer's, people would avert their eyes and clear their throats, even step away, as if Rita too were tainted with something so ghastly it might be catching. It made her wonder if the dead leave different-sized holes in inverse proportion to how much life they got to live.

It's only been in recent months—since Jeannie returned from The Lawns, and the upped dose of pills kicked in properly—that Don has started appearing again. Always when Walter is at work and the kids are at school. Rita would hear the throttle grunt of his silver sports car and know to make herself scarce on an errand. When she returned to the house, Don would be gone, although the scent of his cologne lingered, pungent and peppery. And Jeannie would be languid, wrapped in a white towel, fresh from the bath, steam rising off her pale skin like desire.

Rita tried hard not to think about what they might have been doing. (Picturing the Queen helped. Or Nan's fossil-like toenails that Rita used to help buff.) But then a rude image would slide through her: a finger tracing an inner thigh, the fleshy swell of a buttock. It was hugely confusing. And it made her feel dirty, complicit. She didn't approve. Mothers were meant to be perfect! And yet . . . Rita's heart couldn't help but warm to see Jeannie happy again, the woman she'd once been.

If only Walter's attentions had had the same effect. He did try. Bought Jeannie bunches of carnations she'd let wilt in vases. Cookbooks she never opened. A new carpet sweeper. It was painful to witness: Jeannie's strained thanks, Walter's look of bewildered defeat. She'd overheard enough rows to know he was refusing to grant Jeannie a divorce, doggedly viewing their "estrangement" as a temporary madness that would be cured. He rarely mentioned the baby—"that thing," she'd once overheard him say—and he kept threatening to take custody of the children. Rita despised him for that. But he was also a man who'd been rejected. And she knew how that felt.

She was pretty sure Walter knew about Don, and suspected he was banking on it burning itself out. After all, the "Don Cure," as Rita came to think of it, never lasted. It was fleeting, a lustful fever dream, a way for Jeannie to escape her corrosive sadness. Don walked into a room and blew everything else out of it, and that was what Jeannie needed. Just to forget.

After Don's visit, the clouds would part for a few days; then a new mood would close in. Rita could feel it coming, a distinct cooling under the ornately molded ceilings. Like an animal before an electric storm, Jeannie would grow restless, as if she couldn't settle back into the house or her life. She would keep changing her outfit. Stare at the phone. Pick fights with Walter. Snap at the kids, particularly Hera. She'd be back where she started before Don's visit. Only worse.

Realizing she's been staring at the William Morris wallpaper bubbling on her damp bedroom wall for ages, ruminating about someone else's love life, Rita pushes in the desk chair and walks to the window. She splays her hands on the glass for a cool kiss and flexes her finger joints.

Each rectangular pane is the size of a book, the glass distorted with age, like skin, giving the forest beyond a strange, wavering life. She has the sensation that her mind is stretching, adjusting alongside her eyes, trying to see what's beyond that tree, then the next, unsure if the smoky blue smudge in the distance is composed of sky or glaucous leaf. London is a galaxy away. And this means Don is too. Even if he phones again, they are safe here, hidden like fugitives. So she must waste no more time worrying. She has a job to do. Laundry. Lunch. Keeping the children away from Marge's long list of deadly forest menaces.

10

Sylvie

Definitely beats a bunch of chrysanths." I peer inside the sealed glass bell jar that has mysteriously appeared at the nurses' station. Inside, malachite-green ferns. Moss. A rock. White roots wiggle through the gravelly soil. What's it called? A terrarium, yes, that's it. Very hip. I'm not sure why it makes me feel unsettled.

What would Caroline think? My sister flew back to America almost a week ago now. We talk at least once a day, trying to keep our spirits up. The way forward, we've decided, is hope, not grief. But everything feels tougher without her around. "Did you see who brought this in, Kerry?"

"Not my shift, sorry," the nurse says.

"Bit odd not to leave a note." It strikes me as a generous yet random thing to give.

"Maybe our Rita's got a secret admirer," another nurse suggests, tapping away at a keyboard, gaze glued to a screen.

"Maybe," I say doubtfully. Mum's not so much looked at another man since Dad died. ("I'd sooner get a dog, love.")

I rotate the terrarium to admire it from a different angle. And that's when I see it: a miniature house, the size of a matchbox, rendered in resin, tucked inside a mossy hollow. It changes the scale of everything: the ferns become trees, the stone a boulder. And my unease solidifies into something else. Once I see the forest, I can't unsee it.

※ ※ ※

Back at the apartment, I dump my bag and kick my strappy sandals from hot, sore feet. Something catches my eye and I startle, not expecting to see Annie on the sofa, wrapped in a blanket. I smile, delighted she's making herself at home. "Nice surprise!"

"Hi, Mum," Annie mumbles, checking her phone with that blink-and-you'd-miss-it teenage flick of the eye, fast as a texting thumb. I wonder if she's expecting something from the elusive new boyfriend. Is he decades older? *Married?* I daren't ask.

"How's Granny?"

"Not worse," I say brightly. Not dead! "Hey. Check this out." I carefully lift the terrarium out of my straw shopper and slide it onto the kitchen work top, where the glass winks in the canal-watery light. Still, I see a forest.

"What's that?" Annie sits up.

"A terrarium. Someone left it for Granny. Amazing, isn't it? But plants aren't allowed in the ward. You can have it in your bedroom, if you like."

"Cool." Her eyes are pink-rimmed. She's been crying.

"Granny would still want you to enjoy yourself, you know," I call over my shoulder, reaching for the teapot on the shelf. We need tea. *A nice cup of tea,* as Mum would say. I think of the joy she's always taken in Annie, her willingness to step in whenever work meant I needed emergency childcare, which was often. "This is the woman who gave you and your mates a lift to Glastonbury Festival, remember? *And* who pressed thirty quid into your hands at the gate. She'd strictly forbid you to feel maudlin on her account." I open the balcony windows, and the smell of turmeric and frying garlic wafts in. "She's beyond proud of you, Annie. Everything you've achieved. Math at Cambridge? Hello?"

Annie says nothing.

I barely scraped a pass in math. A restless student—"easily distracted, won't take her studies seriously," teachers would say—I was in a hurry to move to London, earn my own money, fall in love, and acquire the sort of frenetic, glamorous life that would steal me away from myself. Where I came from. Who I was. Annie's an evolutionary leap of a girl.

Steve and I must have done something right. After I'd had four miscarriages, we'd decided to quit further baby-making attempts and put all our resources into our one wonder of a child. Unlike Caroline and me, who were left to our own devices growing up, with a parental shrug of "What will be, will be"—it was the seventies— Annie got violin lessons, tennis teachers, Kumon, and tutors to boost her state education. We always said to her, "Work hard and you can do anything you want, Annie, anything you put your mind to. Don't let anything hold you back." And she hasn't. I flick on the kettle. "Cambridge will be lucky to have you, Annie."

"Can you please stop going on about stupid Cambridge?" she says, with a bite that takes me aback. I turn to face her, frowning. Where did *that* come from?

"I may not make the grades." She nibbles her bottom lip and her gaze skates away. "I may not even want to go."

I almost squeal, "You *have* to go!" (I've already started to fantasize about Annie's high-flying future career with its pensions and security, not subject to the capricious feast and famine of the self-employed, as well as the nice undergraduate she'll meet at Cambridge and go on to marry.) Instead, sensing I'm on shaky ground, I hold my tongue.

The kettle clicks. But something in Annie's expression makes me feel like the day has abruptly pulled away from tea drinking. Something else has shifted too, although I'm not sure exactly what. There's a filter between us, something obfuscating, moving, and delicate, like the fog that wisps across the canal early in the morning. I open the fridge. "Let's have an early lunch. Haven't we got those posh stripy tomatoes from the farmer's market?"

Annie walks over, and leans against the kitchen work top, staring down into the terrarium. "Mum . . ."

"And hummus?" I nudge aside a sticky mustard pot. "Where is it? We have some lurking somewhere."

"We don't." She slides a finger over the terrarium glass, not meeting my gaze. "I ate it."

"Salami, then."

"Ate that too."

I say nothing and reach for a chopping board. "Oh, crap. We're out of bread." The gravelly sound of a boat's engine on the canal below. Someone's on the move. I wonder if it's the attractive boat-man. "I'll run to the deli. One minute." I pick up my purse. Maybe I'll walk past him before he goes.

"Mum . . ."

I become aware of something tangible in the confines of the kitchen. A congestion. Even the terrarium has started to shimmer oddly, as if fireflies are trapped inside it.

"I need to talk to you."

"Oh." My heart plummets. I've been dreading this conversation, half expecting it: Annie saying she wants to live full time with Steve. All the hope I've tried so hard to manufacture this last week starts to ebb away. I miss my mother with a painful pang: she'd know what to say to Annie. "Look, I know it's not been easy, me and Dad . . ." I bluster. "And yes, you're right, I should have been much more hon-est with you earlier on."

"It's not that." She covers her eyes with the palm of her hand. "Mum, it's much worse."

The pink room seems to tip in the passing boat's wake, rolling the silence one way, then the other. And even as I say, "Annie, my lovely, whatever's the matter?" I suddenly know, deep in my belly, that this is going to be one of those conversations with a before and an after—and that nothing will ever be the same again.

11

Rita

Hera and Teddy fly in through the kitchen door, breathless, their hair fluffed, their cheeks glowing cochineal pink. A sort of manic savage glee intoxicates the children in the woods, Rita has noticed. (An outing to Regent's Park never had quite the same effect.) It worries her, since she's unable to follow them around every second of the day. They hop in and out of the holes in the wall, like hares. When she opens the garden gate and yells, "Lunch!" her breath's held, and what was a vague anxiety edges toward panic until the moment they tear out from the trees and the gate's rusty catch clicks shut behind them.

She can't mentally map where they've been in those missing minutes, the mossy gullies they've skidded down—snagging their clothes and fingernails—or their winding routes back to the house. Neither can she gauge how dangerous the forest actually is, if she's worrying unnecessarily. She stops smearing the sulfur-yellow piccalilli into the sandwiches. "You didn't climb the log stack, did you?" She sees it in her mind's eye, the logs precariously balanced, ready to roll like huge, spine-crushing ninepins.

"Don't worry, Big Rita, I pulled him away from certain death just in time. Stayed close to the house, as ordered." Hera gives a mocking Girl Guides salute, drops her knapsack to the floor, and prowls the kitchen for something to eat. "Although those funny-colored mushrooms were tasty, weren't they, Teddy?"

"What?" Her stomach goes pitchy.

Teddy and Hera snort with laughter, delighting in teasing her.

"You shouldn't joke about such things," Rita says sharply through her relief. But she's pleased to see the camaraderie, the sort of sibling solidarity that comes from idling away the hours together, blocking out worries about their mother, who's lying in the soupy silent gloom upstairs. It's just as well the children have to amuse themselves much of the time here. And there's a lot of time to be had, the days at Foxcote loose and baggy, bookended between the din of the dawn chorus and the sunset whorl of the bats, since Rita doesn't like to leave Jeannie alone for long.

If they'd stayed in London this summer, it would have been different. Even if Jeannie had been struck low, she'd have been able to roam her London house, with all its comforts, the reassurance of routine. And Rita would have been able to do her job properly, get out and about, give the children the summer they deserved, with visits to the British Museum, the magical Palm House at Kew, or an afternoon mudlarking on the Thames's sticky shore. All the excursions that Jeannie was more than happy to delegate and Rita loved. She could never believe she was actually being *paid* to do them. Remembering these things now—the warm, sweet smell of a cocoa tree at Kew, a silt-furred chip of a Victorian vase in her palm—makes her ache for London.

"And you shouldn't be so scared of the forest," Hera says, interrupting the tug of Rita's thoughts.

"I'm not!" Rita fibs, trying to inject an as-if scoff into her voice.

"If I was as tall as you I wouldn't be scared of *anything*." Teddy's heavy sigh lifts the curls from his forehead. "I want to grow faster."

"Patience. You'll be taller than me one day." Rita smiles even though it's almost painful to imagine Teddy as a grown man, his boyhood lost in time, like a message in a bottle thrown into a vast, rolling ocean. She untangles a burr from his curls. Then she sniffs, uneasy. "What's that cindery smell?"

"Only a small bonfire," says Teddy cheerfully.

Hera shoots him a silencing look and folds a slice of cheese into her mouth. "It's fine, Big Rita. Out now."

Something in Rita runs cold. She pictures the London house as she last saw it, standing out on the lovely crescent, like a rotten tooth in an otherwise perfect row, its stucco blackened, the wisteria withered. "You can't light fires willy-nilly!" she flashes. "Okay, matches. Who's got them?" She spreads her palm and glances from Hera to Teddy, who looks the guiltiest of the pair.

But it's Hera who reluctantly wiggles them from her tightly stretched shorts pocket and hands them over with a small grunt of resentment.

Rita kicks herself for not noticing the matches were missing. But Foxcote, like the forest itself, is still so unfamiliar, a place where potential disaster lurks in the most mundane guises. The cellar floor is littered with the rusty jaws of metal animal traps. Axes. A machete. There's a collection of old shotguns in a cabinet (unlocked, no key she can locate). She's even found a small handgun in a biscuit tin. When she'd asked Marge about this, she'd simply shrugged and muttered something about having a gun herself, as if keeping lethal weapons hidden among the Garibaldi biscuits was perfectly normal.

Rita slides the matchbox onto the top shelf of the Welsh dresser, among the chipped creamware, out of reach. She checks on the Savoy cabbage, destined for supper, bathing in cold salted water in the Belfast sink, approvingly notes the drowned slugs rising to the surface, and picks up a jug of lemon squash. "Here, Teddy. Be Mother," she adds unthinkingly.

Teddy carries it to the wooden kitchen table, leaving a trail of sticky splodges on the terra-cotta-tiled floor.

"Sit down, Hera," says Rita, wondering why she's still standing there, slightly sheepishly. "What is it?"

"I picked these. For Mother." Hera bends down and takes a small bunch of lilac-blue flowers from her knapsack, fanning them carefully on the table. She looks up, less sure of herself. "Do you think she'll like them?"

Something about the uncertainty and need in Hera's pale eyes loosens feelings in Rita. She suddenly remembers her own acute insecurities and loneliness at a similar age, a funny age really, too old for the comfort of doll's houses yet too young to have any control over your own life. Both dreading and yearning impending womanhood. Still in desperate need of mothering. "Oh, Hera. How could she not? Let me put them in some water." She arranges the flowers in a jam jar.

"But I haven't got Mummy flowers," blurts Teddy, who is sitting on a stool now, breathing hard, his soft dark hair curling over his sun-faded yellow T-shirt. "It's not fair if Hera gets to give her flowers and not me," he says.

Rita puts a sandwich on his plate and, leaning over him, cuts off the crusts. "It's not a competition, Teddy," she says gently. Although it strikes her that while they may be close rambling about outside, in the house the siblings are like forest plants, competing for their mother's warmth and light.

"I thought of it first," says Hera, staking her claim.

"No, you picked them in sneaky secret." Teddy goes to kick her shin under the table but misses, his leg too short. He slides a slice of cheese out of his sandwich and licks off the piccalilli instead. A moment passes. Rita wonders how she might cheer him up, and is about to suggest digging out the Meccano set when Teddy says, "Mummy needs flowers because Mummy's unwell again?"

"She's . . ." It's much harder to lie to Teddy than to Marge. ". . . feeling a bit under the weather." She gives him a reassuring squeeze of the shoulder.

"That's code, Teddy," Hera says unhelpfully, reaching across to swipe his crusts. "You know what for." She glances at Rita, and, with a mouthful of bread, protests, "*I'm* not going to lie to him!"

Teddy's bottom lip puckers and he reddens with the strain of not blubbing like a baby in front of his sister. "But I want Mummy to get better."

"She will in time, Teddy."

Teddy looks at her blankly. Rita remembers she had no concept of time as a child, either. Good things happened in a flash. Boring things went on forever. And time didn't solve anything, like grown-ups promised. It just made you older.

"Come here, you." Rita pulls Teddy onto her lap and hugs him tight. He smells of pickle, soil, and damp wool.

I love these kids, she thinks, with a physical force, like a sharp kick in the stomach, that takes her aback. She quickly checks herself. In a year or two, Teddy will be sent away to board, like his father was (Walter had once told her dryly he'd hated every minute of it), and she'll be forgotten by all of them, just a large hazy figure at the edges of family photographs. She knows this is the nanny's lot, the loving of someone else's children followed by the unacknowledged grief when the job ends. But she also knows that none of her charges have meant nearly as much to her as Teddy and Hera. And she'll never forget the exact weight and feel of Teddy on her lap, the way he molds and settles into her contours. Or the day, when Jeannie was locked up at The Lawns, Teddy turned to her and said, "Will you be my mummy now?" and she'd longed to say yes.

"She doesn't want to see us, does she, Big Rita?" Teddy's voice is still clotted with bravely fought tears. "She's too ill."

Rita knows he's thinking about The Lawns, his mother vanishing again. She can't bear it. "Follow me. Both of you. Upstairs."

Rita doesn't knock in case Jeannie asks them to go away. Hera and Teddy shuffle in behind her, hanging back, unsure of their welcome. Or which mother they might find today.

Rita places a tray on the bed—milk, sandwiches, a cold toasted tea cake—then sweeps open the curtains, making a circus big top of dust motes rotate in the center of the room. She starts to talk softly, filling the stale silence. There are barn owls in the eaves and a really noisy resident woodpecker in the garden, and Teddy's spotted lizards in the log pile. Rita chatters over her shoulder, tugging open the stiff window so the sweet smell of leaves and earth pours into the room. In the distance, sheep drift through the woodland, like clouds. She pushes back the ivy, and bees whirl up in excitement. Rita flaps them away, safely into the sky.

Jeannie slowly emerges from the burrow of bedding. Despite sleeping all the time, she looks shattered. Her eyes are vague and torpid, the skin underneath desiccated and blue-tinged. Rita spots the small bag of the dead baby's things poking out from under her pillow, and her heart sinks.

"Mummy!" Teddy launches himself onto the bed. Jeannie's fingers twirl in his hair, and she bends down to him, smiling weakly, indulgently. "Why, hello, my little soldier."

Rita beckons Hera, who hovers in the doorway. Holding aloft the little jam jar of wild flowers, already starting to wilt, Hera perches gingerly on the side of the bed, not daring to edge into the intimacy of its center. Rita shoots a smile. Jeannie hasn't noticed the flowers yet. She will.

Jeannie cups a yawn in her hand. "Any more phone calls, Rita?" Rita shakes her head. Jeannie's face falls. *Notice the flowers,* thinks Rita. *Notice* Hera.

"I . . . I brought you something, Mother." Hera rests the jam jar on the tray and watches her mother carefully, sideways from under her jagged fringe.

"Hera went out into the forest and picked them this morning." Rita wills Jeannie to admire them. "Just for you, Jeannie."

"They're so beautiful," Jeannie says, with an ache in her voice, like their beauty hurts her. Rita smiles as Jeannie reaches out and touches a flower. But it immediately shatters over the sheet, the petals like scattered Parma violets. "Oh," says Jeannie. "Oh."

Rita winces. They stare in stunned silence at the bald broken flower, then at the fat tears rolling silently down Jeannie's cheeks, splashing onto the snowy sheet.

"It always goes wrong when I try to make you happy," says Hera.

12

Sylvie

I shake the pregnancy-test stick again. No, like the other two, it's not changing its mind. The line is solid and laser blue. Sitting at the kitchen table, staring at it in woozy disbelief, I become aware of a strange crackling energy in my body, as if the test's confirmation has connected a dangerous circuit buried inside me with a violent, ugly jolt.

"Shit," I mumble under my breath, through my clamped hand, and glance out at the balcony where Annie's pacing, our cordless phone pressed to her ear. Her face is puffed from crying. I can just hear her saying, "I don't know . . ." Elliot. It must be him on the line. And whatever he's saying, I don't like it. "No. I . . . I can't promise . . . sorry," Annie says.

A savage heat sweeps through me. I leap up and thread through the balcony door, opening my hand for the phone. To my relief, she hands it to me without protest and vanishes back into the apartment. A moment later, I hear her bedroom door slam.

The phone in my shaking hand is hot. A grenade. And I realize I'm probably not the kind of mother—reassuring, liberal, and practical—I'd always imagined I'd be in such a situation. Because I want to murder the boy. Shake my fists at the summer sky. Why *my* daughter?

I take a breath. "Hello?" Do. Not. Freak. "This is Sylvie, Annie's mum speaking."

"Helen Latham." A posh voice. Slightly shrill. "Elliot's mother."

For a moment I can't speak at all. I see the hatch opening on the boat opposite. Everything slows.

"I'd like to finish my conversation with your daughter," Helen says crisply, undaunted. "Can you put her back on the line, please?"

"Better that you talk to me," I say, collecting myself, squaring up to her. "My daughter's too upset right now."

"Oh, Elliot's *distraught*," Helen says quickly, with an edge.

"I'd rather you didn't speak to my daughter directly." It's taking an enormous effort to be polite. The boatman sits on his deck and starts strumming his guitar. A Radiohead riff.

"Look, Vicky . . ."

"Sylvie." The heron, statuesque, watches me from the bank. The spores of green light the canal throws up seem to mix with the guitar notes. And everything is swaying. I feel dizzy. Jesus, my life is a disaster. It's unspooling. I need my mother back.

Helen clears her throat. "I want this matter sorted out as soon as possible."

"She's not had any time to process it," I say after a beat, trying to contain myself. *Matter?*

"Is money a problem?"

"What? No." So Helen's one of those wealthy London women used to buying her way out of problems. Anger starts to rumble through me, dark and unfocused, its meaning murky but its power abdominally felt. I grip the cool metal balustrade with one hand, squeeze it.

"Can I remind you that an innocent young man's future is at stake?"

"Not that innocent." My voice trembles.

"Elliot's only twenty-one. He's trying to make his way in the world. If Annie was imagining . . . well, to put it nicely, he's in *no* position to be a father."

"Annie's eighteen and has a Cambridge offer."

"Cambridge?" Satisfyingly, she can't hide her surprise. "Well," she says, making a minor mental adjustment, "we're on the same page then, aren't we? I'll call back after the weekend. When she's booked her appointment."

There's a click and the line goes dead. Damn it. "Bitch!" I shout, more loudly than intended. I screw up my eyes and cover them with my sticky palms.

"You all right up there?"

I remove my hands and there's the man on his deck, leaning over his guitar, looking up at me. My body floods with heat. "I . . . No. Yes, of course," I call back, then flee into the apartment.

"Annie?" The bathroom door is closed. I talk through it. "Elliot's mother should never have phoned. Whatever she said, ignore it. Hey, you okay in there? Can I come in, sweetie?" Annie doesn't answer. I push open the door. The bathroom is empty. The pregnancy-test boxes are scattered around the sink. My heart skips a beat. I run to Annie's bedroom, clock the rummaged mess on her bed, the trail of underwear from the chest of drawers, and feel it, like a drop in altitude, a rush of blood. Annie's gone.

13

Rita

Four forty-five A.M. Rita's mind is busy as a hive. The iron bed wobbles precariously as she sits up and reaches for her dressing gown, which in the dim light looks like a person hanging from the back of her door. There's no point lying in bed any longer, trying and failing to fall back to sleep, thinking about Jeannie, the children, and the perils of that forest pressed up against the garden wall. And, as Walter might tersely point out, she's not paid to think. Her job is to keep them all safe. And to do that, she needs to map this place. Get a grip on it. Master it. Since she's got this rare hour to herself, now would be the perfect time.

Downstairs, the house creaks and murmurs, like an elderly lady settling into a chair. She tiptoes across the kitchen's chilly tiles, swiping a biscuit from the side, and opens the back door. The sky is still bloody in the east, as if aglow from a distant forest fire.

Pushing this unsettling association from her mind, she tugs on the men's boots that Marge took from the woodshed—a good fit, annoyingly—and tightens the cord on her dressing gown, its pressure on her waist reassuring.

The broken paving of the garden path rocks under her feet. The trees click with birdsong. Near the gate, she pauses at the swell of a huge hydrangea, glowing fish-belly white in its late summer flush, and glances back at the house. The tiny ferns growing in the mortar wave at her, like babies' hands. Foxcote looks cozy and safe from here. Beyond the wall, not really. She lifts the gate's latch, then freezes.

She wants to do this, pin the forest to her mind, like a butterfly on a board, so that it's no longer a malign mass outside her window. To shrink its scale until it feels no more threatening than the clumps of plastic trees in Teddy's Hornby train set. She wonders if that will ever be possible. Standing there, alone, she realizes her fear of it is carved into her bones, the very crook of her pelvis. It goes way beyond Marge's list or concern about the children.

While she was growing up, Nan would never talk directly about the car accident that killed Rita's parents—it'd be like staring into the noon sun—but she'd say woods were places where "bad men" lurked. And "worse." (Never specified.) She didn't own a car, never would: "coffins on wheels." She wanted Rita indoors. Immobile. Safe on the settee.

What she never said was this: Do you remember, Rita, how your parents, Poppy and Keith, loved the open road and the outdoors, the woods and the mountains, and sleeping under the stars and stirring baked beans in a battered billycan, and the spit and crackle of a campfire?

But suddenly Rita *does* remember. A memory dislodges: she's sitting on the beam of her father's shoulders, the light beer-colored through the leaves. She's not sure where they were, or when it was, if it was the weekend of the accident. But she can feel his heft and hold—she has no fear of falling, not with his giant's hands on her ankles—and she can hear his laughter, booming under a roof of leaves.

She shuts the gate behind her.

❊ ❊ ❊

The moon jumps between branches. She disturbs slumbering sheep. She can sense other presences too: a crunching under hoof; the chirring of insects. An unseen owl hoots. The sound hangs in the air, round as a smoke ring.

She hesitates, then takes the path that curls past the tree stump and the pyramid-stacked log pile—yes, definitely lethal—and decides to loop the house, the route the kids seem to take. She's soon distracted by a deer. Then at stage left, a fox blazes, carrying a rabbit in its jaws. She stops to admire some moths on a gigantic fallen tree. Toadstools. She bends down, hands on her knees, frowning: are these the dreaded death caps?

Something else snags her eye. Persil white. Out of place. Curious, she picks it up. A baby's bootee. Still puffed into the stub of a tiny foot. Recently dropped. It's an odd thing to find in such dense woodland—no pram would make it here. And it reminds her of the other bootees—ornately laced, never worn—that Jeannie treasures. She hooks it on a low-hanging branch, as she used to stick lost kids' gloves on London railings.

She keeps walking. But the path has gone. And it's dimmer, the trees' canopies having locked over her head, like umbrellas on a crowded London street. Roots rise up from the ground and wrap around boulders or dangle from branches. With no warning, a hollow cleaves open beneath her feet, and she grabs at the bracken to halt her fall.

Recovering herself, she kneels down against the huge trunk of an old oak, folding her dressing gown around her, like wings, and taking out her custard cream. She's glad the kids can't see her. How they'd giggle at her lostness. Still. The biscuit helps.

But there's something at her back. She cocks her head. A noise. Twigs cracking. Footsteps? She tenses, remembering what Marge said about oddballs and fugitives being attracted to the forest. The weirdo called Fingers. Not daring to twist around, she pushes back against the tree trunk and its tourniquet of thick itchy ivy, and tucks in the sides of her dressing gown, wishing it wasn't such an unnatural pink. The footsteps stop.

It's not her own fast breathing she can hear now. It's someone else's. Fear twists with defiance. She hasn't survived car crashes and house fires and Fred's saying "No man on earth is going to want you now, Rita," to meet a sticky end out here. She walks her hand through the scuff of fallen leaves toward a large stick. Another footstep. Her heart slams. Her fingers twitch. She's ready.

14

Hera

The forest bursts into life outside my cracked window. I don't need an alarm clock at Foxcote. En route to the bathroom, I see Big Rita's bedroom door is ajar and peep in. A rumpled bed; a pile of novels on the bedside table, a blouse hanging on the back of the chair. But no Big Rita. Where is she? I think of the French nanny who bolted back to Paris one night, without saying good-bye. The mother's help did the same. I nibble the skin around my fingernail, ripping it down to the raw bit that tastes like knives.

But Rita wouldn't desert her terrarium, would she? Or leave without making her bed first. Also, she doesn't have anywhere to go. No family. No home. This is one of the best things about her. I pull open her desk drawer to check that she's not taken the photos of her dead parents and feel a bounce inside when I see them, smiling like they're going to live forever. There's a notebook too. I pick it up and flick through. "Sunday: Jeannie still feeling under the weather. Ate three rounds of Marmite toast." An entry for every day we've been here. Why is she taking notes on Mother like she's a patient?

I shut the drawer, worried: is Mother sicker than I thought? I go to check on her. Her bedroom is dark, and a bit stale, like night breath. But at least in sleep Mother doesn't look like someone who'd start sobbing just because a wild flower shattered.

I sit quietly on the chair beside her bed, grateful she's here, her room only three doorknobs down from mine. At least Daddy's not around to cart her back to The Lawns. No Don, either. I managed to swipe his letter from the doormat yesterday before anyone noticed, recognizing his bold loopy handwriting from postcards he's sent over the years. I fed it, unopened, into the campfire I made in the woods. The envelope corner caught in the embers and made the most perfect leap of vein-blue flame.

I watch Mother and try to remember what she was like before she lost his baby and herself. It's difficult. Like trying to remember someone who moved away ages ago. But I do know that when I left for school in the morning, I always looked forward to coming home. I didn't dread it as I have this last year. And if Mother was in a different room, she was still tangibly around, a presence, bustling and busy, light on her feet. Now the more I'm around her, the more I miss her. She makes a different noise walking up the stairs.

Everyone was drawn to her then. They didn't cross the street to avoid her. If she was on the front steps clipping the wisteria for a vase, a neighbor would pop up, wanting to chat, peering over her shoulder into our hallway, hoping to work their way inside for a good poke about and a slice of my mother's famous toffee flan, which smiled inside your mouth. If that failed, they'd take the back route: I knew I was invited to other girls' houses just so their mothers could meet mine. Maybe get a seat at one of my parents' famous dinner parties.

I loved those, the laughter and chatter and chink of glasses, the orange noses of cigarettes moving about the dark garden. It was my job to stab the foil-covered grapefruit halves with skewers of cheddar cheese cubes and pineapple chunks and to take guests' coats as they came in. After that, I'd settle on the staircase, forehead pressed against the banisters, and enjoy seeing things I wasn't meant to see. Snooty Mrs. Pickering crying, facing the wall, dabbing her mascara, then gliding back into the party, cocktail in hand, smiling like she was having the best evening of her life. The woman from the big house on Regent's Park, switching my mother's seating placements so she was put next to Don at dinner. I'd tell Mother all this the next day and she'd erupt with laughter, cracking the greenish clay of the Avon face mask she liked to use the morning after a party. "No secrets, Hera," I remember her saying with a wink. "You can tell me anything." And I'd puff up with happiness. Like it was us against the world.

And then it changed. After the baby, I couldn't tell her anything. Nothing that mattered, anyway. I didn't want to make her sadness worse. Daddy said we had to pretend the baby hadn't happened, that this was the kindest thing.

Looking down at Mother now, her forehead crinkly, her elbows sharp points, I'm not sure he was right. Also there's a corner of a yellow cot blanket poking out from under her pillow, making me wonder if she sleeps with it every night, like Teddy sleeps with Koala. Although waking her up and asking, "Do you think about the baby all the time too?" still feels like a very bad idea, I find myself talking quietly, under my breath, confiding how much I miss my baby sister. How I looked down from my bedroom window that night into the bundle in the midwife's arms but still can't remember what I saw: my brain fogged up like a cold winter window, all the images scrubbed out.

At this, Mother sighs and turns onto her side. I have to fight the urge to scramble into bed and spoon against her, like I used to as a little girl.

I lean closer, my elbows digging into my knees, watching her, and a nice warm feeling spreads in my chest, like a color. It feels good being honest, more like it used to be, just the two of us, chatting, confiding secrets, and I hear myself telling her about the notebook I found in Big Rita's room. The moment I've said it, I feel bad, like I've betrayed Big Rita. Worse, Mother's breath catches and changes, quivering the lace panel of her nightie. I cover my mouth with my hand, wondering if I've said too much. If she's not as asleep as I thought. But then she starts snoring lightly, like a purr, and I realize she can't have heard, and it'll all be fine.

15

Sylvie

The column of holiday traffic inches slowly west in the heat. I drum my fingers impatiently on the steering wheel and glance across at the adjacent lane, at all the family vehicles stuffed with duvets and bags. Frazzled mothers twisting round in their seats trying to placate their kids with rice cakes and electronic devices. They still think that's the difficult bit.

When the traffic grinds to a halt, I call Caroline to break the news. At first she thinks Mum's died. She can't comprehend what I'm saying. "Slow down, Sylvie, *what?*" So I repeat it. No, she hasn't misheard. Pregnant. No, not me! Christ. Annie! An accident, yes, of course, the Elliot boy. A massive cluster fuck. Steve's in bits. Yesterday Elliot's awful mother called and said God knows what to Annie. Annie stormed out. None of her friends have seen her. She texted me last night: *I'm safe. Just need some space. x.* And her cell phone's been switched off since. I'm going out of my mind.

"A backlash maybe," I wonder out loud. Until this summer, Annie's freedom has been of the risk-assessed sort. Steve's tracked her location via her phone, following her on his iPad, like one of those sky maps on the back of airplane seats. I've searched for the houses of proposed sleepovers on Google Earth, looking for signs of disrepute and fighting dogs. And phoned the mother, just to check. We've been overprotective, made her too trusting . . .

"Is she at Mum's?" asks Caroline, cutting through the white noise of self-recrimination. "If I were her, I'd go there."

"That's what I thought too," I say, relieved I'm not going completely mad. "I'm on my way."

❊ ❊ ❊

The village is hugged between bulky cliffs. It forces you to wind toward it along a meandering coast road, past the dairy farm, with its dank manure gusts, the pub, then the stone harbor wall from which I'd jump as a teen, whooping, into the jelly-green water. I drive farther down the hill, past the old church, with its fishermen's graves staring out to sea, then swing into my mother's drive.

"Crap." Annie's car is not here.

Once I'm inside, the cottage has never felt emptier. I walk down the hallway, past the watermarked antique maps framed on the walls. The wooden sign Annie made Mum years ago: RITA'S BEACH RETREAT. On the console table, a clutter of family photos and a wooden bowl full of redundant keys. On the floor, the heart tug of my mother's hooflike old clogs, and Dad's chunky fishing-rope doorstop, always hazardously placed so you tripped coming back from the pub, tipsy in the dark.

No sign Annie's been here.

But in the kitchen, my spirits soar. There's a half-drunk mug of tea on the table. Cold. Not moldy. Upstairs, the beds are still made. Could Annie have slept on the sofa? She's always enjoyed sleeping on sofas, under a blanket, like a puppy. I peer into the living room. Yes, the sofa's messy, strewn with blankets. She's been here. I call Steve. There's a woman's voice in the background as he picks up, a voice that suddenly goes silent. I don't care who she is this time. I'm distilled into one thing only, Annie's mother, like a rapid contraction of a pupil to a tiny black dot.

We agree it's best I stay put rather than risk missing Annie by going out to look for her. After dutifully watering Mum's wilting potted plants, I'm not sure what to do with myself. My mother's absence lies heavily on this house. Little things she's left behind: reading glasses, open on a shelf; library books, now overdue. Time reels back to other summer evenings spent here, mundane enough at the time, now weighted with an almost unbearable poignancy. It's all so familiar it hurts. The nougat scent of my mother's bourbon roses outside the kitchen window. The taste of the tap water.

On top of this, my body pines for Annie on a cellular level, as it did when I'd leave her at nursery and my day was marked in beats until we could be yoked together again. I had work to distract me then. But here each tick of the wall clock is like a peck. My head keeps stumbling into the wrong places: the cells inside Annie's womb multiplying; the electric pulse of a heart; the curled shrimp of an embryo; tiny fingernails forming, like buds. Stop. Don't go there. She can't possibly have the baby.

I wander restlessly into the sitting room and collapse onto an armchair, head in hands. It's only when I look up I see it. There on the coffee table, a faded yellow A4 folder. I read the label on the front once, twice, not processing, the shock delayed. Written in my mother's confident curlicue-heavy hand: *Summer 1971.* Jesus. Where on earth did Annie find this? I've not seen it before.

The past breathes on the back of my neck. After a while, I risk lifting the folder's lip. A ruffle of yellowing newspaper pages. As I start to part them with shaky fingers, the doorbell rings. My heart drums double time. I fling down the folder.

✳ ✳ ✳

Not Annie. He's over six foot. Wearing baggy skate-boy jeans and a New York baseball cap. He peers hopefully over my shoulder into the hall. "Is Annie in?"

"No. No, she's not." I look at him more sharply, wondering, holding my hair off my face in the salt sting of wind blowing off the sea. "Excuse me, but you're not . . . ?"

"Elliot." He smiles, then blanches, guessing who I am.

So this is the mysterious Elliot. He's quite something, athletic and handsome in that scruffy, privileged English way, with eyes of boy-band blue, ringed by thick dark lashes. I can understand how eyes like that could get a girl into trouble.

I can't stop staring. I find myself stupidly wondering what their child would look like. "I'm Sylvie. Annie's mother."

"Hi," he says inadequately. He swallows hard, his Adam's apple rising and falling, and takes off his baseball cap, revealing floppy dark blond hair.

"Do you want to come in?" I'm already stepping aside.

He clearly doesn't but is too well mannered to say so. In the kitchen, he's all shoulders and enormous feet, too big for the room. Too young for the mess in which he finds himself. Perspiration beads on his forehead.

"Would you like something to drink?" The question does nothing to ease the fundamental awkwardness of the situation. "Tea? A glass of water?"

"I'm good, thank you." His eyes look trapped and I notice the half-moon smudges of stress shadows beneath them. A muscle twitches on the side of his jaw. Stubble. He hasn't shaved today. "I should go . . ." he starts to say apologetically.

"Annie's been here," I say hurriedly, riding a fresh wave of anxiety. "But she's gone out. And her phone's still off." Why is Annie even thinking about distant family history when her future is pressing so urgently? I take a breath. "Have you any idea where she might be?"

"I don't know. Sorry." Beneath his private-school bluster, there's a disarming vulnerability. Sweetness mixed with just the right amount of damage. Annie would have been drawn to that. "She just told me she was heading down to Devon, that's all. She was, like, pretty abrupt. Didn't want to talk."

"She did? Hang on a minute, let me get the timing straight." Something about his wary expression makes me wonder if I look slightly unhinged. My mind is racing at a million miles an hour. "You spoke after your mother phoned her, right?"

"My *mother*?" It's his turn to panic. He steps back and crashes into the sideboard, like a clumsy animal banging against the sides of his pen. Plates rattle. "My mother called Annie?" he repeats in disbelief.

"At the apartment. You didn't know?" Helen hadn't asked his permission. Wow. "She upset Annie. A lot. She should have told you."

"What . . . what did my mother say?" He winces, bracing.

"You'll have to ask her."

"Man." He turns toward the door, clutching his phone. I suspect Helen's about to get an earful.

"Oh, don't go yet." I grab his arm. He glances down at my hand, which I quickly remove, fearing I'm overstepping the mark. "Given the circumstances . . ." He has the decency to blush. I do my best to smile encouragingly. "Annie said you're from London?"

He nods. "I just drove down."

"I don't mind if you wait here. Really. I'd like it." Oh. That came out wrong. He looks terrified, as if I've just propositioned him. "I'm sure Annie won't want to miss you," I add quickly.

"Actually . . ." For a heartbreaking moment he looks like he might cry. He bites the inside of his cheek. "She didn't want to see me. I should be respecting her space."

He's edging down the hall. He can walk away from the whole situation. Annie can't.

"I'm so sorry."

"I can see that" is the kindest thing I can say. He's sincere at least. Seagulls cackle overhead.

Outside on the drive, the sunset sends my stress levels soaring. How much daylight have we left? I think of those cliffs, their putty-like crumbling edges, the jagged teeth beneath. Annie slipping like Mum. Should I phone the coast guard? The police? Go looking for her myself? I'll give her another twenty minutes. No, ten.

I watch Elliot fold into his vehicle sideways, like men with long legs do. A silver four-by-four. The sort of car wealthy Londoners think is essential in Devon, as if all our roads were dirt donkey tracks.

"Nice to meet you, Elliot." Wondering if this may also be the last time I see him, I bend down to the window, hands on my knees, and peer inside: a scuffed paddleboard across the back seat, an empty Pepsi bottle, a battered Lee Child paperback, and a dirty pair of trainers. A small glimpse into the young man with whom my daughter's spent her summer—someone Mum said Annie was head over heels with not so long ago. Watching his car accelerate gustily into the mackerel sky, kicking up clouds of dust, I can see why Annie fell for him. But I don't understand why she's kept him a secret.

16

Rita

Rita prods the potatoes under the boiling water with a wooden spoon. "Anyone getting that?" she shouts to no one in particular. "Someone's at the door."

A moment later, Teddy skids into the kitchen in his socks, arms aeroplaned. "*Neeeoooaw* . . . It's Robbie. He wants to see you, Big Rita."

"Me?" The blood rushes from her head. Her newly shaved legs burn. "I'm cooking. Tell him . . . I can't."

As if yesterday morning wasn't humiliating enough. She's still cringing: she'd leaped at Robbie with a fallen branch and yelled, "Get back, Fingers!" like some sort of banshee. He hadn't even flinched, just politely inquired as to why she was wearing his boots.

"I'm used to signposted streets. One tree looks much like another," she'd explained briskly, shivering. He covered her shoulders with his heavy and slightly whiffy waxed jacket. She'd noticed his big, not very clean carpenter's hands with flat square fingernails, like windows. Hands out of proportion to his height. He came up to her nose, so she got a bird's-eye view through the unbuttoned opening of his frayed shirt, the plank of a lean, hard torso, corded with muscle. He caught her looking too. And his speckled mud-brown eyes were the creasy, dancing sort. Laughing at her.

He'd refused to take the darn boots back. Said they looked much better on her. She took this to be some sort of weak joke at her expense. Men were always doing this, short men especially. Worse, the joke prompted them both to glance down and witness the legs she'd not shaved since London, pelted with hair, emerging from the boots. A furry leg shouldn't matter—she'd sworn off men for good—but somehow it did. Somehow it mattered a lot. After that, she'd rushed inside, her dressing gown bristling with thistle burrs, and bumped into Hera, who was emerging from Jeannie's bedroom, looking extremely shifty.

It felt like they'd both been in places that they shouldn't that night.

"I'll tell him." Teddy pirouettes on his heel, arms flung open, ready for takeoff. But it's too late.

There he is. Standing by the kitchen door, smiling shyly. Rita stirs the bubbling pan more vigorously. She prays Teddy will not say anything silly. He teased her about the misadventure at breakfast, and Rita told him to shut his cakehole, which wasn't very Rita-ish at all, and made Hera and Teddy laugh so hard, she feared Teddy was choking.

"Are you okay, Rita?"

She sneaks a sidelong glance. He's smiling—gloating?

"Without question." She also notices he's carrying something in his hand, a wrap of brown paper, like a roll of sliced ham. "I'd have found my own way back, you know."

"I brought something." He walks closer and tries to hand her the parcel. But she has to put down the spoon first and wipe her damp hand on her apron, and both small acts seem exaggerated and clumsy. When their fingertips brush, something in her abdomen tightens. "It's nothing much," he says. Hera and Teddy bob closer, impatient for her to open it.

She unfolds the paper, trying to keep her expression neutral. Inside: *leaves?* Leaves. Each one named in pencil on a parcel label, tied with string to the stem: *silver birch, oak, holly, beech, elm . . .*

"A forest map, if you like." His chest has flushed pink under his undone checked-shirt collar. She has the urge to cool it with the flat palm of her hand. "Once you know your trees, you got your street signposts," he adds.

She doesn't know what to say. How long has it taken him, collecting the different leaves, labeling them like that? Why would he bother?

"For teaching the kids," he says, popping something inside her like a bubble.

Of course! How awkward it would have been if the leaves *were* for her. Still, she knows she'll lay them out on her bedroom floor later, when everyone's gone to bed. She'll study their colors and shapes, and whisper their names under her breath until they're imprinted on her brain. "Thank you. Perfect, eh, Teddy?"

Teddy nods and grins.

Hera takes one and turns it by the stem, unimpressed. "Well,

Big Rita's made a forest in miniature," she says proudly. "Under glass."

"Really?" He looks at her with intense curiosity. There's a smile in his voice.

"A few ferns in a little glass case, that's all." She wishes Hera would shut up. She feels baldly exposed. "A terrarium."

Rita worries this reveals something odd about her. Self-conscious under the directness of his gaze, she folds the leaves back into the paper, puts the parcel on a shelf and turns to the stove. She spikes a fork into a boiling potato to see if it's soft enough to mash: it bounces, hard as a stone, and pings against the side of the pan; less of an eternity has passed than she thought.

"There's a dance tonight. Would you like to come? With me, I mean."

The fork slides from her grip into the bubbling pan. The heat from the stove has transferred to her face and is chemically reacting with the razor rash on her leg. She's on fire. "I'm working. Sorry."

The silence is heavy and wet, and smells of potato starch. Hera plucks out an eyelash with her fingers and examines it.

"Teddy, why don't you see Robbie out?" Rita says stiffly.

A moment later, Teddy returns, looking pleased with himself. He pulls two wooden dining chairs together and bridges across them with his upturned body, hands on one, feet on the other.

Hera circuits the kitchen, grazing. She picks at the charred rump of Marge's fruit loaf and skewers a sultana, then pops it into her mouth.

"You have to go dancing, Big Rita," says Teddy, upside down.

"Don't be a goose." She removes a colander from a hook on the wall.

"I told Robbie you secretly *do* want to go." A dungaree strap unclasps itself, the buckle landing on the floor with a clink. He starts to sag in the middle.

"For goodness sake, Teddy!"

"But you can dress up!" he protests. Hera giggles through a mouthful of cake.

"I'm not here to gad about. Stop that. You'll hurt yourself, Teddy. Hera, leave the fruit loaf."

Teddy lands in a heap on the floor.

Rita lowers the copper colander to his head. "You, on the other hand, can wear this."

Teddy pulls it down, his eyes glinting through the holes. "I'm a cabbage."

"You said it," says Hera.

❄ ❄ ❄

"I say, who was at the door?" Jeannie's voice swims toward them.

Teddy's eyes widen and glitter through the colander holes. Hera's mouth opens. Rita whips around. And there, unbelievably, is Jeannie, chalk-faced, wearing a glassy smile and a pearl-white silk dressing gown, edged with marabou feathers. She leans against the doorway, trembling like a moth.

Rita is shocked by her appearance, the porridge-gray skin, the dry, frizzed hair. Jeannie used to have fat dark curls that shone like watered silk. Eyes like jewels. Today she looks like she's been rubbed out.

"Mummy!" Teddy charges at her, still wearing the colander. She hugs him with fumbling urgency and laughs. The colander falls off and clatters across the floor.

"So who was it?" Jeannie asks more insistently. Her eyes are glassy.

"Robbie. Robbie Rigby." Rita enjoys the roll of Rs.

Something in Jeannie's face dims. "Oh." She tenderly combs Teddy's hair with her fingers. "Any letters for me?"

"No post at all. I was wondering if we even got it here, actually."

Jeannie glances at Hera, then back at Rita again. "We should."

Out of the corner of her eye, Rita sees Hera tuck one foot behind the other, looking uncomfortable, and wonders why. "Sorry, Jeannie."

"Anyone phoned?" Jeannie's voice pitches with hope.

"Someone did ring last night. But it went dead as I picked up." Rita doesn't say she pressed the handset buttons down with her fingers, cutting the caller off. Anything to avoid questions from Walter. It only occurred to her afterward that it might have been Don Armstrong, trying his luck again. And she was doubly glad she'd done it.

"Will you go to the fete tomorrow, Mummy?" Teddy grabs Jeannie's hand and waggles it, delighted with her. Hera is more wary.

"Fete?" Jeannie yawns.

"Marge says the coconuts are all nailed on." Teddy taps the side of his nose. Hera ruffles his hair.

Jeannie shoots a look of alarm at Rita. "*Marge?* Has she been here a lot?"

"She does like to pop in," Rita answers diplomatically, trying to shield her.

"Every day," Hera needles. "Twice a day."

"I've explained you've been under the weather." Rita feels uncomfortable repeating the lie in front of the children. "Migraines. Hay fever."

"Yes, yes, terrible hay fever." Jeannie steadies herself on the chunky newel-post. "Gosh, yes."

"Take my hand, Mummy." Teddy tugs her forward carefully, as if his mother were extremely old. "That's it. Careful."

In the kitchen, Jeannie nibbles at a dry salted cracker while the children watch her, fascinated, as if a unicorn has joined them for tea. "What did Robbie want?" Jeannie asks.

"Oh, nothing really." Rita plunges her hands into the warm soapy water, searching for the cutlery swimming along the bottom.

"He invited Big Rita to a dance tonight." Teddy edges onto his mother's knee, gingerly, not sure if he'll break it.

"Then you must go, Rita," Jeannie says.

Her hands still under the water. "Oh. No. Really, Jeannie. I don't want to."

"You mean you don't dare leave me in charge?" There's a catch in her voice. "Rita, I want to look after them. I'm their mother, after all. Not you."

Rita's face grows hot. It's been too easy to forget that these last few days. She's just the nanny. She'll always be just the nanny, the cuckoo in the nest. And Jeannie wants some time alone with her children. She wants her out of the way. Natural enough. Emptying the sink, she loops the plug on its chain around the tap, feeling oddly flat.

"One should never turn down an opportunity to dance, Rita. Don't worry about us. We'll have fun." Jeannie smiles, and Rita can sense how desperately she wants to please her children. "What do you fancy doing this evening, Teddy? Hera? Anything you like?"

"A bonfire," says Hera, not missing a beat. Teddy claps his hands.

17

Sylvie

I'm standing on the bones of a long-dead fisherman in the grave-yard, frantically scanning the horizon, when I see Annie's car winding along the coast road. My heart leaps. I pinball away from the church, down the lane, the hill, my feet tripping over each other. She turns and sees me and laughs. She actually laughs. "Mum!"

I grab her and hug her tight. I'm so primed for another disaster, a bit of me can't believe she's actually alive at all.

"What are you doing here?" She pulls back, astonished. "You look completely mental. What's happened?"

"What's *happened*?" I try not to lose it. "Bloody hell, Annie, you left the apartment yesterday without saying good-bye and didn't say where you were going. Sent me some cryptic text. And your phone isn't on!"

"You're always telling me to turn my phone off. Digital sunset."

"Not now! Me and Dad have been climbing the walls."

"Sorry." She winces, grasping the trouble she's caused.

Holding Annie by the arms, I search for signs of emotional distress. Yet she appears to be billowing with hormones and youth—

and a breezy insouciance quite out of kilter with her situation. "Are you okay?"

Her eyes gleam with sea light. "I'm fine."

You're not fine, I think, *you're fricking pregnant.* "Come on, let's get you inside."

"Mum, I'm keeping the baby," she blurts.

I turn very slowly. "*What?*"

She puts a hand on her flat stomach. "I'm not getting rid of it."

"But . . . but . . ." The world tilts, changes, like something picked up and put down again on its side. "You don't need to make a decision straightaway."

"I've decided."

"What? But . . ." My voice wavers. I barely recognize the girl standing in front of me. She's never felt less mine, more herself. Scared of pushing her into a corner, I pick my words carefully. "You've been very upset about Granny. When death feels close, it's easy to be drawn toward new beginnings . . . new life."

She's shaking her head.

"It's natural for someone your age to want a baby, even subconsciously," I blather on. "It's hormones. Humanity ensuring its survival. A . . . a biological trick."

Her face flushes scarlet, like it does before she starts to cry. She looks away, biting her lip. "I knew you'd freak."

"I'm not freaking." I am. "Annie, please . . ."

"I didn't want to get pregnant, okay? It's a major disaster. But it's happened. And I can't bear the thought of . . . It's not a moral thing, Mum. But the baby feels real to me. I . . . I didn't expect it to."

Annie blows out, as if trying to explain exhausts her. "Look, can we just go for a walk along the beach or something? I'd rather talk there. Granny's house without Granny in it makes me feel weird."

The rays of late-evening sun varnish the sand's hard, rippled ridges. We swing our shoes in our hands. If it weren't for the snarl-up that our family life has become, this would be a picture-perfect mother-and-daughter moment. And this makes it worse. As I listen to Annie, my eyes swim with tears.

"I've been googling it," she's saying earnestly, reinvigorated by bracing sea air. "There are crèche facilities for Cambridge undergraduates now, bursaries and things. I'm not the first, honestly. I can still do it all. Just in a different way. And a year later."

Do it all? Her naiveté and courage make me want to sob. My little girl. Not yet finished. "Annie, you're eighteen."

"Nearly nineteen."

"You've got your life ahead of you. I can't . . . I can't tell you how *big* it is. Motherhood. It's just huge. It'll limit your choices, your freedom. And it's . . . undoable." I daren't tell her about the moment she was born when, still waxy from the womb, she lay on my stomach and peered into my eyes, as if to say, *So there you are.* How it was—still is—the most profound moment of my life. "No one knows. Not before. You think you do. But then it hits you like a heavy goods train."

"Thanks."

"Oh, Annie, I've loved being your mother. Having you transformed my life. I . . ." Appallingly, I start crying, like I'm somehow making it all about me. There are so many forces at work, too many feelings I can barely articulate hissing under the surface of the conversation. And I *am* culpable. Guilty. If I hadn't left Steve when I did, she wouldn't have fled down here for the summer and she wouldn't have met Elliot with the boy-band-blue eyes.

"It'll work out, Mum."

This kills me. "I should be the one reassuring you."

"But you can't, can you?" she flares.

I can smell suppressed anger, muffled and dense, like the slumps of blackening seaweed on the shore. The tide crashes in and we jump back up the sand. "I'm not going to pretend it's going to be easy, Annie," I shout, over the rumpus of the water. "I'm not going to lie to you."

She snorts. Her jeans are wet. And there's a quivering drop of sea spray on one of her long red lashes.

"Annie . . ."

"So you're not worrying about what your friends will think?"

"No!" Although, now she's mentioned it, I realize it's hardly going to be a smug granny-to-be Facebook announcement. No midlife freedom signaling for me. I wonder who Annie's told already, if the word's out, if the mothers have already started frenziedly texting one another, exchanging horrified faux sympathy, then marching their daughters down to the doctor's to get hormonal implants. There's always been an unspoken fear that pregnancy, like suicide or eating disorders, might be catching. Our brilliant golden girls, ready to change the world, not nappies.

"You've always told me to listen to my gut and not to care what other people think."

I immediately wish I hadn't.

"Granny would understand." Her voice breaks.

What would Mum do? Embrace it, probably. Move in with Annie if she wanted, offer up her services as a great-granny-cum-nanny. There's nothing Mum loves more than a baby. The tide hisses back.

"Where's Elliot in all this?" I ask carefully.

Annie stares out at the darkening sea, arms crossed, hair blowing. "Not with me."

I wonder if in my efforts to prove I'm okay I've made single life look too easy. "We're not islands, Annie."

"My body."

"For sure."

"His mother said on the phone that Elliot's already dating someone else." She looks away, biting back tears. "I'm not under any illusions."

"Well, he still called around earlier. To check you were okay."

Annie whips around to me, her mouth an O. "*You* met Elliot?"

I nod. "He drove all the way down from London. But he wouldn't wait around. I guess he didn't want to hang out with me. It was kind of intense. Sorry, I should have told you straightaway." I try to smile. "You threw me a bit."

Her face seems to flicker with millions of tiny shocks.

The tide is gushing in faster now, the current lassoing my ankles. My toes are numb with cold. "Annie, one other thing . . ." I take a breath. "You left a folder out on the coffee table." Annie blinks rapidly, her skin paling under her freckles. "*Summer, 1971* written on the front?"

"I . . . I found it, in Granny's desk." Her eyes glint defensively. The horizon darkens to a squid-ink line. "Is that not allowed?"

Distrust starts to curdle around us, like the sea. I kick myself for mentioning the folder. Why didn't I just pretend I never saw it? Brush the whole thing off? Our family history is barbed and tangled, unwieldy as the mound of fishing line farther up the beach. Certainly not for Annie at this point in her life. She bristles and turns to walk up the marshy beach. "Let's get back," I say, running alongside her, burying the conversation. "You need to eat."

I register the rumble too late. One moment Annie's shouting, "There you go again! Let's never talk about that summer—let's pretend it never happened . . ." The next a monstrous rogue wave is exploding against our backs, thumping us into the churning salty black.

18

Rita

Acouple on a bicycle whiz past, the woman on the saddle, her arms around the pedaling man's waist, her red dress puffed like a sail. They throw the bike against the village-hall wall and, holding hands, run inside. Another woman totters by wearing stiletto heels, green as a Granny Smith.

A familiar feeling of being in some fundamental way wrong empties over Rita. Why did she think it a good idea to wear her dreary navy A-line skirt and flat brown shoes again? To shove her one flattering blancmange-pink cardigan back into her drawer? She didn't want to look like she was trying and be silently mocked for failing. Nor did she want to attract attention. But she has a habit of solving one problem by creating another, and she now stands out in her plainness, like a turnip in a flowerbed. She realizes how entrenched she's become in her job, how far she's drifted from carefree people of her own age. Robbie, she notices, stealing a quick sidelong glance, has made an effort, even if it does give him the air of a boy dressed by his mother. His shirt's pressed. His wavy hair is greased and swept to one side, already sprouting loose. "Shall we?" he asks.

She nods, even though she wants to say, *No, thank you very much, we most definitely shall not.* They walk inside the village hall, under the flapping Union Jack bunting, into the music and sweat and laughter.

"Don't fell her by mistake, eh, Robbie," calls out a young man in a checked shirt, clutching a sparrowlike girl and blowing cigarette smoke carelessly into her blond hair.

"Or cut her down to size," another bellows.

"Stop it, Alf." The blond girl laughs. "Just because you'd like another few inches."

It's already worse than she imagined.

"What can I get you to drink?" Robbie doesn't defend her or wisecrack back at the blokes. Fred's butcher's fists would have been whirring: he relished any invitation to fight. Instead Robbie smiles at her, his eyes searching and receptive, as if they're collecting information. "They're just jealous."

It takes a moment for her to believe he's not teasing, that he's perfectly sincere. "A Babycham. Thank you." She prefers beer. Earth-brown ale, like her dad used to drink. But girls can't order beer. Tall girls especially—or they look like brickies.

The bar is a crowded trestle table near the toilets. It takes Robbie an age to get served. She has to stand alone, feeling like Exhibit A. Only one gangly man with an explosion of blond-white hair and pinkish eyes smiles and waves at her across the room. She smiles back, grateful for a friendly face.

"Careful. Or you'll never shake him off." The bicycle girl in the red dress leans over and whispers behind her cupped hand. "Fingers Jonson."

"*Oh.* Right. Thanks." The Green Man? He's white as a grub. She feels a bit sorry for him, standing there alone, fidgeting, cracking his knuckles.

"You're most welcome." The girl takes a sip of her drink, little finger fancily extended from her glass, showing off her flamingo-pink varnish. She's robustly pretty, not beautiful, and the more attractive for it, with an uncontainable embonpoint. She smiles like she knows her own worth. "I'm Casey, by the way."

"Rita." She notices how cotton threads hang from the hem of Casey's dress, giving the impression she's sewn it hurriedly herself the night before. The only thing Rita sews is children's buttons. Or holes in their school socks. An awkward longing to make herself a flirty red dress like Casey's rises in her. She quickly dismisses it. Whatever she wears she looks like herself anyway. Graceless and big. Made badly.

"Got yourself a good job there." Casey's left eyebrow, lined in oily black, lifts. (It's never once occurred to Rita to do anything with her eyebrows: now she wonders if she should.) "With the Harringtons. Nice and respectable. Not some wacky forester family who'll pay you in chickens."

Rita laughs. *If only you knew,* she thinks.

"Wouldn't want to work with little 'uns myself, though." She shudders. "We'll all end up with pramloads of our own screaming brats soon enough, won't we?"

Rita's smile freezes. That future has gone, wiped out. She's simply a heart for hire.

"If we stay here, at least. I won't, though." She taps her nose. "Not me. I've got big dreams. And plans. Hollywood. Broadway."

Rita can see Casey's name up in lights. Casey on a red carpet, blowing kisses. And it makes her feel inadequate, as if she should have a big dream too, a plan to make her mark on the world beyond the Harringtons. She's relieved to see Robbie steering the drinks through the crowd, sloshing his beer as he goes.

Casey nods toward Robbie. "You make a right odd couple, you two."

"Oh, it's nothing like that," she says quickly, embarrassed, patting her cowlick. Still pinned into submission. She tries to think of a funny girlie aside to change the course of the conversation, but she can't.

"Well, you be careful." Casey speaks over the rim of her glass, staring out at the hall with an air of amusement. "There's something in the water here."

Rita smiles blankly, not understanding.

"Easy to get into trouble, like. In a forest. I'm not sure there's a baby in this village conceived in a proper bed."

"*Oh.*" Her blush spreads from her cheeks to her neck and then splatters across her décolletage like a red-wine stain. She thinks of the forlorn baby's bootee she found in the forest and glances around at the other girls in the hall. She can only imagine how a pregnant unmarried girl might be shunned in such a rural community. (Poor pretty Penny McGuire from school: you learned what happened to her and you kept your legs crossed.) She and Fred did it twice—a few juddering minutes; then he'd pull away and she'd try to finish the job with her hand—but *only* once they were engaged. He was old-fashioned like that, he'd said. Even though she knew he'd been less old-fashioned with other girlfriends, which made her feel depressingly resistible.

"Three's a crowd." Casey winks at Robbie and sashays away in that red dress.

Robbie's eyes don't track Casey, unlike every other man's. He hands Rita the drink and watches as she sips, as if the sight pleases him in some secret way. She half wishes Casey would come back and grease the silences with her easy chatter. But Casey is dancing now. Most of the forest girls are dancing: passionate and feisty, they steer the boys across the floor, the boys clearly in thrall, their eyes blotted with . . . No man has ever looked at her in that way. Ever. Then the music slows and the men rope their arms around the girls' waists and tug them closer, pelvis to pelvis, and it looks, frankly, extremely rude. But she finds she can't not watch. Or wonder what it must feel like to be held so close.

Fred never wanted to dance. He said she'd show him up. What with her size and all that.

Robbie's not asked her to dance, either. While this is a blessed relief—he's four inches shorter!—it still makes her feel bad and wonder what she's doing there. She's beset by a sudden terror she might cry. She considers feigning sudden illness to put both of them out of their misery. A stomach upset from Marge's fruit loaf, for example. Plausible.

"Rita." Robbie leans closer. His breath smells of hops. And, very oddly, prompts a distant hazy memory of her father. "Want to dance?"

Not bloody likely. But girls can't say no, not if they've already said yes to going to the dance in the first place: she's trapped; he's trapped. They both have to pretend. "Okay."

Robbie doesn't move. He watches her some more. Something about her seems to settle in his mind. "Or we could just finish our drinks and walk in the woods?"

❋ ❋ ❋

A bramble snatches at her skirt. As she bends to unpick it, Robbie whips a penknife from his pocket and slices through the tough stem as if it were a celery stalk, then starts sliding the thorns out of the fabric with surprisingly deft fingers. "We can't let this ruin your lovely skirt."

It appears he isn't joking, that he genuinely can't see how frumpy the C&A skirt is or how she hides in it. When a finger accidentally, fleetingly, brushes against the skin of her calf, a tingle travels up her leg.

In her head, she hears Nan's voice: Has she taken plain leave of her senses? What's she doing walking home with this rough knife-carrying man in the middle of a *forest*, of all wretched places, letting him put his hands on her skirt?

On the bright side, at least she won't get lost. (Neither will she have to dance in public.) And she should get back to Foxcote: she can't suppress her worries about the bonfire for much longer. Is Jeannie to be trusted around fire? Is Hera?

They quickly fall into step with each other. As other people's shyness makes Rita shyer, Robbie's ease in this environment, his trust in it, flows into her. She starts to relax. She allows herself the small satisfaction of wearing flat shoes. (How far would the woman in the fancy green heels have got? Exactly.) Even her skirt develops a sensuous swish as she walks, the stiff fabric seeming to soften. Pied wagtails loop the air, hunting flies. Above the tree line, a goshawk rises, like a giant coat hanger.

It's easier to talk in motion too, without all that eye contact. Robbie nudges questions into the conversation, like notes under a door, so she doesn't really notice them. And she finds herself answering them in far too much detail. Mostly about growing up in Torquay: the derelict beach hut she'd hide in as a child and read her library books; her first cactus called Burt. She catches herself, but not before he turns to her and says, with a huge, delighted smile, "*Burt?*"

"Tell me about the forest," she says tightly, changing the subject.

But he doesn't show off his knowledge, like Fred did. (Fred could bowl anyone over with gruesome facts about abattoirs.) Rather, it spills out of Robbie, like coins from a hole in his trouser pocket. He picks a bit of antler velvet from a branch and rubs its fuzz against her hand, sending strange tingling sensations shooting up her arm. He blows on the edge of a beech leaf to imitate a roe deer's mating call. (She blushes stupidly at the word *mating*.) He tells Rita how the dead bits of a forest are as important as the living, the rotting matter home to millions of insects, all essential food for the birds. In a forest, "Life and death kiss one another." (Her blush intensifies.) "It's an ancient place, Rita," he says with quiet reverence, "once a royal hunting ground for the Anglo-Saxons, Normans, and Tudors, where history nests among the owls and wood warblers. The oak timber here was used for shipbuilding from the seventeenth century, and Nelson, worried about a dwindling supply, ordered the planting of *thirty million* acorns, which is why there are so many oaks here now, Nelson's oaks, still alive." He explains how tree trunks are structured like spider's webs; how rooks can be eaten, like rabbits, and very tasty they are too, with a good dollop of ketchup; about poachers and culling, and how shooting in a forest is difficult because the trees break the sight line and a bullet can pass right through the body of a stag and keep on traveling. You should never fire a gun without knowing where the bullet will end up.

Rita listens, hungry to be educated. And slowly he takes apart the forest for her, chipping it into smaller pieces. He points out the skyscraping Douglas firs at the top, then the oaks and sweet chestnuts hovering over what he calls the *understory*—she loves this, since stories aren't always about what you think at first, either—of hazel and silver birch and elder. She finds herself peering through the forest's lacy lattice of twigs and branches into the layers of undergrowth and seeing the tiny life-forms folded within—the liverworts, bugle and moss, the lichen stars on a nub of bark, the furry underside of a leaf. Even the bacteria spores on the ground, digesting the dead into a rich black paste.

"Look up," he says, stopping on the path. He points. The fine gold hairs on his muscular arm catch the low sunlight. She wants to run her fingertips over them. His love of this place moves her. "Nest. See it?"

Her body tilts back and into him as her eyes bore into the uppermost branches to what looks like a wicker laundry basket rocking in the wind. Everything spins then, the branches wheeling, she and Robbie the only still point. She giggles.

"You're swaying." There's a smile in his voice. "You'd better sit down." He gestures toward a branch growing horizontally across the ground.

"I'm not used to Babycham," she says, even though she senses it was something else that made her head turn and has made all her blood rush to her inner thighs. Maybe it's the forest that's cast a spell on her this evening, filling her with a funny sort of euphoria, and . . . this *wanting*, as if she's hungry or thirsty, even though she's neither of these things.

"Not the fanciest route home. Sorry, Rita." He doesn't look very sorry. He has an unexpectedly good smile. His lips are full and curved and he has unusually pointed incisors, high in the gum. She commits the smile to memory, scared she might fall into it, and pretends to be fascinated by the spotted fungi on the ground.

"I'll drop you home in my truck next time." He picks up a small stick from the ground, then pulls the knife out of his pocket; it no longer worries her, the knife. (*Next time* does. Is she leading him on? Does it matter?) She watches his hands idly skinning its bark, the green wood emerging, pale as the inside of a pear. He has nice hands. "You must miss London, the parties and things?"

She's too embarrassed to admit she's never been to a party in London, not as a guest anyway. So she says, "Yes, very much," then wonders if *things* is a code for boyfriend.

Robbie stands up and tosses the stick into the undergrowth. "I'll get you back, then."

They walk on in silence. Something has changed. Something

adjusted, a tiny possibility snuffed like a candle flame between fingers. They are no longer strangers at least. She hopes they can be friends. It'd be nice to have a friend here.

Light rain releases the Christmasy smell of pine needles. She starts to recognize landmarks: the charred lightning-struck tree; the wigwam of sticks Teddy built yesterday. Then the smoldering remains of a bonfire, still pulsing orange in its center. Not an inferno, thank goodness. She was worrying for nothing.

When the garden wall appears through the trees, a feeling she doesn't quite understand spreads cool in her chest, like a shadow. She's glimpsed another world of red dresses and young people dancing, pelvis to pelvis, and a man's hand picking thorns from her skirt, and she wants to grab Robbie and say, *Take me back.* In a moment the garden gate will click shut. The sunlit evening will be over. Robbie will be gone. She'll be stuck inside the big brown house, with her duties and her job. Washing up. Counting out Jeannie's pills. Fending off Marge. Calls from Walter. Writing in that hated notebook.

"Shh." He touches her arm lightly, making her skin tingle. "Hear it?"

She stops too. She listens. The sound is faint. It winds toward her, through her body, fishhooking under her skin: a *neh-neh-neh* cry, an inhaling pause, then . . . just the drip of raindrops.

"What *is* that?" She's not sure why she whispers. Or why the hairs on her arms are raised, straight as pins.

He squints into the trees, frowning, filtering through all the sounds of the forest that he knows. "Young," he says, after a beat. "A lot of animals sound like babies. And it'll have a fierce old mama nearby. Come on."

Rita glances over her shoulder: there's nothing to see. Whatever infant animal was there has gone. But the cry hangs in her ears. For her own peace of mind, she has to check. "Robbie, I'm going to turn . . ." she starts saying. But his hands are already on her hips, tugging her body toward him. His mouth on hers.

19

———— ❊ ————

Hera

A fox's scream. Something that isn't a fox. The sky is streaky with dusk and the forest is darkening, its shadows like caves. Tiny birds zip between the branches, like they're trying to find a safe place before night collapses and the owls start to bomb down, button-eyed, talons outstretched. I sort of regret leaving my bonfire, a triumph of twigs, pinecones, and balled-up pages of newspaper.

But there didn't seem much point in staying after Mother and Teddy left. She stood up suddenly, her hands in her hair, all lost and bewildered-looking, like she'd no idea how she'd got there. She brushed down her dress, saying she felt tired and wanted to go back to the house. Needed her cardigan and a hot cup of tea. I bit the inside of my cheek, realizing we wouldn't lie back together on the grass, holding hands, picking out the star necklaces of the Plough and Orion, like she'd promised. She took Teddy's hand and said I could stay if I wanted, as long as I didn't eat too many more marshmallows.

I ate the marshmallows, wanting to get fat to spite her, sucking off their crinkly charcoaled skin and blistering the roof of my mouth. After that I hated myself a bit more and worried about Big Rita's night out. You can catch love more than once. It's not like measles. So sending her off to a dance with Robbie Rigby was a stupid thing for Mother to do. What if Rita likes him? What if she likes him more than *us*? And that's when I heard the funny cry. A sound that didn't belong here.

I followed it like bread crumbs through the wood. I followed it here. Almost to the house. To the big tree stump, a few yards from the front gate.

There's a blankety bundle on top of it. The bundle is moving. A sack of unwanted kittens or puppies? A tiny arm sways unstably in the air.

I look around for a mother. A nanny. A pram. Anything to make sense of this real live baby, who is glowing in a cone of midgy evening light, like she's been beamed down by God. But there's no one. The only hint of a grown-up having been here at all is a grocery bag at the base of the stump. I wonder if both baby and bag have been left behind, after the shopper got lost in the woods. This seems unlikely. But then so does the baby.

The air closes in, electric with trouble. My shadow stretches out, corn dolly long. I wonder if I'm being watched, if this is some kind of test. The French nanny would leave out ten-pence coins on the sideboard to see if I took them. (I did.) Whatever happens next will be my fault. I know I should walk away, leaving the baby for someone else to find. I move toward the baby anyway.

A girl, I think, since she's dressed in pink. Her monkey face is nettle-rash bumpy with insect bites. She's crawling with ants.

There's a hollowed dip of skin on the top of her head that is not bone. It's pulsing.

I touch her hand. Her skin is silky and firm, like the white of a hard-boiled egg. Her fingers wrap around my thumb and don't let go. "Hello, you," I whisper.

At the sound of my voice, the baby chokes on her cry. She fixes me with glossy blackbird's eyes. Her face changes color, patchily, pale to red and back again, like weather's moving underneath it. I want to stare at her forever. But it's getting dark. I don't know what to do or where Big Rita is. And I'm not ready to share the baby with Mother.

Also, a little voice inside is saying, *Finders, keepers. She's mine. Like my little sister never was.*

I snatch the scrappy note that's attached to her blanket with a nappy pin, stuffing it into my pocket to read later and pick up the bag at the base of the stump. She screams and screams, her body rigid, her feet punching out of her blanket, like wooden blocks. "Shh!" I plead. "Someone will hear you. They'll find us."

Her neck wobbles, like it might snap, and I suddenly remember that you have to support babies' heads. The skin of her scalp is cold. I press her tighter against my T-shirt, my heat. She feels really nice, like a pet.

But the crying starts up again, quiet at first, then louder, brighter, like a flame traveling along a string to a cartoon bomb. I jiggle her up and down. No good. I stick my finger into her mouth, mustaching her upper lip with bonfire soot. Her tongue folds around my finger and she sucks. Silence. The absence of scream.

I start walking away, my finger in her mouth, humming under

my breath. For some reason, I can't remember the words to any lullaby. It's like in a dream, when you grab at words and they run away from you.

We're by the stream now, which is gushing through its narrow gully, excited by the rain. My arms are starting to ache. I sit down. She fits perfectly in the sling of my crossed legs, the dough of my thighs, like a missing bit found.

I wriggle the note out of my pocket: *Please look after me. I am a good baby who needs a home.* Just that. Like she's Paddington Bear. No useful tips at all! Not even a name. If I were her mother, I'd have written a detailed manual, just in case, like the one in the glove compartment of the car.

The bag is more helpful. I spread its contents on the grass: cartons of milk powder, two glass bottles with rubbery brown teats, Babygros, and nappies. Hungry? Maybe that's why she's doing that funny stretching sideways thing with her mouth, like a swimmer. I'm going to save this baby. Like I didn't save my little sister.

I rest her on the mossy bank. She likes it there, listening to the water, turning her hands slowly in front of her eyes, astonished, like they're starships, not hands at all. The more I look at her, the more things I notice: her teeny ammonite ears; the little white spots around her nose; the crust on her scalp, flaky like candle wax. I press my finger onto the soft hollow on her head and imagine her blood rushing underneath it, like the stream.

Then I remember. She needs milk.

The stream? Clean enough. I hold a glass bottle against the current so the water sloshes into it. I shake in the powder, but it goes everywhere and the powder that does fall into the bottle won't mix properly and floats in cratery chunks. She spits out the teat and starts to whimper. So I give up on the milk and hold her tight until she stops, mid-scream. She slackens in my arms. Her eyelids close.

I am the world's best big sister at last. Hugging her warmth to my body, something strange happens. I feel myself being pulled back in time, day by day, month by month, like paper folded over, until I'm in my Primrose Hill bedroom again, the night my baby sister was born.

The ambulance is waiting. The midwife's clomping down the front steps. I'm looking down through the wisteria into the blanket in her arms, spotlit by the lantern over the door, and I can suddenly see what I've not been able to recall this last year: the gash where her nose and mouth are meant to be. I also know this: it would have made no difference. With or without a proper face she'd be my baby sister. I'd have loved her just the same.

20

Sylvie

"You were found by a lovely young girl in a magical forest one warm summer's night, safe on a tree stump," my mother would whisper to me at bedtime. I'd immediately beg her to tell me the story again, enchanted by it in the same way I was with Santa Claus or the possibility of fairies at the bottom of the garden. It didn't feel real, but it did feel true, like all good stories. My parents first told me when I was five: "There's something you need to know . . ." Apparently I shrugged, nonplussed, and asked for a biscuit. It wasn't just that I couldn't grasp the enormity—and wouldn't until I was much older. My mum and dad had searched for me and loved me so much they adopted me as their own: I liked this. As Caroline was also adopted, a few months after I was, this was our normal. We both knew what it was like to be *chosen,* not simply born.

I'd always known a vein of wildness ran through me. Like Caroline loved dolls, I was drawn to trees. I'd climb the old apple at the bottom of our garden every day and sit on the highest branches, sniffing the sea. I couldn't concentrate in the classroom—my mind hopped about like a sparrow—but outside, in a tree, something in me would still.

Anyway, I decided, not every girl got to star in her own bedtime story and close her eyes and hear the feathery brush of an owl's wing or the burrowing of hedgehogs through crispy leaves, all while tucked up in the comfort of her bed. Or gaze at the bedroom walls in the dark and see a forest, like Max in *Where the Wild Things Are*. Neither were other girls discovered, like a rare species of butterfly, as I was: Sylvie, a name of French origin, meant "from the forest." So I enjoyed my foundling story on a childish level. What I didn't understand was why my mother's voice went croaky in the telling or why, if I ever asked her questions, the air went crackly.

When I was about nine, everything changed. It was recess at school and raining, the drops dancing on the corrugated outdoor-play roof. For some reason I thought this a good moment to confide my birth story to Donna, not an ally, who was standing next to me with her Heidi blond plaits and boasting about her pony. Donna's eyes widened. "So your real mummy didn't want you and left you to *die*?" I'd trumped her pony. But at some personal cost. That evening I told Mum I didn't want that bedtime story anymore. (I'll never forget the look of relief on her face.) I didn't climb the apple tree ever again, either. I dug out my one neglected doll from the toy box, brushed her matted hair, tied in pink ribbons, and dressed her up so she looked neat and shiny, not wild or foresty. I'd pick the forest out of me too. And I told myself that life starts only when you can remember it.

My first real memory—the one with the grainy photos to prove it, along with thumb shadows and the requisite red eye—is of me sitting on a damp slab of beach, Dad bending down, pawing at the sand with a spade. Caroline is gripping his hairy shoulders and shrieking with delight. My mother is wearing the tiniest of crochet bikinis, with beaded bits dangling down, a top like two triangle-cut sandwiches, and holding up the big black camera that I loved. Sticky ice cream is trickling down my arm. I am three. Sylvie—me—has begun.

But the fear remains. Is there someone else, dormant, curled inside, like a young green nut in a shell? Could my brain reach further back if I let it? Into that void between being born and being found? And what about Caroline? Might she remember stuff too? Even if she doesn't want to. And she doesn't. She never has. She's more past-phobic than I am, which is saying something. We made a vow. Shook little fingers on it. Sisters. Strong and loyal. Not victims.

I read once that the hippocampus, where memories are stored, is not fully developed in a baby's brain. But the amygdala, where emotional memory lives, is already up, its engine running. And this worries me, the possibility that memory is more about retrieval than storage, that the memories might be there, like unread books buried deep in underground library stacks. Fortunately, most of the time trying to imagine my abandonment is like peering into a block of gray ice. There's nothing to see, just the ice. It's only on rare days, raw-edged, disintegrating days like these, after a big shock—and Annie's keeping the baby is an earthquake in my brain—that shapes start to form, not so much a memory but something else, an untold story I can somehow feel without the language to describe it.

I feel it now potently as Annie and I crawl out of the sea foam. "Are you okay? You sure?" I pull her up to her feet. She's shaken.

Neither of us was braced for that boom of water to the back of our legs. We're soaked. Sand in our hair. Our mouths. It could have been much worse. I glance nervously over my shoulder. The rogue wave has retreated to a frothing tongue of shallow water. But I can feel its big sister farther out at sea, pulsing in the dark, gathering energy, starting to roll. And I immediately think of the folder of newspaper clippings, waiting back at the house, secreted by my mother all these years. Like that wave, energy moving through matter, intent on release.

21

Rita

There it is again. The cry Rita heard earlier in the evening with Robbie. Her heart beats faster, percussive, as if her body already knows something she doesn't. She can't turn back. Under the carapace of an enormous yew, she stops and listens. Nothing. Perhaps she imagined it. Her head's scrambled by the kiss.

She pushed Robbie off, of course. Big, plain Rita, fine for a fumble, not a dance! And she'd run back inside the house, only for Jeannie to mention Hera had not yet returned. But Hera wasn't beside the bonfire when she'd passed it, as she'd have expected, and it was far too late for her to be out alone. Her thoughts flicked to Fingers. Her own neglect. She should never have left the children alone with Jeannie . . . Anxiety squeezes her ribs.

She hesitates where the path forks: log pile or stream? Left, yes. Hera loves the stream. She starts walking, quicker now. Where is she?

She can smell rain. She cups her hands over her mouth. "Hera?"

"Over here," comes a voice.

Rita squints into the gloom, frowning. Yes, she's there, the scallywag. Thank goodness. But why is there a doll on her lap?

Hera beckons giddily.

"What's going on?" Rita rushes over. A baby? A baby *here*? She touches the infant. Alive. But the forehead is cool as plastic. "Where's her mother? Is the baby hurt? Goodness, give her to me. Quick, quick."

The baby is small, dainty, no more than a few weeks old, and almost weightless in her arms. Her fingers are white-tipped, as if frost pockets are forming under her nails, and her face is scoured with insect bites. Rita lightly strokes her sore cheek, trying to bring some comfort. The baby whimpers and watches Rita's mouth speculatively, as if this might offer a clue as to what is happening, what she must do next to survive. Rita tucks the baby under her cardigan for warmth, folding the wool around her body, like a blanket, cradling the curve of her spine with one spread hand. "Hera, what on earth . . ."

Hera's gabbling an explanation. Something unlikely about the baby being left on the tree stump. "See."

Rita believes it only when she sees the crumpled note from Hera's pocket. The bag containing the baby gear. Such a pitiful collection of things. So Dickensian. "My god." The cruelty of the world takes her breath away. She rubs the baby's back with the pad of her thumb, relieved at the hum of body heat. "Are you sure there's no one around?"

Hera shakes her head. "I looked."

Rita peeps under her cardigan at the baby, who stares back with wide blue-black eyes. Her vulnerability opens something inside

Rita. She can feel it, like a muscle stretching, a valve opening. Despite the ravaging of bites and cold, the baby's exceptionally pretty, not one of those squashed babies that look like Winston Churchill. She's silent now, as if Rita's body is all she needed. "You should have got an adult straightaway, Hera," she admonishes.

"I thought I'd get into trouble." Hera doesn't mention that the only adult around was Jeannie. Neither does Rita.

Rain starts to fall in fat drops.

❋ ❋ ❋

Jeannie's waiting for them in the hall. "So there you are, Hera! I told you not to do anything silly, didn't I? You've made me look a quite hopeless mother. And now Rita's had to go searching for you and got soaked to her . . ." She stops talking. She frowns and stares, puzzled, at the bulge in Rita's cardigan. "What's that?"

Rita swallows. She has no idea how Jeannie will react. The silence stretches. Their sodden clothes drip onto the wooden floor. The baby wriggles against Rita's ribs. She grabs fistfuls of cardigan.

"Rabbit? Baby deer?" Jeannie frowns and laughs thinly, looking from Hera to Rita and back again. "Dinner? Show me."

As if in answer the baby starts to cry, a low *huh-huh-huh*.

It sends a volt of electricity through Jeannie.

Hera grins. "I found you a baby."

"No," breathes Jeannie, shaking her head. "Don't say things like that."

Rita lifts one side of her cardigan. The baby peers out, like an animal in its pouch.

"For the love of God." Jeannie covers her mouth with her hand. "Hera, what have you done?"

❅   ❅   ❅

Outside the kitchen window, a silver-foil sky flashes. But the baby, who has survived, but only just, Rita thinks, is safe, bottle-feeding on her lap, frantically sucking, her toes curling. Hera and Teddy press close, fascinated, their faces tender and alert, as if the baby is both a previously unimaginable wonder and someone they'd been waiting for to arrive. Only Jeannie maintains a terrified and awed distance. Her eyes are wide, startled, revealing too much white above the irises. She cannot look away.

The soft wet sounds of the baby's feeding fill the room, and they all listen in silence, rapt, like an audience of exquisite chamber music. The baby takes one last loud slurp and her eyes close heavily. A calm settles over the kitchen, soft as the silence after a night's snowfall. And for a magical moment, it feels like they're all knitted together around the baby, a world apart.

"Can I?" Jeannie asks, her voice tremulous. She walks slowly toward them.

Rita passes the baby over, apprehensively, wishing she didn't have to. She has a strange sense that she'll always remember this moment, that something is ripping through the fabric of her life as she's always known it. The baby leaves a small indent on her navy skirt, and the warmth of her remains for a moment or two after she's gone.

"I'd forgotten," Jeannie whispers, marveling, tentatively pressing the baby to her chest and closing her eyes. "I'd quite forgotten."

Half an hour later, Jeannie still won't let go of the baby. She's lying on the sofa, her eyes vague and dreamy, the baby spread-eagled across her chest. In the firelight Jeannie's face has a soft lambent glow, a flushed placidity, as if the baby's vital life force is transfusing into her. The children seem to sense it too, sitting on the floor, leaning against their mother's legs, the silky pool of her dressing gown, staring up at the baby's fingers opening and closing like stars.

So no one else notices the streak of movement at the window. Only Rita. A face? A flash. Something pale. She walks toward it and presses against the flaking paint of the sill, the cold draft leaking through the ramshackle window frame.

Outside, the storm throws itself violently at the trees, like a living thing, rocking them by their roots. The sky is a glowing charcoal gray, flecked with angry embers of orange. Rita squints into the garden, seeing more now her eyes have adjusted. But whoever or whatever was there has gone. An animal probably, she decides. Or a falling branch. Still, it tips her mind to the world outside. It makes the hairs rise on her arms. "Shall I call the police now?" she asks, turning to face Jeannie.

Jeannie's eyes snap open. "What? No!"

Rita is taken aback. She doesn't understand. "But the authorities will know what to do next."

"I know what to do." Jeannie sits up and rearranges the baby in her arms, more tightly. The baby's downy fluff of black hair spreads over her pale forearm. "She's just arrived. She can't leave yet." She looks down at the baby, her eyes flashing, fierce and protective. "Can you, sweet thing?"

The cuckoo clock squawks. Although it feels like the baby's stopped time altogether, it's been well over an hour. Someone somewhere will be out of her mind with worry, Rita thinks. Her heart starts to race. "Shall I call the village doctor, then?"

Hera shakes her head. "The doctor will call the police, won't he, Mother?"

"That's right." Jeannie shoots a warm smile at Hera. "Well said, darling."

Hera seems to grow two inches. Rita feels more confused.

"No police. No doctor." Jeannie lifts the baby up and blows the fuzz of baby hair lightly, watching it move with delight.

"Jeannie, she might be poorly," Rita points out, with a surge of panic. "And someone will be looking for her. Her mother."

"Sick babies don't feed, Rita. And whoever left her on the tree stump knows exactly where she is." Jeannie's face hardens. "Let's not forget that that beast of a woman abandoned her. She could have been taken by a fox, had her eyes pecked out by crows, anything. It doesn't bear thinking about."

"She was left there on purpose, Big Rita," says Hera, enjoying siding with her mother. "Near Foxcote. Near us."

"For us." Teddy grins, joining in and waggling the baby's foot. "Like a present. Baby Forest."

"Oh, Baby Forest, I do like that, Teddy," coos Jeannie. "I like that very much."

"Me too," says Hera, making Teddy beam. She repeats, "Baby Forest," a couple of times under her breath, like an incantation.

Rita can only imagine Walter's take on this. The knife Jeannie kept under her mattress glints like a warning in her mind. Then the entrance to The Lawns, the stone pillars and soaring iron gates, topped with impaling spikes. "Jeannie, we really have to contact the police. I can drive her to the station."

"Drive? You? I don't think so. Christ. Take a look out of the window, Rita. It's wild out there. Lethal! All those flying branches." Jeannie strokes the baby's cheek. The baby looks puzzled. Starts to bleat. "There, there. You're safe with us, my little poppet." She glances up at Rita. "Just one night, okay? To give this poor little thing a chance to recover from such a horrific ordeal."

Rita's aware of something intractable taking shape. A wrongness. "But . . ."

"Shush. Can you hear it?" Jeannie holds a finger to her mouth. "You want the baby out in that, do you? You really want to get behind the wheel?"

Rita listens to the awful sound, too close for comfort, a deep groaning, as if the earth itself is splitting in two, then a scalping rip and crash as the first tree falls. "I guess we should wait for it to blow over," she concedes reluctantly, sensing a different sort of storm stirring, not outside Foxcote's walls but within.

22

———— ❈ ————

Hera

The gigantic tree lies across the lane, upended with a huge skirt of earth, its pale roots thrust in the air, like legs. I feel so sorry for it but am glad that it keeps Marge—and any other visitors—at bay. Two days since I found the baby, and still no one knows we've got her. The only problem is Big Rita, who is behaving sort of strangely, like she's growing her own private opinions. Like she doesn't love Baby Forest as much as we do. Like she might snitch.

She'd have gotten through to the authorities this morning if I hadn't pulled the telephone cable out of the wall last night and said something about it coming down in the storm. And she might even be on her way to the village now, if I hadn't been watching from the bedroom window and tipped off Mother.

"Wait," I shout from the porch as Big Rita lowers the baby into the car. Mother runs past me—I can't remember the last time she *ran* anywhere—and snatches the baby off the passenger seat.

"What's wrong with you, Rita? The lane is blocked."

"I . . . I thought I could drive around the tree somehow," Big Rita mumbles. "Take her to the doctor's."

"What a ridiculous idea. She's not ill, Rita! Do you *want* this little thing to be carted off to some children's home? Is that it?" Mother is so full of fight again I feel like clapping. She's back. *I* brought her back. I cured her sadness. By finding the baby.

"Have you any idea what those places are like?" Mother continues.

Big Rita says nothing. But something about the way she lowers her eyes makes me think she does. I can see her lungs inflating and deflating beneath her blouse. Her mouth goes tight and pouchy, like when you're trying not to cry.

"Babies in metal cots! Rows of them! Dirty nappies. A matron who . . . who will farm her out to be fostered by any old brute. A council house! Anywhere."

I'm pretty sure Big Rita grew up in a council house. She doesn't say anything, though.

"Honestly." Mother gazes down at Baby Forest, her eyes softening: she can't stop looking at her—none of us can. She's the most beautiful baby alive. "You've not had children of your own, Rita. You wouldn't understand."

Something crumples in Big Rita's face then. She stares at her hands on the steering wheel. After a while she says, "It doesn't feel right, Jeannie."

"*Right?*" Mother steps back, her face sharpening. "You mean moral? Well, if you want to talk morals, Rita, we can start by discussing yours, can't we?"

Big Rita's knuckles whiten. The air feels crackly again.

"I know you're writing notes on me for Walter." Mother lowers her voice to a whisper. There's a tremble in it. "Spying."

My body floods with guilty heat: I remember sitting beside

Mother's bed as she slept, mentioning Big Rita's notebook. But then Mother might have found out in another way. Marge could easily have poked through Rita's things. She's always scuttling around upstairs, in and out of bedrooms, clutching a stack of bed linen to her chest.

"Jeannie, if I hadn't agreed, he'd have sacked me on the spot and hired someone else," Big Rita stutters, her words all clumsy and rubbery, falling over each other. "I didn't want to desert the children."

Mother shakes her head. "I always underestimate my husband. He exploited your sweet nature, Rita. Your lack of confidence, you know that?" Something in her eyes goes flinty. "Have you written notes these last two days? Spoken to Walter?"

Big Rita nods. She looks on the verge of tears. Her neck is mottled red. "A couple of nights ago. He said the house would be ready soon, the painters are already in. And he was coming back the last week of August."

I can see Mother calculating dates, like I am: we've got less than two weeks. She studies Big Rita. Her voice goes soft and a little bit scared. "Did you mention the baby?"

"I—I wasn't sure what to say. Then the line cut."

Mother exhales. "You did the right thing, Rita. I think it's best the baby isn't mentioned to Walter. Not yet. I have your word. Don't I?"

Big Rita touches her forehead with her hand, like she's got a headache.

"Come back into the house. Please?" Mother bends down inside the car, the baby over her shoulder. Her voice wheedles. "This baby needs you. She's ravenous. Look at her. Sucking at my neck, like a little octopus. How about you fix her a bottle?"

Mother doesn't do the bottles. I'm not sure she'd know how. She doesn't change nappies, either, or wash them out in the bucket, like Big Rita's been doing every morning before breakfast, the long pale tubes of her arms pummeling the nappy in the stinky brown water.

Finally, slowly, Big Rita gets out of the car and walks back to the house, even though the expression on her face doesn't look so obedient. "You're a good girl, Rita," Mother says.

At lunch Mother eats three whole potatoes and half a lamb chop. Big Rita sits silently, burping the baby over one shoulder, and barely eats anything, which is not like her either. In the garden, the gate bangs on its hinges, like it does when someone's just used it. Worrying that it might be Marge, I run into the forest and look left and right. I can't see anyone. But I swear I can feel a presence—someone who hasn't gone along the road, which is blocked, but threaded through the maze of woodland at the back.

After roly-poly pudding, oozing Marge's seedy sweet jam, I forget about the gate, the funny watched feeling. Everything is our new normal again. Me and Teddy help Big Rita change the baby in the living room. Teddy holds his nose. A large speckled brown feather blows in through the open window and rocks on the floor. I pick it up, decide it's an owl feather, and brush its thistle-top fluffiness against the baby's bare foot. She curls her toes. Mother appears, all excited, holding frilly bootees and a silver rattle, which is tinkling, hooked around her little finger. Our baby's things. The stuff Big

Rita rescued from under my parents' bed in London. "I think the time has come," she says.

Big Rita gasps.

"Aren't they perfect on her?" Mother bends down to tie on the little bootees and presses the rattle into the baby's tight damp fist. She shakes it and the room fills with silvery sounds and dead-baby ghosts and my mother's smile. She jiggles Baby Forest around the room, trailed by me and Teddy. I don't see Big Rita go upstairs. But when she doesn't come down for ages, I go and find her.

Big Rita is hunched over her suitcase and throwing clothes in really fast. She glances across at me—eyes pink—then carries on packing, pushing her murder-mystery novels into an interior pocket. But the terrarium is on the floor, next to another bag. I draw some comfort from this. As long as the terrarium is here, ready to be packed, so is Big Rita.

I suddenly remember an evening in London last year, a bedtime after a bad day—I'd got caught stealing at school, a twist of another girl's pear drops—and how Rita had stroked my hair out of my eyes and told me that, as a kid, one night she'd gone to bed, all sad and angry, and the next morning she'd woken to find a harvest of buttercups growing in her terrarium. She could find no explanation for it other than that the spirit of her dead mother had sprinkled them inside while she slept. And I think how Big Rita's the only person I know who says just the right thing, the thing you least expect. Panic charges through me again. "You can't go."

"I can't stay, Hera." She tucks in navy socks. "Somewhere there's a young girl crying her heart out, regretting what she's done. And someone is bound to know her. Someone is bound to tell."

I remember the garden gate moving back and forth. The watched feeling.

"This is a small community. And if we keep the baby any longer there will be trouble—the big sort, Hera."

Tears burn my eyes. She sounds so certain. I think about The Lawns and feel scared, balled-up inside.

"It's not right that you and Teddy keep such a big secret from your father, either."

"But that's just what families are like."

"Not all families, Hera," she says softly, and shakes her head.

Something flares inside. "I bet you keep secrets!"

She flinches. I know I've got her. "What's your secret, Big Rita?" I tease, trying to stop her packing.

Her lips twitch. "Leave me be, Hera."

I charge at the suitcase, flipping down the lid and landing on it with a crunch. The cardboard side caves. "I won't let you go."

She rolls her eyes. "For goodness sake, Hera. I shouldn't have come here in the first place, okay? It was a mistake. Now scoot."

"You can't drive down the lane anyway."

"I've got legs. I'll walk."

"What about Robbie?" I cast around desperately. "You like him, I know you do."

"Don't talk nonsense," she says, all lemony again.

"You've got nowhere to go. And—and you'll miss us."

She looks at me. And something passes over her eyes, like a shadow. "Terribly," she says, almost a whisper.

I glance at her terrarium, and I'm struck by an almost overwhelming urge to jump on that too, so it shatters, and the thought scares me, the destructive force of it. Every time I feel loss—that thin, angry feeling, like a stringy bit of bacon fat—I want to smash something up.

"You're going to grow up into the most fantastic young woman," she says, like she can smell my fear of myself. She has a knack for that. "You'll be just fine without me, Hera."

My tears start to curl behind my ears. "But I keep thinking I'm going to do a bad thing, a really bad thing, Big Rita, and someone will get hurt. And you're the only person who can stop it." I'm not lying, not exactly. She stares at me, tussling with something. Outside the window, the woodpecker pecks tiny little holes in the silence.

23

Sylvie

After checking that Annie's soundly asleep, I pad, barefoot, down the cottage's narrow staircase. The dark grows fibrous and intimate. In the hush, I can hear the pulse of waves outside, the night's high tide sucking back, millions of sand grains dancing in its wake. My breath quickens, feelings churning inside me too.

In the living room, I snap on the lamp, creating a monocle of light, and tentatively slide out the *Summer 1971* folder from under an old magazine on the coffee table. My fingertips leave clammy prints on the age-washed cardboard. I hesitate and consider calling Caroline, but I know she'll say, "Jeez, don't open it. Mum hid it for a reason. Anyway, we made a vow, remember?" And I remind myself that I've waited all day for this private communion with my past, quite possibly an ugly one. I need to do it alone. Unwatched.

With shaky hands I carefully pull out the newspaper cuttings my mother has stashed away all these years. The paper feels dappled and old, well handled rather than forgotten. I read in the light, braced, waiting for the hurt to start.

"Police Appeal for Abandoned Baby's Mother." The appeal will fail. More than forty years later, she still hasn't come forward or tried to get in touch. She could have. She hasn't. The past is set and cannot be rescued. The lump in my throat is a small rock. "The baby was reportedly taken in by an unnamed local family . . ." reads the article, as lightly sprinkled with facts as my mother's bedtime story. Yet it still somehow diminishes the rest of my life—as big and messy as anyone else's—and recasts me to one tragic line of ink.

I wipe away a rush of bitter tears with my arm. Unable to linger in that place any longer, I curse beneath my breath, lick my finger, and turn to another cutting: "Body in the Woods." I freeze. Even the sea outside seems to still, the waves silencing. I bring it closer, the paper crackling, my heart thumping, and read it again. I note that it's dated three days earlier than the foundling story. Mum's never mentioned *this*. And as I read, I slowly begin to grasp why.

"The death is being treated as suspicious." Murder? The victim? I scan the copy for further details. But the report is from the immediate aftermath. "The police will not release further details at this time." The body isn't named. Only the house, Foxcote Manor, and its owners, the Harringtons, the name of the family who took me in.

I pace the living room's shadowed edges, clutching the newspaper to my nose, as if I might be able to smell what happened next.

Was Mum trying to protect me? But from what? I peer out of the window at the sea, the rippling ladder of moonlight on the water, and try to arrange my thoughts into some sort of rational order. The dates suggest I was with the family at the time of the death, which might explain Mum's evasive secrecy. After all, she sold me the fairy-tale version—"You were found one magical summer's night"—and in the way a photograph can become a memory, replacing the event itself, that story became my story. The last thing Mum would have wanted was to bloody the sweet tale with murder, so it became something more akin to a creepy seventies movie, all *The Shining* dark pines and sulfurous skies. And what if the killing was in some way connected to my appearance in the Harringtons' household? What if one of my parents was the unnamed victim? The idea riots in my head.

Turning away from the window, I sit back down on the sofa and hunch under the light. Pictures. Scissored out of larger articles, as if Mum wanted to keep their memories untainted by the scandal that surrounded them. Strange, given that she never spoke of the family at all. Nor has she ever shown me a photograph. Did I ever ask to see one? No, of course not. I'd pushed the Harringtons into the cupboards of my mind, where suppressed thoughts huddled and scrabbled like mice.

Jeannie Harrington. The wife? A thumbnail portrait. All raven hair and milky skin. She could be a vintage Elizabeth Arden face cream model, if it weren't for the arch glint in her gaze—a hint, perhaps, of something less compliant. There's an individual photo of a Mr. Walter Harrington too, a tall, gaunt fellow in a good suit, paparazzi-snapped, briefcase in hand, on the desperate car-to-courthouse dash, dazzled by the bank of photographers' flashes. Not a flattering picture. Was it kept for a different, less sentimental reason?

The nicest photo, the most thumbed and dimpled, is the family standing in front of a stucco townhouse, under the drip of wisteria. Jeannie's hugely, gloriously pregnant. Tugging on her dress is a little boy. To the left of him is an older girl, plain, plump, with an unsure smile, and an intense gaze that wires right into the photographer's lens. Is this the girl who found me in the woods? A grim possibility starts niggling. Was she the victim? Or her cute little brother? If so, the crime might be so disturbing my mother felt she couldn't share it.

Queasily, I flick through the remaining three cuttings. No more articles about me or the Harringtons. Just a few photographs of the Forest of Dean. I smooth the largest one with my palm, wanting, like a child, to step into the picture. It's a grainy image of sculptural, witchy trees, the type that have contorted faces and might start talking. A woodland borrowed from antique ornate bookplates and movies featuring satyrs or hobbits. A complete and alternate world, caught within three square inches of ink, a portal into my past. And the place, I realize, with a small stifled sob, where I began.

❋ ❋ ❋

The next morning I wake to the wheeling shriek of hooligan gulls in my old bedroom, breathing in the familiar laundered smell of my bed. Then it hits me. *Body found in woods.* It's not the same childhood. Now there's a different version.

I rub my eyes and sit up against the pillows. My body feels stiff and toxic after the stress of the last two days; it aches where the wave thundered into my hamstrings. Above my head an old, much-loved mobile turns. Wooden cutout trees, suspended by string, ready to tremble at the slightest breeze, turning my mind back to the photograph of the forest again.

I part the curtains. Outside, the sky is a fresh lawn-cotton blue, overwritten with aircraft trails. The sea is as flat as glass. It doesn't look capable of last night's mischief. How strange to emerge into a new day so radically different from the one before.

"Morning." Annie appears, sleepy, yawning. Looking about twelve.

Yesterday's declaration, *I'm keeping the baby*, hits me again, like a blow to the back of the head. Will she change her mind today? My determined, stubborn wonder of a daughter. Is she unconsciously trying to right past historic wrongs by keeping the baby, doing what my biological mother evidently didn't? This possibility terrifies me.

A shrink would say, "Let's talk about that." Habit says, "Let's not." I simply want to press pause. Rewind. Plait Annie's hair or comb for nits and pat her down after a bath, with a rub-a-dub-dub, and laugh as she puts her tiny feet into my high heels and teeters across the bedroom, her world still guarded and safe.

* * *

The clothes we hung over the radiator last night are still damp, so we ransack Mum's wardrobe, tugging on her too-long jeans and swampy jumpers, which is both funny—Mum would think it a hoot—and unbearably sad. I run to the corner shop, jeans and cardigan sleeves flapping, imagining what my private clients, all those groomed SW3 ladies, would think if they saw me now. I buy croissants and milk. My phone beeps with texts from Steve, in full patriarch meltdown: *FFS! Just TELL her she can't have a baby!*

At the kitchen table, where Mum should also be sitting but isn't, Annie wolfs two croissants. I drink builder's tea, too fried to eat, aware of the moment's fragility. Annie's beef may be that I never tell her the truth—and this chafes against my need to smother it—but it's my turn to ask questions this morning. "So where did you find that folder?" I watch her over the rim of my mug. "Annie?" I say, when she stares down at the table silently.

"It was the night before she fell . . ." She looks up. Her eyes are complicated. "Granny didn't hear me come in, you see. And she was sitting at her desk, bent over this bit of newspaper. When she saw me, she quickly slipped it back into the folder and shoved that into the desk drawer with this startled caught-out look. I thought, *Hello, what's that?*" Her eyes water. She bites down on her lip. "I was going to ask. But I never got the chance."

For a moment I can't speak. The image of my mother alone, looking at those old newspapers, suggests she lived much closer to the past than I ever realized. "Go on," I say huskily, struggling not to cry.

"Coming back here, two days ago, not knowing what I was going to do about the baby, everything, I wanted to feel close to her . . ." Something about the way Annie says this doesn't quite ring true. Her gaze skids away. She prods a croissant flake from the plate onto her finger and eats it.

Outside the window, there's a murmuration of tiny black birds, lifting, swelling: newsprint letters on a page.

"Why didn't you ever tell me about the dead body in the woods, Mum?" There's an edge to her voice, old resentments surfacing.

"Sweetheart, I didn't know."

"I—I presumed . . ." Her eyes widen. "Wow."

A moment passes. The birds outside the window scatter, re-form, and twist into a different shape. My thoughts do the same. Something about Annie's expression makes me realize I've made a mistake in assuming she's been too busy with school and friends to give a stuff about the dusty brown analogue seventies.

"I googled it," Annie says more cautiously now, unsure how I might react. "But there's nothing online."

"Different world. No internet."

"Didn't you and Granny talk about all that stuff?"

"Not really." I force a breezy smile, aware of how odd this sounds to a generation used to sharing their souls as casually as a bag of popcorn. "Rest assured, Annie, in those days this amounted to an enlightened approach to a taboo subject."

"Still does in our house," she mutters.

"Well, I had a keen sense of self-preservation. I didn't want to know. Which suited Granny just fine."

When I was Annie's age, questions did flutter lively inside me. But asking them meant thinking about "it." The threat of my own dissolution. And in the end, I'd always tell "it" to sod off—*I'm not that baby. That's not my story*—and walk away, hands thrust into my faded Levi's 501 pockets. I'd choose the present over the past: Madonna, self-made and starlight-blond; boys; fashion's shiny surfaces. The simpler explanation is this: My birth mother walked away. She left me on a tree stump and walked *away*. And I set out to reject that part of my life—as I was rejected. But it's too painful to explain this, even to Annie. "We're meant to be talking about you, not me," I say quickly. "Not the past. I'm old news."

"Nice change of subject." Annie slams herself back into the chair. She rolls her eyes. "Always the same."

I feel my own defenses rising.

"Dad's always said, 'Don't ask Mum about that stuff,'" she huffs. "'Don't upset Mum.' It's, like, I don't know, electric-fenced off."

I blanch. Can't deny it. Only my closest friends know I was abandoned, and most wouldn't dare mention it. I can't shrink the enormity of what happened into a dinner-party anecdote. Or face the pity in their eyes.

When Annie was born, what my birth mother did became more incomprehensible and, devastatingly, less abstract. I was engulfed by love for my newborn. How could she not have felt the same? Did she not marvel at the miniature perfection of my fingernails? Ears? Toes? Did she not watch me as I slept? Kiss me. Sniff me. Did I not feel like part of her own body? Clearly not, since she had dumped me in the woods and *walked away*.

As Annie grew up, I determined not to pass on this legacy. And like all new parents, I wanted her exposed only to life's honey, not its sting, naively believing I could curate her world, sugarcoat it. (As my own mother had tried to do for me, of course.) So I kept back my birth story for as long as I could. Too much for a sensitive kid to process: it'll skew her view of the world. What family means.

Steve's always stoked this secrecy. Although he'd never admit it, I'm sure he sees my start in life as slightly grubby and shameful, a bit *Jerry Springer*. A tragedy I've overcome—with his help, the stability of marriage—and shouldn't let define me. For all his metropolitan ad-man tics, at heart he's a fairly conventional bloke from the lawn-sprinkler suburbs, who comes from a long line of nuclear families and sacrificial matriarchs, who stayed married to philandering hus-bands "for the children's sake." It was black and white to him. What my biological mother did was "unnatural and unforgivable," he once said. (My biological father was demoted to a rogue spermatozoon, not held to account.) "You don't need to go there, Sylvie," he'd say if we ever brushed against the subject with a jolt, as a bare leg might a scorching radiator. "Remember that's not who you are." And I would nod and fill the kettle, wondering who I was.

"There you go!" Annie laughs hollowly. "You've put your 'I'm not talking about this' face on!"

"I've got a face for that?" I try to wipe it with a smile. But I can hear the serration in my voice.

"Yes, you really *do*." Her gaze is unflinching, the teenage sort that comes with a bullshit detector fitted. "Which is why I started asking Granny questions about our family history—my history too, just saying—when I first came down here in June." Her face clouds. She looks away. "I was sick of not being told anything."

Although I know that my mother is more likely to discuss a bladder infection than the summer I was found, my heart hammers under her soft old checked shirt all the same. "She told you about the mystery corpse in the woods, did she?" I say, trying to make it sound like a jolly whodunit.

"Hardly! She's almost as bad as you."

Master of sweet white lies. Spinner of grubby old yarn into beau-tiful silken threads. Nightmares into fairy tales. That's Mum.

"*But* in a funny way . . ." Annie laces her fingers over her almost-flat belly. And I can feel it coming, like a distant beat, distorted, carried over the water. ". . . the little she did say led me to Elliot." She nods down at her hands, and a chill sluices through me. "So, I guess, whoever's inside here too."

24

Rita

A wisp of black hair curls at the back of the baby's neck, like a question mark. There are lots of those. Rita picks off the dark fluff that beads between the baby's fingers and toes. She lays her down under the old apple tree on a blanket—covered with a clean white sheet—so she can gaze up at the baubles of hard red fruit. But the baby's gaze stays on her face, as it always does. She's been here only four days, yet she's locked on to Rita in a way Rita finds disconcerting. The baby reminds her of a duckling that hatches and decides its mother is the first living creature it sees, irrespective of species. And any pleasure her presence brings is spoiled by the brute sadness of this misconception.

Rita turns to her wicker basket of never-ending washing and starts hanging the damp terry nappies on the line. Her thoughts roll to Robbie. His mouth. The slow spread of his smile. The golden hairs on his arms. The intense concentration on his face when he used a chainsaw on that fallen tree yesterday, the noise and whir and mesmerizing violence of it, before he expertly bound the sections with ropes to his truck and dragged them out of the lane.

She smiles to herself, wondering if it's the very mindlessness of the task that allows her to mentally wander to secret, slightly steamy places. If this is women's way of escaping their domestic lives, inhabiting them but living elsewhere. If that's what Jeannie did too, only she let the thoughts spill from her brain to her bed. She's sticking up the last nappy, a wooden clothes peg in her mouth, when a shadow drapes coolly over her neck.

"Nothing wrong with this one, is there? Very bonny." Rita whips around to see Marge hunkered over the baby, prodding her with a thick finger. She looks up at Rita, eyes gleaming with small triumph. "Thought you'd hide her from me forever, did you?"

Rita panics. Instinctively she swoops down, picks up the baby, and presses her tight to her chest. What to say? *Anything you do say will be taken down and may be given in evidence* . . . It can't really be abduction. Can it?

She keeps anticipating a policeman's rap on the door. The clink of handcuffs on her wrists. She's also jittery, constantly worrying that someone's watching them, shadowing them in the woods and peering through the holes in the wall. But all her senses feel heightened— she's not sure if she's imagining these things. Turns out she'd have been better off listening for the wheeze of Marge's rusty car instead.

"Well, don't stand just there, Rita. You look like a carp. Mouth opening and closing like that. Don't worry. I won't say anything." Marge taps her nose. "You can trust me."

She doesn't trust Marge. Not an inch. There's something urgent and blinkered about the woman, a bitterness Rita can't help but find repellent. She stares down at the sheet and the imprint the baby has left on it, like a snow angel. Even that squeezes her heart. She should have left while she had the chance.

Hera stopped her. Hera and the grave thing she'd threatened to do, preventable only by Rita's presence. How could she go after that seed was planted? She suspects now that Hera knew exactly what she was doing.

"A foundling, eh?"

Rita flinches. "I didn't say that."

"Didn't have to, love."

Rita finds Marge's lack of shock unnerving. Guns in biscuit tins. Babies left in woods. She feels like she's been drawn through a portal into a different world entirely, unshackled from normal behavior. No wonder feral men hide in these woods. Anything goes.

"Not as unusual around here as you might believe, I'm afraid." She tsk-tsks. "The pretty ones, usually. It goes to their heads."

Out of the corner of her eye Rita can see Hera's face, white and round as a moon at her bedroom window, then Hera frantically wheeling away, probably to tell Jeannie.

"Half the time they don't realize they're pregnant until the baby's head's crowning." Marge clicks her tongue. "I blame their mothers, don't you? Show me an unmarried local girl who gets into trouble, and I'll show you a mother who's not been paying attention." She tweaks the baby's foot. "Still. A wild stroke of luck for the Harringtons, eh?"

Luck? Luck is winning something in a raffle. Or being born to grow to less than five foot eight. Not this. "I'm not sure what you mean."

"To lose one baby . . ."—Marge raises her hands to the sky, like a preacher—"only to find another!"

Rita's unease builds. Earlier that morning, she saw Jeannie, in a long lacy nightie, showing the baby the garden, pointing out the flowers and birds, and it had made her think of those drifting women in the grounds of The Lawns. "But the baby can't stay here, Marge."

Rita might as well have said they'd be feeding the baby to wild pigs. "I *beg* your pardon?"

"Obviously, we're going to call the authorities." She can hear her own voice—and belief that this will ever happen—wobbling slightly. "Just one more day," Jeannie keeps saying. But then night falls, there's another shattering dawn feed, and that day merges into another.

"Heavens, no. Rita, you listen to me. You want to ruin this little jewel's life chances? 'Course not. Then keep her here, secret—you hear me?—until the end of the summer." She grabs Rita's sleeve roughly. "Don't tell a soul."

Has the world gone mad or has she? "But, Marge . . ." she begins, with a disbelieving laugh.

"You're too young." She snorts dismissively and a puff of moist air lands on Rita's cheek.

"But we're surely breaking the law, Marge."

"The law?" Marge scoffs as if this were the most ludicrous thing she's ever heard. "We foresters have our own laws. You think some busybody from the council knows what's best for this baby? I tell you, Rita." She waggles a sausage finger. "Those bureaucrat types, those box-tickers, clueless, the lot of them. Respect the authority in here." She slaps her chest so her meaty bust judders beneath her overall. "And here." She taps her temple. "And there." She stabs her finger at the forest. "You can't trust many people, Rita, but you can trust an oak."

Rita struggles not to giggle. But nothing is funny. It's calamitous and quite, quite mad.

"Worried you're going to get into trouble, eh?" Marge dismisses this with such an energetic wave of her arm that Rita leaps back, protecting the baby's head in her hand. "No need! When the time comes, you can say you phoned and left a message. Some council secretary must have not passed it on. Oh, *and* you sent a letter, a letter that never arrived. They won't be able to prove you didn't. Post goes astray all the time here. The left hand never knows what the right does."

The baby's sucker mouth latches on to her neck. "I'd better get on. She's hungry."

"You know what they'll say?" Marge shuffles closer. "How clean she is! How well fed! How she loves her new family! Look, she's even got a devoted nanny thrown in!" Something ticks behind her eyes. "The Harringtons will be able to adopt formally then." She curls a wisp of hair around the baby's ear with an air of grandmotherly satisfaction. "No one will turn down such a good family, or such a wealthy one. Walter Harrington could fart and the mayor would applaud."

"Is that how social services work?" Rita says weakly. "It doesn't sound right."

"Is round here, love."

She has to say it. "Mr. Harrington doesn't know about the baby, Marge. And he's due back very soon. In a week, probably."

"Ah. Perfect timing. You get to show the baby to Mr. Harrington before you phone the services."

"B-but . . ." she stutters.

"I've known Walter Harrington all his life, Rita. And let me tell you, when he sees how much happier his wife is, he'll embrace that baby with open arms. Contrary to appearances, he's not made of stone." She seems so sure of this that it makes Rita question her own judgment. "Here, give her to me. She needs burping. I can't bear to watch you faffing any longer."

Marge slings the baby over her shoulder and starts whacking, far harder than Rita ever would. Rita wants to snatch her back. A belch erupts. "Better out than in," Marge says approvingly, lifting the startled baby above her head and giving her a shake so that her bare feet waggle back and forth. "One day . . ." Another shake. The baby starts the *heh-heh* sound Rita has learned precedes an eardrum-puncturing cry. ". . . our wee forest flower here will be all grown-up and rich and happy as any Harrington. Don't forget that." As if sensing Rita's doubt—she's never met a child more troubled than Hera—Marge freezes the baby midair and her eyes narrow to beetle-wing slits. "So what's more important, Rita? Blabbing the truth to make yourself feel better or doing what's *right*?"

25

Sylvie

My mother is falling. Spinning. Skirt parachute-puffed. In a whirl of shredded newspaper cuttings, like a deranged Mary Poppins. My stomach lurches. I step back on the cliff path and rapidly blink away the image until I can just see blue sky again. So far this walk with Annie—to stretch our legs before the drive back to London—has done little to soothe my rattled mind.

When I glance back at Annie, she's a couple of steps behind, resting her hands on her knees to catch her breath, a symptom I suddenly remember from my own pregnancy, that altitude-like thinning of the air. "Shall we sit, sweetheart?" I suggest, walking back to her and putting an arm over her shoulders. "Rather than hoof farther over these cliff tops?" She smiles and nods gratefully.

The bench, facing the sea, is an old favorite of Mum's, rickety, lichen-spangled, and dedicated to a long-dead village couple "who loved this spot." I think, if Mum dies, I'll get her an inscribed bench too, then push away the painful thought. She won't die. It's not her time.

I concentrate on the light. Beautiful. That's what I miss most about this place when I'm in London. There's no city haze here. Colors sing. Like on an old masterpiece after its dark varnish is removed.

My phone beeps in my bag. My fingers twitch. But I guess it's another panicking text from Steve, and I don't have any desire to speak to him or to interrupt things. It feels like Annie's finally opening up to me this morning, revealing her summer love affair, petal by petal, a bud unfolding. "So you were saying how you met Elliot . . ." I nudge, careful not to appear too ravenous for information.

"*I was . . .*" she says teasingly.

I bang her knee with mine. "Well, go on, then!"

"At the beginning of the summer, Granny let slip the name of the Harringtons' company." She raises one eyebrow, pauses dramatically. "Harrington Glass."

"Interesting. I didn't know that." Unable to see how this might relate to Elliot, I wonder if she's going off on a tangent.

"Thing is, I wouldn't have thought much of it if she hadn't looked so totally *weird,* Mum," she continues, twisting a strand of hair around one finger. "Like she'd said something she hadn't meant to say. It felt like brushing against something underwater and not knowing what it was. Do you know what I mean?"

My childhood was peppered with such febrile tiny moments: a certain inflection in my mother's voice if I ever asked about her work as a nanny, a swift change of subject. Or unexpectedly charged reactions disproportionate to the event. Like the time I set fire to my bedroom curtains, having a sneaky cig, and she yelled, really yelled—she rarely raised her voice—and accused me of almost burning down the house.

"Yep, know what you mean, Annie."

"So, obviously, I googled the company." She lifts her face to the sunshine and shoots me a sidelong glance under her long lashes. "It's still going, Mum."

"Is it?" I shelter my eyes with my hand and scan the sea for a sighting of seals or dolphins, those childlike shadows slipping beneath the surface, much as in this conversation.

"And *that* was where I first saw Elliot's profile. On the Harrington Glass website."

"*What?*" I turn to her with a small crack of a laugh and immediately see she's not joking. So *this* is why she's been cagey about how they met and not told me anything about him. Not married. Not an ex-con. I should be relieved. I'm not.

"He kind of stood out." She animates when she talks about him. Her eyes shine. "Didn't look like the rest of the headshots, all the old suits. On the staff list, it said 'digital brand ambassador' or something, and linked to a Twitter page that made me laugh. And then, well, I ended up going down this wormhole online. Don't look at me like that, Mum! It was just a distraction from what was going on with you." A wave smashes onto the rocks below: my guilt, with sound effects. "Okay. And Dad," she adds, as a sweet, conciliatory afterthought.

"And what did you find?" My mouth is dry. "In this . . . this wormhole."

"Dark web opiate-delivery service."

"Christ."

She smiles affectionately, and I realize she's winding me up. "He was 'gramming Devon beaches, Mum. Look." She points to a distant bay, a wedge of golden sand. "Turns out he was staying there with a friend at weekends. Surfing. I started liking his photos and we got, you know, chatting."

No, I don't know. Annie makes it sound so easy.

She's silent for a moment. She blushes. There's more, I think. Oh, crap.

"He was working at Harrington Glass for a few weeks because his mother had an 'in' at the company." She makes quote marks with her fingers. "Some contact. No big deal, is it?" She's seeking reassurance. "I mean, he doesn't work there anymore."

"No biggie." One of those unpleasant surprises tossed up by a digital world that connects people who wouldn't ever normally cross paths. "But, Annie, it does concern me that he was just a random stranger off the internet."

She frowns. "Er, how *else* are you meant to meet anyone?"

"At a party? On a train?" A boat. A canal boat. What's *wrong* with me? I've left my husband. My teenage daughter is pregnant. My mother's hovering in a nightmarish no-man's-land between life and death. I haven't worked in ages. I've not even buffed my nails. Or had my roots done. And I'm having disrupting thoughts about a bloke ten years my junior. Tragic.

"A *train?*" She giggles.

"Okay, I'm a dinosaur." I put my hands up, catching her giggle, realizing how much I've missed these confidences. "What happened when you actually met in real life? Did you like him straightaway?"

She nods. "There was this attraction, this *thing.*" Her voice is soaked with longing. "It felt like . . . like it was . . . right."

That feeling. I felt it once too. But a lifetime ago. The weekend I met Steve we sat up talking all night at a festival in the rain. I remember the soft glow inside the leaking orange tent that smelled of spilled beer and sleeping bags. Lying side by side on the boggy ground sheet. Midges whirling around our heads. Falling asleep at dawn, holding hands. Waking to the dazzle of sun, fat and gold with promise. We were so young. We were different people.

"I know it sounds corny."

I smile. "It sounds like you fell in love."

Annie doesn't deny it. But she picks a lichen flake off the bench, self-conscious, as if I've caught her off guard. Waves boom beneath us. The tide is turning.

"Granny met him, right?"

Annie stretches out her long legs, polished and tanned nut brown after a summer spent surfing and not wearing nearly as much sunscreen as I'd have liked. "A couple of times."

"Did she know where he worked?" I ask curiously, warily. Mum would dread the wrecking ball of the past colliding with her beloved grandchild in any way, I know that.

Annie nods. She bites her lower lip. "I told her that on the walk." A cloud covers the sun, tipping the sea from turquoise to a bottomless navy. "Just before she fell," she whispers, rasping with the horror of it still.

"Oh, Annie." I take her hand, remembering what she told me and Caroline: *Granny fell because of me.* "It doesn't make her fall your fault."

"I don't know why I even said it." Annie starts to cry. The tears stick her hair to her cheek. I pick the strand off gently, wanting to take the weight from her shoulders too—and her place on the cliff path that day. "So stupid," she whispers, shaking her head. "It just spilled out of me and made her start, like I'd plugged her into the national grid or something." She closes her eyes, screwing them up, the memory flickering across the minute muscles in her face. "Then she . . . she stepped backward. And Granny was gone."

※ ※ ※

Half an hour later, Annie comes down the cottage stairs with her bag slung over one shoulder and my old childhood mobile, the little wooden trees on strings, bouncing off one finger. "Can I have this? For my baby."

My baby. The overwhelming sense is of loss, and powerlessness. I have to remind myself of how, when Annie was growing up, each stage seemed set and unsolvable. I'd felt like I'd always be leashed to a pram I couldn't figure out how to fold, nap times and feed times, worries about meningitis, vaccines, choking on raisins, never sleeping properly again. But then a new Annie would emerge: toddler, preschooler, tween . . . I'd loved each one with such passion, mourned and marveled when she morphed again, never quite finished off, never quite ready. This too is a stage, I tell myself. A point of transformation. I just need to hold my nerve. "Of course, Annie. You have it."

She grins. "It'll go nicely with the terrarium, I reckon." The mobile starts to turn and twist. "Babies love to stare at things like that, don't they?"

The little forest under glass left at the hospital for Mum. In the whirlwind of the last two days, I'd forgotten all about it. "Oh, yes, they do," I say absently, distracted, niggled by a half-formed thought.

"Mum . . ." She fiddles with the car key in her hand. "I never told Elliot about Granny working for the Harringtons."

"You didn't?" I can't hide my surprise. The way Annie talks about Elliot—and the look in her eyes as she does so—suggests the union was a meeting of minds as well as bodies.

"Or me first seeing him on their company website."

"But I thought you'd got close."

"We did. I mean, it was perfect. That was the problem. I . . . I didn't want to ruin things. And it sounded, I don't know, stalkery. Complicated. It still does." She winces. "Please don't say anything either. Not to him or Helen or *anyone*. Promise? Please."

I hesitate, thinking of the photo of the Harrington family standing outside the lovely stucco house. That there's a link, however gossamer delicate, between them and Annie's situation is like a stitch in the brain. "Not if you don't want me to, of course not, Annie. But—"

"He doesn't want me to have this baby," she interrupts, jiggling the mobile from her finger. "His mother thinks I'm a gold digger. Why make things *worse*?"

"He did drive all the way down from London yesterday," I point out. "I bet he's phoned."

She presses her lips together, which means he has. And she probably hasn't taken his call.

"He seemed genuinely concerned about you."

"No. His monster mother dispatched him from London to make me change my mind, that's all." She blows the mobile, one puff, two, harder, and it starts to spin. "I'm doing this on my own," she adds vehemently.

A shadow forest flickers against the pale wall. As the tiny trees slow to a stop, I feel something still in me too, a dawning realization. Annie's body is not mine: I can no more alter its inner workings than change the course of a satellite circling the moon. And if it weren't for *my* inability to confront my own past, she'd never have felt the need to start probing into it . . . So this is my mess. My responsibility.

I bend down and blow the mobile, so it dances on her fingers once more. "You're not on your own, Annie. We've got this, okay? You and me."

26

Rita

Rita stares down at the puzzle of strings, wire, and half a dozen or so wooden trees, each the size of her palm, yet thin and flat as a fingernail, just as smooth. They're attached by a large brass hook, which she instinctively picks up so that the strings hang down from a circular central rim, like one of those jellyfish that would wash up on the beach near home. The sweet scruffy collie, sitting beside Robbie, glances from one of them to the other, as if following a silent conversation. Her heart rears in her chest. Has Marge gossiped already? Leaked the mad plan to keep a baby hidden at Foxcote until the end of August? Fear mixes with the smell of fresh pencil shavings.

"I made it last night." His eyes smile right inside her. She pictures him cutting and sanding, oblong thighs spread, leaning over a workshop table, an alchemist, pulling something exquisite and delicate from a lump of wood, where it's been hiding. "For the baby."

"The baby?" she stutters.

"The baby I can hear over the garden wall." He nods at her collar. "The baby that's left a patch of milk on your blouse."

Oh, no. She rubs frantically at the bobbly scurf of milk, where Baby Forest nuzzles. She wonders if it's Robbie she's sensed on the grounds this last day or two, if that would explain why she can't shake the feeling she's being watched. Sometimes, walking in the woods, she'll hear something, glance around and no one's there, and she's left rattled. The other night, burping the baby in the drawing room, pacing and jiggling, she could have sworn she saw something at the window. But when she ran over and looked out, she could see no one. Just a slick of moonlight. She began to feel a bit silly then, thickheaded from broken sleep.

"One sec." She collapses the mobile back into the paper and closes the front door so they're standing alone in the porch, awkwardly, the site of the fumbled kiss, a few days ago yet light-years away. "A friend of Jeannie's got into trouble. We're helping out. It's all very hush-hush."

He nods. It's only the slight sharpening in his soft brown eyes that makes her wonder if he believes her.

"You mustn't say anything. It'd be a right old scandal. There's so much at stake." This is true, at least. Heaven knows what Walter will do.

He phoned yesterday, his questions forensic: "Has Jeannie been eating properly and managed to put on any weight? How much?"

"Do her eyes look swollen from crying in the morning?"

And the worst one: "Has my wife mentioned me?"

She reported back, yes, Jeannie's mentioned him a lot—honking lie—and her spirits were much improved. Not a lie. When he'd asked if there'd been any "distracting" visitors—she could tell from the timbre of his voice he meant Don Armstrong—and she'd said no, she could feel his relief down the phone. "I told you Foxcote would restore her, didn't I, Rita?" Walter had said, obviously heartened. "A break from . . ." And then a pause and Rita felt Don slip into it. ". . . her normal routine. I can't wait to see you all."

His sister Edie also phoned. That didn't go as well. Rita didn't cup the receiver with her cardigan in time: the baby started to mewl in the background. "Have you got animals in the house or something?" Edie said, with a small laugh followed by a pause. "Shit, Rita, you've not got yourself into trouble, have you?" Cars beeped manically in the background. The sounds filled Rita with an agitated longing, and a fear that she might never get back to the city. It felt as if an unbridgeable gap had yawned open between that world and Foxcote's. "Rita? Are you still on the line? Do you need my help, darling?" So she'd had to lie to Edie too. She hated that. She'd always liked Edie, her particular kind of worldly brisk kindness. After Edie had hung up, Rita had just stood there listening to the pips, feeling utterly alone.

"I won't say anything to anyone, Rita."

She believes him. She can't imagine Robbie gossiping. A silence thickens. "I wouldn't judge if . . ." He stops. "I mean, if I can do anything to help, Rita."

"The baby's not mine!" She stifles a gasp with her hand. "Is that what you're thinking? It is! I can tell from the look on your face."

"I didn't know what to think. Sorry."

She starts to giggle at the awful irony. The idea that Baby Forest is *hers*. But she's also touched by his sweetness. And the package in her hand. All so confusing. She'd hated him for lunging at her after the dance and thought him a brute, grabbing her like that, his hands like carpenter's clamps on her hips. But he isn't a brute. In fact, people never seem to be who she thinks they are. She wonders if she's the exception. Or if she'll surprise herself too. "Thank you for this," she says, feeling oddly humbled. "It's beautiful."

He looks away shyly, but can't stop his spreading smile.

"Big Rita, Baby Forest wants you," shouts Hera, from inside the house. Then the front door flings back and there is Hera, the baby whining in her arms. "Oh!"

"Hera, it's all right. Robbie knows we're looking after *Jeannie's friend's baby*," Rita says, with slow deliberation. Hera nods, cottoning on.

"Look. He's made her a mobile. Will you take it upstairs and show your mother?" She reaches for the baby. "I'll take her." The baby grabs a handful of her hair. "Ouch." She smiles, unwinding the little fingers.

"Hello, baby." Robbie grins, cocking his head to one side. He cups his not-quite-clean-enough hand around the fluff ball of her head. The dog brushes up against his legs, competing for attention.

Rita remembers how Fred claimed to love babies. "I can't wait for our nippers, Rita," he'd say, patting her belly, as if it was his Ford Cortina's bonnet. But he'd always gravitate to the Anchor rather than spend time with his infant nephews, "ankle biters," he'd call them. "Uncle Fred will be back when you're old enough to help me butcher a lamb, boy."

"She's a beauty, Rita."

Rita feels herself puff with pride, as if Baby Forest was hers, then catches herself. She's promised herself not to get sentimental or too close to this child, since she'll soon be going away. She must be professional. It's proving difficult. No wonder Jeannie's got so attached.

"What's her name?"

"We call her Baby Forest." She's gently discouraged Jeannie from giving the baby a proper name, the sense of possession that comes with it. She clears her throat. "Discretion's sake, you know."

He says nothing, processing this odd detail. He strokes the baby's head with a tenderness that makes Rita look away, confused. "She's hungry," he says.

"Always hungry."

He laughs and a tension she wasn't aware of dissolves. She allows herself a glance at his compelling mouth. How could it have been such a clumsy collision of a kiss? Such a total disaster?

"Rita, I'm sorry. For that night." He rushes into the apology, like a man trying to get through a crowd with his head down. "I'm not . . . I'm not like that."

She focuses on the constellation of milk spots on the baby's forehead.

"I don't know what came over me. Well, I do . . . I mean . . . Ach. Someone shut me up."

She bites back a smile and longs to say, *No, don't stop now, tell me exactly what you felt, in your heart, in your trousers. What made you pull me toward you like that?* She wants him to prove she was the focus of his desire, not just a lumpy female body that happened to be there, a few beers into a warm summer's night.

"I'd better go," he says instead.

She looks up. Their eyes lock, and something crackles between them, like a radio broadcasting in a foreign language she doesn't understand. "Bye then." She watches him step into his truck, yearning to call him back to ask for help. The baby, agitated by the quickening two-step thump of Rita's heartbeat, starts to cry.

27

Hera

The tree stump has a funny draw. I keep returning to the squat
column of wood with its bulging root toes, reliving the moment I found Baby Forest, lying there sweetly like a pudding on a
plate. It's a good place to sit alone, unbothered by the others, far
enough away from the house not to be seen, with a good view into
the dappled shade of the woods. If you sit very still, like I am now,
you can see deer, the trusting fawns, the nervous mothers.

Movement! A flash of something reddish. A deer? I visor my
hand over my eyes. But the trees chop up every view, so you see in
sections and can only fill in the missing bits by moving from side to
side and revealing your presence. Whatever was there vanishes.

I wait a bit—it doesn't come back—then start to swing my legs,
brushing the bare soles on the bristly bracken. I like my feet today.
They don't look like fat girl's trotters anymore. They're tanned or a
bit grubby—it's quite difficult to distinguish between the two. My
soles are hardening, padding out, adjusting to not wearing shoes.
They make me feel free. Soon my zigzag fringe will tuck behind my

ears, and I won't think of Mother screaming, "Oh my god, what have you done to your hair?" every time I look in the mirror. The sun is out, streaming through the branches. And the light is really nice, amber and soft. Like looking at the world through a bar of Pears soap.

I smile. It feels like the baby's changed everything. She brightens Foxcote's shadowy corners too, filling the house with her funny sounds and smells and bits and bobs: bottles and rubber teats on the draining board; the silver rattle on the sofa; baby clothes draped over the fireguard, like happy little ghosts. She has had a magical effect on Mother, who is so different from a week ago, no longer sleepy and switched off, like a cold dark room in a basement. She hasn't worn her sunglasses once. I feel proud: I found the baby, after all. I'm sure the baby knows this. She smiled at me last night: Rita said it was wind, but it wasn't.

The baby sits in the middle of my thoughts and swats at them if they go in the wrong direction. For one, I keep forgetting to steal food. My knicker elastic no longer pinches or leaves a red mark. This morning my stomach actually rumbled. It suddenly feels possible that we're not actually stuck being ourselves, either. Or trapped in the families into which we were born, like the plants in Big Rita's terrarium, pressed against the glass. Families can form without blood ties. Good things *can* happen. You can walk into the woods and stumble across a beautiful baby, for example.

"Big Rita wants you!" Teddy bursts out of the trees. He's only in his pants, and he looks hot and excitable and biscuit brown. "In the house. Come on!"

I jump down from the stump and run back into the garden to find Big Rita changing the baby on the lawn, making cooing sounds under her breath and pulling silly goofy faces. Seeing us, she stops, looking caught out, like she'd forgotten herself for a moment. She says Mother's upstairs having a much-needed rest and we should all get out of her hair. How about a picnic?

Big Rita's the one who needs to rest. She's got purple rings under her eyes and never seems to stop scrubbing down work tops and scouring with the Brillo pad: "Babies need things to be squeaky clean." But it feels like she's trying to rub away something the rest of us can't see.

After she's ordered me and Teddy to put on our shoes, we set off. She carries the baby in her arms. "Like a big bag of spuds," she says, but she won't let anyone else do it. My job is to hold the wicker picnic basket and shepherd Teddy, who keeps darting off, trying to climb trees. As we walk through the woods, the buttery light thickens.

Teddy stops to pick up sticks because Robbie's going to teach him how to whittle them—really just a ploy to visit Big Rita. Mother was delighted by this. "What a good idea. You don't want to end up like your father, Teddy, a man who struggles to carve the roast!"

Her comment brought it all back, those disastrous family Sunday lunches, Daddy hunched over the gray leg of lamb, teeth gritted, sawing fiercely at the meat, like it was Don Armstrong, not lamb at all.

We pick our spot by the bank of the stream, where the blackbirds and skylarks shelter from the afternoon heat and sing on the highest branches. Big Rita throws down a holey old blanket. I arrange the cake on a plate, licking its jam filling off my finger. Teddy strips and jumps into the stream naked, making us laugh. Tanned to the shape of his pants, his bottom is bright blue white. The water comes up to his thighs, but it's crystal clear, roping around him, the tiny fish scattering, weaving between his knees.

I change into my swimming costume under a towel, like I do in the school changing rooms, so no one can see my mouse-nose nipples and jiggly belly. I leap in, gasping at the blazing cold, and hide under the water.

Big Rita hitches up her cotton skirt and wades into the stream too. Very slowly, she dips the baby's foot in, then out again. We hold our breath, waiting for her to cry. But she doesn't. Her pretty monkey face grows intent and serious, as if considering this strange stuff, water. Again and again we dip her foot in, and she starts to gurgle with pleasure. We laugh. The sun beats down on our backs, baking us. Teddy dunks himself and emerges like a mad thing, his wet curls flat against his head. I forget about what I look like in my costume and just enjoy the tug of the water on my body. And it feels like it'll go on forever—the sunshine, the yellow lilies lining the bank, the blue dragonflies, the hunk of sponge cake waiting in the wicker picnic basket. Or that I'm already remembering it from a distance.

After the picnic, Big Rita pats dry the baby with a tea towel, changes her nappy, and dusts her body with Johnson's baby powder. She announces it's time to go. "Too many midges. This place gets itchier the later it gets," she says, fastening the poppers of the

Babygro. Teddy and I protest: it's the most fun we've had in ages. But Big Rita isn't listening to us, only to the baby, who is gazing at her with enormous eyes and making soft ooh sounds, like she's trying to speak. So we seize the moment of distraction and leap off the bank into the stream again, shrieking, the water spraying into our faces.

"For goodness sake," Big Rita groans, fighting a laugh. She lays the baby on the blanket, next to the picnic basket. The baby reaches out and scratches the wicker with her tiny razor fingernails.

Teddy and I start swimming with the current, fast without trying. We're soon quite far from Big Rita. The stream bed shelves and we plunge deeper into colder water. Teddy starts dog-paddling. I can hear Big Rita shouting something, but not the words, what with the water fuming into my ears and nose. I can taste silt at the back of my throat.

I'm still giggling when Teddy ducks. And I'm thinking, *Wow, my brother really can hold his breath,* when there's a huge splash, an explosion of water, and Big Rita is in the stream, all legs and arms and floating wheel of skirt.

She lifts Teddy, gasping, to the bank, and asks him over and over if he's okay. Teddy nods and coughs. Scrambling out of the stream, up the muddy bank, Big Rita squats next to him, dripping wet, her thick bra strap showing underneath her blouse. "Crikey, you gave me a scare." She looks far more shaken than Teddy. "Don't do that again."

Feeling bad that I didn't notice Teddy was in trouble, I glance back at Baby Forest. Something looks different. At first I can't work out what. Then I realize she's on the other side of the blanket, no longer scratching at the wicker basket, but on the opposite far edge, on her front, her toes digging into the grass. "The baby's moved."

Big Rita turns slowly and blinks, like she might be imagining it. Then she walks over, suddenly nervy.

I offer Teddy a piggyback and go to join Big Rita, my steps weaving under Teddy's weight. "She's crawling already. I knew she was super clever."

Big Rita frowns and mutters something about the baby being too young to crawl. She glances around us, squinting into the trees. But it's impossible to see anything because the bright sun makes the understory pitch-black. "I suppose she might have sort of flopped over and . . ." She shakes her head and stares at the basket, then the blanket's frayed edge, as if they're part of a puzzle she can't solve. "I shouldn't have left her. Not even for a second." Then Big Rita does something she never does, not in front of us anyway: she kisses the baby's head. "Let's go."

We walk on in silence. My back starts to ache from Teddy, who forgets to cling, half asleep, his chin resting on my shoulder. I'm glad to see the log stack through the trees, like an ancient monument. The garden wall. I peer up at Mother's bedroom window, impatient to tell her about our afternoon. Her curtains are still shut. The glass looks misted. She must be very tired.

We walk around to the front of the house, chatting about what Mother might want to eat for supper. One: Marge's haddock and egg pie. Iceberg lettuce. Two: a ham hock salad. Big Rita says we all need a good scrub in the bath before we go anywhere near the kitchen. And everything feels right and good and sunny again . . .

until we turn the corner by the front gate. We all stop—time stops too—and stare, barely able to believe it.

A silver sports car is parked at a wild angle in the drive, swung in at great speed, to leave scarring skid marks in the gravel—and our golden afternoon.

28

Rita

"Y ou should never shoot a gun into the trees without knowing
where the bullet will end up," Rita says, repeating Robbie's
words. She's still reeling from the sight of Don's car, glinting ma-
levolently in the drive yesterday, its dents a reminder of the thrill
seeker who drives as he lives. Who probably shoots like that too.

"Is that right, John Wayne?" Don cocks the gun and fires again,
the crack ricocheting into the woods, echoing in her eardrums. A
distant tree showers its leaves. He turns to grin at her wolfishly, revealing the intimate pink tissue of his gums.

"The bullet may just keep going. To shoot safely, you have to
know the bullet's path." She can't help relishing her recall of Robbie's knowledge. "And you don't."

"I see." He raises one eyebrow, in a way that manages to be both
belittling and carnal.

Rita looks away and bends down to Teddy, who is enjoying the
noise and threat of violence immensely. "Indoors," she whispers.
"*Now.*"

Teddy's smile collapses. "But Don promised to show me how to shoot."

"I'm not saying it again, Teddy."

"But—"

Don winks at him. "Another time, little man."

Rita watches Teddy as he stomps back to Foxcote, protesting about the lack of fairness, making a show of kicking up twigs to impress Don. He leaves the garden gate swinging. *Bang.* She needs to oil it or something, whatever you do with gates. *Bang.* And she suddenly remembers how she got up this morning and discovered it wide open, even though she always makes sure the house is as secure as it can be—given those holes in the wall—before she turns in. She also noticed the flowerbeds were crushed under the drawing-room window, and a trail of flattened oxeye daisies leading back to the paved path. She supposes it *could* have been a curious deer. She'd rather it was a deer. But her mind keeps twitching to Fingers, the albino Green Man. And then, with a shudder that travels down her spine, the sight of the baby yesterday, *not* where Rita had left her on the picnic blanket. As if someone had picked her up while she was watching Hera and Teddy. But surely the baby had maneuvered herself somehow. Rita must put it from the muddle of her tired mind.

"I wish you'd talk to me like that, Rita," Don says, dispersing her swarming thoughts. His absurdly blue eyes spark under heavy, indolent lids, and he smiles at her in a way that suggests he's mistaken her for a different sort of woman, someone more attractive.

He's also stripped off his white shirt, entirely gratuitously—it's not hot today—and a thick *V* of curly dark hair arrows down his tanned torso, as if deliberately signposting the bulbous bulk of his groin, its topography alarmingly obvious in his tight flared jeans. She tries hard not to look, but she's got a feeling he's aware of her effort, and it thrills him. "Do you slap buttocks as well?"

Her face heats. She shields her smarting cheek with her hand and glances back at the house, anxious that Jeannie, who is upstairs with the baby, might peer out her window and think she's trying to linger alone with Don. Or, god forbid, flirting with him. (She can't flirt, like she can't dance, but Jeannie may not know this.) Still, she won't leave until Don puts the gun away. "Please, can we stop the shooting now? Teddy might dart back here at any moment, and Hera's always slinking off outside on her own."

He laughs. "Amazed that girl can slink anywhere."

She glares at him. "It's not safe." She can't keep the anger from her voice. How dare he talk about Hera like that? And she hates this blood lust. Just as well that, for all his bravado and swagger, he doesn't seem able even to shoot a squirrel.

"You can be safe when you're dead, Miss Rita." He aims into the trees and shoots again. More leaves fall. (Nothing dies.) "Anyway, Teddy needs to be able to handle a gun."

Rita could have shot Teddy herself when, at breakfast, he'd delightedly informed Don, "We've got a gun in the biscuit tin. *And* shotguns in the cellar." Don's eyes lit up. He gave Teddy a soldier's salute, holding on to a slice of toast. "You and me, Teddy. Hunters, eh?" And Teddy pretty much exploded with joy.

With a vulpine smile, Don disables the gun over his knee. "Happy now?"

She's not. Yesterday, she calmed herself—and a near hysterical

Hera—by saying that Jeannie wouldn't do anything to jeopardize the situation with the baby and would send him rapidly packing.

Today that seems rather less likely. She has had to keep the television on most of the morning to block out the noises erupting from Jeannie's bedroom. Jeannie actually *squealed*, like a stepped-upon cat. (When Rita and Fred had made love, she'd been far too self-conscious to make any noise. Let alone squeal. Frankly, there was no reason to squeal.) At breakfast, like a bad dream, there was Don with his booming laugh, leaning back in the kitchen chair, his arms behind his head, revealing dense tufts of hair, like hedgehogs, under his arms. Worse, when Rita leaned over to put his cup of coffee beside him, she smelled . . . sex. Definitely sex. She can't stop thinking about it.

She catches the same sweet-sour musk now and, with a flush of shame, remembers how last night, while she was damning the immoral transgression taking place a few steps down the landing, her body became hot. "Lunch," she says curtly, and starts walking back to the house.

Don follows. He stamps and crunches through the undergrowth noisily, in contrast to Robbie, who makes barely a sound. "Shooting always makes me ravenous. What's cooking, Miss Rita?"

"I don't know yet." Fish fingers probably. Hedgerow crumble. It's been much harder to get to the shops since the baby arrived.

"You don't know?" he gasps with mock outrage. "Isn't that the point of you? Lists and menus." He pauses. "Plotting."

Heat rushes through her again: Jeannie has warned him. Don's arrival will create another glaring omission in the notebook. She wishes the pages would write themselves, like an invisible hand on a

Ouija board, then flutter across the world and slide, anonymously, under Walter's hotel-room door in Africa.

As she walks through the garden gate, he touches her bare arm, a gesture that says, *Wait.* The tips of his fingers are surprisingly soft, like a small girl's, as if he's never chopped a log or scrubbed a floor in his life. She can smell the ripeness of the last of the summer's roses going over. The tang of salt in his sweat. His skin. She can see the lines where the tropical sun has etched brackets around his mouth, the lips so full they expose their paler moist insides—she wonders where those lips have roamed, then sharply checks herself—and the pencil dots of morning stubble on his chiseled jaw. "The baby. I mean . . . Christ." His face grows serious and his lidded eyes kind, blue as swimming pools, momentarily distracting her from who he is, what he's doing. "Not the best idea, given the circumstances, is it?"

"Jeannie won't let me call the authorities. She won't listen to . . ." She can't say the word *sense.*

"Well, I'm here now," he says with a worrying note of permanence. His mood changes. The concern drains from his face, and it sets with something else, a ruthlessness that makes Rita instinctively step away. "That woman will damn well listen to me."

❉ ❉ ❉

"The baby's not your problem, Jeannie," says Don, making a show of pouring the tea into the chipped white china.

Walter's probably never lifted a teapot in his life, Rita thinks, *let alone poured Jeannie a cup,* and she wonders if this is why Don's doing it, try-ing to inveigle himself deeper into Jeannie's affections.

"She's not a problem, Don. She's a gift." Jeannie smiles down at the baby sleeping in the wicker vegetable trug on the kitchen floor. "Aren't you, poppet?"

Don leans back in his chair. "My god, you are one crazy lady," he says, with such a vexing mixture of contempt and affection that it makes Rita study her hands—and spot their bare feet fiercely ca-ressing beneath the table, like mating otters.

Afterward, when they've gone upstairs for "a nap"—the sort that makes the ceiling plaster powder down—and Rita's elbow deep in washing-up, Hera rushes in, sparking like a plug. "Who does he think he *is?*"

Teddy, sitting at the table, licking clean the crumble bowl, says, "Don's a big-game hunter. He's killed seven lions. He's going to teach me how to shoot rabbits."

"He's just an idiot," splutters Hera. "The rabbits will laugh at him."

"Teddy, give me that dish. Thank you. And don't talk nonsense. Now, go and play in the garden for a bit. There's a good boy." She glides the dish under the suds, wishing she owned some rubber gloves. Her hands feel ten years older than the rest of her.

Hera presses against the draining board. "Make him *leave,*" she begs. As Rita suspected, the new sweet Hera was as delicate as a robin's egg. And she's cracked. "Please, Big Rita."

She scrubs harder. She thinks of all the times in London she's wanted to tell Jeannie to be careful. Confide that Don brushed against her body as he walked past, and once, to her mortification, called her Legs. But she never dared. She felt somehow complicit, guilty, even though she couldn't work out what she'd done to encourage him. And it'd be reckless for any nanny to complain about such trivial things. Everyone knew it went on all the time, and pretty young nannies were wise to wedge chairs against their bedroom door handles before going to bed. You just had to keep your wits about you and your head down. Now she wishes she'd spoken up. "I'll try."

❋ ❋ ❋

It's tricky to catch Jeannie on her own. As the sticky afternoon drifts on, Jeannie and Don remain inseparable. A crackling electricity surrounds them. The way Jeannie looks at Don, so hungrily, it's almost male.

In London they could never be this free. Nor would they dare. Not in front of the children. But here in the forest, inhibition appears to have been peeled off, like a silky dress. It's fascinating, shocking, and she can't rip her eyes away. They don't notice her looking. She's never felt more like a bit of furniture, a large kitchen dresser perhaps, gliding around on soundless casters.

She discreetly tugs back a curtain and peers out of the drawing-room window. Yes, there they are, outside on the daisy-studded lawn, sprawled on a blanket, the baby wedged between them. Two glasses. A wine bottle. Empty. They look like a young family—that's the worst thing. She feels a jab of sympathy for Walter, followed by alarm. If he knew, she can't bear to think what would happen. And if Marge sees them like this, she'll know for certain what's going on under Walter's sagging roof.

She watches Teddy rush toward them and tug Don, laughing and protesting, away by the hand, talking about shooting in the woods. Jeannie waves them off.

Anxiety taps its way down Rita's spine. She hopes they don't go too far. Or pick any mushrooms. Or fall into a disused mine. She'll take the dried washing upstairs, keep her hands and mind busy until Teddy returns safely. Half an hour later, she hears Jeannie's light footstep on the stairs.

Here's her chance. She knocks gently on Jeannie's bedroom door. "It's me, Rita."

"Come in!" Jeannie calls out cheerily.

"I just—*Oh*. Sorry." Jeannie is dressing, wrestling with a bra strap and stepping into an oyster-satin dress. "I'll come back later."

"Don't be silly. We're both women."

She's probably got more in common with the wheelbarrow in the garden than with Jeannie in that liquid halter-neck dress, more lovely than Rita has seen her in months. "Thought I'd scrub up properly for once." Jeannie turns and lifts teased, oiled curls off her neck. "Would you do me up?"

Rita fumbles with the tiny pearl button. She can't help brushing Jeannie's skin, smooth and unblemished, with her own roughened fingers. "I was wondering how long Don might be staying."

Jeannie spins round and holds her gaze a little longer than is comfortable. "A few days. Then he's off to Arabia. Since you ask." The sisterly warmth of a moment ago has gone. "I'll do the fastening."

How will they survive a few *more* days? Also, next week is the last of August. Walter's due back in the country. And the plan is to call the authorities. Or is Jeannie not considering that Walter might actually turn up here? She seems to be refusing to think about everything else.

Time's slipping between their fingers. The seasons are changing. Angry wasps have replaced the corps of white butterflies. The late-August air is blood warm, the sky a tired, bilious blue. And at the dawn feed of the day, she's started to smell autumn seeping through the cracks in the windows, sweet and acidic, like the brown bruised flesh of fallen apples. Rita aches for the sea.

"You're not to mention Don's visit to Walter." Jeannie tries to sound nonchalant. "Let's not make a fuss."

Rita stares down at the unraveling edge of the old Persian rug, feeling as though she's fraying too. "What should I tell Marge?" she asks quietly, not looking up.

"Just say a family friend is staying."

As if she'll believe that. Marge is a bloodhound. She glances at Jeannie's unmade bed, the twisted sheets, and imagines Marge lifting them to her nose and sniffing.

"Best to instruct *her* not to mention anything to Walter too," says Jeannie quickly.

"She's unlikely to listen to me." Marge believes she's a rank, no, a whole species, above Rita.

"Well, Walter can't easily be contacted for the next few days. What with the mine business. Isn't that what he said to you on the phone?"

Rita nods. For some reason, she's not sure if she believes Walter.

He's as likely to phone—or even roll up, with no warning, straight from the plane—to surprise them, catch them out.

"Anyway, Marge can't exactly mention Don to Walter and forget about the small matter of the baby, can she?" Jeannie perches on the edge of the bed and snaps a paste-jeweled cuff bracelet on to her slender wrist. "It's all or nothing."

The same goes for her note-taking. The whole summer is off the record now, a gaping hole where truth no longer lives. Only the story Jeannie has shaped: this fantasy family in the dreamlike Arcadian woods.

"Marge cares about the baby, Rita. She's bigger-hearted than I gave her credit for."

Rita's not sure about this, either. She suspects Marge gets a thrill from being in on a secret. And the power it wields. A silence pools.

"Look, Rita, I know you don't approve of Don."

She can't bring herself to deny it, even though it's not her job to approve or otherwise.

Jeannie turns to the mirror and lifts her chin, examining herself. "And I wish Hera didn't hate him. It's all very awkward, given how fond Don is of her." She adjusts the cuff on her wrist, then glances at Rita sharply, as if rebuking judgment that Rita hasn't yet expressed. "Nothing's black or white. Not how it seems when you're young."

Rita gives the smallest of nods. She'd never be unfaithful to her husband. She knows this in the same way she knows that she'll never be short or not love ferns.

As if reading this, Jeannie's eyes start to swim with tears, endangering her mascara, the catlike sweeps of kohl. "I don't love my children any less, you know. In fact, the opposite. I feel like a proper mother again, not some—some dreary black cloud." She catches a tear deftly on the edge of her finger. "Given everything that's happened, aren't I allowed a few crumbs of joy? Answer me that, Rita."

A difficult philosophical question. And one she's saved from answering by the muffled gunshot outside.

29

———— ✳ ————

Hera

The deer was alive a few seconds ago. The closeness of death, just a breath, a bullet, away, brings a swooping sick feeling. I stick my finger into the warm hole in the young deer's flank and recoil. What have I done?

Watching me, Don starts to laugh. "Bravo. Your first kill. Now taste it."

I shake my head. Teddy, standing next to me, one hand resting on my leg for comfort, is trying really hard not to cry.

"All talk then, Hera? Thought so."

I bring my finger to my mouth and suck. It tastes of blood and copper coins and something else. *Power, I think. My own.*

"That deer's life force has just transferred into you. Feels good, eh?" With no warning, Don lunges at me, hugging me to his bare chest. My face is pressed against the nub of his nipple, the scratchiness of his hair. I don't like it.

He resists as I pull away, his skin sticking to mine. I can't stop looking at the deer. And I'm struck again by the starkness of its being alive one moment, a carcass the next. "Teddy, come on. Let's go." I grab Teddy's hot paw of a hand.

"Wait." Don reaches down to the animal, dips his finger in the wound, and wipes the stickiness across my forehead. "There you go. Blooded. Little hunter." He frowns, as if something's bothering him. "It's hard to shoot anything in these damn trees." He hasn't hit anything that breathes. "Didn't aim for the head, either, like an amateur. The mouth is still full of grass. See? She didn't see the bullet coming. Who taught you?"

"No one," I say truthfully.

"A natural."

It would feel like a compliment from someone else. I turn and run, tugging Teddy with me, away from the blood and the deer's open surprised black eyes.

In the bathroom, I wipe the smear of blood away, over and over until the tissue disintegrates. I pour myself a scorching hot bath that draws a red line on my thighs and I start to cry, thinking of the young deer, how it must have a mother somewhere, and I wonder if she saw, if she'll come back and nuzzle it and try to make it stagger to its feet again. And I hate that there's a link between my pulling that trigger—Don breathing over my shoulder, Don hissing, "Now!"—and the end of that deer's life. I think of the bang on my shoulder, the wrong feeling it gave me—and I wish that Don had been lying there, not an innocent animal.

"Hera? Are you okay?" Big Rita knocks on the locked bathroom door.

"I shot a deer. I hate myself."

Stunned silence. I wonder if she's also picturing the dainty deer on its side, tongue lolling. If she hates me too. She once found a baby bird on the terrace in London and carried it back up to her room—a nest in a shoe box—and got up every two hours in the night to feed it bits of worm. Here at Foxcote she pulls hair from our hairbrushes and leaves it outside in tangled balls for the birds to line their nests. "I'm sorry," she says eventually, in a soft voice, as if she knows, without my telling her, that the deer's death has stolen something precious from me too.

When I go back into my bedroom, pink and boiled by my bath, Big Rita is waiting for me, sitting on the carpet, cross-legged. In front of her is the terrarium, glittering. "I thought you might want to take care of it this summer. Dot and Ethel and all the others. I'm so busy with the baby." She smiles like it's no big deal, when I know it's the biggest. "You're good at looking after things, Hera."

I should thank her. But the words won't come.

"You don't want it?"

"It's your favorite thing."

"I trust you, Hera."

No one trusts me. I've wanted this little glass case of plants from the first moment Big Rita pitched up in London, smelling of the sea, unpacking her blouses and books and then, to Teddy's and my astonishment, this terrarium stuffed full of plants—with names! I think of the bedtime stories she used to tell us—ships moving across the globe, bringing exotic jungle plants to the gray skies of London. No one had brought them back alive before. "I swear on my life I'll take good care of it." I reach over and hug her. She feels soft and safe, the opposite of Don.

"Right, shall we find its perch? We want sunlight but not too much. Not too direct. Not too little. You're east-facing here, that's good." She drags a side table near the window and my bed, then lifts the terrarium onto it. "Ta-da. Perfect. You can look at it before you go to sleep, Hera. I used to love that as a kid. Focusing on it until my eyes went blurry. Forgetting all the bad stuff."

That night I lie on my side in bed and gaze at it. But when my eyes go blurry, the bad stuff doesn't go away. Instead I see a deer running through the ferns, then pronking—leaping, back arched, legs stiff—at some unseen threat behind the glass. And when I sniff my fingers, I can still smell blood.

30

Sylvie

F avorite smells?" Kerry asks, sliding the clipboard back at the
end of the hospital bed. I'm not sure if the nurse is humoring
me because I feel so bloody helpless, and she's walked in and heard
me saying this to Mum (as in therapy, you develop a taste for the
one-sided conversation). "Flowers? Her perfume. Yours maybe?
You always smell delicious, Sylvie, if you don't mind me saying."

I laugh. "Not today. Bit of a rush this morning. But thank you."
I make a mental note to buy Kerry a bottle of my scent, a light fresh
Jo Malone. She enjoys the beauty freebies I bring her and the other
nurses as inadequate little thank-yous.

"And what about music? Does our Rita have favorite songs? Play
them to her. Any sounds, really. Things that might jog a memory.
Mean something . . ."

A scribble of an outlandish idea takes shape.

I hurry home through the crowded city streets, trailed by a disconcerting reflection in the mirrored glass of office blocks: a woman
who has slept badly, leaped out of the bed with a mound of messy
hair—over forty, not so cute—and plucked sweatpants from the

overflowing laundry basket. I turn onto the canal path, wondering if I should discuss my idea with Steve, if the new rules of our co-parenting, eggshell-stepping, demand it. But I know he'll say it's an insane thing to do, the very *last* thing I should do. And he'll have a point.

"Brewing one, if you fancy."

I startle. The canal is talking.

A head appears in a porthole window. The boatman. "Beautiful morning."

I hadn't noticed the weather. But I notice his eyes. One blue. One hazel. Did he really just offer coffee?

"Have to be some upsides to being self-employed and living in a floating bathtub, right?" He leans farther out of the boat window and sticks out a hand. "Jake."

"Sylvie." His handshake is just the right side of too firm. I can't stop staring at his eyes. They gleam with a sort of delicious amusement.

"I've seen you. On the balcony." He nods up at Val's block. I become aware that I'm smiling at him, almost involuntarily.

I should probably pretend coquettishly that I don't know this but find myself saying, "Yes, you too. With the guitar."

"Talent and enthusiasm not always fairly divvied up. You wouldn't be the first neighbor to complain."

So he doesn't think he's the new Ed Sheeran. This is a relief.

"So what size cafetière should I use?" he asks, with just enough of a sidelong smile to make me blush.

"Sorry?" I say, stalling for time. I'm so bad at this. I need some sort of intervention from my single female friends. Dating seems much more complicated than it was the first time round. If this is dating.

Standing there—confused, flattered, vaguely alarmed—I remember how I used to tell myself to be more French about Steve's affairs. I could have an affair too: even things up! Only I didn't. But if I had, where would I be now? With whom? My mind boggles. Married life is an editing process, I realize, a discerning closing down of other options. It's like choosing a capsule wardrobe—navy, black, and cream—over fleeting extravagances, throwaway fast fashion. You tell yourself: understated day-to-night dressing, this works, this is me. But what if you're wrong? And how do you ever know what turn your life might have taken if you'd sashayed to the school gate in a leopard-print jumpsuit instead? None of this helps.

"Would Sylvie-from-the-balcony like a coffee?" he perseveres.

Hearing him say my name brings an unexpected sexy jolt. A tightening. Then it occurs to me that no one but Steve's seen my body naked for years. All its bumps and moles and stretch marks. But he's suggesting coffee, not a shag! How ridiculous. "I . . . I'm kind of busy, I'm afraid. Thank you for the offer, though." I sound like an old lady thanking him for giving up his seat for me on the tube.

"Another time," he says, meaning, *I won't ask again.* Our eyes lock; then he vanishes back into the porthole.

I'm left with a funny hollow feeling, like when you flake out of a party at the last minute and spend the evening wondering if it might have changed your life. The heron spreads her wings and flies away. Deflated, I turn into the concrete cool of the block, trying to persuade myself that the last thing I need is a date.

Slightly breathless from the stairs, I stop on the open-air walk-way. *Who's that?* There's a woman outside my front door.

Skinny, blond, and perfectly coiffed, she's wearing a navy bouclé jacket with gold buttons that squeals Chanel and a pair of tailored white trousers, and she's lifted off the dirty paving by patent leather heels. Mid-fifties? Hard to tell. She stands very upright, with a look of jaw-gritted focus, as if she's doing secret pelvic-floor exercises. Clearly not a resident.

Who is she? Why is she at my door? I've got things to be getting on with. A mission to plan. The woman holds her handbag to her chest, as if expecting a mugger to come steaming toward her at any moment. She glances in my direction.

"Oh, excuse me." Cut-glass accent. A small, strained smile, re-vealing a perfect row of veneered teeth. She has the nervous pale blue eyes of a whippet. "I'm looking for a Sylvie Broom. Am I in the right place?"

It can only be one person. "Helen?" I ask tightly, trying not to sound like I'd like to toss her back down the stairwell.

"*You're* Sylvie?" she says, processing my Nike trainers and sweat-pants and shock of undone hair.

"I don't normally look like this." She doesn't laugh. "Annie's at her dad's today. But, as I said on the phone, I'd rather you didn't contact her directly, if that's okay."

"It's you I wanted to talk to."

"Oh." I blanch. "Well, you better come in. Sorry about the mess. It's been a bit of a morning."

I worry about her stiletto heels on Val's Danish wooden floor but don't quite have the guts to ask her to remove them. She'd prob-ably refuse anyway.

"I hope you don't mind me popping over. I was just around the corner," she says, and we both know she's lying, no more likely to frequent this post code than a polar bear the tropics. She wants a heads-up on what sort of girl her darling boy has got up the duff. Her gaze is like an airport scanner. It sweeps into every corner of the tiny apartment, hovering over the new eye shadows and lipsticks scattered over the coffee table that I haven't yet sorted through, and look like a shoplifter's haul. A dirty plate. Annie's dropped socks. Pale pink walls and houseplants and white sofas can only go so far.

"I'm renting this place from a friend," I impulsively explain.

She tries to frown through her Botox. "Separated?"

It's not a question. She's been digging. "Since June. Amicably."

A smile flickers at the corner of her mouth. Like she knows better.

"Annie splits her time between us," I overexplain. "Steve, my husband, is in the family house for now. A couple of tube stops away." The thought of that dear little house, its teal-blue kitchen, where historic Christmases and Annie's childhood birthday parties seem to be embedded in the walls, makes my voice go high. "Until we decide what to do next."

Something in Helen's face changes. "What? *You* should keep the house. The woman should always keep the house," she declares, without sympathy but with a sort of flat common sense that makes me warm to her a bit. "He should be in the council block, not you."

"It's not a council block. Most of the flats are privately owned," I say, despising myself for lowering to her snobbish level. I glance at her left hand, but it's so crusted in jewelry it's hard to distinguish a wedding ring. "Are you married, Helen?"

"I was. To Elliot's father," she says, with an emphasis on *father,* drawing attention to Annie's very far from married state. "But he died a few years ago." Her face betrays no emotion.

A widow. I wasn't expecting that. She fits the bitter-divorcée mold better. "I'm sorry."

She leans toward me intensely. "Elliot's all I've got now, Sylvie. You understand?"

"Annie's my only child too." She considers this a moment and something in her face softens slightly. "Can I get you something? Tea? Water?"

"No, thank you. This shouldn't take long."

Ominous. I walk into the kitchen area sensing her at my back, that spiky skinny woman's energy, the self-righteousness that comes from self-denial and rigorous self-control. Her perfume, very eighties, overloaded with heavy, smoky notes, follows us too, like a hormonal mood. I open the balcony doors, hoping to dilute it discreetly. "Do sit down."

Helen plucks a scrunched-up tea towel from a chair and hesitates before she sits, as if it were a grubby seat on the Northern Line.

We assess each other, shiftily combative over the kitchen table. I know she's examining me as closely as I am her. A shaft of sunlight reveals a facelift, scars neatly tucked behind her ears, and—educated guess—neck work too. Her nose has the unnatural childlike snub that comes courtesy of the surgeon's scalpel. It's not a bad nose as worked-on noses go, and I've seen some honks, but I do yearn to tell her she's gone too far with the lip fillers, when all she needed was a decent lipstick, the same shade as the inside of her cheek. Laura Mercier, probably.

I know about reinventing oneself to get on: I understand this. I'm with her. Do what you can to fight the drag south, absolutely. But I also know that when women start surgically tinkering, like my wealthy private clients all do, there's rarely a point when they say, "Enough. I look bloody fantastic. I'm done." Like when you paint one room in a house, all the others start to seem tired and scruffy.

I know Helen. I've worked for lots of Helens. Women who consider a private makeup artist a necessity, like a good gynae, rather than a luxury. Hair colorists. Facialists. The nail lady. All on speed dial too. These women are hard to please but also needy, easy to hurt, and too often living with the (not irrational) fear they'll be replaced by a younger version of themselves. But I've never moved in the same social circles. And it's hard to believe there might be any sort of link between us, that our DNA is actually mingling in my daughter's womb. Even stranger, that our families have a peculiar historical intersection, a path where they randomly cross. What in did she have with Harrington Glass? How well does she know the family?

I itch to ask outright. But I promised Annie I wouldn't. And I can't risk rocking that boat now, for Annie to push me away again.

"So has Annie changed her mind yet?" she asks abruptly, interrupting my thoughts.

"She's set on keeping the baby."

She closes her eyes, and the shimmery lids quiver. "Really? Please tell me there's a chance she'll change her mind."

"Look, I know Annie. Once she's made her mind up . . . We're both going to have to embrace it, Helen."

She looks truly rocked. "I really thought . . ." She startles again. "But that means you and I . . ." She stops, with a look of dawning horror. "Good god. We're going to be *grandmothers!*"

"Makes one feel ancient, doesn't it?" I can't help but smile while a part of me yelps. I wonder what Jake would think if he knew. A grandmother. He wouldn't be offering me coffee then.

She leans forward across the table. The perfume is so strong it's as if she's breathing it out. "I simply must talk to her."

"Helen, you upset her so much last time that she ran away."

"I was only offering money!" she splutters. "To make it all easier."

"Exactly."

Helen looks genuinely mystified.

"Can we be clear? She's not going to get rid of the baby. She's not after your family's money. She's determined to manage all this on her own."

"But your . . . your situation." Her hand flutters around the room. "This block. This neighborhood."

"I love this neighborhood!" As if on cue, Jake starts playing guitar on his boat deck, bluesy strumming, the odd dropped note. It does nothing to persuade Helen.

"Oh, come on, Sylvie. This is no place to bring up a baby. There are gangs! Armed with knives! Lurking in the stairwells!"

"They're just teenagers knocking about, and they live here too," I say, pitying her. How sad to view the young with such suspicion. I wonder if she's had a bad experience, was a victim of some sort of crime, but daren't ask.

"The flat is the size of a utility cupboard! And Annie's age! Basically a child. How in God's name is she going to *manage?*"

A tightness in my chest. "I only know my daughter's resourceful and determined and . . . just a remarkable girl."

Helen looks shocked, as if she's never heard a mother talk about her child like that. Then she shakes her head, dismissing it. "What if she can't cope? What if she doesn't bond with the baby? Succumbs to postnatal depression? Much higher in younger mothers, the depression thing. I know. I've read up about it, Sylvie."

"I'm going to support her," I say quietly. My heart has started to pound, like it does when you know someone's spoiling for a fight, and you can't see how to get out of their way.

"This is ridiculous," she mutters under her breath, the implication being I can barely support myself.

I say nothing, cross my arms over my chest and wait for her to take the hint: please fricking leave. She doesn't. So I say, "I'll be in touch, of course. When we know more. The due date."

"The due date? Christ." She stands up with a shudder. The gold buttons on her jacket wink in the sunshine. A heavy jacket to be wearing on such a warm day. And her foundation is far too thick, one of those old-fashioned formulas, more like stage paint. I decide Helen's one of those self-flagellating women who feel most themselves when they're pinched into high shoes, too hot or too cold, slightly in pain. I decide she's a nightmare.

"Thanks for dropping round," I say, trying to stay civil for Annie's sake.

"I suppose we'd better swap numbers," says Helen, looking faintly shocked by the idea, despite suggesting it. I don't naturally belong in her address book. "Call if . . . anything changes."

We awkwardly tap each other's details into our phones—"Eight, did you say? Oh, damn, sorry, bungled it. Can you repeat that, Sylvie?"—Helen's long shellacs hitting the screen with a flinty click. Afterward she hesitates by the front door, once again positioning her handbag tightly under her arm, ready to run the gauntlet of the communal walkway. She takes in the lewd graffiti on the wall opposite and the peeling paint, with a *moue* of distaste. "Sylvie . . ."

I steel myself. "Yes, Helen."

"This is all very well. Terribly . . ."—she gestures around her, struggling not to be offensive—"modern. But you won't realize how precious a family house is until you've really lost it. That's all I'm going to say." She frowns. "All those memories. Don't let your husband waltz off with them."

"Right." I wasn't expecting that. "Thank you. But don't worry, I won't." Sooner rather than later we'll have to sell the house, divide the assets, if we're both to buy places of our own. Even though I'm no longer living there, the thought upsets me. And now Annie's pregnant, it feels too disrupting to suggest it.

"Right. Lecture over. I can see you're itching for me to leave. Where does one get a black cab around here?"

"Turn left at the bottom of the stairwell. Right at the kebab shop."

She flinches at "kebab," in greed or disgust, I'm not sure. She looks like a woman in need of one, rather than a blowout of popped quinoa.

I watch her walk away, listening to the sound of those expensive heels meeting grubby concrete, and think about what she said—families, memories, houses—and something solidifies in my mind. I hear Kerry's voice: *Any sounds, really. Things that might jog a memory.*

I hunt down my laptop, buried under last month's *Vogue*. I open up Google Maps, swing the little yellow cursor over the Forest of Dean, and land it on a junction of the main forest road. The camera twists and zooms in. The image pixelates, then clarifies: trees in the distance, in the foreground fields. I'm standing at a crossroads, with wooden arrowed signs that look like they were stuck up there decades ago and left to rot. Which way? Damn.

Foxcote Manor, I type. Reload. Zilch. Have I remembered the name wrongly? Misspelled it? Hall, maybe. House. I frantically type, trying different versions. Still nothing. I fling myself back against the chair, frustrated. Has the house been razed to the ground? Whatever was there is no longer. Foxcote Manor has gone.

31

❋

Rita

The Morris Minor stalls at the crossroads. Rita can't blame it. She'd like to stall too. Or reverse back down the road. But she can't. (Not just because she can't drive backward in a straight line.) She didn't like leaving the baby and the children in the care of Jeannie and Don this morning. Not after the dingdong last night. Not after seeing the bruise swelling into a plum beneath Jeannie's left eye at breakfast. Just the thought of it brings a fresh high-pitched flute of panic and a compulsion to return to Foxcote urgently.

She restarts the ignition and skids left toward Foxcote. A maroon estate car appears in the rearview mirror. Rita tenses, aware that the back seat is covered with baby supplies she's bulk-bought at a shop far enough away from Hawkswell so as not to cause gossip. She drives a little faster, scaring herself, sweat gumming her back to her seersucker blouse.

Muttering, "Don't crash, don't crash," beneath her breath, she straightens her arms on the wheel. They feel like stiff steel rods: the faster she goes, the more anxious she is, the worse her driving, as if the steering shaft connects to her brain.

Today it feels like there's no membrane between her and the rest of the world, like her skin's been flayed. And she's bone-tired. She didn't know such tiredness was possible, her body a lumpen burden to be dragged around. The strain of keeping the baby secret means her stomach has been cramping. And around three in the morning, every morning, then again at five, she's up, anticipating squalls, forearmed with a warm sterilized bottle of milk, a fresh muslin cloth. Now, far worse than any of this, there's Don to worry about too. A violence she hadn't seen before.

Rita feels like the household has tipped off the edge of the civilized world and they're all disoriented, drunk on the absinthe-green light. Only Don, she suspects, grasps the madness of the situation with the baby and his own presence at Foxcote, Walter due to arrive any day. But Don's either too arrogant to be fazed by it or, more likely, gets a kick from the risk. *No doubt he's convinced he can brazen it out,* Rita thinks, slowing into a bend in the lane. Or he'll wriggle his way free of the situation, like a slippery Thames eel through the fingers.

They've just got to get through the next four days, she reminds herself, the dog end of August. Then Don leaves for Arabia and Jeannie will finally, finally—please God—make contact with the authorities. Although this plan still strikes her as completely bonkers— why not turf Don out and call now?—it's less bonkers than not having one at all.

On the other hand, containment for even another afternoon seems ambitious. Robbie or Marge could let something slip. Teddy has no filter at all, bless him, and has only to pick up the phone when Walter calls and gabble it all out. And she still can't shake that eerie *watched* feeling, especially at night when the house is lit up and the darkness rubs against the windows, thick and furred, like a black bear's back. *Who is it?* she wonders with a shudder.

Robbie? Oh, she'd hate it to be him. Fingers? Ugh. The other likely culprit would be Marge. But Rita doubts her capacity for subterfuge: why skulk around when you can just charge in?

She did this yesterday, cornering Rita in the scullery. "Who, in heaven's name, is that man marauding about the woods half naked?" she'd demanded, lantern jaw tensed, the lone hair on her chin mole quivering. "Is it his ridiculous car?" The "good family friend" line didn't wash, of course. Marge looked apoplectic, as if she was about to sweep the tins of baked beans and tuna off the shelves with her burly, work-thickened fists. "He'll ruin everything for the baby and Mrs. Harrington. Talk about attracting attention! He bellows in the woods, like a stag in rut!" And this image—uncannily accurate—made Rita giggle, and Marge even crosser, stamping her foot and accusing her of not taking the situation seriously.

What could be more serious? Rita is constantly terrified of doing something wrong, the baby being hungry, cold, or ill or simply feeling unloved. Although she's trying to be professional, to view Baby Forest simply as an independent living organism who needs nurturing, not unlike Ethel the fern, with every hour that passes, Baby Forest crawls a little further under Rita's skin. They've developed a sort of understanding that circumvents language. When the baby needs her, Rita just *knows*. It's like an alarm clock ringing in her brain. She'll wake up with a start and, sludgy with sleep, stagger across the bedroom in the gloom to the cot Robbie has made especially, sanded smooth. Baby Forest will always be wide awake, waiting for her to arrive. And Rita will rest her chin on the cot's side and sing a lullaby—"*Bye, baby bunting, Daddy's gone a-hunting*"—and watch the mobile's shadows flickering on the wall, until the baby's eyes start to close again. Other times, if the child is grumbling and wriggling with colic, she does what she knows she shouldn't, taking the baby into bed with her, snuggled in the crook of her arm, the only tactic that ensures both of them will get a few unbroken hours of sleep.

Baby Forest's too easy to love, that's the problem. In other families, the mother is the natural barrier between nanny and baby, like a monolithic Easter Island statue, a reminder not to get too close, not to try to compete. A nanny must be efficient, kind, and discreet: never more maternal, prettier, or preferred by the children (let alone the husband). But the situation is different here. Jeannie's attention is constantly tugged in different directions now, like hands pulling on a skirt.

Rita senses that Teddy is starting to fret at the baby's permanence, the threat to his position as the cherished youngest. He gets clingier and more boisterous by the day. Hera seethes at Don's presence, her own growing ever more fraught and charged, like stretched elastic the moment before it's pinged. And Don? Well, Don wants to keep Jeannie to himself, of course, always pawing, stroking, and resting his hand on the neat curve of Jeannie's bottom, with a brazen casual possession. A sensual fleshy fug surrounds them. Worst of all, he wanders around after his morning bath, dominating every room he enters, looking for Jeannie, a towel around his waist, sexuality bared like teeth.

Maybe this is why the baby's eyes always follow Rita, not Jeannie. When the baby cries, Rita knows she's the only one who'll be able to soothe her and has to watch, hands fidgeting at her sides, while Don and Jeannie jiggle her too energetically, trying to distract her—never works—when all she wants is to be pressed close, held firm, made to feel safe.

When the baby wakes in the night, Rita struggles to go back to sleep. She's on high alert, feeling as though something bad might happen if she lets down her guard—that the baby will forget to breathe if she's not watching the tiny mammalian chest rise and fall.

She's developed her own insomniac routine, a sort of mental drift, which always fails to send her back to sleep and involves taking apart the situation at Foxcote, like a jigsaw, and putting it together again in a new way, finishing it with A Nice Ending. This usually involves a kind lady with a mollifying smile from social services arriving at the door. Not a policeman. The lady will carefully tuck up Baby Forest into a shiny new pram and clean blanket and explain that the real mother, a lovely young woman, an Emma or an Anne or a Felicity, has come to her senses and desperately wants her baby back. Who could argue with that? A baby returning to its rightful mother? They will kiss Baby Forest good-bye and promise to write and send money if Emma/Anne/Felicity needs it. Meanwhile Don will vanish through the back door and roar off in his sports car into the arms of another woman. Someone less hassle. Someone less *married*.

That's what last night's row was all about. The married bit.

Shouting woke her, not the baby this time. At first she thought Don and Jeannie were having sex again and she held a pillow over her head. Then she realized it wasn't sex. It was the opposite. Jeannie was screaming, "You slept with Edie? You slept with my sister-in-law? How could you? How *could* you?" and there was the sound of something falling to the floor, a chair or a table, and Don shouting, "Why can't I? I can sleep with whoever I like. You're the married one, Jeannie. You're the one who's cheating on my old friend like a whore." More yelling: words indecipherable. After that came the sound of skin meeting skin, Jeannie's cry of pain and surprise.

A new thought streaked through Rita's head then: what if the knife she found under the mattress in London wasn't to protect Jeannie from Walter, as Rita had presumed, but from *Don*?

This possibility altered everything. It felt like the Harringtons' world had been tilted on its side, exposing a previously unseen cross section, a shocking hidden view, like the first sight of ghoulish worm-white roots in a slab of dark soil.

She suddenly felt Foxcote's remoteness keenly—the bristling woodland, the empty lane, the way you could scream and scream here and no one would ever hear you. Only she *had* heard, hadn't she? So she had to be brave.

She'd knocked once, twice, on Jeannie's bedroom door, and when there was no answer, she'd asked quietly, "Jeannie, is everything okay?"

No answer. Her mind flung to awful places: Jeannie dead on the rug; Jeannie tossed from the window, lying like a rag doll across the rampaging hydrangea beneath. She was turning the doorknob, ready to enter, when Jeannie replied cheerfully, "I'm fine! Go back to bed."

She'd retreated, mortified, wondering if she'd mistaken passion for fighting. After all, what does she know of the former? But at breakfast this morning Jeannie came downstairs alone in her tortoiseshell sunglasses, which didn't quite hide the mark on her cheekbone.

Jeannie didn't chat or fuss over the baby. She halfheartedly stabbed toast soldiers into the boiled egg until it became a mess of broken shell and dripping yolk that seemed horribly symbolic of sex and violence and babies in a way Rita didn't quite understand. After that, Rita couldn't stomach an egg. As she pulls into Foxcote's drive, she's not sure she ever will.

※ ※ ※

"The short-arse woodsman called for you when you were at the shops, Rita," Don says, leaning up against the table, gulping coffee, rubbing the dark wiry hairs on his belly with his free hand. He's wearing nothing but shorts. Rita drops the shopping bags by the kitchen dresser and starts to unload them. "Wondered if you fancied a stroll," he adds goadingly.

Heat prickles around her collarbone, rises up her neck.

Don's merciless. "Oh, look at Rita! There I was thinking you might bat for the other side."

"Shut up, Don," says Jeannie, walking into the room with Teddy, the baby dozing over her shoulder. No longer wearing sunglasses, she's troweled Pan Stik over her cheeks, which gives her complexion a strangely chalky appearance. "Teddy, give Rita a hand."

Leaning down to the bags, Rita smiles at him. Teddy grins back from under his curls, adoringly, a reminder of why she stays.

Afterward, Rita can't stop Don from taking Teddy shooting.

When she inquires as to Hera's whereabouts, Jeannie tells her Hera's gone "off roaming, in one of her funny moods." Rita feels a skewer of worry. She'd like to go after Hera and check she's okay: she's sure Hera will have noticed the bruise beneath Jeannie's eye too. She misses nothing. But the baby's nappy is heavy as a bag of frozen peas. No one has changed it all morning.

Rita lays the baby in the living room on a towel, pin in her mouth, and starts changing her while Jeannie watches from the sofa, lost in her thoughts, nibbling a bit of shortbread. The phone rings in the library. Neither of them moves.

"I can always tell when it's Walter calling," Jeannie whispers. "Don't even think about answering it, Rita."

The phone rings again, five minutes later. It feels like Walter's banging on the front door. They both hold their breath, waiting for the noise to stop.

The baby, delighted to be free of her nappy, to have her bottom in the air, rocks back and forth with a gurgle. But Rita doesn't smile or pull a silly face, like she normally does. She feels scared and stuck. The world outside Foxcote is closing in.

"I'm sorry if we disturbed you last night," Jeannie says.

Rita doesn't know what to say or where to look. Neither does Jeannie. Now the phone's stopped ringing, it feels like the deafening silence that follows a scream.

"I'll do the nappy." Jeannie jumps off the sofa and rolls up the crepe de chine sleeves of her pale blouse. "Take a break, Rita. A walk? If you see Hera, will you send her back to the house?"

Rita hesitates. She's never seen Jeannie change a nappy. Does she even know how to do it?

Jeannie picks up one of the new pink Babygros. "I won't prick her with the nappy pin, if that's what you're thinking."

Closing the heavy front door behind her, Rita wishes she hadn't missed Robbie and feels a pang for the walk they could have had. There's something reassuring and solid about Robbie. She can be silent with him, neither of them speaking a word, and feel like they're having a conversation. That she's not entirely alone here.

But she is alone. And the forest's never felt more alien.

She drifts for twenty minutes or so—neither Hera, Teddy, nor Don to be seen—then returns. Unable to face going back into the house, she sits on a rusty iron bench in the garden, under a canopy of wild roses. She rests her chin in her hands and closes her eyes. Her skin feels numb, like it belongs to someone else. She can smell the throaty tang of smoke. It reminds her of something, and she has the peculiar sense of being tugged back in time. A memory surfaces, like a splinter working its way out of the body and up through skin, then another: thick smoke and thicker heat; the numbness in her little-girl legs; hands yanking her out of the car window; looking back, over her rescuer's shoulder, and seeing her parents' car engulfed in a hellish ball of flame, her mother's hands banging on the wrong side of the glass. With a groan, Rita bends over and is sick into the geraniums, just missing her shoes. As she looks up and wipes her mouth, she realizes the smoke smell doesn't belong to a distant memory, after all. It's twisting, like a sheer black stocking, from Hera's bedroom window.

32

Hera

I didn't expect my little fire to make so much smoke. Or for Big
Rita to see it. She throws back my bedroom door and just stands
there, mouth parted, staring at the terrarium on the window seat.
The water dripping down the glass. The black smoke still curling
from the little pile of sticks that I'd arranged to look like the log pile
outside, as a nice surprise.

"There was a gust through the open window. The dry bark just
went u-up," I stammer, then stare down at the floor and wait for her
to yell.

But Big Rita doesn't yell. She stands there for years, then walks
slowly toward me and hugs me so her chin is resting on my head. She
smells of the baby. Good things. I smell of smoke. And I suddenly
know I always will.

"I'm sorry." I start to cry and keep apologizing, but this does not
remove the soot from the glass or the burning taste on my tongue,
or make me a nice girl. She'll leave us now.

"Hera." She pulls back, holds me by the shoulders, her fingers
sinking into my disgusting fleshiness. "You think Dot and Ethel

will expire at a whiff of smoke? They're tougher than that. A bit of vinegar on a cloth will clean the glass too. Hey, look at me." I raise my gaze slowly, daring to believe it might be okay. "Why, Hera? Why did you light those sticks?" she asks, like this question matters more than anything else. More than the fire itself, even.

But I don't know how to explain that the urge began last night, when I heard Mother and Don shouting, and it grew this morning, after I saw the bruise on Mother's face. And then the urge was bigger than me.

"You could have started a proper fire. Burned down the house." Rita pauses. Something in her eyes is scared. "Is that what you wanted?"

"No." I study the empty glass rolling on the rug. The beads of spilled water on the wool. And I wish I could thread them together into a necklace and give it to Big Rita, make everything right again. And I hear her say, "Are you sure?"

And the way she asks it makes me not sure at all, so I don't answer.

"And London?" Her voice goes strange and raspy. "Did you light that fire, Hera?" Her big sandy-brown eyes run over my face.

I consider lying. But it's Big Rita, so I whisper, "I thought it was out."

She takes a sharp breath. Outside the open window, birds start clacking in the trees, and it sounds like slow clapping, getting faster. After a while she says, "You've told me something big. Something that makes me worried."

"I won't do it again." I'm not sure she believes me either.

"Tell me what happened. That night in London."

I press my lips together. My mouth is full of too many feelings. They all have different flavors. None of them nice. "Will you tell my mother?"

A frown quarrels between her eyebrows. "I should."

"Don't, Big Rita. Please."

"Just tell me what happened."

It suddenly feels easier to be truthful. Like, if I tell, the worry of it might leap from me to Big Rita, like a nit. "Everyone was asleep and . . . and I sneaked downstairs to get something to eat."

She almost smiles. "Right."

"Those pink wafer biscuits. I wouldn't have bothered for anything else. I wanted to eat them on my own in the dark."

She nods, like she knows this already. "How did you light the fire?"

The question is like a jab of a needle. My body flinches. "I only singed the edge of the curtain on the lightbulb, just to see what would happen. I squashed the scorchy bit between my fingers."

She cocks her head to one side and looks at me in the same concentrated way she does at newspaper crosswords. "But it must have hurt?"

"It stopped me feeling anything. That's why I . . ." I stop. Unable to say it. "Then I went to bed."

She waits patiently for the next bit. I can hear the woodpecker now. His machiney pecking, like he's at a typewriter, taking down evidence.

"I thought I'd pulled the curtain clear of the lamp and turned the lamp off," I explain truthfully. "But I can't have, because later I smelled smoke. So I ran into your room and woke you up."

When I shook Big Rita's shoulders, she went from sleepy to awake in a second. I've never seen anyone move so fast. She launched into Teddy's room and slung him over her shoulder, then grabbed my hand and we ran to the floor below to wake Mother, who was all woozy from the pills. Big Rita pretty much had to carry her down the stairs too. I'm not sure anyone would have survived without her. Other people get medals for this sort of thing. Rita got sent to Foxcote.

"What did you not want to feel?" She won't let it go.

The question skims too close. I don't want to risk feeling it again by answering, so I press my lips together and taste the pink wafer biscuits I ate earlier.

Big Rita loops her arms around her legs. "When I was six I saw my parents die in a car crash."

"That's really sad." I'm relieved not to talk about me.

"But I couldn't remember it for years, even though I was there." Her face grows sad and a million years old. "It was only today, in fact, I just remembered fully what happened." She disguises her voice breaking with a cough. An expression I don't recognize ripples across her face, like a reflection on water. "You're the only person I've told, Hera. And, you know, I feel much better for telling you."

I rub her arm, glad she feels a bit happier. I wonder if I would too, if I told her what I think I saw when I looked out of my bedroom window at the midwife running down our front steps, the baby in her arms.

"I think if we keep the dark things shut up inside," she goes on, "they grow big. Like weeds. They smother all the flowers and block the sunlight." She takes my hand and holds it tight, squeezing all secrets out, like the last bit of toothpaste from a tube. "So what did you want to forget, Hera?"

"My baby sister. Mother and Don's baby."

Big Rita's eyes pop open like umbrellas.

"And when I looked out of the window, the night she was born, and the midwife took her away—" My breath goes all raggedy. "She didn't have a proper face, Big Rita. Her mouth and nose were . . . like one big hole. And . . . and there's something else. The baby . . ." The words scratch inside my head, trying to get out. "She wasn't dead, Big Rita. Her little hand was moving. When the midwife carried away my baby sister, she was still alive."

33

Sylvie

So this is it. Annie and I are on the motorway, hurtling toward a house that no longer exists, and a place in my heart I've spent a lifetime trying to eviscerate. Oh, yes, and the sounds of a forest that we'll record and play to Mum in the hope of jolting her back to life. This is the original reason for going, I remind myself, although it feels like other forces are pulling me toward the forest now, a whirlpool suck. The provincial suburbs soon peter out, and the landscape—inside my head, out of the window—starts to change: rushing rivers; pea-green valleys; excitement; trepidation; and at the edges, molar-powdering anxiety. It feels like the past is rushing toward me at seventy miles an hour.

The bottles of craft ale drunk on an empty stomach yesterday evening are probably not helping.

After Helen's unexpected visit, I spent an hour of manic searching on Google Earth; at that point, my head felt tight, stretched, as if it was straining to grasp the tangled mass of recent events. Seeking clarity, I went for a walk along the canal towpath. Jake was on his boat deck, wrench in hand, fiddling with the engine. Admittedly

I'd noted this from the balcony already and had punctuated my exhausted-looking face with red lipstick. There was something endearing about his absorption in the task and in the way the complexities of the engine seemed to have beaten him. He didn't even look up as I passed. Just asked me how it was going from under his hat, as if he could thermally detect my presence. Rather than answering, "Good, thanks, you?"—the only polite answer in London—and walking on, I committed the faux pas of *answering* the question, as if we were in 1950s rural Ireland. My life—Mum's accident, Annie's pregnancy, Helen the psycho mother—tumbled out in a huge messy overshare. He'd put down the tool and said, "No wonder you turned down a coffee. You need alcohol."

"You've no idea how much."

He offered me his hand and held mine firmly as I walked down the gangplank, my eyes locked to his mismatched Bowie ones, feeling a surge of excitement I hadn't felt for years.

After that time wheeled away, like unexpected perfect evenings do. I learned about boat crankshafts and pistons and rotary motions. How he's a techie and hot-desks in an office in Kings Cross with an on-site churro machine. Six months single—she wanted kids, he didn't—he plans to travel the world on his motorbike, "before I'm forty," he said, as if this was a bucket-list deadline. He's *thirty-one*. "You're a baby!" I hooted.

"And you're about to be a grandmother," he replied with a lazy smile, and for some reason this was the funniest, most unlikely thing I'd ever heard, and I laughed so hard the beer came fizzing up through my nostrils in an appalling way, not caring one bit. When I left, he kissed me on both cheeks, disappointingly chastely. He smelled of oil and sweat. He smiled right into my eyes and said, "Sylvie-from-the-balcony, your life is completely mental," which is man code for *Run away, run away, the woman's a wacko.* But the way he said it didn't make me feel like that. I simply felt understood. And the evening was like a mega-dose of effervescent vitamin C. Unfortunately, the effects are rapidly wearing off.

Caroline's words repeat in my head. "In what way is this *not* a bad idea, Sylvie?" she said when I called her last night.

I didn't even try to describe my strange new craving to see the forest or that I'd been dreaming of it every night, a twisting path through the trees, leading me endlessly forward—even this felt like a sisterly betrayal of sorts—but I said it mattered to Annie, that the pregnancy had sharpened her curiosity, lent it a new urgency and a sense of entitlement to my history, or "*her*-story," as Annie corrected. But, of course, the most important thing was recording forest sounds for Mum. As the nurse suggested.

"But you could stand in Hyde Park and record it! You can download birdsong!" Caroline protested.

"Not the same, Caro." The conversation tautened between our respective continents.

Eventually Caroline said, "I'm worried about you, Sylvie. You seem . . . not yourself." She paused. "What if it stirs something up? You don't know how you'll react. I mean, if it were me . . . if I ever—" She stopped short of mentioning her own provenance. But her breath caught on it. "The whole thing makes me a tad anxious, that's all, sis," she added more warmly, stepping back and refocusing on me, like always.

I was relieved I'd trusted my instincts and not mentioned the folder. With all the worry about Mum in the hospital and every-thing else Caroline's got on her plate, it didn't seem right to throw her a curve ball like that. Not when she's so far away. "It's just a place, Caroline," I insisted. But as I drive toward it, I know this isn't true.

"Oh, no!" exclaims Annie, interrupting my thoughts. Sitting be-side me in the passenger seat, she's been absorbed in a pregnancy calendar app on her phone for the last half an hour. "I might start getting stretch marks from next *month*. No way. I'd rather die."

I laugh and change gears. "I doubt it. You're so young you'll ping back to shape like a pair of Falke tights."

"You didn't," she says breezily. She's in a good place today, ex-cited about this trip. She didn't believe me at first when I sug-gested it.

"You weighed in at nine and a half pounds, thank you very much."

Annie crosses her legs. "Eek. Not hereditary, I hope."

I say nothing. I don't know my birth weight. Or my true birthday.

She shoots an apologetic glance at me, realizing the significance too. After that we sit, not talking, like you do when there's too much to say and a high likelihood of a conversation veering off in the wrong direction, like the car.

❋ ❋ ❋

"Turn left at these crossroads!" Annie shrieks two hours later. "Google Maps says follow the signpost for the village of Hawkswell. No, no, left, Mum!"

I turn on to a narrow country road and wonder if my mother made the same journey, decades ago, if she ever drove down this particular road. I like to think she did, that these are ghost routes I'm retreading.

Annie points out of the windscreen and waggles her finger excitedly, as if she's spotted a herd of elephants. "Forest!"

At the first sight of it, that looming swampy green, all the blood rushes from my head. I try to concentrate on the road. But it's getting closer and closer, filling the expanse of the windscreen, making my heart knock so hard in my chest it feels like it's going to smash its way out. I'm struck by the irony of being in a place with so many trees, when I was born with no known family tree of my own.

"Mum, what you doing?"

I pull up at the side of the road, feeling an unstable slipping sensation, a foot on black ice.

"Mum, are you having a moment? A funny turn?"

I shake my head. It's more like being hit by an asteroid. Or having a stroke. Christ. Am I old enough to have a stroke? When I peer at the trees ahead, I feel a dull tugging, dragging-down sensation, as if the forest has its very own dream logic and centripetal pull. "Long drive. I need some air."

I wind down the window. The woody scent of bark and leaves. But also the ripe tang of decay.

"You're scaring me. No offense."

"It's a proper forest, right? Sorry, I think I was expecting something more like Hampstead Heath. I've been in London too long. A toffee, please." The sugar hit works. "Cured. Let's go."

"You sure? We don't have to do this, Mum. I mean, I'd love to see the forest, but not if . . . Well, I guess it must be kind of weird."

"Annie, do I look like a woman who is intimidated by some old trees?"

"Er, yeah." And we both laugh. Only mine fades quickly. I suddenly remember how fearless I'd once been as a young girl, before I realized being discovered meant being abandoned. I think of the apple tree in my parents' garden, how I'd climb it—small hands gripping, bare feet swinging upward, knowing every twist of twig, every eye and dimple on the bark, the joyous weightlessness of sitting in the upper branches, like a bird in its nest. What happened to that girl?

In the rearview mirror, the exit is no longer visible. Low, twisted branches scrape against the windows. I feel a tremor of panic, then awe.

The forest is monumental. Dwarfing. Disorienting. At the side of the road, the gouging scars of old mines. Tourist signs to caves. A knock-kneed heap of old railway tracks.

This is not a nurturing fairy glade or the twinkly arboretum Mum would describe to me as a child. Oh, no. This is a darker, wilder place. Indifferent to my survival. And I can't help but wonder if it forged neural pathways into my kernel infant brain, like the veins in a leaf. As we drive, I imagine them flickering into life. I sort of like this idea. It also scares the crap out of me.

I can't imagine this place has changed much since the seventies, only the world around it. Time no longer feels linear, but on a loop. I think about the body in the woods in the newspaper cuttings and wonder if forest noises are the best idea, after all. On the other hand, perhaps they're perfect, just the sort of visceral shock Mum needs. Even if, right now, the shock is all mine.

We pull up in a car park. Startled birds explode from the trees. "You wanted to see your roots?" I say, getting out of the car and pointing to the thick toes of a nearby tree, hiding my nerves behind a joke.

Annie laughs. Her hair is dogwood red against the green. We walk, looking for "the right spot" to record for Mum. I'm astonished by it all. The enormous haggy yew. A yellow fungus protruding from a trunk, like a giant's ear. Mud churned by the wild boars' trotters. The earth is the color of rich bronzer and it stains my white trainers. I imagine the archaeological dig beneath my feet: poachers' bullet cartridges; a steak knife with a criminal history; the skeleton of a baby who wasn't as lucky as me. This forest could hide anything.

"Here," I say, because I don't want to go any farther. "Then we'll go and find a cup of tea and some cake."

"Shush. Don't make a sound. One. Two." Annie holds up her phone. She's pinning so much hope on this that I don't want to say anything negative. Long shot. "Recording."

At first nothing. It takes a minute or so for our ears to tune in. Annie listens rapturously, like those YouTube clips of deaf people hearing for the first time. The drilling of a woodpecker. A twig breaking. The paper-bag rustle of leaves. I try to imagine the noises penetrating the oceanic deep of my mother's brain, lighting up her synapses, like a shimmer of cognitive fluorescence. It suddenly feels unlikely, and my mood dips.

As we walk back to the car, Annie turns to face me. Her eyes are shining. "Aren't you glad your biological mother had you? Even given what she did?"

I know this question is loaded, Annie's way of justifying her own decision. But I can only be honest. "Well, yes. Otherwise there'd be no you, and I'd not even get to be a jostling atom in the universe, which would be pretty rubbish."

"I'm glad too," she says, and I squeeze her hand.

Casey's Café is the only tearoom in Hawkswell, a village name I recognize from the newspaper cuttings. A small, slightly dingy establishment with a sun-faded stripy awning, it looks out at a village hall and a cobbled square. The small round tables are empty, apart from one old woman sitting beside the dimpled glass of the window, warming her hands on a metal teapot. She's weathered and gray and oddly still, like she might have died in the chair a few hours ago and no one's noticed. We sit at the table next to hers, avoiding the gloomier rear of the café. Annie giggles at the menu. "Oh my god, what's lardy cake?"

"Sugar and lard, basically. No smashed avocado on toast here, Annie. Scones. Look. Can't go wrong with scones. Let's order them."

The elderly lady on the opposite table squints at us suspiciously. When no waitress appears, I walk to the beaded curtained door that separates café from kitchen at the back. "Hello?"

An attractive woman in her sixties swishes out, dusting off her hands on a black apron, which hugs her curves and is embroidered with the name Casey. I notice that the kitchen is incongruously papered with old movie posters before the beaded curtains clatter shut. She writes down our order on a notepad with great care and reads it back to me with a softly burred accent. I assure her it's correct—plain scones, not fruit, that's right; cream, yes—and wonder how ordering scones can be quite so complicated, then turn back to the table.

I start. The old woman has Annie's hand clutched in hers. Annie's backed into her seat, horrified. I hurry over. "Is everything okay?"

Annie shoots a *save-me* look.

"She's the spit! Looks just like her!" The woman's eyes seem to swivel in their sockets, hectic in the leathery folds of her skin.

"I think there's been some misunderstanding," I say, gently removing the old woman's hand from Annie's.

Casey hurries over. "Leave my customers alone, eh?" she says to the woman, not unkindly. She rolls her eyes at me, as if to say, *Don't worry, the old dear does it all the time.* "Let me help you to the door, love." She affectionately takes the woman's arm.

"But . . ." the woman protests indignantly.

"Here's your walking stick. Careful. That's it. We'll see you same time tomorrow. Your pot of tea and egg sandwich will be ready and waiting. On the dot. As always." She guides her out and mouths a smiling "Sorry" to Annie. She waves. "You enjoy the rest of your day now, Marge."

But Marge doesn't move. She stands on the other side of the

window, staring at Annie, the swirled dimples in the glass distorting her baggy face, and something in me too. Only when the café owner smilingly shoos her away does Marge reluctantly turn and, hunched over, walking stick extended, tap her way down the darkening village street.

34

———— ❈ ————

Rita

Marge ambushes Foxcote through the garden gate, armed with muddy stalks of broccoli, carrots from her veg patch, and a jar of pickles. Don quips, loud enough for Marge to hear, "Just as well my constitution's been hardened on the Serengeti."

Rita holds her breath. Don's soft in the head if he thinks messing with Marge is a good idea. Nor is it likely to help that he's sunbathing on the lawn in swimming trunks that leave nothing to the imagination. The baby sleeps beside them, wearing a nappy, her soft pudding belly rising and falling. (In a forest small things grow quickly: Rita swears the baby gets bigger by the hour.)

"The child needs her blanket," Marge says accusingly.

"Oh, dear. Has it got a bit nippy? There," Jeannie says, quickly rectifying the situation. "Nice and cozy."

But Marge is not looking at the baby now. She's zoomed in to Jeannie and Don's feet—their toes are just touching—and then, as if drawing an invisible line between them, the fading yellowy mark under Jeannie's eye. Jeannie, sensing this perhaps, slips down her sunglasses, which were holding back her hair.

Too late, thinks Rita. Violence, after all, is proof Don is a lover, not a friend. What sort of friend smashes you in the face?

The broken veins on Marge's cheeks blaze. She looks at Don with such frank loathing it makes Rita's breath catch. It's Teddy who saves them, leaping out of a tree and rolling across the lawn.

"Heavens," says Jeannie, snatching up the baby. "Careful, Teddy."

"Ah, man-cub." Don grins approvingly. He nods up at a towering pine swaying on the other side of the garden wall. "Now go and climb that. Show us what you're made of, Teddy."

Rita grabs his hand and pulls him up. No way is he climbing that. "Come on, Teddy. Let's see what Hera's up to."

"Don says—" protests Teddy.

"Don has no idea what he's talking about," says Marge, more pugnacious than ever.

Don lazily scratches his stomach. His nonchalance puts Rita on edge. Don, she's quickly learning, is a man who can accelerate from docile charm to aggression in seconds, like his car.

"Do what Rita says. Inside, Teddy," says Jeannie, glancing at Marge, silently imploring her to say no more.

"Doesn't know trees." Marge lifts her chin. She snorts. "Doesn't know guns, neither."

"I'll let the hunted animal heads that adorn the walls of my Chelsea flat know." His eyes are sparkling dangerously.

"That's enough," Jeannie whispers. She looks on the verge of tears.

Rita tightens her grip on Teddy's hand and pulls him back to the house. Two days before Don leaves, and the question of the baby is settled. She's started to pray that Marge is right and the

Harringtons are able to adopt easily. The other prospect—the baby taken away, given to another family—is now too unbearable to think about.

"Is this a good time?" comes a voice from over the wall.

Something inside Rita clenches.

"Robbie!" calls Jeannie, clearly glad the fraught scene has been interrupted. She leaps up, smiling too brightly, baby over one shoulder. Her cotton dress sticks to the back of her legs. Even with Marge there, watching him like a hawk, Don grins at Jeannie's bottom. "Do come in," Jeannie calls out.

Rita can't breathe. She's unprepared for Robbie, especially in the company of others. She dreads Don saying something. And she looks awful. She's got a spot on her chin, weepy and adolescent, and bags under her eyes.

Ever since Hera told her about the poor Harrington baby, alive when she left the Primrose Hill house, Rita's moved through her domestic tasks in a disembodied daze, her body leaden, her mind fidgety. She's witnessed a lot of dawns. She can't even be sure that Hera, overtired and traumatized on the night of the birth, didn't imagine the whole thing. Maybe she wanted to believe her little sister was alive so much that she saw movement that wasn't there. Willed hope where there was none. Maybe Don wasn't the baby's father after all.

Nannies, she realizes, only get to peep inside a marriage—the contents of the bathroom bin, the conversations that spill under doors or stop suddenly when they enter the room—but they never *really* know. The Harrington marriage—and the family—is a huge intricate jigsaw, with too many missing pieces.

So many unanswered questions niggle. Does Jeannie know the

newborn left the house alive? She suspects Jeannie was out cold and Walter persuaded the midwife to remove the distressing baby. She can imagine that, Walter being the controlling sort, especially if the baby *was* Don's—unfortunately, this has begun to make a dreadful sense—and soon died at hospital. But why? Of what? No one's ever explained it to her—and it's not something she dare ask.

Irrationally, she feels she might have been able to help. After all, she knows the power of a surgeon's stitches, the way they can mend the most broken and twisted of bodies: she has scars like coat zips, more metal pins and plates than a junkyard. Maybe it's different with a newborn baby, she reasons, with its miniature body, the workings fragile as a tiny Swiss clock. Still, if she had been the mother, she'd have wanted to spend those last few minutes with her baby. She'd have kissed and hugged that poor doomed creature as it turned stiff and blue in her arms. It was still a dear human being. A tiny precious thing.

"What do you think, Rita?" Jeannie's saying.

Rita startles, shocked that she's still standing in the same spot on the lawn: her thoughts have traveled miles, yet only a second or two has passed. Everyone is staring at her oddly. She winds her scrambling mind back toward her, like a skein of wool. She blinks repeatedly. "Sorry?"

Don snaps his fingers and laughs. "And she's back in the room."

"Robbie was asking if we had any use for extra logs?" Jeannie frowns, puzzled by Rita's absent expression.

"Go on, Rita. Give Robbie a hand bringing the logs in. I'll take Teddy and keep him out of . . ."—Marge shoots an acidic glance at Don—"harm's way."

Stripes of sunlight stream through the gaps in the shed's planks. The wood chips on the floor muffle the sound of their voices. She's aware of him watching her as she moves logs from wheelbarrow to stack, then straightens and rubs her lower back, gracelessly, catching the tang of her own sweat. She seems to spend half her life bent over changing mats and she aches, the curse of the tall girl. "Well, that's it, I think," she says. "We'll not freeze in our beds this last week of August."

He looks slightly sheepish and fights a smile.

From the garden, Rita can hear the baby starting to whinge. Calling for her. The sound travels right under her skin, as it's always done. She moves toward the door and reaches for the rusty latch.

"The thing is . . ."—he takes a breath—"I just wanted an excuse to come round and speak to you in private."

The temperature in the woodshed rises. She colors. The conversation suddenly feels almost unbearably intense. "Oh, right," she says, struggling to sound casual. "Why?"

"I don't mean to speak out of turn, but you look a bit . . . a bit . . . trapped here. At Foxcote, I mean. Not in the shed." He grins, and her stomach swoops. "You're free to leave the shed at any time."

Rita lets go of the latch and studies the floor, scared she'll give herself away. Her mouth is dry and, for some odd reason, tastes of burned toast. Trapped, yes. It feels like she's caught in the air bubble inside a heavy glass paperweight. She looks up with a small frown. "Have you been spying on us, Robbie?"

"*Spying?*" He looks so baffled by her question—and hurt—that Rita immediately realizes that if someone is secretly watching them, it's not Robbie.

"Doesn't matter." She feels bad. Presses her lips together. "Sorry."

He steps a little closer. She catches the exertion of the log-lifting on him too, a salty musk. He smells exciting. Robbie lowers his voice. "Look, you don't need to tell me nothing. About what's going on. I don't want to put you in a position, Rita." He pauses. She fights the urge to tell him everything. "But you don't look happy, that's all I care about." He fixes her with his warm direct gaze. "And . . . and you should be. You deserve to be happy, Rita."

She bows her head, unable to hold that gaze because if she does she knows she'll start to cry, like you do when people are unexpectedly kind and understand deep unknowable things about you without being told. "I'm dog-tired, Robbie, that's all," she mutters.

"You must be exhausted," he says, with such feeling it's almost as though he's moving around under her skin, and this makes her feel exposed and vulnerable, in a way she never was with Fred. "You don't like this forest much, do you?"

She looks up. Her pupils are dilated, black and huge. "It's beautiful, Robbie. But it's not home."

His Adam's apple rises and falls. "And never could be?" The question lands softly, devastatingly.

She realizes she can't see his shortness anymore, those missing crucial few inches. When she looks into his earth-brown eyes, they seem completely level to her own. And she wants to say, *Yes, I could live here, maybe,* just to see what he'll say next, what unexpected course the conversation might take. But it'd be an insult to lead such a good man on. She couldn't do it. "I don't think so."

They stand there in silence, digesting their fundamental incompatibility, letting it settle around them.

"We go back to London in a few days. For the new school term." It sounds unbelievable even to her. She feels like she's been at Foxcote for centuries, that she's morphed into someone else here. Will she really soon be pushing Teddy on a swing in Regent's Park? Feeding the fat London ducks?

"I could still cook you dinner tonight?" he suggests, his opportunistic cheekiness defying the somber mood.

"Dinner?" She laughs. She can't actually imagine having *dinner* with Robbie. In her mind, he forages for berries and traps rabbit and eats it raw, with the fur still on. "The thing is . . ."

"You've got to wash your hair?" There's no bitterness in his voice. But some of his bounce has gone.

Oh, no. Does her hair look dirty? She flattens her cowlick with the palm of her hand. "It's not that, just . . ." She stops. Just *what*? The world won't end! The children will survive without her. Marge won't actually pickle Don in a jar—more's the pity. Even Hera's unlikely to try to burn the place down twice in one week. As her resistance to Robbie's invitation inverts, like a current changing course, she feels an unexpected recklessness, a novel thrill, and her body starts to hum. What's the worst that could happen? "Yes, please."

35

Hera

The moment Big Rita's gone, Foxcote Manor feels unstable, like a tent without pegs in a gathering storm. From the drawing-room window, I watch her legs swing up into Robbie's muddy truck. She looks happy, more like she used to, and is wearing her pink cardigan, which she never wears. It makes her look too pretty, less like a nanny. My fingertips tingle, like when you know something bad is about to happen. Just not exactly what.

I mooch around, trying to murder the minutes until Big Rita returns. Don lies on the sofa and blows cigarette smoke over Baby Forest, who is lying on a cushion, gnawing on her fist, waiting for Big Rita. I manage to pocket his lighter, a metal one, Zippo, a satisfying prize. He doesn't notice.

Mother reads her book, her bare leg on a footstool, her toenails newly painted red. Teddy lies across the rug on his tummy and drops a net bag of swirly blue marbles from one hand to the other, making a gritty glass-crunching sound.

"Feels sort of funny without Rita, doesn't it?" Mother observes, looking up from her book. It's a romance, with a woman in a bodice on the cover, the sort of book my aunt Edie calls "kindling."

"Sort of liberating." Don tosses her a Look. Clearly, a "nap" is imminent.

"She'll be back soon, won't she?" Teddy has his worried face on, and I feel for him.

"I don't know, Teddy." Don stubs out his cigarette. "Could be Rita's lucky night. She might roll back at dawn. Wearing nothing but oak leaves," he adds, grinning, like he might be picturing it.

Mother smiles, licks a finger, and turns a page. "Well, I won't complain if she does. She deserves a bit of fun." She looks up again and says firmly to Don, "Robbie's terribly nice."

"Since when did women go for nice?" Don yawns, rubbing his fingers through his stubble.

Mother's lips purse slightly. She doesn't look up from her book.

I don't want Big Rita to fall for Robbie and lose interest in us, but I think she could do with a nice thing happening to her. These last few days I keep catching her staring into space. And I'm pretty sure she was crying as she cooked lunch yesterday. She said it was the onions. But she was chopping celery.

Don lumbers up and wanders over to the drinks trolley. He picks up bottles, reads the labels, and puts them down again with a chink. He shoots Mother another coded look.

On cue: "Hera, darling, could you look after Teddy and the baby for half an hour?" Mother doesn't say the word *nap*. She doesn't have to. She springs up from her chair. "Marge made a mushroom soup. You can heat that up for supper. Give the baby a bottle. You're so good at it."

"Okay." I suddenly know I'll always remember my mother in her sky-blue dress and the baby cooing on the sofa, her dark eyes searching for Big Rita. The sound of glass marbles colliding in Teddy's hands. Don muttering, "Where did I put that lighter?" as he moves to follow Mother out of the room.

"But you said you'd take me shooting!" Teddy propels himself forward on the rug and grabs Don's tanned ankle.

Don shakes him off, as if he were an annoying puppy. "Later, okay?"

In the kitchen, I warm up Marge's soup on the hot plate while Teddy sits next to the baby in the trug and sings "This Little Piggy" and tugs at her toes. The soup tastes like how fungi smell, dank and earthy, the fat pale mushroom stalks bobbing about like bones. Neither of us can eat it, so we fill up on piles of cold apple crumble, swimming in a moat of cream. Teddy lets the baby suck cream off his little finger while I warm her bottle, flicking the milk on my wrist to check its temperature, like Big Rita does. But I'm not Big Rita. And the baby knows it, twisting on my lap, glancing from side to side so the teat keeps popping out, refusing to settle. We decide she may be happier in the drawing room. She isn't.

For no reason, Teddy explodes into tears. The baby is so surprised by this outburst she stops whimpering and fidgeting and starts to feed, which is good.

"What's up with you?" I rock the baby like a dolly as she drains the bottle, dribbling milk over the sofa.

"I have worries, Hera." He struggles to get out the words.

I reach across and rub his shoulder with my spare hand. "Big Rita will be back soon."

"I miss Daddy." He sniffs, wiping his nose on his arm.

"Daddy?" I can't let myself miss Daddy. There would be too many complicated feelings. Like when you mix bright colors and end up with that sludgy brown.

Teddy nods snottily. "I've tried to pretend Don's Daddy. But he's not."

"No, he really, really isn't," I say, making the baby start. I lower my voice again. "You'll see Daddy soon, Teddy. Big Rita spoke to him."

And this is the problem. Daddy doesn't know about the baby yet. I've started to dread the moment he finds out. What if he takes one of his "moral stances" and makes us hand in the baby immediately, as if she were a purse found on the pavement? What if he doesn't *want* her? Back in London, neighbors like the Pickerings will be waiting, peering over the fence, muttering about golf and dinner parties and who's got the best gardener. How will a foundling *fit*? I simply can't work out how we get from this point to that. I'm not sure Mother can, either.

Teddy starts to sob again, harder this time.

"Oh, Teddy. Take the baby. She'll cheer you up. Whoa . . . support her neck. Yes, that's it." Teddy holds her warily. "Smell the top of her head. It'll make you feel better. It just will. Promise."

He sniffs it and lets her worm her finger into his ear.

"Smells like yogurt." He sniffs again. "And Big Rita."

"There you go. And you feel a bit better?"

"Sort of." And I can tell he doesn't, that he's just trying to please me. I'm not even sure he loves the baby as much as he did. His forehead goes ribbed, serious, like a little old man's. "There's something else, Hera," he whispers.

Inside my head, a whirring, like a mosquito you can hear but can't see. "What?"

"I heard Don say to Mummy . . ."—his bottom lip puckers—"'Let's run away together, Jeannie.' That's what he said."

"Well then, he's a twerp, isn't he? Mother would *never* do that." I hug him and the baby. Not wanting to let go. Ever. "She'd never leave you, Teddy." But would she leave me? What if she doesn't want to be a mother at all anymore, but someone else, like Aunt Edie? The thought is like a hole opening up in the floor.

Under my arm, Teddy's shoulders start to heave. I hate seeing him this upset. Desperately try to think like Big Rita. What would she do? "Wait there, Teddy. Don't move."

Carrying down the terrarium from my bedroom, I'm unable to lift my hands and stopper my ears from the piggy grunts sliding out from under Mother's bedroom door. I carefully rest it on the living-room rug. "Ta-da!"

Teddy's eyes bug. He plops the baby on the sofa, like a toy he's tiring of, and kneels down beside the glass case, now sparkling again after the fire, with only a tiny bit of soot in the hinges. He peers into it, his eyes widening, a smile spreading. The baby gurgles happily.

"Playing doll's houses, Teddy?" Don makes us jump. He stands in the doorway, looking like he's run ten miles, his hair sprouting out at odd angles on his head, two red dots on his cheekbones. The baby kicks on the sofa.

Teddy edges away from the terrarium, pretending he's not interested. "I was waiting for you. To go shooting. Boys' stuff."

Don walks over to the drinks trolley and pours himself a whiskey, knocking it back in one. "Better."

Above us, I can hear the sound of Mother's bath taps running.

Teddy jumps up. "I'll go and get ready. Long trousers?"

Don raises his glass. "Learning fast."

I shut the door so Teddy can't hear and turn to face him, my arms crossed. "You're trying to get Mother to leave us! Teddy told me."

"You, Hera, are a riot." He doesn't even deny it.

"You can't tell her what to do!"

"I assure you no one tells your mother what to do. Apart from that bully your father."

"We were happy before you came here." My voice quakes. "Us and the baby."

He glances irritably at Baby Forest on the sofa—she's grumbling and scratching at her cheeks. He looks back at me and his eyes are glinting dangerously, blue as Teddy's marbles, just as hard. "If you were all so happy, why did you lie to your mother, Hera? Hide things from her? Do you want to tell me what you did with my letter?"

My mouth opens and shuts. So Mother was awake that night as I sat beside her bed in the dark, whispering confidences. The world tips. She must hate me.

He steps closer. "And how have *you*, her fiery disappointment of a daughter, made your mother happy exactly, Hera? Tell me." He raises his hand.

I know he's going to hit me, like he hit Mother. But I refuse to flinch. I ball my fists at my sides, bare my teeth, snarl, ready to fight back. But to my surprise, he strokes my cheek instead, which is so much worse. "Hera, I'll let you in on a secret." He brushes a hank of my growing-out fringe from my face. "It was your mother who suggested us running away. Not me."

The kick is a reflex. I get him in the shin. Then again between the legs, in the balls. He roars and grabs his crotch. "You fat little—"

He barrels toward me with his arms outstretched, like he's trying to catch a chicken in a yard. But I take refuge behind an armchair. He charges again. I leap behind another. He's big and slow and clumsy. "Call yourself a hunter?" I tease. The baby gurgles on the sofa, like she's laughing too.

It happens in slow motion. One second Don's panting, hands on his knees, the next he's swinging at the defenseless target with the full force of his right foot, and all I can hear is the sound of my own voice screaming, "No!"

36

Sylvie

I'd really like to know what happened next, that's all," Annie says sleepily, as if we're debating whether to stream the next Netflix episode. "Like who died in the woods that day. And why."

"Me too." I yawn. My jaw pops. The motorway whips past. My eyes are tired, the lights starting to smear. I'm craving the lovely brain blot of an enormous glass of cold white wine. London glows in the distance. Almost home.

"But I guess it *was* a long time ago." She sighs, with a note of resignation.

"Very," I say firmly, not wanting the forest's secrets to linger in Annie's pregnant body, like microscopic fungal spores. I want to nourish her with good things, happy thoughts. So I don't tell her that a part of me is still walking down Hawkswell's cobbled damp streets—and the past feels very close indeed. Or that I can smell the forest faintly, every time I move, as if it's caught in the spirals of my hair, the layers of my skin. Leaf mold. Soil. Resin. Or maybe it's just that the gutsy little girl who used to climb trees is still in me somewhere, despite me spending a lifetime smothering her in sequins, jumpsuits, and Paris-red lipstick. You can't get much farther from a forest than backstage at a fashion show, I realize with a small smile.

"Will you go back, Mum?" Annie asks suddenly. "To the forest?"

The direct question takes me by surprise. "Well, we've got the recording for Granny now," I say, not quite answering. I know I will go back. I *have* to go back. But alone.

I can't get the woman out of my head. Marge. Something was off about her. "She's the spit . . ." she'd said about Annie, and this thought is much more unsettling to me than a corpse in the woods forty-odd years ago.

Whenever I accidentally switch on FaceTime or take a selfie without wearing sunglasses, it's always a shock, the brutal objective evidence of myself, the older face imprinted on mine, waiting in line for me to look like her. It's not just that, like most of my fortysomething friends, I balk at any evidence that I'm not thirty-three. (I feel thirty-three!) It's also the strangers emerging as the years stream past. Generations of unknown women going back through time. The history under my skin. And Annie's, clearly.

One particular afternoon at middle school. On my knee, a plaster that was so much paler and pinker than my skin, like all plasters were back then. The grainy scoop of the red plastic school chair. And the dreaded approach of the teacher, the one who'd asked the class to draw their family tree. Worse, she leaned over my shoulder, with staff-room coffee breath, and asked who I looked most like. In front of everyone. For a moment my tongue was stuck. There was a roar in my head. And I felt hot and ashamed, like I should confess to something, although I knew I hadn't done anything wrong. So I said simply, "I look like me." And I stored the incident—and the teacher's question—away, unexamined. I never mentioned it to Mum.

But now I kick myself for not asking more questions when I could, rather than hiding behind Mum's reluctance to talk about a difficult period in her life and my fear of being hurt, a rejection so fundamental it felt like it might eat me from within if I gave it too much air time. Our mutual evasion was conspiratorial and extremely effective, I think, as the motorway lane starts to slow, clogging at London's approach.

"Listening to woodland sounds will be nicer than all those hospital machines beeping anyway," Annie says. Her voice sounds weary. I glance across. She's leaning her head against the window, crushing her thick red hair—whose hair?—against the glass.

I feel a snag of anxiety. Maybe today's been too much. Was it irresponsible of me to bring her? In my efforts to support Annie and be more open, have I gone too far? The questions roil in my head. "Sleep. Been a long day."

Annie's eyes close instantly, and her breathing changes. She looks so young. And I recall how I loved her with such searing intensity when she was asleep as a small child, that fleeting stretch of peace when I could notice the love, let it wrap around me. And I notice it now, just the same.

A minute later, my phone rings. The caller's mobile number lights up on my dashboard. Not one I recognize. Not the hospital: I live in dread of their bad-news calls. Spam? I won't answer it. Then it occurs to me it could be Jake. He did ask for my number—I couldn't think of a good enough reason not to give it to him. Something like that.

I glance at Annie, trying to judge her level of unconsciousness. No, bad idea. She'd be appalled. I won't answer it. The man thinks I'm a basket case anyway. "Hello?"

"It's me. Helen. I've got a proposition."

※ ※ ※

I stand outside Helen's Chelsea mews house, rallying the courage to press the dashboard of an intercom. Yesterday's epic drive cranks in my upper vertebrae as I peer up. It's a doll's house, smallish— compared to nearby mansions, anyway—but perfectly formed with Georgian windows, the sills painted black, the blinds all shut. Three security cameras swivel and blink at me with red eyes. I glance at my watch self-consciously, feeling observed. Yes, if we've got the timing right, Elliot should be arriving at my flat at any moment.

"I'm going to send him round in a taxi to your apartment for ten," Helen instructed, the reason for the call in the car. "Perhaps we could sit it out together at mine and discuss future responsibilities." This wasn't a question.

Annie was resistant. "He'll just try to persuade me not to keep the baby, Mum," she'd said, crossing her arms across her swollen breasts. I told her to give him a chance. "He's had it already," she snapped, tougher than I've ever been. How many chances did I give Steve? So many. Too many.

"It's me, Sylvie." The door opens slowly and Helen's taut face appears in the gap. Then a small smile. A chain rattles, pulled back. As I step over the threshold, the door slams heavily behind me and the security locks crunch back into position. "Wow," I say, peering around goofily. TARDIS-like, the petite exterior gives way to a soaring pitched-glass roof. "Gorgeous house."

Right thing to say: she looks pleased, and her smile widens, revealing her white teeth. "An old artist's studio. Lucian Freud used to . . ." she enthuses, then checks herself, possibly remembering Val's rather more modest apartment. "Well, I like it." She eyes my strappy silver sandals approvingly. (I've made an effort.) "You'll have a gin and tonic." Again, not a question.

I'd had her down as living in a featureless taupe and chrome interior, bland and expensive, like a posh hotel. This is more interesting. She likes modern art. Enormous high-energy abstracts splashed with red paint, like blood. I wonder if this is what necessitates the high security: panic alarms; CCTV cameras aimed at the glass roof, as if a James Bond baddie might swing down on a rope at any moment.

Although it's still impossible to imagine Helen slobbing out in front of a box set in pj's, she's clearly more relaxed in her own home, wearing a black jumpsuit and kitten heels. On a large velvet ottoman, promisingly, I spot an open bar of dark chocolate. Two squares missing from it. (Who stops at two squares?) I think, *I'll text Mum about that later,* then catch myself. It's just the sort of detail she loves. We'd get a multi-text rally out of it.

"So I said to Elliot, 'Darling, don't despair. She may yet change her mind,'" she says companionably, stirring our drinks with a glass cocktail stick. I take the glass obediently, even though it's far too early in the day for me. It's the most exquisite cut-crystal goblet I've ever seen, like it's been chipped from stars. I take a tiny polite sip and splutter: it's one of the strongest gin and tonics I've ever tasted.

I smile at her brightly. "Ain't happening. She's not changing her mind, Helen. Believe me, I know Annie."

"Well, she and Elliot will never make it work as a couple. Sadly," she says as an afterthought, not sounding sad at all. She clinks down her glass on a mirrored side table. "Elliot can't be tied down at his age. Nor can Annie. They've both got their lives ahead of them." She touches my arm. The unexpected contact is like a small electric shock: she's got such an untouchy-feely aura, a social awkwardness at odds with her privilege. "We have to face the facts, Sylvie."

"I'm not about to pick my mother-of-the-bride outfit just yet," I concede wryly. She fights a smile, the sort that reaches her eyes, which makes me wonder if there's a warmer, more idiosyncratic Helen beneath the cold, polished surface.

I smile back, heartened. There are worse things than being a teenage single mother, I keep telling myself when the reality of Annie's situation makes me bolt upright in bed, as it did this morning, frazzled with panic. There are women who can't conceive or who miscarry, as I did, who spend thousands on unsuccessful fertility treatment and would give their right arm to have a new life budding inside them, however off the timing.

"Well, given that worst-case scenario, we'll just have to crack on and find a good doula—Chelsea is awash with them—and a nutritionist . . ."

There's something almost endearing about Helen's earnestness. "I'll make sure she doesn't live off Kettle Chips and blue cheese, don't worry, Helen."

Helen frowns. "Right. Well, I'll take control of the baby's finances, then."

I laugh, disbelieving of her bluntness. But of course she can't help herself. The woman *is* a control freak. I wonder why I haven't realized this before. I also feel jealous. I'd love to throw my financial largess around, not be the grandmother who's picked apart the family nest at the worst time imaginable. "You are, of course, welcome to contribute, Helen, but I will make sure that the baby has everything it needs."

She looks doubtful, opens her mouth to say something but thinks better of it. She glances at my full drink. "Would you prefer a coffee?"

"If it's no bother. Sorry, not very good on spirits during the day."

"Follow me," she says, turning on her heel, a bit put out.

Excited to see more of the house, I follow Helen's twiggy frame along a narrow hallway, decorated with arty black-and-white photographs. I pause to admire them and puzzle over what they might be. "Palm houses?"

"Kew! At night!" She's unable to hide a passion that suggests I may have stereotyped her—the wealthy walking facelift—rather too quickly. And something changes between us, ever so slightly, a recalibration of who we both might be.

When we emerge into the kitchen conservatory at the back of the house, the south-facing light is blinding. It takes a moment for my eyes to adjust. I blink. Blink again. And then I see them. Rows of terrariums on a stone plinth, all different shapes and sizes. Dozens of plants held captive, trapped inside glass.

37

Rita

Walnut?" Robbie cracks his fist, shakes away the shell, and presses the brain-like nut into Rita's hand. His gaze locked to hers, he closes her fingers slowly, one by one, each tugging some internal string inside Rita's body until she feels tuned to him, like an instrument. "More where that came from." He nods at the majestic tree hanging over his garden. The firelight streams in his eyes. "You won't starve with me, Miss Rita."

Rita bites into the walnut, her eyes half closed. Has she ever tasted anything more delicious? Nothing like the stale, bitter nuts she and Nan ate every Christmas, nervously, due to the fragility of Nan's dentures. This is a different experience altogether. Eating a walnut in the woods! With a fat gold harvest moon hanging above the trees and a dog at her feet! She's fallen into a Laura Ingalls Wilder novel, like the ones she read in the local library as a child.

Robbie's small stone cottage, embraced on all sides by woodland, a fair walk from the road, once belonged to his late parents, "and before that, my grandparents," he told her with simple pride. Inside it's scruffy but ordered, glossy with age and patina. She could have spent hours poking curiously around in his workshop, a barnlike building that extends into the garden, a treasure trove of planes, lathes, band saws, and grinders, meaty lumps of ash and elm waiting to be turned into something else, given new life. But it's one of those perfect summer nights, and the only place to be is in the garden, where they sit on a log next to a spitting fire under an indigo sky, pinholed with stars. The air is so still that the candles, stuck in empty wine bottles, don't blow out. Rita's full of the ham, smoky from being cooked over the fire, tender enough to feather on her fork. And she sloshes with beer when she laughs. Which is often.

"Are you warm enough?" Robbie breaks the forest hush, which feels simultaneously intensely private, a silence that only they can inhabit, and excited and alive, like it's crackling. "Here. A blanket."

"Thanks." Her body absorbs the brush of his fingertips against the back of her neck, the lanolin smell of the wool. She finishes her beer—she's so pleased he has nothing but beer, not something sweet and fizzy in a silly bottle, as if he knew what she liked—and sneaks a glance at Robbie's mouth, the cactus stubble on his upper lip. She wishes she could capture just this, exactly as it is, and trap it under glass.

"Let me." Robbie opens a new bottle of beer, chilled from the plastic bucket of ice, and passes it to her, leaning so that she can feel the muscular ridge of his body. His leg meets hers and stays there. Distance closed. She smiles. The dog looks up at them, glancing from one to the other, like a weary chaperone.

"I mustn't return to duty drunk."

"Don't see why not. We'll walk back. That'll sober you up."

"Good idea," she says weakly, not wanting to sober up. Wanting, in fact, to get gloriously plastered and never leave.

The surrounding forest feels like it's been grown just for them, the trees sculpted like bonsai, teased into shape to let in just the perfect amount of light—dreamy, underwatery—and the densest shadows against which the flames can flicker and lick.

She strokes the dog's hard silky head because her hand suddenly needs to touch something. When she looks up at Robbie, his eyes are fixed on her. She smiles. She peels off her pink cardigan, midday hot all of a sudden, and wonders if there's been some hiccup in the universe. How come she hasn't realized Robbie was this attractive before tonight? When she had a chance. When he actually wanted to kiss her. Now she's a mess of feelings that have nowhere to go. A weight is pressing down on her pelvis.

"So, Rita?" he teases.

"So?" She leans closer, stretching out one leg from under the folds of her skirt, not minding its length for once. Is she *flirting*? Is this what flirting feels like? She likes it.

The evening has been studded with these taut moments, before loosening again and turning into something else. Sparks from the fire flutter up in the wind and blow about. The dog closes his watchful eye and falls asleep.

"We never did dance that time." He has a smile in his voice. The hint of something else too, and it lodges inside her body, sweetly.

"I'm too tall to dance," she says, even though she couldn't care less how tall she is tonight, and neither, it seems, can he. He pulls her up by the hand, easily, as if she were a wisp of a thing.

"You are *magnificent*, Rita."

She throws back her head and laughs, so her cowlick bounces free of the hair grip.

When he kicks off his shoes Rita hesitates, then decides she doesn't hate her feet anymore and follows his example. The ground is soft underfoot. She wants to lift his shirt and sniff his skin. The trees move and sway around them as they dance. The dog slopes away when they roll to the ground, the grass and bracken in their hair, their clothes peeling off, all breath and bodies, until she's there, stark naked in front of a man for the first time in her life, stripped of everything she's spent her entire life trying to hide, exposed, horrified, flying with joy.

But then he sees them. His expression instantly sobers. He traces the zipper-like scar across her stomach with a fingertip. She can't speak. She'll die of embarrassment and desire. The scars are a turnoff. Fred couldn't even look at them.

"What happened to you?" he asks.

Because there's nowhere to hide now, she tells him. Not just the actual accident: the flash of red deer leaping out; the car swerving and hitting the tree; her own escape, the first to be pulled out of the fireball—and the last. But what happened afterward. How she was in hospital for six months and spent most of the time looking at the strip-lit ceiling, metal-pinned legs cantilevered up, reversing events, making time go backward, the smashed car and the broken bodies fling back together. The flames extinguish. Returning the three of them to the safety of the campfire, the hands on her father's wristwatch stuck forever at five past one.

"I'm so sorry, Rita." Robbie presses his forehead against hers, as if to pour the pain from her head into his.

"There's something else. Something very few people know. My . . . my secret." Since she's nothing to lose anymore, she tells him about the day a doctor stood next to her bed and said to her nan, "It's not good news, I'm afraid," and Nan had sucked hard on her teeth, then said, "At least her face is fine."

Nan only explained once she came out of hospital. She lowered her voice in case the neighbors could hear and said, "Never tell a man straightaway, or you'll never pass go. Wait until the time is right, when they love you for you, Rita, and then you might stand a chance."

She explains how the time was never "right" enough to tell Fred. After he proposed, she didn't want to ruin things, not when they saw each other so infrequently anyway, her being in London with the Harringtons, him in Torquay. But he kept going on and on about children, how he needed a son to take on the family business, and how their son would be big and strong, just like Rita, with his father's eye for the meatiest cut of shin and brisket, the juiciest slice of tongue.

What could she do? Once married, she could hardly pretend, month after month, they'd just been unlucky. And didn't he say he loved her to bits? So she called him from the phone box on the corner of the Harringtons' crescent: "I got damaged, Fred. Down there. I won't have kids." The shocked pause went on forever.

"But I'd never have asked you to marry me if you'd told me," he'd said eventually. And she'd realized she'd known that all along.

There. It's out. Rita stares up at the sky. The moonlight falls on her bare skin like rain.

"Lucky," he says.

"Lucky?" she repeats, with a hollow laugh. Her heart is one big bruise.

"You found out Fred's true character before you walked down the aisle." Robbie rolls on top of her, pinning her down, weighting his body's length against hers. She doesn't register she's crying until he wipes her tears away with his thumb. "And I'm a lucky bugger too. Because you're not married to that idiot and this means I can kiss you from your head to your toes."

And every crevice besides. God. She had no idea such sensations *existed*. Lying back on the ground afterward, her body quivering, trying to catch her racing breath, she feels . . . *reborn*. Robbie reaches for her hand and brings it to his mouth, skimming her knuckles with his lips, and she smiles, so lost in him, the warm summer's night, she doesn't hear the distant gunshots, muted by the trees.

38

Hera

I didn't want to kill anything. And I wouldn't have gone shooting at all if Don hadn't kicked the terrarium, and the baby hadn't started screaming at the top of her lungs and Teddy hadn't run in, followed by Mother, bewildered in a flowing black dress embroidered with teeny sequiny chips of mirror. I roared at her, "He's an animal! LOOK what he's done!" But she just stood there, refusing to look at the shattered glass case—or who Don really was.

"Obviously, it was an accident," Don said, rubbing the side of his nose.

Mother said, "Get the dustpan and brush, Hera." She walked toward the sofa and picked up the screaming baby. Baby Forest had never cried like that before. She looked terrified, all bulging and rigid. "There, there," Mother said, cuddling her tight. "It's all right, it's all right, sweetpea." But it wasn't all right. And the baby knew it. She kept on crying, like an alarm going off, arching her back, and I knew, and probably Mother knew, the only person who was able to calm her down was Big Rita. But Big Rita wasn't there. And we had no idea when she might be back.

"So are we going shooting?" Teddy said, hopping from foot to foot, agitated.

I mouthed, "No."

"I don't think . . ." Don drew a hand along his cheek. He suddenly looked exhausted. "Not tonight, Teddy."

Mother, dancing and jigging in little circles with the baby, trying to soothe her, said sharply, "Go, Don. Really. Then I can get things under control here. Shh, baby."

Don shook his head. He looked shocked by himself. In a daze.

"Go!" Mother shouted, panicked by the baby's screams, the red ribbon of noise. "I can't settle the baby with you here. Just go." She suddenly sounded like she hated him too. She turned to me. "Would you go too? Please, Hera." I couldn't say no. I knew she wanted me to go to keep an eye on Teddy. I think Don knew too.

"Jeannie, I really don't think that's a very good idea," he said with a small laugh.

"I'll go," I said. There was no way Teddy was going out with him alone.

A couple of minutes later, like he was trying to prove something, Don pressed a gun into my hand. "Do your worst."

❊ ❊ ❊

We soon lost Don, tracking something or other. I held Teddy's hand so he couldn't follow him. Once Don was out of sight, no danger to us anymore, I roared and turned in a circle and beat my chest, like the stupid silverback gorilla Don thought he was, and we both started giggling. In the hush, the sound grew around us, coming from all directions, as if there were dozens of madly giggling children hidden in the trees. By then we were in the thick copse of pines, where the ground is dry and crunchy, skiddy with needles, and the air is completely still, like the inside of a wardrobe. When we stopped laughing, Teddy got spooked. I led him away from the pines until we could see the sky again, the lights of a plane arcing across it, like a spaceship. My arm was aching from carrying the gun. And I wanted to curl up in the soft, powdery hollow of a tree and sleep, arms around Teddy, rather than go back to Foxcote. Or see the broken glass on the floor. Thinking about the terrarium made an urgent anger hiss through me. And that's all I remember, the sudden fume of fury, and my heart, like a big bass drum, then Teddy pointing at a moving far-off shape and hissing, "Deer! Deer! Shoot!"

The bullet rang out before I decided to fire. The gun punched my shoulder. The evening shattered into a zillion fragments.

We stood there a moment, not saying anything, our ears ringing, like church bells. I imagined the deer bleeding out. Suffering. But I wasn't sure I'd be brave enough to give the animal another shot to save it from further pain. So I threw the gun down and we ran back to Foxcote.

That was almost an hour ago. I clean my teeth with a trembling hand.

A knock on the bathroom door. "Hera? You in there?"

I startle at the sound of Big Rita's voice and drop my toothbrush into the plastic beaker.

"So how was your evening?" She pushes open the door slightly. Through the gap I can see she's grinning madly. Her hair is all messed up, like a herd of cows have licked it. She smells of bonfire and happiness. This tells me one thing: she hasn't seen her precious terrarium. Yet.

I don't answer. She follows me into my bedroom and bounces on the side of my bed, making it creak. Her smile fades. "Teddy's in a flump too. Anyone going to tell me what's the matter?"

It's like someone's died. All the happiness drains from Rita's whitening face. "Smashed?" she repeats, unable to believe it.

"Kicked in." My voice sounds watery. "By Don."

"Don?" she repeats blankly. The clock ticks on the wall. Her eyes start to blaze. Like I've never seen them. Dagger gold, not brown. And she seems to grow bigger, more powerful, as if she could crush Don's skull in her hand, like a ripe peach. "I'll stand up to him this time, Hera." A new Big Rita is talking. She strides to the door. "I'll make the bugger leave. Right." She frowns. She hesitates. "Hang on a minute, where is he?"

39

Sylvie

"My advice, as your older and much wiser sister, is to venture no further than the range of the television remote control," says Caroline, on the phone. There's a steely strain in her voice: she's not joking. I feel disloyal: I've not told her everything. Self-doubt begins to creep in. "Stop it, you!" she shouts, and it takes me a beat to realize she's addressing one of her children, stage left in her American life. "Spike! Alfie's digging up the lawn with a spoon. Sorry, Sylvie, what was I saying?"

"I shouldn't go back to the forest," I say sheepishly, feeling like I've been caught rashly digging up my life too.

"Christ, no. You've done it once. You've got the woodland noises for Mum." She doesn't say they've not had any impact other than to cheer up the nurses. But I know she's thinking it. "Don't be a nutter and go back! Not when you're in such a tizz, Sylv."

"I'm not in a tizz," I huff. I am in a tizz.

"It's that bloody woman again. Elliot's mother and her terrariums. She's thrown you," Caroline says. My pulse quickens at the mention of Helen and the eerie sight of the terrarium collection in her conservatory. "I'm right, aren't I?"

I don't answer.

"Knew it. It's a coincidence, I'll give you that. But these things are fashionable, aren't they? Terrariums, I mean. Not coincidences. Did you mention someone gave one to Mum?"

"No." A reluctance to share the private pain of Mum's situation stopped me. A fear of Helen's indifference. Or, worse, sympathy. The possibility I might break down. "We were there to talk Annie and Elliot business."

"Bet *that* was fun."

"Indeed."

Caroline laughs. After that, an easier silence stretches between us, the comforting kind when you simply listen to the person you love, thousands of miles away, breathing. "Please don't go back to the forest," she says, breaking the silence. "Sisters' proper promise you won't?"

The mobile feels very hot against my ear. I feel really bad. "Too late. I'm sorry, Caro."

"Sylvie. Where the hell are you?"

"Casey's Café in Hawkswell." I lower my voice. "And that old lady, the one I told you about—bit mad with a stick, remember? Marge. Here she comes. Caroline, I've got to go."

I hang up on my sister's protestations. I flick the phone to silent. Needs must.

On time, Marge crumples down at the adjacent table, like a brown-paper bag. An egg sandwich and a pot of tea duly appear, courtesy of Casey. Neither seems to recognize me without my flame-haired daughter. Although I'm not sure I quite carry off looking like a local, either.

I wait for the right moment. Striking up a conversation isn't difficult—an observation about the weather, followed by a compliment on her excellent choice of sandwich, and she's mine. She invites me to her table. Up close, Marge's face is creased with an extraordinary crosshatching of lines, all going in different directions, deeply carved, like a dried-up riverbed. Never worn sun block, clearly. It's the thing my private clients most fear: the marks of a long life lived. But she fits this place perfectly, and the lines bring with them a certain respect.

After a few minutes, she warms up. Pleased to have a bit of company. I wonder if the old woman's on her own a lot, shuffling between doctor's appointments and bus stops, sitting in the café to keep heating costs down at home, like Mum and her nan used to do. I feel for her. She tells me Casey's windows need a clean: newspaper and vinegar would do the job, and she'd do it herself if her arthritis wasn't playing up. When she blames her arthritis on a lifetime of working as a housekeeper—"a hard life and a thankless one"—my ears prick up. Before I can ask if she knew of a house called Foxcote Manor, she's on to the husband who drowned ("drunk as a newt") in the river Severn a year after they married, and left her with nothing, just a mistress knocking at the door, asking for the money he owed her, a son Marge didn't know about, all told with the rhythmic patter of an anecdote relayed before, honed for an audience. She doesn't really listen to me, rather pounces on pauses in the conversation to talk about herself. *Lonely, the poor thing,* I think. Never had her own family, she says, with a sigh, but collected people around her, "the leftovers, like me." I'm soon so swept along by her tale—an unsung story of female working-class hardship, I'm thinking—I'm completely unprepared for the confrontational clink of her teacup on the saucer and the hissed question "Why are you being bloody nice? What do you want?"

Out of the corner of my eye, I can see the café owner, Casey, hovering warily, sensing the change in tempo too. I wonder if she was expecting it. Something tells me Marge won't be fobbed off, either.

"Look, you probably don't remember, but I was here last week, sitting just over there, on that table, that's right, over there, and you seemed quite startled by my teenage daughter. A redhead? You grabbed her hand and you said she was the spit of someone."

"Of course I remember. I may be old, but I'm not crackers."

The café owner moves toward us and smiles quizzically. "Everything all right, Marge?"

Marge glances between me and the teapot, sniffing an opportunity. "This lady's going to treat me to a cream tea."

"Of course. Anything you like, Marge." As soon as Casey's gone, I press her again about the *spit* part. But Marge is more reluctant now, tapping a foot beneath her, staring at me so hard, it's like being poked with a knitting needle. "Why do you want to know?"

"Just curious." I smile too brightly, sure she's going to tell me to sod off.

"A girl. Jo. Same red hair. Used to live not too far from here." Her gaze fixes on the middle distance, gone somewhere I can't follow. It feels like a hand is reaching out of a dim dirty alley and yanking me in. "Big slanty eyes," she adds. "Color of sycamore leaves."

"What happened to Jo?" My heart has started banging. Looping in my head, *She walked away.*

"Oh, she was one of *those* girls." She makes a tsk noise between her teeth. "Got into a spot of bother."

Was that me? The trouble. The mistake.

"Silly girl. No one but herself to blame."

"Does she live here still?" The words come out strangled with anxiety.

"Oh, no. Left donkey's years ago. Moved to Canada, I believe."

A weight lifts. The thought that I could walk out of this café and bump into someone who could be my birth mother makes me feel fractured.

"That's why your girl gave me such a turn, you see. Looked just like her, as she was back then." Marge sips her tea, her lips crumpling over the lip of the cup. "Worked on the cruise ships." She shakes her head. "Anything went on in the cruise ships. Let alone the ports. Didn't even know the father's name. Tsk."

My brain scrambles to make sense of this. I know I'm being ridiculous. What are the chances? And yet. It's a tiny village and Annie's red hair doesn't come from Steve's side. We've always wondered about it.

"Questions, questions." She lurches forward. "Who *are* you?"

I rear back, shocked by the pent-up aggression in the woman's scrunched face. The urge to run away is overwhelming. I glance at the door. I'd be out of here in three springy steps. "I was found . . ." I begin, struggling to say it out loud to a stranger after a lifetime of being unable to talk about it even with close friends. The words dry in my mouth. "As a baby . . ." I try again. It doesn't work.

"What? Didn't catch that?" She puts a hand behind one huge ear, bending the pink flesh toward me.

"Sylvie." I burrow back to a safer place. "I'm Sylvie Broom. My mother used to work for a local family, the Harringtons, as a nanny, one summer many years ago. Her name's Rita. Rita Murphy."

Marge's face changes before my eyes: it's like a cupboard door opening and everything tumbling out. "Not Big Rita?" she wheezes.

"I've not heard her called that." The name makes me smile. Growing up, I loved having a giantess as a mother. It made me feel safe. "She's pretty tall, though."

"Well, I never." Marge sits back in her chair, aghast. Two scones arrive, jam and cream dolloped on the side. She stares at the plate, as if they've dropped there from outer space.

"So you know her."

She nods dumbly.

"Don't tell me you were the housekeeper?" I say, half joking. "At Foxcote Manor?"

Her eyes agitate in their sockets. She opens her mouth to say something, then thinks better of it. *She was. She bloody well was,* I think.

My blood whooshes in my ears. "Mum stayed down here in August nineteen seventy-one."

"Nineteen seventy-one?" As her face opened a few seconds ago, it closes again. Her eyes glint metallically. The big jaw tenses. "You're the police, aren't you? Not Rita's daughter at all." With some effort, she creaks down to look under the table at my legs and nods, something affirmed. "Too short to be Rita's daughter."

"I'm not a policewoman. I give you my word."

But it's too late. She's standing up, walking stick stuck out, a proboscis.

"But you haven't eaten your cream tea."

She snatches a scone off the plate and tosses it into her shopping bag.

I slap a ten-pound note on the table and follow her outside as Casey watches, bemused.

It's raining now, splashy earth-smelling drops. Marge may be old, but she's determined, and makes steady progress down the street, pretending I'm not there. After a minute or two, we arrive at a row of small cottages, their pebble dash dirty, melancholy in the rain. She stands outside the most run-down of the lot. Grubby nets hang at the window. I notice a man's bicycle leaning up against the wall.

Her hand flails about in her leatherette handbag for her key. "You've got no business here."

"Actually . . ." But I can't say it. My denial is so ingrained, pressed into me like whorls in wood.

"There. Thought so," says Marge with a note of triumph. "You lot always give yourselves away. Children playing at cops, the lot of you."

But something beats inside me. I think of Steve, all the years of marriage, in which he'd say, "You're a Broom now. Don't taint Annie with your history." Don't put our friends off their dinner. Okay, he didn't say the last line. But he might as well have. I think of the newspaper cuttings my mother stashed away. And I feel more determined than ever. "I'm just trying to find out about what happened that summer."

"Oh, you're only about forty years too late! Haven't you got proper crimes to solve?" She stabs her key in the door. "We've had three robberies in six months. No one arrested for those!"

"Marge, I *am* Rita's daughter. Her adopted daughter."

"Adopted, eh?" I wonder if something's slipping into place or if it's my imagination. Her eyes narrow again. "Not one of them reporters?"

A gaggle of geese fly above us. "I'm a makeup artist."

She huffs disparagingly. "And I'm Princess Margaret."

"Off duty." I smile, trying to get her onside. "But I do have a large box of false eyelashes of varying lengths in the boot of my car for emergencies. Do you want to see them? I also have a couple of new tester lipsticks in my handbag. Here. Look. Brand-new. I've not used them." I pull out one from my handbag pocket, retro, in a satisfying silvery case. "Would you like it?"

"Bribery now, is it?" She looks at it hungrily.

"You'd suit this shade. It'd bring out your eyes."

"Oh, get inside, then. Watch the packing boxes." She whips the lipstick from my hand, clunks the front door shut behind us, and shouts shrilly into the small dark house, "Fingers! Put the kettle on. We've got company."

40

Rita

The evening with Robbie returns to Rita in small aftershocks, ricocheting up her thighs, across her hip bones. Her body's still humming, despite the terrible sight on the living-room floor. If the terrarium's wanton destruction had happened earlier in the day, she'd have splintered into fragments too. But right now? A feather pillow seems to be wedged between her and the universe.

After bathing Teddy and putting him to bed, Rita has calmed down a bit. (It's hard to stay upset and angry when Teddy's making fart noises with a wet flannel.) Petty and violent, that's what Don is. Nothing more. The smallest of men. She'll spell things out when she sees him, that's for sure. He'll have to leave. She'll say to Jeannie, *It's him or me. Enough's enough.*

Rita presses her nose to the hall's cool window glass, squinting through the gaps in the ivy. She wonders where Don has gotten to. Probably weaving his way back from the pub through the gloaming on ale-legs. Or chatting up a forest girl by the bar. Damn him.

She bends down to the skirting board for Robbie's boots, the ones that started everything, thrilling slightly as she points her socked foot and slowly slips it into the soft, leathery interior.

"Thanks for coming with me, Big Rita," Hera says, watching as Rita tightens the laces. "When I find the thing I shot, I'll feel better. Promise I'll go to bed then."

"Don't worry. We'll find it," whispers Rita, not wanting to disturb Jeannie and the baby, who are dozing upstairs. She wishes she didn't have to go out again, that she could stay and attend to her terrarium plants, pick the glass shards off bit by bit, like fleas from a beloved pet. She also rather hopes any deer is dead, that she won't have the grim duty of putting the poor creature out of its misery. "Come on."

Outside, Rita's not seen a night sky so pretty, all velvety folds backlit by a harvest moon, with a pale gold corona. A mist is starting to stream along the ground. The forest has never looked more magical or benign, a place of sanctuary, not a mass of trees of different species, but a sentient ancient being, with its own moods and soul. She catches herself and smiles. Where's the old Rita gone? She should be peering into these forest shadows, sensing watching eyes and gnashing teeth and hearing the sound of her parents' car crashing over and over again. She inwardly jolts, as you do at the odd moment when one version of yourself becomes another, and you grow up not incrementally but in one unexpected gliding-forward leap, as if taking a step on the moon.

"The logs, yes, we went past the log pile." Hera tugs on her arm, drawing her out of her thoughts. "I think it was this way."

As they walk, Rita feels an unexpected surge of elation. Possibility. The future is pliable. Something she can shape, as Robbie can bend steamed wood. The malignant thing that's squatted over her for years, the burden of her shameful secret, has lifted. Nan warned her against telling anyone. "Not even friends, who'll tittle-tattle," she'd say, and ruin her reputation. But in telling Robbie, opening up, although she's not removed it, she's taken away much of its power and weight. She's considering this revelation when she sees movement, a flicker of someone in the trees. "Don?" she calls. Nothing. She turns to Hera. "Did you see someone too?"

Hera shakes her head and stares into the gloom, her round face mushroom-pale. The mist licks their ankles.

"Don? Are you there? Are you lost?"

Again, silence. Whoever was there has gone. Or doesn't want to be found. Maybe it wasn't him. Fingers? Unease slides silkily over her skin. Her confidence wavers. "Let's go home, Hera. It's too late for this. We can come back in the morning."

"Just as far as the stream? Then we'll turn back. Please."

They carry on walking until they can hear the sound of rushing water. It sounds louder in the dark, like a river. "I really don't think you hit anything, Hera. And if you did, it's trotted merrily home." She takes Hera's warm, pudgy hand. "Let's loop along the other path. Quicker back that way."

A round black cloud slips over the moon, like a sunglasses lens. Oh, for a torch. Still, if they keep going, they'll see Foxcote's brightly lit windows soon enough. And she's not scared. Not even nervous! It's like when pain stops, and even though it was excruciating while it lasted, you can no longer recall it. She wonders if she could live in the forest after all, with Robbie, in his sweet, scuffed cottage, rather than move back to the London house. And she's thinking, *Yes, maybe I could,* when her foot lands on something soft and fleshy and Hera screams and screams, and all those lovely possibilities, all those other Ritas, powder to dust.

41

———— ❄ ————

Hera

Don's eyes are open, staring at the star-spattered sky. Big Rita's boot has left a muddy imprint on his cheek. Blood blooms on his safari shirt, on the left-hand chest pocket. An owl hoots. Once. Twice. A death warning come too late. Big Rita touches the side of his neck and gasps, snatching away her hand.

"Don't look." She presses my face to her cardigan.

But I peer down, fascinated and horrified. The problem of Don has gone. But Don is dead. *Dead.* He no longer exists. My stomach flips.

"We need . . ." Her heart *ba-booms* against my cheek. "We need to get help."

As if she's summoned it, there's a noise behind us. "There you are!" Mother's voice rings out, a laugh inside it.

I can feel Big Rita's heart banging harder.

"Is the rascal drunk?" Mother asks, walking toward us, smoothing her hair, trying to make herself pretty. Her dress glitters, the teeny mirror chips trailing light. "I should have known he'd hunt down a pint in the end, not a pheasant."

Big Rita says softly, "Jeannie . . ." then covers her mouth with her hand because she can't say it. Nor can I. We stare at my mother, pitched on the edge, her last sweet moment of not knowing.

"Why are you looking at me like that? What's going on?" She runs toward him and kneels down and holds his face, smacking his cheeks. "Wake up, my love . . ." It's as though she can't see the blood at all. "It's me. Your Jeannie. Don . . . Don . . . Please."

Big Rita puts an arm around her shoulders. "He's gone, Jeannie."

She lets out a noise that isn't like Mother. It isn't human. I cover my ears with my hands. Her face is a mask, stiff and white, the mouth turned down. Sinking to the ground, she curls around his body. Don's blood glistens in her hair, like one of her jeweled hair slides.

"I don't understand. I don't . . ." Mother's voice is a rasp. A whisper. A ghost. "How?"

The forest stills. Big Rita says nothing. She doesn't even glance at me. And I know this means she isn't going to mention my name, or that I thought I'd shot something. Not someone. I could get away with it. Mother never need know. This makes it worse. And I think how all the thoughts and noises and smells that were Don have gone forever. How I've wanted to kill him for days. "I didn't mean to do it."

42

※

Rita

Rita watches Hera run, legs flashing, until the mist rubs her away. A volt of shock travels down her spine. The nightmare on the ground flashes, pulses—real, unreal. Her brain can't register it. Don is marble white. A fallen statue. Jeannie is cradled over him, mewling, the chips of mirror work on her dress glinting, dark stars.

Rita's mind loops, trying to find a way out. Don is dead. Hera thinks she did it. And Rita can smell blood. Meat. Like Fred's butcher's shop counter. And something sweeter, riper, draining out of his body, sinking into the earth. A stag beetle is already investigating Don's outstretched hand, the stiffening fingers curling inward.

She shudders and tries to collect herself. But she can't think straight. Jeannie is groaning, shaking. The temperature of the air seems to plunge. Rita kneels down, hugging Jeannie's shoulders. She can feel Jeannie's goose bumps against her own skin, a birdlike tremble in her bones. "Jeannie," she whispers. She can't think of what else to say, how to make things better. "Jeannie . . ."

Very slowly Jeannie looks up, her face contorted and ugly with grief. "Hera did it?" she breathes, gagging her sobs with cupped hands.

"I don't know. I don't . . . know." And Rita doesn't. She truly can't believe it. "She thought she was shooting a deer . . ." The words buckle.

"It . . . it looks bad," stammers Jeannie.

Rita can't deny this.

"Hera will be sent to an institution." Jeannie covers her mouth with a hand and groans, that sound again, deep and raw, coming from a place Rita isn't sure she's been. "Like The Lawns. Or worse, much worse. Oh, god."

Rita's horror at Don's death tips into something else. Fear for those left behind. Hera wouldn't survive such a place. She wouldn't last a week. The beetle is on his arm now, a moving black spot.

"The gun?" Something has changed, sharpened, in Jeannie's face. "Where's the gun?"

"Hera dropped it." Rita's teeth involuntarily start to chatter. "I—I don't know where."

"We must dig!" Jeannie grabs Rita's arm, her fingernails biting sickles into Rita's skin. Her eyes grow wild. "Come on." She stands up, pulling Rita with her.

"Dig?" The word curdles sickeningly. "What . . . what do you mean?"

"Bury him. We'll say he left. Arabia. Yes, yes," jabbers Jeannie, manically. "He left for Arabia yesterday."

Rita blinks. She feels cornered. Snared. Her power draining away. Fred was right: she's going down with their ship.

"Hera's life is ahead of her. Don's gone. But we can save Hera. We must, Rita." Jeannie glances about in a frenzy. "No one has seen us. No one will ever know. You'll help me, won't you? For Hera's sake? I can't lose everyone I love. I can't, Rita. For pity's sake, help me."

Rita agitates at the edge of acquiescence. The urge to say yes and relieve some of Jeannie's agony is overwhelming. And yet. Something inside—forged in the heat of her evening with Robbie, a tiny granite fragment—resists.

"Rita?" Jeannie begs. She shakes her by the arms, back and forth. "You are so strong. I can't do this on my own. Please."

The trees seem to lean toward Rita then, narrowing the night sky, entombing her in the dark. She thinks of her mother inside the glowing lantern of the blazing car, her hands splayed on the glass; her mother dying, not growing, like the plants Rita's nurtured all these years, trying, she suddenly realizes, to reverse those forces. The joy she finds in small things. A fern frond unfurling. A crystal of sea salt on the tip of her tongue. New socks.

Her life is insignificant, she knows that. One of a plain single woman, lacking riches or status, never to have a family of her own or anyone to mourn or miss her. But dare she risk that life, however small and modest, for a prison cell? For the Harringtons?

"We need spades." Jeannie tugs her harder now. "Come on."

"I can't bury him, Jeannie." The hardest thing she's ever said. Tears slide down her cheeks. "I'm so sorry."

"What?" gasps Jeannie. "But you have to—I'm telling you . . ."

And then they hear it. The sound of something in the trees. Twig snaps. Footsteps. *Voices.* Rita puts a finger to her lips. They stand rigid, not daring to exhale. And just when they think the people have gone, a beam of torchlight reaches toward them through the swirling mist, like a jailer's arm.

43

Sylvie

"Good riddance, that's what we said." Marge sips her sherry and splutters on it, with a small laugh. The residue gleams greasily on her upper lip. She's enjoying an audience. "Didn't we, Fingers?"

"No, Marge," Fingers hisses through gritted teeth and a rictus smile. "Rest in peace. *That*'s what we said when Armstrong got tragically shot, Marge. Rest in peace."

The live-in carer is odder than his name, tall, shoelace thin, with a shock of ice-white hair and a pearly translucence to his face and eyes. Unable to stay still, he stalks around Marge's living room, like an agitated survivor of a hideous natural disaster. "She gets in a right muddle." He makes an exaggerated whirly sign with a finger at his temple, which only makes everything else seem even more unhinged. He offers me the plate of biscuits. "Another fig roll?"

I shake my head, unable to rip my eyes from the old woman in the chintz armchair, holding the silver-cased lipstick aloft, moving it back and forth for a long-sighted inspection, and murmuring, "Looks just like a bullet, come to think of it."

Fingers stiffens at her side and lets out a strangled laugh.

"I married a man just like Armstrong," Marge continues blithely. She takes the lid off the lipstick and sniffs. "Bastard. Lived a double life. Didn't give a damn who he hurt. This does smell fancy."

"Who did it?" I ask, trying to fill in the headlines of an imaginary newspaper article. My mind winds back to the pap-snap of a broken-looking Walter Harrington, hurrying from courthouse to car. "Who shot Armstrong, Marge?"

To my astonishment, Marge starts to giggle. Fingers looks like he might grab a cushion and smother his charge at any moment. A chilling thought streaks through my head: *He did it.*

Then another. No one knows where I am. I've got scratchy mobile reception. I'm not entirely sure where I parked the car. This stuffy room is fogging my brain, trapping me in 1971 by means of its swirly green carpet and peeling wallpaper, the color of horses' teeth. The cluttered house's desolate air is made worse by the cardboard boxes stacked against the walls, the bin liners, slumped, half full of rubbish: an imminent move into sheltered accommodation. "Won't go," she's already told me defiantly, and I felt for her, knowing she will, and the heartbreak involved in packing up a home, dismantling memories. In the end our houses are furnished less with tables and chairs than with these.

I flinch as Fingers touches my back and I catch the tang of his body odor, almost an animal scent. Like how I imagine an old badger den might smell. "I'll see you out, Sylvie."

"Thanks." I grab my bag, relieved to be going. Caroline's right. I should never have come. What am I doing? I should be with Annie, googling secondhand Bugaboos and debating silly celebrity baby names, not pressing my nose against the past, peering at the horrors inside.

"Oh, but she's Big Rita's girl. Big Rita, remember, Fingers? You had a mad crush on Big Rita once." Marge winks. "You peeping Tom, you."

Fingers's grayish-skinned face blazes. Rain starts to grease the living-room windows.

Marge nods at me. "Now, your mother *could* keep a secret."

And don't I know it.

"Big heart." Another sip of sherry. The alcohol is loosening her. "And feet! Gordon Bennett, those feet. What a lot of trouble *they* caused."

Again Fingers tries to maneuver me out of the room. But I stand firm, sensing the undertow of a different story. "What sort of trouble?"

"Her boot mark on Don's cheek."

Christ. Was Mum a suspect? No wonder she never wanted to speak about it. Then a new possibility, unimaginable seconds before, wheels toward me: Did *Mum* shoot the man?

"She lives in the past, this one." Fingers bends down to my ear. His breath is damp, dank as soil. "But can't remember it right."

Marge rolls her eyes and turns to me, her tone conspiratorial. "Take no notice. I'm all he's got. When you don't have real family, like we don't, you find your own kin. You've always been scared of losing me, haven't you, my little Green Man?"

Fingers bows his head, unexpectedly submissive and boyish all of a sudden. This is not a normal carer/patient relationship, I begin to realize. Something else is going on here. She pats his hand, a maternal gesture and yet also an assertion of dominance. "Settle down or I'll dock your supper," she murmurs under her breath. And for a moment he just stands there, chastised, silent, swaying like a tall tree.

"Anyway, I call a spade a spade," she says, turning back to me, seeming to pick up our conversation about Armstrong again. "Only cared about that truncheon dangling between his legs. Ruining things for that baby, he was."

"Jo's baby?" I test, sure they must be able to hear my heart thumping. My tiny unknown self slips into the conversation, silk over glass.

"Aye." She looks at me, confused, frowning, trying to place me or something I said. Her gaze grows milkier, clouded by age.

She walked away. I can't get beyond this. But I still must ask: "Do . . . do you remember her surname?"

"Why do you want to know?" Fingers asks, springing back to life and widening his eyes at Marge, some sort of warning.

"I . . ." Part of me, I realize, is asking because I think I *should*, because you're meant to want to know. We're told that's how adoption tales play out, the long-lost mother, the tearful reunion . . .

"Did you know Jo?" Marge stares at me, frowning. She taps a yellow thumbnail against her front tooth. "What's the connection again?"

"I . . ." Cringing inside, I whisper out the rarely spoken truth: "I was found in the forest that summer."

Fingers's leg starts to bounce feverishly in the corner of my vision.

"What?" Marge's face scrunches, uncomprehending. "What are you saying?"

"I was the abandoned baby, Marge," I say more loudly, stripping the words of their talismanic power. "It was me." Louder still.

Her face chalks. "You're lying!" she hisses.

Fingers mutters, "Codswallop," under his breath.

I'm so taken aback, struck down by the absurdity that it's taken me this many bloody years to speak the truth out loud—and sober—to a stranger, to claim it as my own, only to be accused of *making it up*, that for a moment I don't know what to say and teeter on the verge of hysterical laughter.

"I'd recognize Jo's baby." Her voice breaks. Her rage ruptures, like a wound. Tears spill down the creases of her cheeks. She turns to Fingers, her voice desperate. "Wouldn't I? Even all these years later."

"Of course, dear." Fingers splays his hand on her frail shoulder protectively, talking over her wispy head. "This is all very distressing for Marge. Quite unnecessary."

I'm baffled and frustrated. After years of burying my story, rejecting it, I feel the urgent need to own it. Because it's mine, I realize. Running through my veins. Part of me. My own beautiful damage. "But . . ."

"Lies!" Marge throws her fig roll at me and starts to sob. "A cruel trick! Out! Out!"

"Well, Sylvie." Fingers claps his huge white hands together with a twisted smile. "I believe we're done here."

44

Hera

Outside the bedroom window, two fuzzy headlights, like glowing eyes, wind their way through the trees toward us. More police? The ambulance? The two police constables who found Mother and Rita in the woods are now on our sofa, their torches on the coffee table, notebooks on their laps. They're "taking us through the evening" and asking questions, in hushed voices, like people in a library. I feel distant, like I'm watching from the ceiling.

The woman wears serious glasses with magnifying lenses. There's a ladder in her tights. The policeman looks flushed. Their radios constantly hiss and buzz. I worry the noise will wake Teddy and he'll stumble downstairs to discover what's happened. What *has* happened? I want to ask the police for details. Or at least to check my version of events against Big Rita's. My brain is a big blank space, like an ice rink, cold and skiddy. Thoughts can't stand up on it properly. Everything slides about. The policeman keeps staring at me.

A member of the public called the station, he's saying, glancing back at Mother. An anonymous tip-off. He can't quite hide the squeaking thrill in his voice. I guess if you're a policeman, finding a murdered man counts as a good day at the office, especially in this sleepy sort of place. I'm not sure they visit many houses like this, either. The policewoman is staring around the room, her gaze sticking to the grandfather clock, the oil paintings, and then, of course, the terrarium, the sparkling wreck on the floor. I wonder if it'll look like my motive for killing Don. I hope it doesn't look like Big Rita's.

Problem is, Big Rita is acting guilty. She's a bag of nerves, her knee bouncing up and down. Sobs crackle up in her throat; then she swallows them. The baby dozes over her shoulder, wrapped in the yellow blanket, and Rita clings to her little body like she's expecting the police to snatch her out of her arms at any minute. But the police haven't even asked about the baby. They're asking about other things. Big Rita keeps tripping over her words, especially when the policewoman mentions the boot print on Don's face, the boots Rita wore earlier and the police have now slipped into a special plastic bag. "So they belong to Robbie Rigby?" the policeman asks intently. "Correct?"

"Correct," Rita mumbles, and wipes away a tear with the sleeve of her pink cardigan.

"Can you confirm this, Mrs. Harrington?"

"Yes, Officer." You'd never know that she and Don were having one of their "naps" a few hours ago. She looks like a mother again. Her legs are crossed at the ankle. She's covered her floaty black dress with a long cream cardigan—a good idea, since some of the tiny mirrors embroidered into it are pink with blood—and tucked her hair behind her ears so she doesn't look deranged, just sad and shocked, like a woman might be to discover "a family friend" dead in the grounds.

There's a sense of mission about her too. Her jaw is set, her gaze steady. And when the police aren't looking, her eyes burn into me, as if they're desperately trying to tell me something. But I don't know what. Only that she hates me and always will and her hate is part of me now. I worry the police can see it too, because when I look up from my feet, I find them both staring, as if there's something about me they find unsettling. Finally the policeman clears his throat and glances down at his notes. "So, Heerr . . ."—he stumbles over my name, like everyone does—"Hera."

I nod. My heart starts to kick in my ears. I realize it might help if I started crying, like normal girls are supposed to, but I can't. My feelings are all stuck.

"It's important you tell the truth, you know that, don't you?" he says, speaking slowly, as if I were stupid.

"Nothing but the truth." I've heard this on the telly.

Mother chokes back a small sob and shakes her head at me like the truth is the last thing I should be telling. This is confusing, because all my life Mother's said, "Just tell the truth, Hera. I'll be less cross with you if you just tell the bloody truth." And who else could have shot Don *but* me?

Also, there's a relief in being caught. I know what happens next. I'll be taken away from Teddy to live with other bad, dangerous children, somewhere harsh and lonely, like the school in *Jane Eyre*. Aunt Edie will likely visit, just not every weekend because she's so busy and abroad all the time. Big Rita will come and arrange her face into a smile. Will Mother? Probably not. Why should she forgive me? She'll go back to Daddy, and Baby Forest will take my place. Teddy will love his new sister just as much. Daddy will be grateful Mother's happy. And I can't blame anyone but myself. Everything's been leading to this point, I realize, from the moment I draped the curtains across the lamp's scorching lightbulb in Primrose Hill. I didn't burn down the house, not completely. But I ended up destroying everything just the same, like I always feared I would.

"So Hera went out with her brother Teddy and the deceased and a . . ."—he clears his throat—"gun?" The policewoman flicks Mother a sideways look of disgust, as if to say, *What sort of mother are you?*

"It was Don's idea," says Big Rita. "He said they were in safe hands."

The policeman raises an eyebrow. "Go on, Hera."

Upstairs, the sound of the cuckoo clock. It makes me think of the woodpecker, the one that lives outside Big Rita's bedroom window, and I wonder if I'll ever hear it again, if they'll take me now or in the morning.

"Can you try to tell us, Hera?" the policewoman says more kindly.

"I thought I saw a deer, something moving . . ."

"Stop!" Mother leaps up, her hands scrunched at the fabric of her dress. "Officer, this interrogation of my traumatized daughter is unnecessary. The poor girl is barely cogent. It's far too soon. And we need a lawyer."

"Mrs. Harrington, please sit down. Your daughter seems quite able to cooperate. We have to establish the sequence of events. We'll all need to do an official statement at the station."

The station? Tonight, then. I go tonight. I feel a surge of terror. Big Rita starts to sob onto the baby's fluffy hair.

"You're wasting your time." We all turn to look at Mother. Something in her voice commands attention. "It was me. The shotgun is still in the woods somewhere. If you look, you'll find it. Now, if you please, I'd like to call my lawyer and my husband."

What? What's Mother doing? I catch Big Rita's shocked eyes, rolling, enormous, full of white.

"The medication for my . . . condition." She taps her temple and winces and lets out a mad little laugh. "It affects my vision, Officer. Doesn't it, Rita? So I shouldn't have held a gun, any gun, knowing this. It was an accident."

I'm no longer sure what's going on. The room cracks and splits with my raggedy breaths and tears. I see Big Rita looking at me, mouthing, "It's okay." But it can't be. Bright car headlights are already sweeping through the living-room windows. The sound of a car pulling up on the gravel.

"You can put your hands down, Mrs. Harrington. I won't cuff you." And I beg them not to take her.

"Get the girl something sweet," I hear the policewoman say to Big Rita.

Big Rita has to hold me back and pull me against her and the baby, who has woken up and started to cry. As the police walk Mother between them out of the room, she grabs my hand and squeezes it. And for the first time in months, I feel her love flow through my skin into my body, like a color, pink and warm.

Foxcote's front door bangs. We whip around. "Jeannie darling, I'm home." A gust of fresh air. Footsteps. Daddy appears in the doorway, hands frozen in the act of loosening his tie. "What sort of welcome party is this?"

45

Sylvie

I'd planned to drive straight home to London, not looking back.
But after the profound weirdness of Marge's house, I find myself
unable to do so. Half an hour after Fingers slammed the front door,
my hands are still unsteady. I feel fuzzy-headed, pixelated. So I sit
in the car, listening to Nick Cave, collecting the scattered bits of
myself together, as the rain patinates the windscreen. I roll the
name Jo around my mouth and wonder why I'm actually relieved
not to have found out her surname too. Is this a normal reaction?
Or just cowardice? Further evidence that I can't face up to my own
pedigree. I taste mascara. I'm crying. The windows fug up.

Then the rain stops. Sun slices through the cloud, hot and irre-
sistible, and I feel a bit silly. Getting out of the car, I inhale the
sweet grassy wet. My head clears. My mood lightens. And I suddenly know what I need to do before I leave this place. See it for
myself. Alone.

A forest, I realize, stepping into it, succumbing to it, reveals its
true nature only to the solitary walker. And it's indifferent to me.

I've got no more right to exist here than a bramble or a fox. I decide I like this. Liberating. Which way?

The path forks. One side leads to a narrow lane, shadowed by the trees that lock over it in an emerald-green canopy. A shortcut back to the village, perhaps. Lanes always lead somewhere.

Five minutes on, set far back from the road, a high wall. A roof rises above it. Intrigued, I walk back into the woods and around its perimeter until I can get a decent view of the house through its garden gate. Gorgeous. Ridiculously so. It is, I realize, with a dissatisfied pang, a Farrow & Ball house from a fantasy life, the one where I got richer, had a flock of charming, feral children, and married the actor Dominic West. My next life, then.

The sign above its main gate reads WILDWOOD HOUSE. If I owned a house like this, I'd call it that too.

As I stand there, gawping, I mentally style a seventies scene: children running barefoot through the trees, owl feathers in their hair; a young nanny chasing them, calling their names. I lean back against the girth of a vast yew—hundreds of years older than me, with more lines. I feel a wave of affection for this tree and slowly sink to the point that I'm squatting above the ground, which is springy and comfortable, still dry, like rush matting. The birds start chattering, alerting one another to my alien presence.

I check my phone: no signal; one missed call from my agent, Pippa, likely wondering if my compassionate leave will ever end; another from a worried girlfriend, who has started to say, slightly gratingly, "You really must look after yourself now," every time we speak, as if leaving a long marriage is a reckless act of self-sabotage, the gateway drug to the dangerous state of not-giving-a-f*** and un-controlled body hair. I'm glad to have the excuse of no signal, since I can't square my London life with *this*. I can't inhabit both at the same time, I realize. I can't function and be both people. So I rope off parts of myself. Which is why I could stay married to Steve for so long, I guess.

I yawn. My body feels catatonically heavy. It's exhausting keeping all the disparate bits separate, the endless collating of self. Am I defeated by such a process or starting to relax? Both, perhaps. I wonder if this is why forest bathing is a thing.

A memory bobs to the surface. Dad and I walking along the beach near the cottage. Dad bending down and picking up drift-wood, pale and smooth, hollowed inside. "Like a skull," I said. Dad saying, "Yes, exactly, Sylvie, just like that," and telling me that if you cut open a human brain, slice it really thin, like salami, and peer at it under a microscope, you'll see trees. Dendrites, they're called. And all your thoughts, all the tiny electrical messages, shoot from branch to branch. "We have woods inside us, Sylvie," he said, then hugged me and kissed the top of my head.

His words feel wise and true today. It feels as if I might even be reconnecting with a lost part of myself, the little girl who would climb trees to feel the sway of the top branches, her head crowned with leaves. I close my eyes and spin out to the aurora borealis wa-vering across my eyelids. The ground seems to rock. And then it happens. A shadowy shape emerges, like a grainy ultrasound image. Me as a baby. Lying on a tree stump. Crying.

"Excuse me, are you okay? Do you need help?"

The noise stops. Oh, god, it was coming from me. I open my eyes, look up, and see dazzling white teeth. A beard.

"The forest always gives one rather wild dreams." The man is looking at me askance, possibly trying to work out if I'm high. He's very handsome, I register slowly. Blue eyes. "Not local?" he asks, trying to place me.

"London." Long story.

"Ah." He smiles knowingly and nods back at the house. "Are you sure you're okay? If you need to come in, you're welcome."

I brush off leaves from my jeans. "I'm fine, really. Just a bit embarrassed." But I do feel tender inside, wrung out, like after a good weep. "If you could just direct me back to the village, I'd be very grateful. My car's parked there."

"Sure. Back up the lane, then . . ." He pauses and frowns. I suspect my dragged-through-the-hedge-backward hair might be giving off mixed messages. And it's starting to rain, falling in fat splatters. "Look, I was just about to drive into Hawkswell. Do you want a lift?"

I hesitate. Was he really about to drive to the village or is he a psychopathic opportunist? I decide that serial killers probably don't wear beautiful shirts with stripy yellow cuffs. Screw it. I'll take my chances.

"Nice car," I say, strapping on the seat belt. A vintage pea-green Porsche convertible, roof rolled up.

"I think so." The car revs deliciously. "My husband bought it for my fiftieth."

Typical. "Nice husband."

He laughs.

I decide I like him a lot, in the immediate gut instinct way you can do with strangers sometimes. "Thank you . . . ?"

"Teddy," he shouts over the growling engine as we zoom down the lane in a whirl of leaves and rain. "My name's Teddy. Hold tight."

46

S ix months later, Rita still plays her last journey from Foxcote over in her mind: the clunk of the taxi door; the whirl of the first gingery leaves down the lane; the big house receding until it was swallowed by the trees. Like it had never existed. The sickening, lightening relief of escape.

By then five long days had passed since Don had died, and hours of circular questioning by the local police, who wouldn't let any of them leave Foxcote. She wished she'd known then that those constables would later be heavily criticized for their bungling of the case. At the time she was terrified, the possibility that she might be sacrificed to save the Harringtons' reputation never far from her mind.

As she'd once yearned to be at the heart of the Harrington household, she was now desperate to struggle free of it. A family could be the least safe of places, she knew that now, not the harbor she'd idolized since she was a child. In the end, you had to rely on yourself.

As the slow, anxious hours ticked past, she began to see, with thumping clarity, how she'd been sucked into the Harringtons' world—drawn by an irrational longing for her own mother, a family of her own—and lost her bearings. She tried to explain this to the policewoman. But she'd listened with narrowing eyes, taking rapid-fire notes. Rita, scared that she was somehow incriminating herself, was quickly silenced.

A couple of days after Don died, a woman from social services wearing a boxy gray coat arrived. She plucked the baby from the trug on the kitchen floor, as if she were a lettuce. When Rita begged her to wait or at least say where the baby was going, Walter hurried the woman out of the door. That night Rita tucked the Babygros under her pillow, just as Jeannie had once done, and inhaled their milky sweetness.

She couldn't sleep more than an hour or two. Neither could anyone else. She'd go downstairs at night and often find Hera rummaging through the larder. Or Teddy padding around in his pajamas, confused, asking where his mother was.

Everything felt shattered, just like the terrarium. Walter shoved its Don-wrecked remains into the dustbin and bashed it down with a stick for good measure, as if the little glass case was responsible for it all, which, in a way, it was.

But Rita still crept back to the bin once Walter had gone, defiantly pulled out Dot and Ethel and secretly planted them in the loamy garden bed by the gate. She knew it didn't matter how mangled a plant's leaves were: if the roots were still there, they had a chance. And this thought comforts her. *Children are not unlike plants,* she thinks.

Rita wonders what Hera and Teddy are doing on this cold March morning as thick gray fog rolls over the Hackney rooftops and she shivers in her bedsit. No fat on her now to keep her warm, she's all angles—how the model agency likes it—jutting hip bones and tight skin.

She's been banned from ever trying to contact the family again—a court order, Walter said. The officiousness of such a thing terrifies her, even if she doesn't understand it. Hating the thought of the children feeling abandoned, at Christmas she'd risked a short letter to the Primrose Hill house, addressed to Hera, with her new London details—the bedsit in Hackney, with a cantankerous landlady called Mrs. Catton, blind in one eye, who knocks on the wall if she turns on the radio—but it was returned unopened: *Unknown at this address.* Shamefully, she was relieved. At least Walter hadn't intercepted and read it.

She likes to think that Hera and Teddy, through the force of some as yet unknown physics, are aware she's thinking of them as she stands in chilly workshops, seamstresses pinning fabric around her slender body. But Baby Forest . . . No, the baby is too painful to think about, although that doesn't stop her doing so. All the time. Where is she? Not knowing the baby's whereabouts or fate torments her.

The missing is so physical, a whiplash of pain, she struggles not to cry out. Rita misses her damp, dense weight, the pad of her palm, her musical oohs and aahs, the way she'd nuzzle her wet face into Rita's neck, and those glossy dark eyes always following her around the room. She must have changed so much by now. Sitting up. On solids. Trying to crawl? No. Mustn't go there.

She's tried to follow the story in the news, but there was only one mention of Baby Forest, appealing for her mother to come forward, and many more of Don's death. She's stored some of the articles in the suitcase under her bed, cutting out photos of the family so she doesn't forget their faces. But it's been hard to know what to believe. One tabloid implied Don had taken his own life, revealing staggering debts and rumors he was being hunted down by unforgiving East End gangsters. (Marge was quoted: "He was a shady character. He was trouble.") While in *The Daily Telegraph*'s obituary, Don was described as "a charismatic polymath, raconteur, and man of the world—the very best of Etonians." Soon the story vanished, superseded by some new horror in Northern Ireland. A couple of months later a footnote in *The Times* announced that there hadn't been enough evidence to charge anyone in connection with Don's death. The case remained open. It was, the reporter said, a mystery: there was some ambiguity over whether the fatal bullet matched the suspected gun. Jeannie Harrington was of unsound mind and recovering in an institution, her confession not backed up by hard evidence. Who else had been in the woods that night? the reporter asked. Then: Is this yet another hush-up by the elite classes? Of course it was! Rita had little doubt. Walter—with his winking portly male friends in high places—would have done everything he could to make the story go away. It was bad for business. She also knew he'd been a suspect initially and had suffered the indignity of being taken "down to the station" to account for his whereabouts—until his hotshot London lawyers had got involved.

In those strange dazed days at Foxcote after Don died, Rita was astonished that Walter didn't blame Jeannie for any of this, not even the affair, which he persisted in seeing as a symptom of an illness, something that would be cured. He refused to believe she had it in her to shoot Don, and told the policewoman so, slowly and loudly, as if she were slightly deaf. (He preferred "dealing with the chap.") No, it was easier to blame Rita, not for the murder, although he would if he could, but everything else. She'd "conspired" with Don, he'd hissed, ripping out the damningly blank pages from the notebook and tossing them across the garden, where they'd whirled in the wind, catching on the trees like doves. He never mentioned Baby Forest: it was as if she'd never been there. He was devastated about Don's death—she'd hear him sobbing in the library, muttering his name. "My oldest friend would still be alive if you'd told me what was going on earlier," he'd say. "And my wife would be here. You stupid girl." Part of her knew this to be true. In her determination to do everything right, she'd got it all wrong. But she'd also started to realize that the Harringtons' fateful course was plotted before she'd even joined the family. Jeannie's dissatisfaction in her marriage—including that gilded domestic life—had been the force that had set things in motion, as an exhaled sigh can make the delicate trees on Robbie's mobile start to turn.

It wore her down, gnawed at her, not knowing who'd fired the gun. She kept changing her mind. Hera believed she'd shot him, albeit accidentally. So was Jeannie protecting Hera, her love for her daughter trumping her passion for Don? She hoped so. Then she thought of the ripe bruise Don's fist had left under Jeannie's eye. Jeannie's readiness to bury him in the forest, fodder for the worms and fungi and larvae. And she wondered.

When the police finally allowed her to leave the area, Walter gave her twenty minutes notice before the taxi arrived. All she could do was pack what she could grab and hug the children one last time.

She thought about diverting to Robbie's house but realized she had no idea where it was—"Maybe that way, through the trees?" wasn't really an address, as the cabbie kindly pointed out. She didn't have Robbie's telephone number. Did he even have a phone? And why would he want to say good-bye? She'd caused him enough damage. He'd emerged from the police cells with a shiner and a broken rib, apparently. "The cops would pin it on him if they could," Marge had confided. "Close the case quickly. Keep Walter Harrington and all his lawyers sweet. You know, Rita, it'd be better if you don't contact him again," she'd advised protectively. "He needs to stay out of it, love."

Rita was glad she didn't have his address. Otherwise she might have given in to temptation and selfishly knocked at his door, just to see him one last time. At least they'd had that magical night. She was sure most people live entire lifetimes and never experience anything close.

Seeking what's left of him, she kneels down on the bare boards, avoiding the exposed rusty nails, and pulls her suitcase from under the bed. The leaves he gave her that summer, parceled in paper, are in a bit of a state now, dried and powdery, shattered to just the stem, like fish bones. But she can still read the handwritten tags—*ash, birch, elm . . .* —and likes to do so most days.

The mobile he made is also carefully stored, wrapped in a pair of old tights. She took that for Baby Forest, vowing one day to find her and return it so she'll know there was once a man kind and skilled enough to make that just for her, as a father would; that she was once indulged and treasured, like every other baby in the world.

Peeling back the hosiery, she strokes her index finger over the delicate tiny trees, then collects herself—she can't risk tears or a puffy face today: she's got a casting. Pushing the box back under the bed, she thinks of Jeannie, who hid precious things under her bed once too, and how we all hide the tender bits of ourselves. They feel safer like that. And it's often the only place they fit.

She's pretty sure the landlady, Mrs. Catton, has rummaged through the rest of her things, searching for contraband. ("No alcohol. No smoking. No male visitors. No hot bath deeper than six inches.") It was definitely a mistake to tell her she was modeling to pay the rent.

Anyway, she could hardly have applied for another nanny job, even if she'd wanted to. Modeling has been an unlikely godsend.

She'd been doing twelve-hour days waitressing in a restaurant in Mayfair when the woman from the agency tapped her on the shoulder with a French-polished fingernail. Had she ever considered modeling? She'd thought it was a cruel joke at first. But the woman wasn't laughing: she was sizing up her newly skinny figure, all bones since she'd lost her appetite. Nothing puts you off food like working with it, and she didn't feel she deserved nice things anymore. Suspecting the woman needed her eyes tested, Rita took the stiff cream card and used it as a bookmark for at least a month. The idea that she could model was absurd. Models were beautiful. She was plain. She'd always been plain. Apart from that night with Robbie, when she'd felt like a goddess. In the end, though, curiosity—and money—got the better of her.

Now she earns more in five hours than she did as a waitress in twelve. For the first time in her life, her height is an asset. Her body is on her side. She's found it reassuring and empowering to meet other towering girls with size 10 feet, girls you wouldn't necessarily call pretty, either. No one's laughing at them now. "It's a 'look,'" as the agency woman says, puffing on her cigarette. And one she no longer minds so much.

The work consists mostly of behind-the-scenes fitting model stuff. It was mortifying at first, standing there in her underwear, until she realized she was simply a mannequin and her thoughts were her own. And she liked the brisk, matronly seamstresses, their precision and industry, their light, cool fingers, the maternal way they talk to her sometimes. Her scars mean she can't do catwalk, although there's one photographer—dead famous, sounds like a Cockney market stallholder—who is desperate to photograph her naked and record the scars, "like tribal markings." But she feels strongly that they are her story, not his, and she stubbornly won't do it, much to the frustration of the agency. The last thing she wants is fame. Just money. Independence. Never to be reliant on a man like Walter Harrington again. Any man actually. Soon she'll have saved enough to put down a deposit on a flat of her own. Beyond this, she can't imagine. There's a fog in her brain, like the one over the city today, where her old plans and enthusiasms and the future used to be. She wonders what advice her mother, Poppy, might give, if she were alive. And the wondering makes her feel sad and cheated.

The landlady's distinct three-knuckled rap.

Rita tenses. The old bat. "Yes?"

Mrs. Catton shoves open the door. Her working eye rolls around the room, checking for signs of disrepute. The other, milky and blank, stares straight ahead. She takes a puff of her cigarette—"a landlady's prerogative"—and steps over the threshold. Rita hates the invasion. It always takes her a few minutes to reinhabit the room after she's left. "I've told you the rules, Rita."

"You have," Rita says coolly. Even her voice sounds older and deeper now: she's grown up fast. A few months ago, she'd have been hopping about trying to ingratiate herself. She won't anymore. Not after her experience with the Harringtons. The meek don't inherit the earth. She's no longer scared to take up space. "But I don't believe I've broken any, Mrs. Catton."

The landlady exhales a yellowy twist of Rothmans. "Not yet."

Rita frowns, fighting irritation. "I'm not following, sorry."

"No male visitors," the landlady barks. The puff of breath is putrid.

"I have had no visitors, male or female, since I moved in, and don't intend to. Now, if you don't mind, Mrs. Catton, I've got to get myself ready for work . . ."

Mrs. Catton glances over the hunched bulkhead of her shoulder into the dark communal stairwell, the cigarette balancing between her lips. "Well, there's a fella at the door. I can't get rid of him. Says he has news about some baby."

47

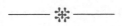

Hera, Now

A cloud of melon vape hangs like the ghost of a fruit salad in the hall. I flap it away with my hands. "What is that dreadful stuff? I preferred it when you smoked like a power station, Edie."

"Darling, you think I don't? But times have changed. And so have I." Edie stuffs the vape machine—it looks unsettlingly like a pistol—into her handbag. "Thanks for an impeccable cup of Earl Grey. Better shoot. On a deadline."

I eye my aunt dubiously, suspecting she's making excuses to leave and escape the conversation and all my angsting. "Really? You haven't got your deadline face on."

Brow furrowed. Bottom lip bitten. The metallic clatter of typewriter keys. I grew up with all of that. Edie was preoccupied a lot of the time. She'd ask me and Teddy about our homework but wouldn't listen to our answers—she was thinking about her writing. "The rabbit did it for me," I said once, as a test, and she said absently, "Great work, darling," and banged out another line of copy. But when the article was finished, she'd always bundle us on to the top of a bus for ice-cream sundaes in Hyde Park or lunch in Piccadilly.

We loved those days. But I haven't tasted ice cream for over twenty years. Or taken the bus in five. Or the tube. Not when the city grows more violent by the day. The flu strains more virulent. And the panic attacks that started after my husband died—and I lost my last buffer against the past—became harder to disguise. Without him, I feel peeled, shucked, vulnerable to every shove and cough. Since the latest family drama kicked off—I mean, when will it end?—I can feel the rev of panic again, the fear that I might unravel like my mother.

"Well, not a deadline exactly. But I'm extremely busy." Edie looks worryingly pleased with herself and waits for me to ask about the source of her latest busyness.

"What with?" I ask, dutifully playing along.

Her lips twitch into a smile. "Setting up an Instagram account."

"Heavens. What on earth about?"

"My newsmag years. Feminism. Fashion. I'm going to turn myself into a national treasure." She grins and rattles the chunky resin bangles on her wrist. "Hell, why not?"

I stare at her for a moment, my tiny withered bright-eyed aunt, framed against the Colefax and Fowler foliate wallpaper, like an exotic bird. "I'm going to put that on your gravestone. *Here lies Edie Harrington, who looked at the world and asked, 'Hell, why not?'*"

She giggles. "I doubt it. Since I'll outlive you, vaping my melon sorbet. Now if you don't mind . . ." She brushes past me, trailing the sharp citric men's cologne she's always worn.

I feel a mix of affection and neediness, as I always do when she leaves, and an urge to hug her, which I never act upon. Most people I've hugged in my life have either died or disappeared. But Edie and

I understand each other, and that's enough. She knows she saved my life.

The leukemia knocked at our door with no warning. Mother was dead two weeks after diagnosis, four months after coming home from The Lawns. The young, bored nanny who'd replaced Rita upped and left, saying the job was too difficult. Daddy tried to be Mother, but he couldn't boil an egg and had business abroad. So Edie gave up her rented apartment and foreign post and moved in to look after us. Nobody could believe it or expected it to work. She couldn't boil an egg, either, but knew where to eat out. She got an editorial job in London, on a magazine, and filled the house with hacks and artists and people who needed a bed for the night. It was a revelation. The conventions and anxieties that had governed my parents' lives simply didn't apply to Edie. She never married. She had a job and a million friends instead. And us. She was the first and only person in my life to say, "Don't worry what other people think, be who you want to be. *Hell, why not, Hera?*" So I did. I reinvented myself. Years later, I even took a photograph of Mother to a plastic surgeon and said, "Can you fix me a nose like hers?" I still look nothing like her.

When Mother was discharged from The Lawns, she didn't resemble herself much, either. She had lost so much weight, and her dark hair had turned white and started to fall out in clumps. But she was delighted to be home, which was, by then, a house in Bloomsbury, smaller and scruffier, far away from the gossips of Primrose Hill. She and Daddy had separate bedrooms with an interlinked door that I think Daddy hoped would one day be unlocked. (It never was.) In a funny way, we were the closest we'd ever been in that house. Everything felt tender and quiet but hopeful, like after surgery.

Edie said to me, "Only the trees know what went on in the woods that night." My father wouldn't speak of it, or of Don. They never discussed the case in front of me. I'd later learn it had fallen apart. Father sold the mine and company shares to pay for the lawyers. I once tentatively asked Mother if she'd really shot Don, and she'd hesitated, her face a cross-stitch of feelings I couldn't read, her eyes full of tears, then replied, "It wasn't you. You mustn't ever think it was you, Hera. That's all that matters." But a part of me did. A part of me still does. I'd shot something that night. And although I didn't try to kill Don, I'd wished him scrubbed from the face of the earth so many times.

Officers would occasionally still come round, and my parents would quickly usher us upstairs. Teddy and I would sit, terrified, huddled together, in case they took Mother away again. Lawyers appeared. Doctors. Newspaper reporters would knock on our front door, and we'd be told to duck from the windows and pull the curtains shut. I've never lost the sense that the world might shoulder-barge into my life again and take away someone I love. I still feel comfortable in my house only with the blinds shut. So Edie's new enthusiasm unnerves me. "Don't put any photos of me on social media, Edie, will you?"

"Cripes, I wouldn't *dare*, darling." Edie opens the front door and grins at the city, the cars and people swimming past. She winks. "You'd break the interweb."

"Internet. It's called the internet, Edie." I touch her sleeve lightly. "Before you go, tell me what to do, Edie. Please." There's only one opinion that counts.

"I've never told you what to do." She purses her lips together, so that all the old smoker's lines ray out. "I don't believe in it." A police helicopter whirs overhead.

"I've tried throwing money at the problem. I've tried reason."

She turns to face me, more sternly. "Have you tried giving up?"

"What?" I laugh, the idea preposterous.

"It's out of your hands, darling. So you either give in fighting. Or you give in with grace and kindness." Edie smiles at me, slightly exasperated. "You'll make yourself ill if you go on like this." She squints down the street. "When's the next number 22 due?"

"God invented taxis for a reason." To save us from crowds and crime and norovirus and me breaking into a cold sweat, unable to breathe.

"Well, you're missing out. The conversations on buses, my goodness. I take notes!"

"You would."

"Good luck." Her clawlike hand squeezes mine. "Let me know how it goes, Hera."

"Don't call me that."

"Oops. The ancient mind slips, darling. Sorry." She doesn't look very sorry. My aunt is constitutionally incapable of regret. But she's kind. "You'll always be Hera to me, my dear plump mad Hera."

"For goodness sake." I shake my head.

"Well, at my age . . ."

"Edie, I've been called Helen Latham for thirty-three bloody years." I flick a bit of lint from her navy jacket collar. "And I weigh one hundred and ten pounds. Thank you very much."

48

Sylvie

Elliot and Annie are sitting a continent apart on the sofa, their eyes drilling into the floor. "How's it going?" I ask unnecessarily.

"Great," Elliot answers when Annie says nothing. The air crackles.

I've given them an hour's privacy: a fake mission to buy a pint of milk. "Did Annie tell you we've bought a cot?" I slide the milk carton I don't need into the fridge. "Two, actually. One for here. One for her dad's. Hugely reduced. A bargain." Still a fortune. Annie made me buy them. I'm a softer touch than Steve. "Didn't expect them to arrive quite so soon, though, did we, Annie?"

"No," Annie says quietly, coloring.

If it were up to Annie, she'd have bought everything by now. Maybe all new mothers try to buy a bit of confidence, not realizing that when the baby's screaming at four in the morning, the brand of changing mat really won't matter. But for Annie I think it's also a way of staving off her fears for Mum, whose condition remains perilous. Partly for this reason, I haven't told Annie about my trip to the forest last week, not wanting to add Marge or Jo to the mix. "A beer, Elliot? I've got some cold ones here."

Annie shoots me an eye-widening look that says, "*Mum.*" Okay, perhaps the meeting to discuss "practicalities" hasn't gone so brilliantly. And I'm making it worse.

"Annie can't drink, so I'll do the same." He shoots a cautious glance at Annie, who looks regally unmoved by such sacrifice. A moment later she glances back at him, pretending not to. I'm aware of a certain hormonal heat in the room.

Elliot stands up, pulls on his shirt cuffs nervously. "Guess I better shoot, then." He waits for Annie to say, *No, do stay.*

She doesn't. "I'm off too."

They both leap up from the sofa with awkward synchrony. "Bye then," murmurs Annie, not meeting his eye.

To my surprise, and Annie's, Elliot reaches out and hugs her. "Let me know if there's anything I can do," he whispers into her hair.

Annie closes her eyes—I'm about to creep away, discreetly—then pulls back roughly, as if coming to her senses. "I'm pregnant, not disabled."

Christ. "He *is* trying," I mouth to her as he shuffles dejectedly to the front door. My heart aches for them both.

❊ ❊ ❊

"It's Elliot's baby in there too, Annie," I say afterward.

Annie picks up her handbag. "It's going to be a Broom, not a Latham."

"I just wonder . . ." I say carefully.

"What?" Annie's nostrils flare, alert for any disloyalty.

"There is a palpable energy between you two. I can feel it."

"A sort of you-screwed-my-life sort of energy?"

"No. A spark. An attraction. The way he hugged you, Annie . . ."

She scoffs. But her eyes fill with tears. She looks away, trying to hide them from me.

"Could you not *try* to make it work, sweetheart?"

She bites down on her lip and shakes her head, muttering something about Elliot not wanting the baby, Elliot wasting no time moving on to someone else.

I wonder if it's the same girl Helen described on the phone to me. "Family friend, works at Christie's. Very tolerant of the Situation," she'd said. "Maybe you could have a little chat with Annie about it." The cheek.

"Anyway, it's much better for the baby to have always known their parents separated, than to try and fail and psychologically damage them with a split," she says. "All the experts say so."

Ouch. I bite my tongue, trying not to take it personally.

"I'm going to see Granny." She walks to the front door and opens it. London rushes in, humid and heavy. "Play her the forest recording again. The woodpecker."

My thoughts run, screaming, arms in the air, back in the direction of the forest. Marge. Fingers. "Okay, Annie. Good luck."

❋ ❋ ❋

I can't stop thinking about Marge's ramblings. *Muddled*, Fingers said. But she's certainly not gaga. In fact, she seemed relatively lucid, albeit off message. I don't know what to believe.

I've picked up the phone to call Caroline many times, then put it down again. I don't want to send her loopy too. Also, old habits die hard: I can't shift the belief that if I keep all this secret, I can contain it, shape it, stop the past spewing onto the present. And the present is growing more urgent. Every day, Annie's unborn baby journeys closer to the cot in the bedroom, over which the tree mobile hangs, quivering, waiting.

I've done my bit, haven't I? Taken Annie to the forest, at least. Why risk digging deeper? Mum was protecting us from something, I'm sure of that now. In this strange hinterland between life and death, a place where I cannot grieve for her or move on, I make a decision to leave it alone. Right now, my focus needs to be on the baby. Annie. Mum. Work.

I write an email to my agent, trying to sound dynamic: *Dear Pippa, How are things? Can we have a catch-up on the phone this week?* I press send. The doorbell rings.

"Sylvie." Helen marches into my apartment. Intense. Wearing flats. Something's up. Has Elliot reported back already? Maybe he doesn't want his firstborn sleeping in an end-of-line bargain cot but instead in something festooned with antique Parisian lace. "How was the cold war summit?"

I hesitate. Settle on optimism. "They'll get there." She looks worried at such a prospect. "Helen, come and see the nursery." For once, Annie's room is scrupulously tidy due to Elliot's visit. I can risk it.

"Very early to do the nursery, Sylvie. You don't want to tempt Fate." For a moment she seems frightened, as if the worst thing wouldn't be Annie's having the baby but Annie's losing it.

"God, I know. But the cot arrived yesterday and Annie insisted we erect it and see what it looked like. I spent hours in flat-pack purgatory last night. You've no idea. Have a peep. Annie's out. She won't mind." She will. But I want to reassure Helen that we're more together than we appear. Also, she suggested Elliot coming over today. Her razor edges appear to be blunting a little.

I open Annie's bedroom door. The light from the canal is wavering on the walls. The room is aglitter. "Sweet, isn't it?"

She stands in the doorway, her hands steepled over her nose. I wait for her to say something. She simply points to the windowsill, where the terrarium basks in the sunlight.

"Oh, Annie loves that."

"It's one of mine. I . . . I have a company. A small terrarium company."

The hairs on my arms prickle. "Someone gave it to my mum. She's in hospital . . ." I stop, seeing the expression on her face.

"Good Lord. That . . . that." She points at the forest mobile over the cot, slowly spinning in the breeze from the open window. "Where did you get that?"

"Oh, it's very old. My father made it."

"Your *father*?" she splutters.

"He was a carpenter." Pride swells my voice. "A very good one."

At this news Helen appears to short-circuit, her mouth opening and closing, her eyes bugging. "Who was he?" She clicks her fingers. "Name. Name!"

"Robbie Rigby. His stuff's quite collectible now. Have you heard of him?"

49

Hera, Now

I hear myself make a small ugly gasp. Sweat glues my silk shirt to
my spine. It's like riding a nuclear menopausal flush. I lower myself to Annie's bed, covering my mouth with my hand, trying to
soothe myself with the familiar chemical smell of new gel nails. I
must contain the feelings. The panic. Breathe, Helen, breathe.

I can't make sense of it.

Hanging over the cot is the wooden tree mobile that's turned in
my dreams for forty-odd years. Beside the window is the terrarium
I had made especially by my company's finest craftswoman a few
weeks ago.

"Your mother in hospital." My voice comes out as a croak.
"What's her name?"

"Rita." She hesitates. "Rita Murphy." I glance at the tree mobile
again, shaking my head, unable to take it in. Sylvie adds, "She kept
her maiden name."

"Big Rita," I whisper, the words sweet and as rare as cheesecake
in my mouth. So she *did* marry Robbie. And she had a family of
her own. Feeling a mix of joy and childish envy, I stare at Sylvie,

searching for likeness. Although much darker, she looks a bit like Robbie, with those high cheekbones and glinting forester eyes. But Big Rita? No. She certainly didn't get the legs. But then, there's not much of Mother in me.

"It wasn't you who left the terrarium at the hospital for Mum, was it?" Sylvie asks with a nervous laugh.

"I wanted to replace what my family destroyed."

"Your family?" Sylvie steps away from me. Her eyes flash black gypsy gold. She crosses her arms over her chest.

"Your mother was my nanny. When I was a girl." As I say the words, I fight a frightening surge of emotion. It suddenly feels like the protective rind over my heart might split like a dry heel. "Sorry. May I have a glass of water?"

Sylvie doesn't answer. She doesn't offer me water, either. Her eyes are narrowing to sickles. A question is moving behind them.

"The accident was in the newspaper. The cliff fall." I talk into the awkward silence, feeling the need to explain myself. "After all this time. There she . . ."—my voice cracks phlegmatically—"was."

Sylvie's hands, dexterous makeup artist's hands, flex and fist at her sides. Her face has drained of color, and all that's left is a powdery frost of highlighter on her cheeks.

"I called the hospital, the one mentioned in the paper. Learned she'd been transferred to a specialist unit in London." I wince, recalling how I intimidated the young assistant on the desk into giving me the information. "Is she out now? Better?"

"Not yet." Sylvie's lower lip convulses minutely. She's staring at me with a discomforting intensity.

"I had no idea she was your mother. Didn't even know your mother was ill. Elliot doesn't tell me anything! Nothing! I have to read him like a rune stone. We're not close . . ." My voice fissures again. I disguise it with a cough. My eyes sting, as if I'm slicing shallots. I blink the tears back. I never cry. I *can't* cry. "Your mother . . . gosh, your mother, she was . . . an inspiration. A complete inspiration. For my company. Everything. They were for her. Shattered things mended. Broken glass recycled, blown again . . ."

"I know who you are."

Something inside me jerks. I reach for the scars behind my ears, the seam between Hera and Helen. She doesn't know. She can't. "I . . . I beg your pardon?"

"The girl from the old newspaper my mother kept." Her voice deepens with a dawning certainty. "The Harrington girl."

No, no. Not her. I lift my chin, arrange my face into Helen, and try to smile. "I think you must be mistaken," I say weakly, and both of us know she's not.

"Your eyes." Sylvie squints, like she's looking right through me. "Just the same."

I'm about to protest, deny it all, but outside the window, a man starts strumming a guitar. And for a reason I cannot fathom, I find I can't lie to the sound of that guitar, the notes vibrating with summer and hope. Or to Sylvie.

"I'm right, aren't I? Helen?"

I bow my head. The exposure is raw and painful, like skin peeled back.

"Shit, Helen." Sylvie sits down on the bed and drops her head into her hands. She looks up at me, dragging at her cheeks with her fingers. "Does Elliot know Annie's granny once worked for your family? The connection?" Her voice is faint.

I shake my head. "Elliot wouldn't even know Rita's name." My foot starts to tap involuntarily, slacks tightening over my skinny thigh. "I've never told him . . ." I stop. "Something terrible happened to my family once. A long time ago. We were pariahs. Our world fell apart. I . . . I changed my name, you see. Married. Built a new life."

She's frowning at me. "But why didn't Elliot mention your terrarium business to Annie? If he had, she'd have said something when she saw that one over there."

"I guess he didn't want to talk about me." I lower my gaze, humiliated. *Screwed-up woman,* she's no doubt thinking. Not close to her son. *Liar. Pretender. Bad mother.* But when I look up again, Sylvie's eyes are soft, like she understands. "Helen," she says, "there's something about me you should know."

50

Rita, October 1972

A half-chewed Farley's Rusk pulps in Sylvie's clutched fist as she sleeps behind the stripy windbreak. Rita removes it, flicks away the sand bugs, and covers her little girl carefully with a pink blanket, one she hand-knit on summer evenings. Today is one of those glorious late-autumn days, unseasonably warm. But the breeze is cool, hinting at the winter months, the stews, roaring fires, and hunkering down to come.

Rita picks her shoreline finds out of a red bucket, her hands working quickly, deftly, and spreads them in an arc, like a deck of cards. "There," she says, glancing up at Robbie with a smile, and feeling that immediate catch, weakening, whatever it is, that still happens low in her belly every time she locks gazes with her husband.

Robbie is lying on his side, resting his head on his hand, his expression receptive and quiet. His hair has grown longer since their wedding in May—Hackney register office, a short white Miss Selfridge dress, a model friend as a witness, drinks in the pub afterward, bliss—and is sun-bleached from his daily sea swims, as far out as the fishing boats, cove to cove, like a native. There's a wallet-shaped faded square on the front pocket of his jeans, their house keys bulging in the other. Behind him, the sun is gold as Devon butter, and starting to sink.

"If I had some string, I'd tie labels to each item, like you did my leaves," she adds teasingly, feeling a beat of pleasure just looking at him. "For reference. Lest you forget."

His smile spreads slowly. He has a self-taught, encyclopedic brain and never forgets anything. Slightly annoyingly, he can already identify all the different seaweed that washes up on their little local beach—gutweed, red rag, egg wrack, oyster thief, dead man's rope . . . He says he's well on the way to becoming an arenophile. ("A what?" "A sand lover.") She hopes so. His cottage has sold now, and the forest is a place to which they daren't return.

They moved to Devon from London last month. Although a bit of her misses the city—Robbie does not—she's glad to be out of their poky rental apartment, and Sylvie can breathe fresh air, not the fumes from the number 30 bus.

Every morning she wakes to the gulls' cries and a novel set of feelings: she's on holiday; she's come home. Not just the abstract idea of home, like she had before, that confused mash of yearning and other people's houses. But home as a simple place of belonging.

They have big plans. Self-sufficiency. Veg. Fruit. Chickens. And a carpentry studio, which he's started to build in their generous garden, the woodworking equipment under a tarpaulin for now. The house itself is tiny and tongue-and-grooved, like a ship's cabin—she can stretch out her arms in Sylvie's nursery and touch the opposing wonky walls—but it's all they can afford. And it's about as far from the forest as they could get without falling into the ocean.

Home is wherever they are together, Robbie says. His adaptability amazes Rita. And yet she's aware of the sacrifice he's made. Sometimes she'll find him on the beach, a silvered lump of driftwood in his hands, his fingertips running over it, as if communing, absorbing its long journey from seedling to sea.

"Urchin." She points to each shell in turn. "Artemis. Razor clam. You don't want to step on that. Common whelk. Periwinkle. You can eat those. Needs a good squirt of lemon, though." He nods, listening carefully. But in typical Robbie fashion, he doesn't say anything, lets her jabber on. "Oh, and this is actually a seabird bill. Probably an oystercatcher. See the shape? To hammer open mollusks . . . Don't you dare ask me for the Latin name!"

He laughs and reaches toward her, holding her face in his hands, rough palms light on her cheeks. They often end up like this, just staring at each other, grinning stupidly. But today is different. Today there is something else hovering. Unresolved. She can see it in his eyes, a cloud, a question mark.

Sylvie, ever attuned to moments of parental intimacy, wakes and strains to pull herself up and totter off. A feisty and inquisitive infant, she's drawn to the sea, always making a break for it. They have to watch her like hawks.

"Come here, you." Robbie brushes the sand from Sylvie's pudgy feet, then lies back, wheeling her above his head so she giggles, her delight growing frenzied.

Rita watches them, smiling. But something nags. She tries to identify the feeling, the vague sense of misplacement. But it slips away. She just knows it's made worse by perfect family moments like this. The wispy beach grass waving in the wind. The dark jewel of the sea. The sheer *excess* of loveliness.

Robbie shoots her a sidelong glance. Sylvie tugs his nose, wanting his attention, Daddy's girl. "You're thinking about it again, aren't you? What we talked about last night."

Rita nods and lowers her eyes.

Robbie lies down, Sylvie on his chest. She paddles her feet and snatches fistfuls of sand, throws it. "It's a risk, Rita. Even attempting to . . . I mean, Walter . . ." He stops. His face darkens. Walter's name is never spoken without a hard swallow afterward.

Rita doesn't want to push their luck, either. They've got so much. She didn't think it was possible to feel this happy. "Yes, mad idea."

Sylvie lurches forward and grabs the periwinkle shell, turning it in her fingers. When she tries to taste it, Rita takes it from her mouth and shakes her head. But she doesn't remove it. This is Sylvie's world, hers to explore. Robbie is adamant about that. He even sits Sylvie on an alarmingly high apple-tree branch in the garden, holding her carefully, but letting her enjoy the sensation, her legs kicking free. Rita's glad the lady at the adoption agency never got to see that.

"Rita." Robbie nudges her bare foot with his own. "We can't rescue everyone."

"I know, I know." She hinges down beside him, stretching out her long brown legs, and stares up. The sky is huge, the clouds feathered, like the flesh of a freshly cooked fish. *This is enough,* she tells herself. *Just this.*

Then Robbie says quietly, "But we could try."

51

Sylvie

"Is it really you?" Helen touches my face as if I were a dead child come to life. I stiffen. "Good Lord," she rasps. "Baby Forest."

I stare, fascinated, shocked, as tears slide freely down her cheeks, cutting tramlines through her foundation. Helen is dissolving in front of my eyes. The distance between us is closing.

Outside the window, Jake's guitar, the sound of a different world. *Keep playing,* I think. *Please keep playing.*

"You had eyes like a blackbird." She looks radiant, as if the real Helen has broken through the Botox. It's the first time I've seen her truly smile. "Ant bites all over you. Red raw cheeks."

Mum never told me that. Or that I was called Baby Forest.

"I mixed your milk powder with water from the stream."

"You did?" It's like seeing a line drawing emerge on a page. Tears bulb between my lower lashes.

"Thankfully, you refused to touch it."

I feel weirdly proud of my baby self.

"I wanted you all to myself." She sniffs, ugly crying, not caring. "So did Mother . . ."

Jeannie. With the flawless skin and dark curls in the newspaper photo. Jeannie pregnant, outside a stucco house, smiling, a little boy tugging her skirt. And I suddenly long to meet her.

"But you only had eyes for Big Rita," Helen continues, her polished demeanor rupturing. She snorts back the tears. She wipes them on her shirtsleeve. "Your gaze followed her around the room. If you were crying, she'd swoop down and pick you up and soothe you, like a nanny, yes, yes, but also like she was born to do it."

My heart throbs. It feels like a door to the past is being pushed open, inch by inch. Behind it I see a young Rita, vertical and full of life. A woman born to graze ceilings and stars. A natural mother. The contrast with how she is now, horizontal, on a hospital bed, slays me.

"You two . . . Gosh. It was like you recognized something in each other. I . . . can't explain."

I miss Mum so intensely then it hurts.

"Never in a million years . . ." She digs in her pocket for a tissue. "You say you have a sister too?" Her face clouds. "All my life I've longed for a sister. You were mine for a short while." She brightens again. "What's your sister's name?"

"Caroline," I say, and finally lose it. "Can I borrow your tissue?"

"Let me." She dabs my eyes. I can smell mint on her breath. Possibly gin. She pulls back and stares at me intensely, a question forming. "What were you told about it all, Sylvie? Growing up."

Something inside me twists. "I didn't want to know," I say.

A gleam in those pale whippet eyes. "Well, do you now? Could you stomach it?"

I think of the little girl I was in the apple tree, all the bits of me

I've suppressed. Steve's saying, "Don't go there, Sylvie. Remember, that's not who you are." And I hear Jake's guitar, louder now, more insistent, beating across the still green canal. One strum. Two. "I want to know everything."

✳ ✳ ✳

The British Museum flashes past the taxi window, a déjà vu stream of columns and stone and amulet-blue sky. A few minutes later, the taxi swerves into Great Portland Street. "We're here." Helen can't hide the anxiety in her voice—like a plucked untuned violin string—and it makes mine worse.

We're buzzed into a tall building, grand, frayed at the edges. She still won't tell me where we're going or why. All I know is that she made a furtive call before we left. "Trust me," she says.

I don't, not quite. But for the first time in years, I'm beginning to trust myself to be able to deal with the truth, not to be sunk by it.

There's a lift, small, metal, like a shark cage. Helen won't set foot in it—"I'd rather scale the drainpipes"—so we pant up five flights of stairs. The apartment door isn't locked—someone's expecting us. My heart starts to knock in my chest. I hesitate. My feet are weighted like stones. Helen beckons me in and closes the door behind us with a high-security metallic crunch. It's dark in here. Stale. The walls are stamped with sad exotic trophies, the head of an antelope, a huge rhino. There's a moth-eaten tiger skin on the floor. It feels like an old gentlemen's club, the kind that excludes women, leathery, stuffed with hunted dead things.

"We've got company," I say, gauche with nerves, gesturing around at the taxidermy.

"Ugh. Don's horrible stuff. Daddy won't be parted from it," she says. It takes a moment for me to connect. The newspaper stories, hidden for so long by Mum, are starting to flesh. I'm about to find out the answers, the bits she scissored away. My heart beats faster.

Glass eyes follow us as we cross the lobby and go into a smaller, darker room, scratchily overheated, furnished with polished antiques and dimly lit with green-shaded lamps. It's the kind of room children instinctively misbehave in. Again, Helen shuts the door behind us. I feel a prick of claustrophobia. Two eyes—bromide blue, Helen's eyes, Elliot's eyes—stare out of the gloom.

A thin, rather sickly-looking elderly man sits upright in a battered leather chair. He's wearing a jaunty spotted navy bow tie at a lopsided angle, as if he's hurriedly tied it on for the occasion. And he's still recognizable as the fraught man in the newspaper, dashing out of the court.

On a table beside him is a bowl of walnuts. A silver nutcracker. A wicker basket containing a blown ostrich egg. Everything is clammily still. Loaded with meaning. I immediately want to leave.

As Helen kisses him briskly on each cheek, he squints over his shoulder at me. "Daddy, this is Baby Forest." Her voice fills with wonder again. "The foundling. Found."

Painfully slowly, her father puts on the spectacles that hang on a chain around his neck and peers at me, frowning, with an expression of dispassionate curiosity.

"As I explained on the phone, Daddy, she's Big Rita's adopted daughter. And . . . yes, hold on to your hat, *Annie's* mother. I'll explain how that happened later. Teenagers on smartphones basically." Her father looks understandably confused. He scratches the folds of his scraggy neck. "Sylvie, this is my father, Walter Harrington."

I struggle to smile. My armpits are wet. I can hardly breathe in here. There's something toxic, cloying, caught in the dust our feet kick up.

"Dear girl, I owe you an apology." There's a wheezy rattle in Walter's voice.

An apology? For what? For a moment, I just stand and stare at him, forgetting my manners. My heart flutters.

"You'd better sit." Helen steers me to a nearby chair, like a fussing aunt, and pushes me into button-back upholstery. "There's no easy way of telling you this, Sylvie."

I glance at Walter, adjusting his bow tie, his expression stern. There's a drop in pressure in the room, headachy. The visit suddenly feels as if it could detonate in any direction. Why did I trust Helen? Why am I here?

"Daddy and his housekeeper, a psychopath called Marge, they planned it." Helen's voice vibrates with fury. A vein pulses under her eye. "You being found in the woods."

Even the wooden African masks on the wall scream, "*What?*"

"Marge put you on that tree stump." Helen shakes her head, as if she can't quite believe it herself. "She left you there. Your birth mother couldn't bear to do it."

"Is this some sort of joke?" *She walked away.* Only it wasn't my mother? It was Marge? Marge of the flying fig roll. The room swims in the green lamplight.

"No, I'm afraid not." Helen's face sags with regret. "The rest of us had no idea at the time. None at all. Please believe that. Big Rita never knew, did she, Daddy?"

Walter nudges up his glasses, which leave an indent on either side of his nose. "Correct. Although I was scared she'd guess."

My feelings hurl around like angry children. I don't know how to be in my skin. What to say. What to do. I don't care about who died now, who killed. I must leave. But when I try to move my legs, they're useless mush.

"After Don died, Daddy cut Big Rita out of our lives. Brutally." Helen's mouth thins to an angry line. "Took out court orders. You like a lawyer, don't you, Daddy? Threatened her, said if she ever spoke to the press, to anyone about that summer, he'd hammer her life into the ground, drag her name through the mud."

"You . . . you . . ."—I feel faint with rage—"*arsehole.*"

Walter puts up his hands in surrender. "In my defense, I was crazier than my wife by then. I just didn't know it at the time."

"Just say sorry, won't you?" says Helen icily. "For once in your life, Daddy."

Walter bows his head. His pate looks fragile and pale, like the ostrich egg in the bowl. "My deepest apologies, Sylvie."

I cannot look at him, this reserved, entitled man, who thought he was above the rules and treated a baby like a doll.

"I selfishly thought the baby, you—gosh, how strange life is—would save my marriage. Rescue my beautiful Jeannie." Everything starts to feels unreal. Dubbed. "I stayed out of the way, even when I got back from overseas, and I hid away here, in this apartment, just to give her a chance to bond with you, the baby she craved, quietly, in the woods."

Feeling vulnerable, unshelled, I try to stand again, but my legs are still not working, and I sink back into the chair.

"I'd never have thought of such a preposterous thing on my own. Marge presented it, like a once-in-a-lifetime opportunity, a . . . a stroke of luck." He drags at his wizened cheeks with long, thin fingers. "I wasn't thinking straight."

I grip the sides of the armchair, like Caroline in an airplane seat during turbulence. I want Caroline. I should have told her I was coming here. She'd have stopped me.

"We need a drink." Helen starts clinking glasses at a trolley. She presses a gin and tonic into my hand. I take a swig, feeling as though I'm slipping through the protective net I've sewn around myself. Trying to grab things to stop my fall.

"Marge kept everything about you rather vague." He nudges his glasses up his nose with his thumb. "But I can tell you that your mother was young, nineteen, I believe, and very, very pregnant when she realized. I'm afraid she didn't know the father's full name. A sailor of some sort. She gave birth at home, in secret, her own mother as midwife, if I remember rightly. Lived on the other side of the forest, a strict religious family. Dirt poor. Private people. But Marge knew them—she knew everybody, made it her business—and offered a way out." He grimaces, and something that might be guilt flashes across his features. "I'm not sure she'd have had much choice, your mother. Not like girls do now."

The ice in my glass cracks. Something inside me does the same.

I'm struck by an overwhelming urge to reach back in time and pluck the baby away from all these people—not just the rural family into which I was born, but the Harringtons too. The next moment, as a swig of gin burns down my throat, it occurs to me that this *is* what my parents did. The "truth" is less about that blood-soaked summer than about the legacy of my adopted parents' daily small acts of love—what was created anew, rather than what was lost. It's like seeing myself in the mirror for the first time.

"I'm sure your birth mother was the anonymous caller who tipped off the police the night Don was shot." Walter is silent for a moment, sifting through the event. "Of course, she was meant to have gone by then. On a ship."

"A ship?" I breathe. Jo.

"A cruise ship," Helen confirms. She hands me a tissue. "She worked in the kitchens."

This hurts my heart. There can't be many workplaces grimmer than a greasy boiling kitchen under the waterline.

"Wanted to see the world," said Helen, her voice choking up. "Isn't that right, Daddy?"

He nods. "And she got to Canada in the end. Just not straight-away." There's a hint of annoyance in his voice. "Not like she was meant to."

Canada. She couldn't have got much farther from her family. I wonder if she ever forgave them, if she's got one of her own now, a nice husband, grown-up children. And if she's ever told them about me or if I'm a tiny precious secret.

"But that summer she hung around, checking on you. Marge

couldn't get rid of her and was terrified she might snatch you back. And the girl might well have if she hadn't seen how well Rita cared for her . . . you, I mean. Held you, sang to you, all that mumsy stuff. Marge said that'd made a big difference. It stopped her." He raises an eyebrow knowingly, as if aware of a closer call. "Just."

Something in me slides. Starts to thaw. I fight this. It's dangerous to imagine my birth mother was anything but heartless. Not young and scared and manipulated. In a different era, Annie. And it's strange, fissuring, to think that it was Mum, then just a young nanny, Helen's Big Rita, who might unwittingly have stopped my birth mother from reclaiming me, rerouting Fate, taking my hand and leading me into a whole different life. I can't take it in.

"It's true, Sylvie. We always felt watched," Helen says. "I used to sense someone out there in the trees, but she was so quick, so deft, like a woodland creature. I never actually saw her." She lays a jewelry-encrusted hand on my arm. "She stayed as long as she could. But she had to bolt after making the call to the police, or she'd have been questioned too. She'd have been rightly terrified."

A new feeling opens inside me, like the heron's wings. Forgiveness of sorts. If not forgiveness, understanding. And a sadness so sharp and sweet it feels like relief.

"So you see, Sylvie." Walter takes off his glasses and rubs his rheumy eyes. "Marge's mad plan failed. And I failed you and your birth mother. I promised I'd give you every advantage and I didn't. The shame is mine, all mine."

My childhood rushes past, imperfect and happy: wind-blistered beaches; the gnarly apple tree in the garden; Dad in his workshop, soft-leaded flat carpenter's pencil behind his ear; me and Caroline rushing into the cottage with handfuls of wild flowers for Mum, and Mum beaming and saying, "Wow. Aren't I just the luckiest, most spoiled mother in the world?" I swallow. Feel a charge of pride and truculence. "I had every advantage, Walter."

"And a bloody lucky escape," agrees Helen, gulping back her drink.

"Look, Sylvie, if there's anything you need, anything at all, property, money . . ." Walter begins.

"I don't want anything from you." I stand up. My legs feel strong again. Made of steel. "Nothing."

"I will make it up to Annie and her baby." Walter splays his hand on his chest. "I give you my word."

I only just bite back, "Screw you," because Annie could probably do with all the help she can get, and stride toward the door.

"Oh, must you go, Sylvie?" Helen says, as if I were leaving a dinner party early. "Stay for another drink."

"After all, here we are," Walter marvels, incomprehensibly. "We end as we began. With a baby." He brings the tips of his fingers together. "There's an excellent bottle of Krug in the fridge." He looks up at Helen. "Perhaps this time we can celebrate. Not grieve."

"Except we didn't need to grieve my little baby sister, did we, Daddy?" The atmosphere in the room switches like a blade. My hand freezes on the door handle.

"Not now, Helen," Walter mutters, with an embarrassed laugh.

"Why not?" Her lip curls. "Are you ashamed of Sylvie knowing?"

The room grows smaller and hotter. I suddenly feel I'm in the presence of a family secret so murky I don't want to hear it.

Helen's telling me anyway. "I had a little sister once, Sylvie. My father told us she'd died in hospital an hour after birth." She speaks with cool ferocity. "But she didn't."

Walter stares into the middle distance. He swallows hard, like he knows what's coming.

"She just wasn't good enough, was she, Daddy? She was flawed. Monstrous."

"She was Don's baby. She wasn't mine." Walter's words come out choked, as if the bow tie is tightening around his neck. "Your mother couldn't have coped."

"You told her a lie! She literally went mad with grief!"

"I thought it was for the best. Everyone did. She was blue. Not breathing properly. And the face . . . the wretched child's face." Walter closes his eyes and presses his fingers to his temples, trying to dam the flow of images.

The room starts to hum. An awful possibility is solidifying. Something so disturbing, my brain bucks away from it like a horse.

"It was a cleft palate, Daddy. Just a cleft palate, I'm sure of it. But you saw a monster. Because you saw Don's child. If she'd been yours . . ."

"She wasn't." His face flushes, turgid with bitterness. "She wasn't mine, damn it."

The humming sound swarms in my head. The room starts to shudder and contract violently. I lean back against the wall.

"Are you okay, Sylvie? You've gone white as a sheet." Helen's face looms closer, all her features smudged, a painting melting.

I try to get the words out. My tongue feels too thick. In my bag, my phone starts to ring. The outside world. Annie? The noise twists into my ears like wire.

"Here, sip, darling." She presses gin and tonic to my lips. My phone rings again. I push away the glass and check my phone, with dread. The hospital.

52

Rita, Now

A woodpecker. A chiseling sound. Beak on bark. Or skull. But Rita can't see the bird. She can't see anything. Someone's turned the stars out. It's dark in there. Robbie's not bothered by it. He can read the silhouette of the trees at night like an Ordnance Survey map under an Anglepoise lamp. Robbie knows where he is on a path by the timbre of the crunch beneath his soles. Rita needs Robbie. She fumbles around, arms outstretched, like blindman's buff, looking for him, like a slipped thought. Then she remembers: Robbie's not there. Robbie's dead. She's alone. She's been alone for ten years now. And if she does get out of this forest, she will still be alone, so she doesn't need to escape, does she? She can stay there. Peacefully disintegrating. Lie down on the soft mattress of earth while the woodpecker pecks and the dry leaves spin from the sky. Easier like this.

Rita's eyelashes knit together, sealing the darkness inside. A hand grabs hers. She tries to shake it away—she's busy dying here!— but it's strong as a carpenter's clamp. She can feel its calluses, the thickened pad of skin under the wedding ring, the small hard scars from slipped hammers and nails, and she can hear Robbie's voice, Robbie who is not there, whom she misses like a severed limb, Robbie, saying, "You damn well don't give up, Rita Murphy. You're needed." Then something about life having the structure of a tree—concentric annual rings, stitched through by radial lines—as he rushes her through the shadows toward the tiniest chink of blue-white light, his hand gripping tighter, and then, out of the silence, a voice saying, "Rita? Rita, blink if you can you hear me."

53

Hera, Now

I tap a fingernail against my veneers impatiently. When will Sylvie be back from the hospital with news? I hate not knowing what's happening. Her apartment seems smaller and pinker than ever, like the inside of a migraine.

I begged to accompany her to the hospital. I even leaped into the lift, overcoming my fear of its clanking cell-like enclosure just to spend a few more seconds in her company. She could barely talk. She just said, in this strange broken whisper, "Tell me about your baby sister, tell me more." So I described how, over twenty years after she was born, a charity leaflet had dropped through the letter box of my Battersea apartment with photos of cleft babies in the developing world. How I recognized my newborn sister's face in theirs and searched for her but could find no trace.

Outside the building, Sylvie sprinted in the direction of the tube. "I'll keep Annie company while we wait for news!" I shouted after her. I'm not sure she heard me.

I was still standing on the pavement, dazed, wondering why Sylvie was asking about the cleft, if she was in any state to get on the tube, when Edie rang. She'd just had a very bizarre call from my father, she said. What the hell was going on? I gabbled it out. No, he hasn't lost his marbles. It was all true. Declaring a state of emergency, she insisted on escorting me to Sylvie's apartment too. So here we all are. Waiting.

It's been over twenty minutes now. From the look on Annie's face, I suspect we may have outstayed our welcome, such as it was: "What are you doing here?"

"But Annie's such a great girl!" Edie exclaimed in a loud whisper, a few minutes after we bustled past Annie into the apartment. "Why didn't you *say*?"

I felt such shame then. I still feel it now, more acutely than ever. I can't meet Annie's eye.

"Just like Venice," Edie calls over her shoulder. She's standing on the balcony, her knotty hands on the balustrade, tapping her feet to music. A young man in a fedora is shamelessly playing a guitar on the deck of his narrow boat below. A straggly heron watches from the bank, one of the ugliest birds I've ever seen.

"No offense, but I have no idea why you're here and I'd like you to leave," I hear Annie say. "This has got nothing to do with you."

I spin around, wishing I could tell her everything. But that's her mother's job. My mouth opens and closes.

Incensed pink dots blaze on her cheeks. "I've ruined your son's life, remember?"

Edie turns from the balcony, silently imploring me to say the right thing. As ever, I have no idea what this might be.

Annie digs her hands into her jeans pockets, revealing a slither of tanned tummy, ever so slightly rounded. The sight of it brings a lump to my throat. I want to rest my hands on the smooth skin. I want to talk to it. I want to say sorry.

"You're quite right, Annie. We'll get out of your hair," says Edie warmly, walking back into the room. She slings on her denim jacket.

When I don't move, Annie turns to me, polite again, despite everything. Well brought up. "Do you have a coat, Helen?" she prompts.

"A coat?" I mutter, at a loss to stall my removal. I want to say, *Let me stay here and get to know you. I'm so sorry. I've messed up.* Instead I say, "Just that jacket on the back of the chair. The Chanel." Stupidly, out of habit. Like the designer matters.

When Annie glances at me, I can't bear to think whom she sees. "Would you like me to call Elliot? Get him over instead? Maybe he could go with you to the hospital later."

She shakes her head.

I have the urge to toss the damn jacket into the canal, if only to show her I'm not that woman. Because, my god, Edie's right. Annie *is* great. Beautiful. Determined. She's also Big Rita's granddaughter. By some trick of the universe—or the internet—I've been given an unexpected second act, a new role, a new family. A second chance. And I've already blown it.

Cruel to be kind, I've justified. Elliot's weeks of lovestruck mooning have scared the pants off me. Just like Mother and her passion for Don. I had to protect him from that disaster, as I protected myself with a sensible marriage built on friendship and separate bedrooms. *Annie will never cope,* I thought. Too young. Too smart to be satisfied by motherhood. Not rich enough. The statistics are against her. At the back of my mind was always the teenage girl who'd abandoned Baby Forest to Marge's mad scheme. So I've told Elliot repeatedly that

Sylvie's confided to me that Annie's said there's no possible romantic future. (Just as I've lied to Annie and Sylvie about Elliot's dating.) He must do his duty, I've told him, and pay his way—rather, his grandfather and I will do that—but he must stay free since one day, when he's older, he will meet someone else, someone he can get serious about. Someone suitable, more like us. *Us? Me?* What on earth was I *thinking?* As if we need another person like us in the family.

"*Helen*, your jacket," Edie says firmly. She's staring at me with an alarmed expression. Not unlike the way the neighbors would look at Mother during one of her "episodes."

"Thank you." The bouclé tweed swings heavy in my hand. How will I ever explain myself to Annie and Elliot? Let alone be forgiven? The thought of telling my son terrifies me.

"It's been a bit of a long day. I'll get her home," I hear Edie say in a conspiratorial tone to Annie. She takes my arm. "Right, come along now, Helen, darling."

"Wait. Can I just say to Annie . . ." My voice wavers.

"I'm not sure this is the time, Helen," Edie says, with a short, uneasy laugh. Her grip on my arm tightens, warning me not to gabble it all out.

"I . . . I just want to say that you're going to make a wonderful mother, Annie. Truly."

Annie's face flames. Too horrified or embarrassed to speak. With Edie's help I pull on my jacket, all fumbling fingers. The fabric feels different on my shoulders. Lighter.

Annie yanks open the front door. The city blasts in. Diesel micro-particulates and the greasy stink of kebabs, yes. But also the caffeinated whiff of life and hope. Just as Annie's shutting the door, she stops, looks up with those serious emerald eyes, and says quietly, "Thanks, Helen."

Something in me soars. It's a start. As if quiet riches the world's held back for so long, that I'd forgotten even existed, are within my reach.

Edie turns to me. "Taxi?"

"No," I say, wanting to prove something to myself. "I think it's about bloody time I tried a bus, don't you?"

❊ ❊ ❊

Three hours later, I check the grainy image on my entry camera. It's not Sylvie, as I'd hoped, on her way back from the hospital finally to share news of Rita. Nor is it Elliot, who isn't answering my calls. It's a gray-haired woman, plainly dressed, holding up a badge to the camera: police. Panic flutters inside my chest. I want to rush back inside the house and hide behind the sofa, as I did when I was a girl. Another ring. Something in me rallies. *You can do this, Helen.* I take a breath and open the door.

"No one's hurt and you're not in any trouble, Ms. Latham," the police officer says quickly. "I'm here to inform you of a development in the Armstrong case." She flashes me her badge again and peers into my house. "May I come in?"

❊ ❊ ❊

After she's gone, I sink into a wicker chair in the conservatory, doors flung back, the terrariums surrounding me, my life's work, a constellation of stars. Over the terrace walls, the church bells start ringing out over the Chelsea rooftops.

I flex the policewoman's card in my fingers, a reminder I haven't dreamed this. Dare I believe the nightmare's over after all these years? Marge Grieves has been arrested, the policewoman said. The suspect handed herself in after her carer, who'd been clearing out the house for a move into sheltered accommodation, discovered a weapon and old ammunition hidden in the loft. Initial investigations suggest a match with those used on Don Armstrong in 1971. Grieves is helping them with their inquiries. Yes, they believe there will be enough evidence to charge.

I can barely remember what else was said after that. Something was already falling inside me, like snow, starting to settle. And it is this: My mother thought I'd shot Don that night. Not only did she forgive me, she did everything she could to protect me. She even returned to The Lawns, shielded behind her apparently "unsound mind," which modern doctors would surely recognize as postpartum depression, or even PTSD, a heart's breaking. She loved me as fiercely as any mother ever loved a child. Hers was the greatest of sacrifices, and the most dogged. I think of her words "You mustn't ever think it was you, Hera. That's all that matters," and lift my face, squinting into the setting sun, until I can see my mother's mirror-chip dress aflutter among trees, my mother, turning slowly, blowing me one last kiss, a smile, then gone.

54

Rita, Ten Months Later

A burly wind skids down the trees, shaking the spring leaves like coins. Having never forgotten Marge's list of forest hazards, Rita instinctively peers up. But no branches are falling. And it was Marge—Marge!—who had turned out to be the most dangerous of all. Lethal as any death cap mushroom. Rita had had no idea.

"One sec, Sylvie." Pausing to catch her breath, she inhales the sweet whiff of wild garlic. The forest furs at its edges. She feels like she's falling through it.

"You okay, Mum?" Sylvie's eyes are so clear today that the forest is reflected within them. "Do you need to sit down?"

"Certainly not." She'd *love* to sit down. She gets tired so easily now. But she refuses to admit it. Hates the fuss. Rehabilitation has been frustratingly slow. She often wakes with a roaming confusion that takes a few minutes to clear. She sieves through everyday words, familiar names, as if beachcombing, rinsing away the sand. But occasionally her jolted mind throws up unexpected gems, long-forgotten treasures: her mother's voice, the smell of her hair, the bristles of her father's beard against her fingertips. She is closer to them at least. And this weekend she's got a feeling she's finally returning to herself too—and to a family changed out of all recognition.

"I just want to take a moment." She buttons her camel coat, a present from Helen, as immaculately cut as any of the coats she ever modeled, with a delicious midnight-blue silk lining. "Are you sure I'm not imagining all this, Sylvie? It's not a side effect of my medication?"

Sylvie laughs, the sort that stays in the eyes afterward. *Jake has a lot to do with that,* Rita thinks approvingly. She's got a good feeling about the boatman.

"Take a look over there, Mum," Sylvie whispers, pointing back to the woodland clearing, where Elliot and Annie are dawdling, shaking off the oldies. Elliot's sitting on a log, Annie on his knee. His chin rests on her shoulder and he's beaming down at the bundle in her arms: Poppy, perfect in every way, with her fuzz of black hair and blue eyes, named after Rita's mother. Her tiny fist rises into the air, snatching at the light and shadow, leaf and sky.

Rita's heart swells. Babies love forests. We're born with a love of trees deep in our souls, she decides. Like a love of the sea. She hopes that when the young family moves to Cambridge in the autumn and Annie starts her studies, they'll still seek out woodland for Poppy to romp around in there too. She suspects they will.

A boom of laughter. Rita whips around. She squints at the footpath ahead. Goodness.

Teddy. She can almost see his 1970s dungarees strap swinging. Edie, sprightly in a duck-yellow fake fur jacket. (Thirty-one thousand Instagram followers and counting, Annie tells her. More than the entire population of Barnstaple. The world's gone mad.) And farther ahead, yes, there they are, Helen and Caroline. Talking. Always heatedly talking.

No, they don't look like half sisters. You could slip four Chanel-clad Helens into a pair of Caroline's Target jeans alone, Caroline says. But somehow they fit together perfectly.

❉ ❉ ❉

A hole where the mouth should be. A baby with no face. It came to Rita one day, a few weeks after adopting Sylvie, the hazy memory of a little boy in the hospital after her own childhood car accident. A boy who hid his mouth behind his hand in shame. She couldn't forget the Harrington baby then.

The search for an infant in care with a bilateral cleft palate or some other craniofacial anomaly, born in London around certain dates, was not as hard as it should have been. No one wanted to adopt the little girl who couldn't smile. On the birth certificate, no father was named. A bit of digging revealed that Jeannie's mother's maiden name had been used. The birth date was also a day out. Walter had clearly done whatever he could to fudge it.

Poor Jeannie was dead by then. Walter wasn't. Rita would wake in a cold sweat, imagining him coming to take Caroline away, poisoning the adoption authorities against them. She carried that anxiety always, pressing on her diaphragm: if you lose your family once, you can easily imagine it happening again. The more you have, the more you can lose. Everything snatched in an instant. Robbie feared Walter's influence too. His brave little girl had already gone through so much, not least with all the corrective surgery. So they were not as open with either of the girls as they'd originally planned. As they should have been.

Mentioning the Harringtons felt like a risk. The less was said, the fainter they became, until they were just shadows flickering at the sunlit edges. She never spelled out the link between the family she'd once worked for years ago and Caroline's birth mother, let alone the suspected father and his brutal end. She'd planned to. She'd kept some of the newspapers. One day.

They didn't even dare take the girls to the forest. Robbie would occasionally return, quietly, anonymously, just to walk on his own. And when he worked in his carpentry studio, he'd talk to the girls about trees, the rings of time inside their trunks, all the hundreds of life-forms one oak hosted. He'd give them blocks of wood to sand and touch. Took them camping and riding in other woods. She'd hoped this was enough.

It wasn't, was it? With the hindsight of age—and the perspicacity that comes from dangling inside death's icy chamber—she realizes she's always been appalling at revealing things when she should, that her fear of losing someone overrides it each time.

Of course, if either of their daughters *had* asked . . . But Caroline and Sylvie were like two little girls on tiptoe, hands reaching up, and together, with their combined strength, bolting a heavy door.

"Mum, we'd better not forget about Walter," says Sylvie softly, tugging her out of her mash of thoughts.

"More's the pity," says Rita, stepping around a spectacular buckler fern she'd love to inspect more closely.

❊ ❊ ❊

Teddy sets the urn of cremated ashes on the ground. His dog circles it, sniffing.

"The dog's licking her chops!" shrieks Edie. "Naughty dog!"

Rita notices that Caroline and Sylvie—standing side by side— are discreetly shaking little fingers. They did this as little girls too. Never told her why. ("Secret!" they'd bark in unison.) In childhood the finger shake was done with overwrought seriousness, today with a wink and a bitten-down smile.

"Right. Where are the young lovebirds?" Teddy holds the dog back by the collar and looks around.

"Oh, leave them be, Teddy." Edie takes a photo of the urn on her phone. "We don't want the baby breathing in Walter."

Rita suddenly remembers Robbie explaining that when a giant tree crashes down in a forest, light and air rush into the cleared space, dormant seeds flower, and new life scrambles up, seizing its chance.

"Well, here goes, Pa old man," says Teddy, kneeling down to lift the lid.

Rita begins to feel peculiar. It takes a second or two for her to recognize that this peculiarity is not her woolly brain misfiring, as it's wont to do, but the old snared feeling, the one she'd felt here decades ago.

"Teddy," Rita says too loudly. Everyone turns to look at her. "I hope no one's offended . . ." She'll say it anyway. ". . . but I don't think I should be here for this bit. No, really. I'm going to head back to the house. For a nice cup of tea." As soon as she's spoken, the trapped feeling slithers away, like a slowworm in the bracken. Sometimes it's a relief not to be young anymore. To be able to say no.

Sylvie runs after her.

"I can't pretend to mourn him," Rita mutters beneath her breath as they walk away.

"Me neither." Sylvie pulls a car key from her pocket and dangles it from her finger. "Fancy a spin in a Porsche instead of a cup of tea, Great-Grandma? Teddy's lent me his car."

"He has? That terrifying-looking thing in the drive?" Rita laughs at the very idea. "No, thank you."

A few paces on, Wildwood's red-tiled roof appears through the trees. *Funny to think that Poppy will inherit the place one day,* Rita thinks. Quite right too. Despite its facelift and name change, it'll always be Foxcote. As Helen will be Hera. (The same angry, agitated fingers that once lit fires now design the most exquisite terrariums she's ever seen. Worlds under glass, a lost sweet joy.) And the garden gate, although a tasteful shade of putty now, is still recognizably the same rickety gate she once crept through at dawn, wearing a lurid pink dressing gown and boots that belonged to the great love of her life, whom she hadn't yet met. It makes her breath catch.

As they get closer, something else snags Rita's eye. A streak of lightning-white hair, a loping flash, vanishing into the bluebell haze. Fingers? Watching them? Eyes and ears of the forest. The Green Man. Revealer and burier of its secrets. She wonders what else he knows.

And it's then that a fuzzy thought that's been niggling throughout this hectic weekend takes on a more solid shape. Fat as a rain-drop about to roll, it feels like the first crystalline, defined thought she's had since the accident.

The gate's well-oiled latch clicks behind them. They walk into the garden, along a path banked by white tulips and delicate feath-ery ferns that bear a striking resemblance to Ethel. Rita's mind ticks over. This is her chance. She's got Sylvie alone. She must say something.

But they're on the drive already, and Sylvie has stopped by Ted-dy's car, gleaming dangerously, its roof rolled down. "Oh, go on, Mum. Wouldn't it be good to escape for a bit? Just the two of us? See a horizon?"

Rita thinks, *My parents died on a forest road. Don drove a car not unlike this.* She says, "It's tiny! I wouldn't fit inside!"

Sylvie opens the car door anyway. And something about her daughter's ease in this forest, the gleam in her eyes, makes Rita slide trustingly into the low leather seat. Her knees almost graze her chin.

Sylvie leaps into the driver's seat and sticks the key into the ignition.

"Wait." Now. Now is the time. "There's something I need to . . ." Rita swallows. She's dreaded this conversation for years. She's con-structed her life to avoid it. "As I'm on the mend, I'd like to help you find this . . . this Jo. Your birth mother."

Sylvie blanches. Clearly she wasn't expecting this. The trees stir around them. Curl back.

"There'll be local leads," Rita continues nervously, thinking of Fingers. "Or the ancestry DNA company Caroline used a few weeks ago. You just rub a cotton bud on the inside of your cheek, apparently." Her voice fades. This is coming out all wrong, as she always dreaded it would.

Still Sylvie says nothing. High in the branches above them, a woodpecker starts to drum, like Rita's heart.

"Of course, I understand if it's something you want to do on your own . . ." Rita fades, losing confidence.

A moment passes. The house peers down, the mullioned windows blinking, waiting.

"Honestly?" Sylvie's pupils have spread, ink-drop black. "If there's one thing I've learned these last few months, Mum, it's that I'm *so* your daughter. No one else's. Just like Annie's mine. And Poppy is Annie's." She starts the engine and the car bucks, then starts to growl.

It rumbles Rita's old bones. She's terrified. Her heart's exploding. "Good Lord."

Sylvie drives slowly out of the gate, the first few bends. But when the road straightens, she accelerates, throwing them back against the seats. The trees stream past, a riot of green. Their hair whips. And Rita laughs and whoops because she's no longer scared, not one bit, and they're moving so fast that in no time at all, they're piercing the forest's edge. And then, look, just look, it's shrinking to a smudge behind them.

Acknowledgments

A huge thank-you to my editors Tara Singh Carlson, Helen Richard, and Maxine Hitchcock. You've all brought so much to this novel, and I count myself one lucky writer—we've a great hive mind! Lizzy Kremer, my agent—heartfelt gratitude, always. Hazel Orme, Maddalena Cavaciuti, Bea McIntyre, Alice Howe, and the inspiring teams at G. P. Putnam's Sons, Michael Joseph, and David Higham Associates . . . thank you, thank you. My fellow author readers: I know you've all got teetering proof piles, and I'm so appreciative. Lastly, my family: Ben, Oscar, Jago, and Alice. In the end, it's all for you. (And the dog!) With much love.